A native of St. Louis, Missouri, **Tiffany Snow** earned degrees in education and history from the University of Missouri-Columbia, before launching a career in information technology. After nearly fifteen years in IT, she switched careers to what she always dreamed of doing – writing. Tiffany is the author of romantic suspense novels such as the Kathleen Turner series, which includes *No Turning Back*, *Turn to Me*, and *Turning Point*. Since she's drawn to character-driven books herself, that's what she loves to write, and the guy always gets his girl.

She feeds her love of books with avid reading, yet she manages to spare time and considerable affection for trivia, eighties hair bands, the St. Louis Cardinals, and Elvis. She and her husband have two daughters and one dog, whose untimely demise Tiffany contemplates on a daily basis.

www.tiffanyasnow.com
www.facebook.com/TiffanyASnow
www.twitter.com/TiffanyASnow

D0549713

PLAYING DIRTY

TIFFANY SNOW

PIATKUS

First published in the US in 2015 by Forever Romance,
an imprint of Grand Central Publishing, a division of Hachette Book Group, Inc.
First published in Great Britain in 2015 by Piatkus

1 3 5 7 9 10 8 6 4 2

A CIP catalogue record for this book
is available from the British Library.

ISBN 978-0-349-41155-2

Printed and bound in Great Britain by
Clays Ltd, St Ives plc

Papers used by Piatkus are from well-managed forests
and other responsible sources.

MIX
Paper from
responsible sources
FSC® C104740

*This book is dedicated to Jill, for digitally
holding my hand as we
slogged through together, one day at a
time. You're awesome, Babe.*

PLAYING DIRTY

PROLOGUE

Parker watched as Ryker's truck rolled to a stop in front of the building. Sage emerged from the entry, scurrying across the sidewalk barefoot before climbing into the passenger seat. The truck pulled away from the curb, lost to sight in moments down the avenue.

He'd heard the door close when she'd gone, leaving him alone in his bed without so much as a word of farewell.

Not that he could blame her.

She'd nearly died tonight. Had been moments away. Viktor hadn't cared if he killed her or not. He'd put a fucking plastic bag over her head and slowly suffocated her.

Parker's hands balled into fists just remembering how she'd looked when he'd pulled her out of that car. Deathly pale, her mouth bleeding from where Viktor had hit her, mascara smeared by the tears soaking her cheeks…

Sage deserved better. Far better. But Parker needed her in

his life...in his job. No matter how tempting it was to want to slip into a more personal relationship with her, he knew he couldn't. Relationships never lasted, and just when you thought you'd found the forever kind of love—it would end. And when it was over...she'd be gone. Permanently.

Better to let her go with Ryker, a man who'd wanted a wife and kids—a family—for as long as Parker had known him, which had been a helluva long time. Ryker had fascinated Parker when they were young. So unlike the wealthy, cookie-cutter kids that had gone to the private school, the poor kid from the south side of town had been a welcome breath of fresh air.

Nearly two decades had passed since they'd first met, but some things never changed. Maybe it had been because he'd been raised by a single mom, but Ryker had talked of nothing else but wanting to fall in love and get married. Especially when they'd been deployed and the future sometimes looked grim. Why he wasn't married already, Parker had no idea.

Unless he still wasn't over Natalie.

Natalie. The woman who'd torn the two of them apart. Obviously, Ryker still blamed Parker for her suicide, his anger and loathing as fresh now as the day they'd found out she'd driven her car into the river.

Maybe he'd marry Sage.

That thought was like a kick in the gut.

Unable to stand the bedroom anymore and unwilling to climb beneath sheets still warm from Sage's body, Parker walked into the living room. A faint glow from a dim light under the kitchen cabinets filtered in through the space, providing enough illumination for him to pour a healthy shot of scotch.

Memories assailed him as he stood in the silent apartment, staring blindly out the window. Memories of Sage and the day they'd first met.

"How many applicants do we have?" he asked the HR rep in charge of helping him find a new secretary.

She set half a dozen files on his desk. "These were the ones I thought were the most qualified."

He glanced through the stack, flipping one open at random, then frowned. "An art history degree qualifies someone to be a secretary?"

"Executive Administrative Assistant," she corrected him. "And that's the least qualified candidate, but she had a solid 3.8 GPA and her application was very well done. I thought an interview couldn't hurt. I can cancel it, if you'd rather. She's scheduled last so—"

"No, it's fine," Parker interrupted, tossing aside the files. "Just send them in when they get here." Surely one of them would work out. And could start immediately. He was drowning under the pile of work and the incessant phone calls.

"Yes, sir." She left the office, but Parker barely noticed, already plowing through his inbox, currently cluttered with over two hundred unread e-mails.

The first applicant was Joanne, a no-nonsense woman who'd spent the last twenty years as assistant to some Wall Street hedge fund manager. He'd retired and she'd moved to Chicago to be closer to her grandchildren. Parker was bored before she'd even gotten to the name of the third one.

The second applicant chewed gum. In an interview. Nope.

The third wore a blouse two sizes too small and a skirt so short he had to look away when she crossed her legs or it would go all Basic Instinct on him. She had a predatory look in her eye and Parker would swear she eyed his crotch when he stood to shake her hand.

The fourth and fifth were both bland possibilities, neither one standing out as particularly ambitious or enthusiastic. Parker wouldn't want to stereotype—that would be politically incorrect—but if he did, he'd say they both seemed like women biding their time in a temporary job until they married and quit to pop out babies.

By the time the last one—the art history major—was due, Parker'd had about enough. This interview shit was putting him even further behind. Accounting had just delivered a stack of billables he was supposed to check, he had a meeting in less than thirty minutes that he hadn't had enough time to prepare for, and he was starving because he'd had to work through lunch. Irritated didn't begin to describe his current mood.

A tentative knock sounded on the glass door and he didn't even glance up as he called out a "Come in." He heard the door open as he shifted a stack of folders. That Carlson file had to be around here somewhere . . .

"Just have a seat," he said. "I'll be with you in a mo—"

Glancing up, his words abruptly cut off.

The woman who'd entered his office was drop-dead gorgeous. Not pretty. No, way more than that—curvy and sexy, with legs up to there, and thick chestnut hair down to there. Her body looked like it had been made for sex, lovingly encased in a peach dress that hugged every delicious curve. The neckline was demure, scooped and only hinting at what lay beneath. The hemline teased, hitting right above her knees. The skin of her legs was so perfect, Parker couldn't tell if she was wearing nylons or not. But then he caught sight of her shoes, bronze sandals that wrapped around her ankle on top of a three-inch heel.

And her toes were painted the exact shade of her dress.

"Hi, I'm Sage Reese."

The voice was throaty and smooth like twenty-year-old scotch, and made Parker jerk his gaze up to her face. She was smiling, a warm, open smile that showed perfect white teeth. Her eyes were the same shade of mahogany as her hair, framed in lush, dark lashes.

She was holding her hand out expectantly and Parker jumped to his feet, thrusting his hand toward her and knocking over the entire stack of Accounting files in the process.

Shit.

"Oh no!" she exclaimed. "That was totally my fault." She dropped down and started picking up the scattered files, treating Parker to first a view down her cleavage, then one of the fabric of her dress stretched tight across her hips and ass as she bobbed up and down.

"Don't worry about it," he said hurriedly. "Just leave it." This time he grabbed her wrist when she placed a file back on his desk. Her bones felt fragile beneath soft skin and he quickly let go. He gestured to one of the two chairs in front of his desk. "Have a seat."

Her smile wasn't quite as wide now, but she sat down. Parker fished through the disaster on his desk, looking for her file while the silence grew long and awkward. He felt incompetent and unprepared, her appearance throwing him off, which was ridiculous. It wasn't as though he'd never been with a beautiful woman before.

The phrase been with *provoked all the wrong kind of images for a work setting and he cleared his throat, banishing those thoughts as he finally laid hands on her file and flipped it open.*

"Why don't you tell me a little about yourself, Sage?" he asked, trying to recover what was left of a first impression. She probably thought he was a disorganized, unprofessional klutz.

"Um, sure. Well, I graduated magna cum laude from the University of Chicago with a degree in art history. I interned at the Art Institute of Chicago—"

"And why didn't they hire you?" he interrupted, glancing up from the pages.

Her cheeks flushed. "I don't know," she said. "I don't think there was an open position."

He'd embarrassed her, and he could have kicked himself for the tactless question. It wasn't like they would've told her a reason for not hiring her even if they'd had a job available.

"Do you have any experience with investment banking?" he asked, hurrying to change the subject. Her eyes were focused on him, deep and fathomless, and he had to look away. He flipped through her application and résumé, barely seeing the words.

"Um, no."

"Any experience with the stock market? Hedge funds? Economics? Finance?" She shook her head after each one, her cheeks growing redder with each word. "Ever been a secreta—administrative assistant—before?"

"No." Her voice was quiet, and even the small smile she'd had earlier was nowhere in sight now.

Parker felt like a schmuck now, but what the hell was he supposed to do? It was an interview, not a date.

"Are you from Chicago?" he asked, wanting to hear something from her other than a No.

"Lake Forest," she replied, naming one of the wealthiest suburbs of Chicago.

"Sisters? Brothers?" Boyfriend? Husband? He knew he couldn't ask the last two, but wished he could. He hadn't spied a ring earlier, but nowadays, that didn't necessarily mean anything.

"Only child."

Daddy's little princess. He could see it on her as clearly as if she'd had it bedazzled on the dress she wore. Which begged the question, why was she interviewing for a job like this when surely she could live with her parents until something in her field opened up?

"I know what you're thinking," she said.

He doubted it.

"You're thinking why would I apply for a job I have absolutely no qualifications for," she continued.

Okay, maybe she did know what he was thinking.

Tossing the file onto the desk, Parker sat back in his chair and waited.

"I'm smart," she said. "I'm a hard worker, and a quick learner."

"You have zero business experience at all," Parker said bluntly.

"I had a minor in business," she said, somewhat defensive.

A minor. Practically nothing more than a few economics classes about how to balance a checkbook. But he didn't say that.

"Can you at least type?"

"Yes, I can type," she said, sounding affronted.

"You're an art history major," he said flatly. "It was a valid question."

The corners of her lips lifted slightly in an almost smile. It entranced him. Then he found he was staring at her mouth and jerked his gaze away.

She swallowed, her next words seeming to take an effort to get out. "I need this job. I have bills to pay. Please, Mr. Anderson. Give me a chance. I won't disappoint you."

Considering her background, it was odd that she'd need a job quite that badly. Had her parents fallen on hard times? Maybe they'd disowned her? He felt a pang of sympathy

*at the thought—uncharacteristic for him—and he frowned,
which was the wrong thing to do because her face immediately fell as she misinterpreted his response.*

*She shot to her feet. "I'm sorry for wasting your time,"
she blurted. "I'll just go." She looked near tears, which was
the proverbial final straw. He mentally cursed his weakness
for tears on a pretty girl.*

*"Wait," he called, halting her on her way out the door.
She turned back. "This job won't be easy and you'll probably be working more than forty hours a week," he cautioned,
wondering if he was out of his mind. Not only was she inexperienced, he didn't know if he could trust himself around
her. And he refused to be the cliché boss screwing his secretary.*

Administrative Assistant.

Fuck.

"I can do that," she said, hope lighting up in her eyes.

"If you don't cut it, then you'll be let go," he warned.

"I understand."

*Coming out from behind his desk, Parker approached her,
noting the subtle scent of her perfume as he drew closer.
Holding out his hand, he said, "When can you start?"*

*Her smile was blinding as she placed her hand in his, and
Parker knew he'd made a huge mistake the minute their skin
touched. He'd just consigned himself to God only knew how
much torture. If he hadn't hired her, he could've asked her
out, taken her to dinner... then to bed. All of which was utterly out of the question now.*

*"Thank you so much, sir," she enthused. "I won't let you
down. I promise."*

*Parker's expression was grim, he knew, so he mustered
a faint smile. "See you tomorrow morning, Sage. Seventhirty."*

"Absolutely." She'd nodded, still smiling, then turned and left. Her scent had lingered in the air of his office. He'd scrubbed a hand over his face in frustrated resignation. He'd made his bed. Now he had to lie in it. If he had any luck at all, she'd hate the job and quit.

But she hadn't hated the job. She'd taken to being his assistant like she'd been born to it, their communication clicking immediately into place. Somehow, she'd understood him, the job, and what he needed almost without trying. In a frighteningly short amount of time, she'd become indispensable to him.

And he'd liked her. Besides being so attracted to her it made concentrating difficult sometimes when she was in his office—like when she was crawling around on the floor in her skirt and bare feet, emptying box after box of documents—he enjoyed her personality. Funny, a bit quirky, almost always lighthearted and positive, she was his own personal breath of fresh air in the stale business environment that sometimes felt suffocating.

In the end he was glad he'd hired her, even though it ruled out anything physical between them, because it meant their relationship could continue. Because if he hadn't hired her and had dated her instead, he had no doubt it would have been short-lived. He didn't do relationships. Not even with Sage. *Especially* not with Sage.

Watching her date other men had been hard, and if someone were to ask him if he'd deliberately sabotaged those short-lived relationships, he'd deny it. But deep down, he knew that jealousy had played a factor in how often he called her when he knew she was out with another man. Was it fair to either of them? No. Yet he hadn't been able to stop himself.

And now she'd chosen to go from his bed to Ryker's. *Jealousy* was too pale of a word to describe how that made him feel, but if the last couple of weeks had shown him anything, it was that he needed to let it go. He'd flat-out turned her down, which had been the hardest thing he'd ever done. To *know*, definitively and not just as a guess, that Sage wanted him had been a heady thing. The feel of her in his arms, the press of her lips against his...the sight of her naked in that bathtub, her soap-slickened hands touching her breasts, her stomach—

Parker tossed back the rest of the scotch in one swallow, forcing the images from his mind. He had to stop obsessing, and stop sabotaging her. It wasn't fair to Sage, and it was just his own fucking bad luck that he had to figure this out now, when she was with Ryker, than before when she'd been dating what's-his-name. The guy she'd said had been bad in bed.

His lips twisted at that. She'd been so adorably embarrassed when she'd blurted that out he'd had a hard time not laughing outright, until he'd realized that she'd only know that because she'd slept with him. Then the green monster had dug into his gut and he'd been viciously glad to have interrupted her date the night before.

But not anymore. Enough. It was done. Parker would exercise self-control and ignore the jealousy, because otherwise he'd never let Sage find someone, and she deserved to be happy.

Even if it was with Ryker, the closest friend he'd ever had, who now hated him beyond all reason.

CHAPTER ONE

Four Months Later

It's amazing how sleeping with a hot guy with rock-hard abs provides motivation to get one's ass to the gym.

At least that's what I kept telling myself as I sweated my way through twenty minutes on the elliptical. I watched the closed-captioning scroll across the mounted television tuned in to the news, increasingly resentful of the female anchor with perfectly toned and tanned legs on display.

Finally, the timer beeped and I turned off the machine, stepping back to the floor with legs that felt like rubber. Megan bebopped up to me, her ponytail bouncing with each step.

"I always feel so energized after I work out," she said, grinning.

I stared daggers at her. "I hate you so much right now," I panted, still trying to catch my breath. Megan was petite and tiny with a personality I adored...usually. We'd worked together at KLP Capital for almost two years now.

"C'mon, Sage, you know you'll feel better after a shower." She grabbed my elbow and dragged me with her to the locker room. "Then we'll have lunch. I know this great new sushi place just around the corner."

The prospect of food made me perk up a little and I glowered slightly less. By the time I'd cleaned up, blown my hair dry, and added some makeup, I was congratulating myself on how healthy and diligent I was to get up early on a Saturday to go work out. Which lasted precisely as long as it took to walk to the sushi place and see the donut shop next door.

"So how's Armed and Delicious?" Megan asked, biting into a powdered donut.

I answered around a mouthful of strawberry jelly. "Ryker's fine," I said. "He had to work late. Was still asleep when I left. So...I guess we're kinda...living together now?" I meant it as a statement but it came out as a question.

Megan's chewing ground to a halt. "Kinda?" she asked, mouth full. She swallowed. "How do you *kinda* live with someone?"

"Well, I gave him a key, because his hours are so weird," I explained. "And now he just comes by when he gets off— whenever that is—and stays. He gets up when I leave for work and has a cup of coffee with me, goes home and sleeps, then the process kind of repeats. So is that living together?"

"Does he have clothes and toiletries at your apartment?" she asked.

I thought about it. "A toothbrush and a few changes of clothes," I admitted. "Sometimes he showers there, so yeah, there's some of his stuff."

"Congratulations," she said. "Your boyfriend is living with you and you didn't even know it."

I rolled my eyes at her dry sarcasm, taking a sip of my

coffee. It was chilly and rainy today—autumn was rolling in—and the coffee was like a soothing blanket.

"So is this a good development or bad?" she asked, peering in the bag for another donut.

"Good, I think," I said. "It just snuck up on me, that's all."

"It sounds like things are progressing," she said. "You're sleeping with him, it's a given that you're together as much as possible, and now you're 'kind of' living together." She used quote-y fingers for *kind of*. "Isn't that what you want?"

Parker's face drifted through my mind. I shoved it away. "Yeah," I said. "It just seems a bit... fast, that's all. We've only been seeing each other for a little over four months. Do you think that's fast?"

She shrugged. "I think that's up to you and Ryker."

"It feels right, I guess. It wasn't like we had a conversation about it. Like last night, he didn't get there until almost three in the morning."

I didn't mention how I hadn't thought he was going to come over, not when he'd called and said he had to work late. But then I'd woken to the feel of his body against my back and his arm slung over my waist.

"What're you doing here?" I'd murmured, reaching behind me to push my fingers into his hair.

He'd nuzzled my neck, his lips pressed to the tender spot beneath my jaw. "Couldn't stand not seeing you," he'd whispered in my ear.

Ryker was a hard-as-nails homicide detective for the Chicago PD. To say he wasn't the type to "share his feelings" was an understatement. So when he said that, my eyes had flown open in surprise.

"Really?" I asked, turning in his arms. Our relationship was still new and we'd both shied away from any big declarations.

"Really."

He'd made short work of the pajamas I'd worn to bed, his hands skating down my hips to my thighs as he moved above me. His lips met mine and I slipped his dog tags around to his back from where they'd rested against me.

I was lost in the memories of what had happened next when I heard my name.

"Hey, Sage. Snap out of it."

I glanced over at Megan, sheepish, but she was grinning.

"You're hopelessly whipped," she said, rolling her eyes at me.

"I'm not whipped," I protested. "I'm just... heavily in like."

"So we're not mentioning the other L-word?" she said, raising an eyebrow.

"It's only been four months."

"Which is longer than any other relationship you've had in the past two years," she said. "I'm surprised Parker's allowed it."

My smile faded at the mention of my boss, Parker Anderson. I knew Megan was kidding... sort of. My work had intruded on my personal time ever since I'd begun my job almost two years ago as Executive Administrative Assistant to Parker Anderson, Director of Investment Analytics at KLP Capital, which was *the* investment bank in Chicago.

Four months ago, that changed. Whereas I used to get calls at all hours—and I did literally mean all hours—from Parker for various work things, now he rarely called in the evening, and never on the weekends. I should be glad for the space he'd given me. And I was.

Sort of.

"It's not up to Parker to *allow* anything," I said. "It's my life."

"And you're sleeping with his arch-nemesis," she reminded me.

"So they had a falling-out. It was forever ago." I shrugged, popping the rest of the donut into my mouth.

"It was over a woman and they still hate each other," she said. "It's not like they're let-bygones-be-bygones kind of guys."

That much was true. Parker and Ryker actively despised each other, which was kind of sad, considering how they'd been best friends all through childhood, even going as far as to join the Marines together. A woman named Natalie changed all that. They both fell in love with her, and now she was dead.

"I thought you were all about me not letting Parker and my job take over my life," I reminded Megan. "You should be glad he's backed off, not giving me trouble about it."

"I *am* glad he's been a lot less of a jerk to you than usual," she amended, primly blotting her lips with a napkin. "I was just kind of wondering if you are."

I didn't have a response to that, and still didn't even after she'd dropped me back at my apartment. Parker and I had always had a good working relationship—professional and intuitive. I'd liked and admired him from nearly the first time we'd met and he'd given me the job, despite my woeful lack of experience. I'd worked hard for him and the job was a good one. I hadn't complained at the hours or how often he began contacting me when I wasn't technically on the clock.

And if part of the reason for that was that I'd fallen in love with him, well, no one had to know that but me.

As an only child to wealthy parents who were still in love even after thirty years of marriage, it was good to feel needed. Because that's how Parker made me feel. Indispensable. Even if he didn't look at me the same way I looked at him.

When I'd finally realized that Parker didn't reciprocate my feelings and never would, I'd decided I wasn't going to let an infatuation with my boss hold me back from pursuing a relationship with Ryker. Ryker was a good man who wanted me, desired me, and made my pulse climb whenever he was near.

As though the thought had conjured him, Ryker poked his head out of my kitchen when I pushed open my apartment door. He'd obviously just showered, since his dark hair was still wet and he wore only a pair of jeans. The dog tags he never took off dangled from his neck as he headed for me.

"You were gone when I woke up," he said, brushing a kiss to my lips.

"I promised Megan we'd work out this morning," I said. His hands had settled firmly on my hips, pulling me against him. "She'd have killed me if I bailed on her."

"What do you want to do today?" he asked.

"You don't have to work?"

"Nope. I'm all yours."

A whole Saturday just to spend together without either of us having to work was an unexpected pleasure. He'd been working so much lately, we hadn't had time to just be together.

"I just need to run home and take care of McClane first," he said.

I grimaced at the mention of Ryker's huge police dog. The canine had flunked out of his training and Ryker had adopted him. I wasn't a dog person, so of course McClane adored me.

Ryker's phone buzzed and as he checked the text message, I began cleaning up the kitchen. Neither of us were amazing chefs, but between Ryker and me, we managed to cook a few nights a week.

"Hey, that's a buddy of mine," he said, coming up behind me. "Texting me, asking if we want to join him on his boat on the lake today."

"What kind of boat?" I asked.

He raised an eyebrow. "Does it matter? It's a beautiful and sunny September day, and winter will be here all too soon."

"I like winter," I protested, loading dishes into the dishwasher.

"You're crazy," he said. "Snow and ice, colds and flu. Winter sucks."

"Christmas and fireplaces, sweaters and a white winter wonderland. It all depends on how you look at it, Mr. Cynical."

Coming from behind me, he slid his arms around my waist and nuzzled my neck. "Maybe if I have you to cuddle with in front of a fire, I won't mind the cold as much."

"Maybe not," I agreed. Things were going well with Ryker. Too well. It was almost scary if I dwelled on it. So I didn't.

"Go change and don't forget your suit," he said, pushing me toward the bedroom.

I supposed there were worse ways to spend a Saturday than lounging on a boat on Lake Michigan with my boyfriend.

I slipped my bikini on and wore my shorts and a T-shirt over it, layering on a light button-down shirt in case it got chilly this evening. I grabbed my sun bag with my hat and sunscreen, slipped on a pair of sandals, and was ready to go.

As expected, McClane was exceptionally enthusiastic to see me when we arrived at Ryker's house, and I grimaced as he tried to lick any part of me he could reach.

"McClane! Sit!"

The dog obeyed Ryker's command—eventually—his tail thumping the ground and his tongue lolling as he gazed up at me in adoration.

"If you'd just say hello to him, he'd leave you alone," Ryker said, heading past me into the hallway that led to his bedroom.

"That is so not true," I muttered.

"I heard that," Ryker called out. I shot a glare down the hall.

Gingerly, I patted McClane's head a couple of times. "Hi, McClane. Now stop trying to lick me." As I'd feared, petting him only encouraged his enthusiasm. I squealed in dismay as he jumped up, placing his paws on my shoulders. A big warm puff of dog breath blew right in my face and I nearly gagged.

"McClane, get off her," Ryker said, walking past again and snapping his fingers. The dog reluctantly sat back down on the floor, his ears drooping. The dejection on his face almost made me feel bad for him. Almost. I heard the sound of dog food rattling in the kitchen and so did McClane. His ears perked up and he was off like a shot.

I waited, not daring to get within McClane's line of sight again, and Ryker came back from the kitchen. He'd changed into a white tank, a worn pair of jeans, and as I'd done, he'd thrown on an unbuttoned short-sleeved shirt over the top. His dog tags glinted in the sunlight as he climbed on his motorcycle and slid on mirrored shades.

Yum.

"Let's go, babe."

No need to tell me twice.

I put on the helmet I so disliked and climbed behind him on the back of the bike—a mode of transportation I was gradually becoming accustomed to, but doubted I'd ever feel safe doing—and wrapped my arms around his chest to hold on. It was hot today, already pushing the mid-eighties, and I could feel sweat trickling down my back.

Thirty minutes later, we were pulling in to a lot and parking. My legs felt numb from riding the bike and my knees were rubbery. The sudden quiet after the engine had been roaring in my ears was a welcome relief.

"So who's the buddy?" I asked, following Ryker as he took my hand and began walking down the pier. I could smell the water now and there was a hard breeze blowing, easing the heat a bit.

"His name's Troy and I served with him," Ryker said, alluding to when he'd been in the Marines. "He's a mechanic now, only works on the high-end luxury vehicles. Does pretty well, I think." He stopped and pointed. "That's his boat there."

Shading my eyes since not even my dark sunglasses were doing the trick in the blazing sunshine, I looked where he was pointing. It was a beautiful cabin cruiser yacht, large enough for several people, and spotless. Yes, it looked like Troy did pretty well, indeed.

"C'mon," he said, tugging my hand.

There were three women and two men already on board, along with two kids running around.

"Hey, Dean!" One of the women approached us. She was wearing a one-piece suit with a pair of cutoff shorts, and was obviously several months pregnant. She gave Ryker a hug. "Good to see you."

"Good to see you, too, Sammy," he said. "How you been feeling?"

"I'm doing well, thanks," she said, resting a hand on her stomach. She glanced expectantly at me.

"This is my girlfriend, Sage," Ryker said.

"Nice to meet you," I said as I shook hands with Sammy. She was a cute girl, probably about mid-twenties like me.

"Same here," she said with a friendly smile.

"Where's Cody?" Ryker asked.

"He's still at work. He should be here soon."

"Hey, Dean! About time you got here."

One of the men had approached. He was a big guy with massive biceps and a bald head gleaming in the sun. His sunglasses hid his eyes from me, but his white teeth flashed in a grin. "Looks like you been busy."

"Tyrone, my man, this is my girl Sage."

"'Bout time you brought a lady 'round here," Tyrone said. Rather than take the hand I held out, he wrapped an arm around me and squeezed. "You need to make an honest man outta him, Sage."

I grinned back, liking Tyrone immediately. "Thanks for the advice."

"Tyrone, leave the girl alone."

I turned to see who I assumed was Tyrone's wife. She slapped his arm playfully and he let me go, then introduced herself as Anisha.

The last couple on the boat were the boat owners—Amy and Troy—who also were the parents of the twins, Robin and Ricky. They were just as nice as the other friends of Ryker's that I'd met. Cody showed up pretty quickly after that and it was obvious he was smitten with his pregnant wife, solicitously making sure she was comfortable and had everything she might need within easy reach.

And only as I watched Ryker help Troy unmoor the boat did it occur to me that all of Ryker's friends were married, several already with children. Could it be I'd actually found that elusive creature…a man who wanted to settle down?

We hadn't talked marriage and family, as I was a faithful adherent to the rule to never be the first to bring that up. Too many commitment-phobic men ran scared at the mere mention of the M-word.

The women were nice and easy to chat with as Troy steered us out onto Lake Michigan. Ryker reappeared with two beers, handing me one.

"Mooching off your friends?" I teased. I took a sip of the beer and tried not to grimace. It wasn't my favorite drink, but I could choke one down if I had to.

He shot me a look. "You should see how much of my beer they drink when they come over to watch the Bears."

I laughed and his lips lifted in a lopsided smile that made my breath catch. He'd taken off his tank and I got a real good look at Ryker's sweat-dampened chest.

"Let's see the suit," he said, nodding toward my T-shirt. I'd gone shopping at the end-of-season sales and picked up a bikini I'd teased him about, but not let him see.

"Okay, but it's fragile and for display only," I warned him. "Don't get me wet."

Ryker's grin widened and I blushed at my unintentional innuendo. He leaned closer. "No promises, babe." His raspy voice in my ear sent a shiver down my spine.

I crossed my arms over my chest and tugged the T-shirt over my head. My apprehension over how the barely there beige crochet tie bikini looked was immediately set at ease when Ryker eased his sunglasses down to peer over them. His eyes drank me in and I didn't hesitate to shuck the shorts, too.

Handing him my bottle of sunscreen, I asked, "Put some lotion on my back?"

"I'd rather put it on your front," he teased.

"I'm sure you would."

The guys all gathered together once the boat was out a ways and the women likewise were stretched out side by side on the deck.

"So where did you and Dean meet?" Amy asked me, adding water to Robin's tippy cup.

I hesitated, wondering how this was going to go over. "He knows my boss," I said. "I guess they used to be friends."

"Who's your boss?"

"Parker Anderson."

Amy glanced over at me, her eyebrows raised. "Seriously?"

I nodded. "Yeah."

"Talk about a small world."

Anisha had glanced over, too, from where she was stretched on the deck. "You work for Parker? What's *that* like?"

I bristled since it was obvious that neither of them liked Parker. "It's great, actually," I said. "He's a good boss. I love my job."

My defensiveness must've shown because Sammy jumped in to defuse the sudden tension.

"That's great," she said. "Not everyone likes their boss and their job, right, Amy?"

Amy's smile was forced. "Right."

But Anisha wasn't as easily placated. "You know the history between Parker and Dean, don't you? What that asshole Parker did to him?"

"I know that it was in the past and it's none of my business," I said, getting to my feet. "If you'll excuse me."

Grabbing another crappy beer from the cooler, I popped the top and went in search of Ryker. He was in the middle of a conversation about a '68 Mustang he was thinking of buying and restoring, so I just settled in next to him. Glancing down at me, he smiled and draped an arm over my shoulders.

I listened to them talk for a while, deciding about two-thirds of the way through my beer that hey, it wasn't so bad after all. When I finished that one, I went and opened another.

Amy stepped up behind me as I was taking a swig. "Hey," she said with a smile. "I just wanted to apologize. Anisha was out of line. We're just all very...protective of Dean. That's all."

"I like him, too," I said. "Or else I wouldn't be here."

"We were just surprised. We haven't heard Parker's name in a really long time."

"So what happened?" I asked. "Why do you all hate him so much?"

"You really don't know?" she asked, scrutinizing me.

I shrugged. "I've heard bits and pieces from both of them, and of course their sides of the story are vastly different. It'd be nice to hear from an outside party what happened."

The wind had torn her hair from its braid and she took it down, tying it back in a ponytail as she talked.

"Well, it all started when they came back from deployment," she said. "Troy and I were high school sweethearts and have been friends with Dean since forever. He and Troy lived by each other in that shitty trailer park. Parker was never really one of us, never really fit in, but Dean liked him, so we accepted him.

"Parker and Dean were inseparable," she continued. "I don't know what had happened to bring them together—neither of them would ever say—but they had each other's backs all through high school and into the service. I didn't think anything could ever come between them. Until they met Natalie."

Natalie. The woman they'd both fallen in love with, the woman who'd committed suicide because of it.

"Tell me about her," I said.

Amy shrugged, her face blank. "She was a little thing. Pretty. Delicate, kind of, I guess. Men like that sort of thing, or at least Dean and Parker did."

"That's all?" I asked when she stopped talking.

"It's unkind to speak ill of the dead."

That was unexpected. I'd assumed, given how Ryker and Parker had referred to Natalie, that she'd been sweet and nice. Maybe I'd assumed wrong. "You didn't like her?" I prodded.

Amy hesitated, turning her gaze out to stare at the water. "I think...Natalie was someone who was hard to know. And I think infatuation can make people overlook things that should be obvious. And both Parker and Dean were very infatuated with Natalie.

"Dean loved her, but she'd slept with Parker. It was hard for him to reconcile her betrayal with his love for her." She shrugged. "That's probably why he took it out on Parker. He couldn't bear to lose Natalie, so all his anger was directed at his supposed best friend." Her voice was bitter. "Then Natalie killed herself, and he's blamed himself ever since."

She took a deep breath and faced me again. "But like you said, it's all in the past."

"And yet, none of you have forgiven Parker," I persisted.

"He broke Dean's trust," she said. "That's not something easily forgiven."

Our eyes met in mutual understanding and I gave her a nod. Regardless of how I felt about the situation, Ryker and his friends believed Parker had betrayed him.

"So you didn't really say how you met," she said. "How long have you guys been dating?"

"A little over four months," I replied. "Ryker was working on a case that involved Parker. We met and he asked me out. Well, he didn't really ask," I amended. "More like told me I was going to dinner with him."

Amy laughed. "That sounds like Dean. He's never had a confidence problem when it comes to women. But I think it's awesome that you've been together this long. I think it's the longest actual relationship he's had in years."

That surprised me. "Really?"

She nodded. "It took a while for him to learn to trust again. I'm glad he brought you today, though. He hasn't brought anyone around for our approval in years."

"Well, I don't think Anisha's going to approve," I said ruefully.

"She'll come around," Amy said. "Especially if Dean is happy."

"You're talking about me, Amy?"

Ryker appeared over my shoulder, his hand sliding onto my hip. "Don't believe a word she says," he said to me. "It's all lies."

"I was just getting ready to tell her about the time you arrested that lady and it turned out to be a man," Amy teased.

Ryker groaned. "That's one strip search I'll never forget."

Amy and I laughed. After that, it was a little easier. Anisha didn't say much to me, but that was okay. Sammy was nice and the guys made everyone laugh with their constant ribbing of each other. All in all, it was a relaxing afternoon and by the time we'd eaten and gotten back to the pier, I'd consumed enough beer to be more than a little tipsy. I'd also deepened my tan and the bikini looked amazing. It was skimpier than anything I'd worn before, but I'd seen it on the hanger and had only thought of how Ryker would react when he saw it. Considering how he'd been using any excuse to touch me all afternoon, I thought it was a pretty good bet that he liked it very much.

Tyrone and Troy were docking the boat while Ryker and I stood at the bow, watching as the sun was beginning to set. His chest was hot against my back and his arms wrapped around my waist. I rested my head back against his shoulder and he leaned down to press his lips to the dip between my neck and shoulder.

Another boat was docked next to ours and I glanced over to the deck. A man stood opposite us, maybe thirty or forty feet away. He had on an unbuttoned white shirt that blew in the wind and his dark hair ruffled with the breeze. He was striking, a charisma about him drawing my eye as Ryker pressed kisses to my bare shoulder. Then he turned, and though he wore sunglasses I knew he was looking at me, and I realized why he looked so familiar.

It was Parker.

His chest was deliciously bare and showing the six-pack of muscles usually hidden underneath his suits. The loose-fitting linen pants he wore hit low on his lean hips. He was holding a glass of white wine, and once he saw me, he froze. I wondered if he knew who I was. Probably not, not at this distance with my hair tousled by the wind and wearing sunglasses. No doubt the bikini had caught his eye—he was a man, after all.

But then he dipped his head, just a little, just enough that it couldn't be mistaken for anything other than an acknowledgment. He took a drink of the wine, still looking my way.

"What the hell is he doing here?" Ryker's growl forced my gaze away from Parker.

"Out on his boat," I said. "Just like us." I'd forgotten about the bill, deducted from Parker's account every month, for docking his boat here. I'd never seen his boat before, though I'd known he had one.

"I don't like how he's looking at you." Ryker's arms pulled me farther back into him.

"He's looking at *us*," I said mildly. "And may I remind you that I'm his assistant. He looks at me every day."

"Not wearing that bikini, he doesn't."

I was distracted from the argument by someone else on Parker's boat. A woman. She'd just come up the steps from the cabin below

She was tall and lean—Victoria's Secret model–type lean—with long, dark hair, and sporting oversize designer sunglasses. Wearing a black bikini that made mine look like a modest vintage piece, she strutted up to Parker, blocking my view of him. She slid her hands around his waist and tipped her head up. The three-inch heels she wore put her only slightly shorter than he was. I saw his lips tilt in a half-smile, then he kissed her.

Well.

Good for him. Really.

There was an ache in my gut that hadn't been there before, but I ignored it. I still had half a beer left and I chugged it, daintily covering my mouth when the very non-dainty burp erupted.

"Oops. Sorry."

But Ryker just laughed and scooped me up in his arms. I squealed as the deck tilted underneath me, clutching at his shoulders.

"You shouldn't do that to someone who's drank as much as I have today," I said. "You're liable to get puked on."

"I'll take my chances," he said with a grin. "I'm ready to get home and get you out of that bikini that's been driving me insane all day."

I glanced over his shoulder to where Parker still stood with the woman. He was playing with her hair now and talking, and didn't look our way. My smile faded.

"Yeah, me too."

Later that night, we sat in my living room eating pizza, and I decided to bring up what had happened today.

"I don't think your friends like me all that much," I said, taking a drink of water. I needed to hydrate.

Ryker frowned at me as he reached for another slice. "Why do you say that?"

"Because I work for Parker and don't think he's the devil."

He rolled his eyes. "Don't be ridiculous. Of course they like you."

"How did you and Parker meet?" I asked, deciding to drop that particular topic. "No one seems to know."

"Why do *you* want to know?" he asked.

"Why don't you want to tell me?" I countered.

Ryker took a bite of pizza and chewed slowly. I remained quiet, hoping he'd open up to me. He swallowed and took a drink of his Coke.

"I've told you before that I had a single mom growing up," he said at last. I nodded. "We lived in a shitty trailer park in a bad part of town. Most days I was lucky if I didn't get into some kind of scrape on my way home from school. Gangs ran that part of town and they were always recruiting.

"My mom was dead set on me getting a decent education, so she paid tuition for a nicer school than the one in my district. Took nearly every spare dime she had, but she refused to let it go. I thought it would be a shitty way to repay her, by joining a gang. So I always said no, which sounds easy, but wasn't. They had all kinds of ways of pressuring you, from stalking you for a chance to rough you up, to threatening your family."

He took a deep breath and I remained quiet, listening. This was more than Ryker had ever told me before about his past.

"Anyway, there was this kid at school," he said. "A quiet kid, kind of a loner. Rich as fuck, of course. Most of them were. He used to watch me. Tried talking to me a couple of times, but I pretty much told him to fuck off. Figured he was just weird.

"One day I was waiting at the bus stop for my ride home. I had to take two different buses so I usually didn't get home until about six at night or later. It was early in the winter so it got dark early. I was waiting, and that was the night I got jumped. Three guys in high school, older than me. I wouldn't join their gang so they'd been told to fuck me over. And they would've, too, if Parker hadn't been there."

"Parker was there?" I asked in surprise.

"Yeah. He was the guy who wouldn't leave me alone. No clue why. Maybe he felt sorry for the charity case, maybe he just thought I could use a friend. The other kids treated me like a pariah in their midst. Not him. He was determined we were going to be friends. He'd followed me that day. He was curious, I think. His parents were way into sheltering him from society's degenerates. Like me, I suppose. Anyway, he flew right at those guys. Didn't even hesitate. Next thing I knew, two of them were on the ground and one was running away."

"What about you? Were you hurt?"

"They'd gotten me with a knife. Might've bled to death if Parker hadn't been there and gotten help. He saved my life that night."

"Why didn't you ever tell anyone?" I asked.

"Because Parker didn't want me to," he said with a shrug. "He knew it would only bring trouble for both of us. The gang would try again for me and might even target him, too, for revenge. As it was, no one really knew what went down that night. Safer for both of us at that age."

"How old were you?"

"Fourteen."

"Wow," I breathed. "That's...really young to be dealing with that kind of stuff."

"Tell me about it. Anyway, that pretty much sealed our friendship. I knew his parents could never stand me or understand why Parker would befriend someone from the South Side, but Parker was never like that. He would've died for me and me for him. Had each other's backs all through our deployment. I saved his life a couple times, and he returned the favor. I didn't think anything would ever—could ever—come between us."

He had a faraway look in his eyes now and his face looked older. Sadder. Impulsively, I reached for him, cupping his jaw in my hand. His day-old whiskers were rough against my skin.

"It doesn't have to be this way," I said. "You can be friends again."

But Ryker's smile was bitter as he took my hand, moving it from his face to rest on his thigh. "No. What he did was unforgivable. Sometimes, you can't go back. This is one of those times."

Natalie.

I didn't know why, but I felt as though I needed to do all I could to patch up Ryker and Parker's relationship. They were the two most important men in my life, and they meant something to each other. But in order to do that, I needed to know everything that had happened all those years ago. I needed to know *Natalie*, and I wasn't sure how to go about finding out.

CHAPTER TWO

It was the usual morning routine for me: running late because I'd decided to change the polish on my toes—*Kiss Me on My Tulips* didn't suit my mood, so instead I swapped it for *I Don't Give a Rotterdam*—and I nearly missed the bus. Luckily the driver liked me and knew my schedule, so he always gave me an extra thirty seconds or so to get my butt there.

"Thanks, Bob," I huffed with a smile, trying to catch my breath as I scrambled up the stairs and into a seat.

"Looks like you got some sun," he remarked, glancing in the overhead mirror at me.

"Yep. May be one of the last nice weekends we have," I said. "What did you do this weekend?"

We chatted on the way to my stop while I finished my makeup. Bob had been driving the same bus route for nearly five years and he always had a story or two come Monday morning. I'd given him homemade fudge last year for Christmas and he'd loved it so much, I'd made a mental note to give him a double batch this year.

My cell buzzed on my way into the Starbucks a couple of doors down from the office building. Pulling the phone out of my purse, I groaned when I saw the caller ID.

"Hi, Mom," I said, glancing at my watch.

"Good morning, sweetheart! You didn't call me back yesterday."

I held back a sigh. She'd left a voice mail Sunday evening, but I'd gone out to dinner with my friend Lilly, who lived in the apartment directly below me, conveniently not returning home until late.

"Sorry, Mom. I meant to call today." I winced at the white lie. It wasn't that I didn't enjoy talking to my mom, she just...asked a lot of questions.

"How's Dean?" She always asked this, ever since I'd broken the news to her a couple of months ago that I had a boyfriend. Usually, I didn't bother telling my parents until after the relationship lasted beyond the standard eight-week trial period.

"He's fine. We're fine. Everything's fine," I replied, heading off what I knew the next two questions would be.

"Wonderful! That's perfect because your father and I are going to be in the city tomorrow and want to take you and Dean to dinner."

I stopped in my tracks, then nearly got knocked to the ground by the flow of pedestrians behind me. I scurried on, weaving my way to the Starbucks door.

"What? Um, dinner? Well, I don't know if Ryker can make it. He has to work a lot—"

"I'm not taking no for an answer, young lady, and neither is your father. You've been seeing this man for several months and your father wants to know what kind of man is dating our daughter. If he's worth his salt, he'll want to meet us, too."

I winced. My mother was a cupcake, but my father was an entirely different matter. He hadn't built up an entire distribution company by being stupid. Smart and confident, he intimidated most people. Good thing Ryker wasn't like most people.

"Okay," I gave in. "I'll check and see if he's available."

"Good," she said, pleased satisfaction in her voice. "We'll pick you up at seven."

"Thanks, Mom."

"You're welcome. Love you, darling."

"Love you, too."

I absently ordered the usual grande coffee for Parker, ordering the grande pumpkin spice latte (extra whip) for me, as well as choosing an egg white panini with spinach and ham for his breakfast.

What would Ryker say when I told him my parents wanted to meet him? That was kind of a big step. Would it send him running for the hills? All his friends were married and having babies. Was that what he was looking for in this relationship? Was I?

I went through the motions of setting Parker's breakfast on his desk, putting away my purse, and checking voice mail and e-mail without really focusing on what I was doing. I didn't know if I was ready to be in a serious relationship. All of Ryker's friends had seemed so close-knit yesterday, whereas I'd been the outsider, no matter how friendly they were (or weren't, as the case with Anisha had been).

At exactly straight-up eight o'clock, Parker Anderson stepped off the elevator and came striding toward me.

It was secretly my favorite part of the day, a guilty

pleasure where I could watch him without seeming creepy about it. He was in a good mood. I could tell because he'd worn a light blue shirt rather than white—but not a great mood because he'd chosen a dark tie. If he'd been in a *great* mood, the tie would have been a light shade like a yellow.

"Good morning, Sage," he said, tucking his folded newspaper underneath his arm. He carried his briefcase in one hand and reached for the stack of messages I'd set on the chest-high counter that served as the "wall" for my cubicle.

"Morning," I replied, wondering if he'd say anything about seeing each other Saturday. His hair had the usual wave that made a lock of it fall over his forehead, which always made my fingers itch to push it back.

"Did you have fun this weekend?" he asked, still flipping through the messages.

A generic kind of question. I decided to push a little. "Yes. A friend of Ryker's has a boat he invited us on."

"Thought that was you," he said.

"It was." I was dying to ask about the woman, but I didn't dare. It wasn't like I hadn't known Parker dated around; I just hadn't seen a face to put with the fact like I had yesterday. Ever since he'd turned me down so blatantly a few months ago when I'd been up front about wanting more with him, we'd gone back to our professional interaction. Nothing too personal. Just business. I didn't talk about Ryker, and he didn't talk about the women he saw.

"You have a nice boat," I said, hoping it would coax some more information out of him, but he just smiled and said, "Thank you," then it was back to business.

"Conner left a message that he needs to reschedule," he said. "See what I have open on Wednesday."

"You had a two o'clock so I moved him there," I said, scrolling through his calendar on my computer.

"I thought I had the Bartholomew meeting with Gash and Knight then?"

"That's Thursday," I said. I knew Parker's schedule better than my own.

"Great. And make reservations for two at Everest for to-morrow night, will you? Eight o'clock."

"Sure," I said, jotting it down. Everest was this awesome restaurant I'd been dying to go to. Maybe Parker would bring in his leftovers for me. "Which client am I billing?"

"It's not for a client. It's personal."

Reflexively, I glanced up at him. Rarely did Parker go out to an expensive, exclusive restaurant on a weeknight unless it was with a client. I couldn't remember the last time. On the weekend, yeah, he'd take a date somewhere I guess; I didn't really know since I never made those reservations for him. He'd take care of those himself, so this was new on two fronts.

"Um, okay, yeah, sure," I stammered, my mind immediately flying back to the woman on the boat.

"Thanks, Sage." Then he was gone, disappearing through the glass door into his office.

I made the reservations, having to name-drop Parker in order to get them on such short notice. Then I was immersed in the day-to-day work of my job, filing a stack of trades that had come in from last week, replying to e-mails that Parker sent with requests for documents, and a thousand other things that filled up my morning.

"So how was your weekend?"

I turned to see Megan leaning on my counter. She was holding two Starbucks cups and handed over one to me.

"Thanks," I said, taking a sip. Megan was awesome—

she never forgot to have them add extra whip. "It was good. Went on a cool boat with Ryker Saturday and met some of his friends."

"Ooh, the friendship test," she said. "How'd it go?"

I shrugged. "It was going better until they found out I work for Parker. Apparently, they all hold a grudge."

"Wow," she said. "I get friendship and all, but that's a little much. It's not like you had anything to do with it."

"I know, and they came around. Well, most of them did." I decided not to worry about Anisha. "But that's not all that happened," I added.

Megan leaned forward, her unerring spidey sense twitching that I had something juicy to say.

"Tell me tell me tell me," she said, rapid-fire.

I glanced around, but no one was near, so I said in a low voice, "Saw some chick with Parker on his boat, which happened to be right next to ours."

Megan loved gossip the way I loved Reese's Peanut Butter Cups, and she eagerly leaned forward for more. "Really? You usually don't see his flavors of the month," she said. "What did she look like?"

"Thin. Tall. Gorgeous. Big tits." I rolled my eyes.

She grimaced in understanding. I'd told Megan about how close Parker and I had come to taking our relationship to a different level, and how he'd turned me down. I'd decided to move on, but it didn't make seeing his new, beautiful girlfriend any easier.

"Not surprised," she said. "It's not like he's looking for a woman who *can* actually walk and chew gum at the same time."

I grinned at her description.

"Wanna go to lunch today?" she asked, but I shook my head.

"Can't. It's Monday, you know. Parker will eat at his desk so I'll need to get his lunch. I'll grab a hot dog like usual."

"That's right. Sorry, I forgot it was Monday," she said. "The day's been so long it already felt like Wednesday."

I laughed. "I hear ya."

"Catch you later," she said, moving off.

"Thanks for the coffee," I called after her. She gave me a finger wave and disappeared around the corner.

At eleven-thirty, I headed to the restaurant where I always ordered the lunch special on Mondays for Parker. I munched on a plain hot dog as I went. A particularly unpleasant mishap with mustard and my blouse kept me from ever adding any condiments.

By eleven-fifty, I was on my way back and precisely at noon I was putting the finishing touches on folding Parker's linen napkin in the shape of fan. The aroma of the roasted chicken and mushroom risotto made my mouth water. Parker had stepped out to go talk to one of the managers who worked underneath him, but I expected he'd be back any moment.

Heading back to my desk, I glanced toward the elevators and stopped in my tracks.

The woman from the boat had just stepped off.

She looked like a fashion plate, wearing black trousers and a black corset with a delicate ivory lace overlay wrapped around her tiny waist. A matching ivory jacket cut high with pointed lapels, a heavy gold necklace, and black suede booties with four-inch heels completed her outfit. I felt downright dowdy in my gray pencil skirt and black blouse. Yes, I'd splurged and worn my red platforms, but still.

"Can I help you?" I asked as she paused a few feet away, glancing around uncertainly.

"Yes, please," she replied. She had a heavy French accent

and my stomach sank. "I am looking for Parker." The way she said his name, with the R rolling in the way I never could perfect back in high school French class, had jealousy inching its way into my gut. Yes, I could certainly see why Parker would be dating her. She'd been gorgeous from afar yesterday. Up close, she was stunningly flawless.

"He's not available right now," I said, knowing I probably shouldn't feel as satisfied to be able to say that as I did.

She frowned, her perfectly shaded coral lips curving down. "But we are to have lunch together," she said.

"You must be mistaken," I said. "Parker never leaves the office for lunch on Mondays."

"Monique, glad you could make it."

I turned to see Parker striding toward us, all smiles. For Monique, of course. When he turned to me, it was for a dismissal.

"Heading to lunch, Sage. I'll be back shortly." Taking Monique's elbow he began to steer her toward the elevators.

"But your lunch is on your desk," I blurted. I told myself my dismay was because he was wasting the lunch I'd gotten and *not* because he was taking Monique to lunch.

Parker glanced back, but didn't pause. "Oh yeah. Sorry about that. Forgot to mention it. Just toss it, will you? Or you can have it, if you want." He shrugged, then they were disappearing inside the elevator and I was left staring after them with my mouth hanging open.

I stood there like an idiot for a moment. The ugly twisting sensation inside my stomach felt too much like bitter jealousy, but I wanted to focus on that rather than the feeling of utter sadness that lurked right behind it.

Hurrying into his office, I grabbed the plate and napkin, channeling my jealousy and despair into anger. The least he could have done was tell me. It wasn't like this was a new thing. I got his lunch every single Monday and I'd done that for almost two years. It wasn't like him to be so thoughtless.

I'd worked up a good head of steam by the time I got to the kitchen and I viciously tossed the whole plate, chicken and all, into the sink. It shattered into several pieces, the silverware ricocheting off the side. I stood there, staring at it and breathing hard.

Did this change in his usually sacrosanct schedule mean he was serious about Monique?

No, he couldn't possibly be. He'd told me he didn't do relationships. This was just…an aberration, that's all. A one-time thing.

I shouldn't care. I was with Ryker and had just been wondering this morning if I wanted things to turn serious between us. Begrudging Parker the same thing was just… really small of me. And not fair to Ryker, either.

Upset and confused, I went back to my desk, throwing myself back into work and barely glancing up when Parker returned ninety-seven minutes later. Not that I was keeping track. And no way did I log in to his credit card account to see if he'd made any hotel charges today (he hadn't).

I knew I was in a sullen, bitchy mood, so I avoided conversations until I could shake myself out of it. Which might not be until tomorrow, I realized with a sigh. Thankfully, it was quitting time and I'd managed to go the whole rest of the afternoon without having to talk to Parker.

"Sage," Parker called over the intercom. "Can you come in here, please?"

Shit. I'd nearly been out the door. Setting my purse back down on my desk, I steeled myself. Plastering on a pleasant expression, I walked in his office. "Yes?"

"Did you make those reservations for me?" he asked.

I gritted my teeth. He could've asked me that over the intercom, or better yet, e-mail. "Of course," I said. "Was there anything else?"

"Sorry again about lunch today," he said.

I shrugged and forced a fake smile even though my cheeks felt like they were carved in wood. "It's not a problem. Will this be a weekly thing?" The question popped out of its own accord.

"Maybe. I'm not sure."

I kept smiling, my lips stretched tight. "Okay then." I turned to go.

"Sage—"

"Yes?" *Please just let me leave...*

"Monique thought you were quite pretty," he said. "I just thought I'd let you know that."

Dear God, kill me now. "How...sweet of her," I said. "She's...striking. Wherever did you, um, meet her?"

"A client introduced us," he said. "She's from Lyon. She's a model."

I'd been right. Not only the real-deal French, but an honest-to-God model. I hated her with every fiber of my being.

"That's so nice," I lied. "And you're taking her to Everest."

"She's French. She's a foodie."

"Of course."

An awkward silence descended, but I was too irrationally upset to bother trying to break it. I just stood there in front of his desk, waiting.

"How are you and Ryker doing?" he asked.

"Fine," I said stiffly. "We're fine."

More silence.

"Was there anything else?" I asked.

He studied me, the blue of his eyes piercing, until I flushed and looked away.

"I don't mean to be curt," I said, trying to push back my emotions and react the way any normal person would in this situation. "I'm glad you met her. She...seems nice."

Maybe it hadn't been that Parker didn't want a relationship. Maybe he just hadn't wanted a relationship with *me*.

The thought hurt, which made me feel even worse. I'd thought I was over Parker, over wanting anything between us. I cared about Ryker. A lot. Maybe I was even falling in love with him. So why was I so upset that Parker had maybe found someone, too? I should want him to be happy. If I *really* cared about him, I'd want him to be happy no matter what.

With that echoing inside my head, I blurted, "I hope you're happy. With her, I mean." My throat thickened and I swallowed hard.

"Sage—"

"Yeah, I gotta go," I managed, backing toward the door. "I'll see you in the morning." I didn't wait to see if he had more to say; I grabbed my purse off my desk and jumped in the elevator just as it was about to close.

I had to get a grip, I decided as I unlocked my apartment door and headed inside. Control my emotions, not the other way around. Chocolate would help with that. Specifically, peanut M&M's.

Digging into my cabinet, I pulled out the cookie jar my mom had given me one year for Christmas. I never put cookies in it, because frankly they wouldn't last very long, so I filled it with peanut M&M's. Dangerous to have around, which is why I kept it on a high shelf in the back of my pantry as a deterrent, which didn't matter one little bit when I wanted them. But I could still pretend.

Ryker called as I was heating up a microwave dinner and sipping on a glass of wine.

"Hey, babe, how was your day?" he asked.

"Fine. The usual," I said. I never went into great detail about my work or mentioned Parker at all, if I could help it. "You?"

"Cracked a case, made an arrest. Think we even got enough evidence to put him away, which is nice."

"Congrats," I said.

"Another day in paradise," he joked.

"Speaking of which, my mom called today." I reached for another handful of M&M's.

"How's she doing?"

"Fine," I said as I munched. "But her and Dad are going to be in town tomorrow night and...they want to take us to dinner." I swallowed and took a breath before blurting the bad news. "They want to meet you." I had no clue how he was going to react to this. We hadn't discussed being serious or even exclusive, but had let the relationship kind of progress at its own speed.

"That sounds great," he said.

"Really?"

He laughed, a low chuckle that thrummed in my ear. "Yes, really."

I smiled into the phone. "Okay then. They said they'd be here at seven."

"I'll probably have to meet you at the restaurant," he said.

"Okay. I'll text you as soon as I know where we're going. Are you coming over tonight?"

"Gotta take a rain check on that, too," he said. "But I have a few minutes if you want to talk dirty to me."

I snorted. "Yeah. That'll happen. Go arrest some bad guys. I'll talk to you later."

We disconnected and I went back to my M&M's and wine, which wasn't as bad a combination as it sounded.

* * *

The next morning, I'd resolved not to think at all about my confused feelings for Parker. How I was able to compartmentalize, I had no clue, but work went on as usual. Megan showed up at my desk for a mid-afternoon gossip break.

"So how's Todd?" I asked. Todd was relatively new to the company, an attorney from Omaha who'd wasted no time in asking Megan out a few months ago.

Megan grimaced.

"Oh no. What happened?"

"We had a fight," she said, looking glum. She leaned her hip against my desk as she scooted a little closer. "About his ex."

"What about her?"

"They're still communicating," she said. "You know, decided to be friends or something because he wanted to move here and she didn't, so they broke it off."

"That's not good," I said. "What if she changes her mind? Or he does? Is he still in love with her?"

Now Megan looked downright dejected. "Yeah, I think so. I told him I wasn't comfortable with him still being so close to his ex—I mean they text like all the time—but he said they were just friends and I shouldn't worry."

"Which means you should worry."

"Exactly."

"And to top it off," she continued, "Brian's been turning up again, sending me random texts about work stuff."

"No way is he texting you again," I said in disbelief. Megan had crushed on the eccentric and socially awkward IT guy for quite a while before giving it up as hopeless.

"I know, right?"

We commiserated for a while on the sometimes inexplicable behavior of men before we had to get back to our mutual jobs. But Megan talking about Todd still being hung up on his ex had me thinking about Natalie.

A few months ago, I'd found a photo of Ryker, Parker, and the woman I'd assumed to be Natalie tucked away in a dresser drawer in Ryker's bedroom. Keeping something like that made me think that maybe Todd wasn't the only one still hung up on an ex. And I was confused as to the conflicting reports I'd heard about Natalie. Ryker made her seem akin to a saint when he spoke of her, whereas Amy hadn't appeared to like her very much at all.

Was Ryker over Natalie? That was a question I wanted answered before I could decide whether or not "serious" was in the cards for us.

* * *

It was late in the afternoon when Parker called me into his office to work on a file for one of our biggest clients. It took a couple of hours and I kept glancing surreptitiously at my watch, wondering if I was going to have to cancel dinner with my parents. This last time, Parker caught me at it.

"Something wrong?" he asked, raising an eyebrow.

"No, I just—"

"Have a date with Ryker?" Parker interrupted.

"No. My parents are coming to take me to dinner," I said, omitting the information that Ryker was coming, too, and that he was in fact the entire reason for my parents driving into the city.

"Ah. I see." Parker settled back into his chair from where he'd been pacing as he talked through the case and I'd taken notes. "You know, I'd like to think we're still friends, you and me."

"We are?" Parker and I had never discussed our relationship after I'd left his apartment—and his bed—in the middle of the night.

"Of course. Which is why I told Monique I wasn't going to fire you."

"Excuse me?" Surely I had misheard. "I thought she said I was pretty."

"Oh, she did. That was the problem. She doesn't like the idea of me having a secretary who looks like you."

"Executive Administrative Assistant," I automatically corrected him. My immediate thought was, *what a bitch*. My next thought was to wonder why he was telling me this.

"I told her she was being ridiculous. And you're probably wondering why I'm telling you this," he said.

My internal *um, yeah* must've shown on my face.

"I like Monique," he said. "She's an...interesting diversion. But you...you are a fixture in my life and I wouldn't dream of firing you, especially at the whim of a temporary girlfriend."

"Is that what she is? Your girlfriend?"

"For the moment."

"I see."

"Is Ryker for the moment? Or a fixture?" he asked.

That gave me pause. Since when were we discussing our personal lives at work? Or anywhere, for that matter?

"Why do you care?" I asked.

"We're friends, Sage. I care. I just want what's best for you. Like you said last night, I want you to be happy, too."

He seemed genuine in his concern, his eyes locked on mine as he leaned forward onto his desk, his arms folded on top of the polished wood surface. The tie at his neck was loosened, a slight concession to it being after official working hours, and his jacket had been tossed on the leather couch in the corner. I'd been wanting to go hang it up so it wouldn't wrinkle for the past thirty minutes.

"Ryker and I...haven't really discussed the future," I said, deciding to be honest.

Parker got up and walked to the old-fashioned antique highboy where he kept his liquor and took out two glasses. "But he's meeting your parents tonight," he guessed.

Unsurprised that he'd figured that out, I nodded, watching as he poured an inch of amber liquid into each glass. "I met some of his friends this past weekend. People I think you know, too."

"And I bet not a one of them had a good word to say about me," he said, handing me one of the glasses as he took a sip from the other that he held. Returning to his chair, he leaned back, his hands folded on his abdomen, which caused my gaze to briefly wander before I jerked it back up to his face.

"It seems everyone knows all the details about you, Ryker, and Natalie," I said. "Except me." I took a drink of the scotch, the liquor burning a smooth path down my throat to warm my belly.

He shrugged. "I told you everything I thought you needed to know."

"Why does Amy not like her, but Ryker speaks of her as if she were a saint?" Maybe I could get more information out of Parker than Ryker.

Parker's lips twisted. "Ryker was always blinded to some darker spots in Natalie's nature. We both were, at first, but then I began to see her for who she really was. I tried to talk to Ryker, but he wouldn't listen. He just insisted that I'd stolen her from him, the love of his life." The last bit was said with more than a little contempt.

I hesitated, then decided since he was in a talkative mood,

I'd take advantage as much as possible. It wasn't like anyone else was going to tell me what I wanted to know.

"I saw a photo," I said. "Of the three of you. It looked like you were all friends."

"That's how it began," Parker said. "Natalie was very… manipulative. Very charismatic and charming. She knew how to get what she wanted."

"What did she want?"

"Both of us."

CHAPTER THREE

I was waiting outside when my parents pulled up. Shultz was driving them, as he'd driven them for the past twenty-some-odd years, and I didn't wait for him to get out and open the door to the car for me. I always felt guilty making him get out and come around, especially when I could just open the door myself.

"Hey, Mom. Dad," I said, giving them each a hug before taking the seat opposite them. The familiar cloud of my mother's perfume filled my nostrils.

"Where's Dean, dear?" Mom asked, glancing out at the sidewalk.

"He had to work so he's going to meet us at the restaurant," I said. "Where are we going?"

"Oh, your father wanted to go to Everest, since we don't get into the city very often anymore," she said. "He's been reading about it in those magazines he gets."

My father thought himself a foodie, though he was from

Chicago's South Side and the fanciest thing he ate growing up was hot dogs on an actual bun instead of a rolled-up slice of white bread. A few years ago, he'd taken up cooking as a hobby.

Then I remembered.

"Everest?" I blurted. "Uh, isn't there someplace else you want to go? I hear it's hard to get in there, like you have to make reservations weeks in advance." I really didn't want to watch Parker with Monique tonight. Seeing them together on the boat had been quite enough.

Dad just looked at me strangely. "Since when has your old man ever had a problem getting a table at a restaurant?"

"How's work going for you?" Mom interjected.

"Fine, it's fine," I said with a sigh, knowing it was futile. With any luck, though, we wouldn't see them. After all, Parker's reservation wasn't for another—I glanced at my watch—half hour. Pulling out my phone, I sent a quick text to Ryker.

"You always say 'fine,'" my mother complained. "You know your father can talk to some people, see about getting you on at the museum. You don't have to be a secretary, Sage."

"Executive Administrative Assistant," I corrected her. "And we've discussed this. I don't want Daddy to pull strings to get me a job. I keep applying whenever there's a position open. If it's meant to be, it'll happen."

"Sometimes things that are meant to be need a little help," she replied.

"I'll keep that in mind." My parents meant well, I just wanted to get a job at the museum on my own merit, not because of how much money my father agreed to donate.

"Here we are," my father announced as the car slowed and pulled up to a curb outside the Chicago Stock Exchange.

I followed my mother out of the car and waited as she

slipped her hand through Dad's arm. My father may have grown up dirt poor, but he'd fallen in love with a woman who brought out the best in him, including treating her like a princess. He offered me his other arm.

"Shall we, my lovely ladies?"

I grinned up at him and he pressed a quick kiss to my cheek, then the three of us went inside and took the elevator up to the fortieth floor. As he'd predicted, once the maitre d' saw my father, he had no trouble finding a table for us. It wasn't just his imposing presence at over six feet combined with a formidable girth that made him recognizable, but also his name. Joe Muccino was a name anyone familiar with the liquor business in Chicago knew, and even those who weren't still knew of him.

It had been so bad in school that I'd taken my mother's maiden name as my last name when I'd gone to college. Not that it wasn't nice to have people know your father was a wealthy and powerful man, but I'd just wanted to make my own way without the special favors.

The sommelier brought a bottle of wine, opening and pouring it for us as I checked my phone. Ryker had just texted that he was on his way and should be there any moment. I settled my hands back into my lap, gazing at the pretty candle and flowers on the table. The flickering light reflected off the silverware and crystal glasses. While the restaurant was full, it wasn't loud, so you could have a conversation without any problem.

I looked over the menu as Mom leaned over toward Dad to read him the entrees. Although he needed reading glasses, he absolutely refused to get them. But Mom didn't seem to mind translating.

Taking another sip of wine, I glanced past them... and almost choked. Parker had just entered the restaurant. Though

I'd been hoping not to see him tonight, there he was, like fate was having a big laugh at my expense. Monique wasn't with him yet and I figured he was meeting her here, just as I was doing with Ryker.

I stared at him, aghast, and prayed somehow he'd pass by without spotting us. But as if he could sense my presence, Parker turned his head and his gaze locked right on mine.

Oh no. He was *so* going to think I'd chosen to come here because I'd known he was bringing Monique. Would he think I was spying on them? God, that would be so embarrassing. I scooted down in my seat, hoping beyond hope that he hadn't recognized me. It was possible. The lighting was low enough he might think he'd been mistaken.

"Don't slouch in your seat, dear," my mom said mildly. Of course, I couldn't tell her that I wasn't slouching—I was hiding. Maybe Parker would just go sit down.

I watched as he followed the maitre d' to a table only two away from ours—the universe hated me—and breathed a sigh of relief…that was abruptly choked off when he thanked the maitre d', turned, and headed our way.

"Mr. Muccino, I thought that was you," Parker said, holding his hand out to my father, who took it and gave it a firm shake.

"Mr. Anderson, it's been a while since we've seen each other face-to-face," Dad said. "I take it my investments are doing well?"

My jaw had dropped open in shock at this exchange. I'd never told Parker who my parents were and while they knew I worked at KLP Capital, I'd always referred to Parker as just "my boss." And I'd had no idea Parker handled business for my father.

"Absolutely. Don't doubt that," Parker said with a warm smile.

"Anderson, this is my wife, Barbara," Dad said. Mom smiled and held out her hand.

"Please call me Barb," she said.

"And my daughter, Sage."

My smile was weak, but Parker's had a bit of the devil in it as he took my hand. His eyes met mine, and I suddenly knew he wasn't a bit surprised to see who my parents were, the shit. How long had he known?

"You have a lovely wife and daughter," Parker said, all charm as he pressed his lips to the back of my hand and his blue eyes danced with humor.

I thought my heart skipped a beat, maybe two.

"Sit down," my father invited, gesturing to the empty chair at our table.

"He can't," I blurted.

Everyone turned to look at me.

"I-I mean, I'm sure he's not alone, right?" I sent a frantic message with my eyes to Parker.

"Actually, my companion had to cancel," he said smoothly.

"Then that settles it," my dad said in his no-nonsense voice. "You're joining us for dinner."

I choked on air.

"Are you all right?" Mom asked. "Here, have a drink of water." She handed me my water glass.

I swigged the water, my gaze inexorably drawn to Parker, who seemed to be even more amused now. This was turning into a nightmare. Not only would Ryker be meeting my parents for the first time, but it seemed Parker was going to be a witness to it.

"If you're sure," Parker said, his eyes still on mine and his lips twisted in a half-smile. "I'll just be a moment."

The next few minutes were a daze of *this-can't-really-be-happening* as my father flagged down the waiter to order more wine and Parker fetched the maitre d' and told him he wouldn't need a table after all.

I was trying really hard not to let my irritation and stress show, but Parker knew me too well and I saw him hide a smile as he sat down next to me. I pulled out my phone, checking to see if a miracle had occurred and Ryker'd had to cancel or something.

"It's rude to be on your phone at dinner," Parker said in my ear, his voice low so only I could hear.

I sent him a glare that would have withered any other man, but he just smiled benignly.

"I take it you've never told your parents about me?" he asked.

I glanced at my mom and dad, who were asking the waiter about tonight's specials as he uncorked another bottle and poured.

"No," I hissed back. "You're just my asshole boss that barges in on dinner with my parents, makes me work the weekends, calls at all hours—"

"Not anymore," he interrupted.

I frowned, looking quizzically at him.

"I don't call you at all hours anymore," he said, reaching for his glass of merlot and taking a drink.

Yes, that was true. I'd just thought it was coincidence, but the way Parker said that made me think it was something he'd done on purpose. Which kind of sucked. He'd been de-liberately putting distance between us, actively working to decrease his dependence on me, and though it had been good for my and Ryker's relationship, it still gave me an ick feel-ing in my stomach.

"Ryker *is* coming, isn't he?" Parker asked. "Because I'd sure hate to miss this."

"Anderson, do you know Sage's boss?" Dad interrupted. "He works at KLP, too. I'm sure you know him. Perhaps you can put in a word. He works her much too hard. Just two weeks ago she couldn't come home for her aunt Iris's birthday party because he made her work on a Saturday."

My cheeks burned. Parker hadn't made me work that weekend. I'd had plans with Ryker, so had fibbed to my parents about the exact reason I couldn't come home. I steadfastly refused to look at Parker, and his silent presence beside me felt like a monolith of judgment.

"Yes," Mom emphatically agreed. "You must talk to him, Parker. Sage needs time off like anyone else, especially when it's to visit family."

"Mom, Dad, stop," I blurted. "Parker *is* my boss."

They both fell silent and looked at me as though I'd sprouted wings.

"What do you mean?" Dad asked.

"She means that she wasn't sure exactly how to tell you that she works for me," Parker smoothly interjected. "And you're absolutely right. Sage works much too hard. I apologize that she missed Aunt Iris's birthday party. It won't happen again."

My eyes slipped closed as now shame warred with embarrassment. Not only had Parker caught me in a lie, he'd taken the blame for something that wasn't his fault.

"Have you tried the foie gras?" Parker asked, changing the subject. "It's really excellent."

"We have not. Joe, let's order some of that, shall we? It sounds delicious." My mother was a master of conversation. She could make anyone feel at ease and smooth over awkward moments, such as now.

And the bump in the road that was me was effortlessly transitioned into dinner talk. I shot my mother a grateful

look and she smiled a bit, though I knew I'd have some ex-
plaining to do later.

"I'm glad to see you tonight," Parker said to my father.
"There was an opportunity I wanted to discuss."

He launched into business-speak with my dad and I
sipped my wine, glancing at my watch nervously every few
moments. By the time the foie gras came, Dad and Parker
were talking like they were old buddies instead of business
associates, laughing at some joke Dad had made.

"My girl here is your secretary, eh?" he asked.

"She's my assistant, yes," Parker replied, glancing at me.
"The best one in the company, as far as I'm concerned, and
irreplaceable. I have no idea what I'd do without her."

That made me feel way too warm and fuzzy inside. I
could tell both my parents liked that and my mother got a
gleam in her eye as she looked at Parker that I didn't like
the look of *at all*. Mom had been waiting for me to meet Mr.
Right since I'd graduated college, and I could practically see
the wheels turning inside her head.

Feeling Parker's gaze on me, I glanced up and our eyes
met. I could swear he was sitting closer to me than he had
been just moments ago, and I could smell the warm, spicy
scent of his cologne. It was the closest we'd been in proximity to each other since I'd been wrapped in his arms in his
bed.

Perhaps the same thought flashed through his mind, because his eyes darkened and suddenly it was harder to
breathe.

"Sage?"

My stomach bottomed out as I spun around to see Ryker
standing a couple of feet behind me. I nearly tripped in my
haste to get up out of my chair.

"You made it!" I said, somewhat breathless. I stepped

into his arms for a quick kiss, and while he obliged, I could tell he wasn't happy by the tension in his body. Taking his hand, I led him to the table. "Mom, Dad, this is Dean Ryker. Dean, my dad, Joe." I deliberately left off the last name.

My father stood to shake his hand. "Pleased to finally meet you," he said.

"Likewise," Ryker replied. His smile was genial enough, but I could tell it was forced as his gaze kept twitching back to where Parker sat, unperturbed.

"We happened to run into Sage's boss," my father continued, gesturing to Parker. "He's joining us for dinner as well."

"How nice," Ryker said, his icy gaze meeting Parker's, who just gave him a nod and a bland smile.

"This is my mom," I hurriedly said, introducing them.

We sat down and that's when I realized I was sandwiched between the two men. The table sat six, but there was an empty chair between Ryker and my father. Oh lord, as if this evening wasn't awkward enough already...

"Nice shirt," Parker said to Ryker, making my head swivel around. I hadn't noticed, but Ryker had dressed nicer than usual. He still wore jeans and boots, but his shirt was button-down and he wore a sport coat underneath his leather jacket. Granted, it wasn't a suit, nor was it the quality or caliber of Parker's or my father's attire, but I was glad he'd made an effort.

I leaned closer to him. "Yeah, you look really nice," I said in an undertone. I smiled at him, hoping to put him a little more at ease, and he finally smiled back. A real smile that softened his eyes.

"Would you care for some wine, sir?" the waiter asked Ryker.

"Do you have any beer?" he asked instead.

"Yes, sir. Which brand would you like?" He rattled off a list of at least a half-dozen.

"Just a Budweiser, if you have it," Ryker said.

"Absolutely. I'll be right back with that, sir."

"So you're a police officer," my mother said, pulling our attention to her. "What kind of police work do you do?"

"I'm a homicide detective," Ryker replied.

"And is that dangerous?"

He hesitated, and I could see where this was going. "It can be," he answered honestly.

My mother shot me a look that said loud and clear what she thought of that.

"What about your parents?" Dad asked. "Was your dad a police officer, too?"

"My father left my mother when I was young," Ryker said. "I haven't seen him since."

Awkward silence.

The waiter returned with a chilled glass and poured a bottle of beer into it. No one spoke until he'd finished and set the glass in front of Ryker, then left again.

"I'm sorry to hear that," Mom said. "Does your mother live close?"

"She moved to Florida a few years ago," Ryker said. "The warm weather was preferable to Chicago winters."

"I can't disagree with her there," Mom said with a smile. "She sounds like a smart lady."

"She is," Ryker agreed. "Raised me on her own in a part of Chicago most people try to ignore exists."

"Which part?" Dad asked.

"Englewood."

"I grew up not far from there," Dad replied. "I still have some cousins on that side of town."

"Really? What're their names?"

I wanted to slap my hand over Dad's mouth, but he was proud of his family and how not only had he made something of himself, but so had my uncles.

"The Muccinos. Maybe you've heard of them?"

Ryker blanched, his accusing gaze swiveling to mine. I gave him a weak smile.

"I have, actually," he said, still looking at me. His gaze flicked briefly to Parker, then back to my Dad. "I didn't realize Sage *Reese* was Sage *Muccino*."

Dad laughed. "The one and same."

And things only went downhill from there.

By the look on his face, I didn't think Ryker liked most of the things on the menu, and ended up getting the steak while I had the duck and Parker ordered the halibut. My mother asked Ryker a lot of questions, but his answers weren't elaborate. I knew he was pissed about Parker being there, but it wasn't like there was anything I could do about it.

I think Dad figured out pretty quick that Ryker wasn't in a chatty mood, so he focused his attention on Parker as they discussed the relative strength of the dollar and the Asian markets. I tuned them out. Our food took an excruciatingly long time to arrive, by which time my mother was glancing helplessly at me and I was on my third glass of wine. Or was it the fourth?

"So I imagine you must deal with a lot of the seedy side of Chicago," Dad asked Ryker as he cut into the lamb he'd ordered.

"Homicide isn't known for rescuing kittens from trees, no," Ryker replied dryly, which I thought was a little rude. I shot him a look, but my father just chuckled.

"True. How long have you been a cop?"

"Seven years," Ryker replied. "Shortly after I was discharged, I went into the Academy."

"Discharged? You were in the service?"

"The Marines."

Dad turned to Parker. "You were in the Marines, too, weren't you, Anderson?"

"Yes. Coincidentally, in the same platoon as Detective Ryker."

Both my parents looked up from their plates at this, glancing first at Parker, then Ryker.

I took another gulp of wine, draining my glass. Raising my hand slightly, I signaled the waiter for a refill.

"So you two know each other," Mom said.

"It was a long time ago," Parker evaded.

Ryker's cell phone buzzed and he dug it out of his pocket. "I'm sorry, I need to take this," he said, pushing back from the table.

My father waved him on as the waiter cleared our plates and dropped off the dessert menu.

"So you know Ryker," Dad said to Parker. "Tell me, is he the right kind of man to be dating my daughter?"

"Dad—" I interrupted, mortified. He held up a hand to shush me, which really sent me over the edge. "Are you shushing me?" I hissed at him, but he shot me a look, and since I'd seen that look many times growing up, I snapped my mouth shut. But I still glared at him.

"I trust Anderson here with my money. I trust his opinion on this." He glanced back at Parker. "Well?"

Parker hesitated, considering his words carefully. "Ryker is a good man, an honest man."

"That doesn't answer my question," Dad replied.

"It's not up to me to say if he's the right kind of man for Sage," Parker said. "That's up to her."

Well at least one of the men here had some sense.

Ryker stepped back to the table again but didn't sit down.

Instead, he swung his leather jacket back on. "I hate to do this, but I need to go," he said. "That was work and I'm needed down at the precinct."

"Of course we understand," Mom said graciously. "It's been lovely meeting you."

My Dad stood to shake his hand and I pushed back my chair, too.

"We'll chat again soon, Dean," he said.

"I'll walk you out," I said.

We didn't speak in the elevator as it had several other people in the car with us, but to me it felt as though the tension between us was thick and heavy.

In the lobby, he turned to me as others moved past us and the space emptied. "Stay inside," he said. "It's cold out and you left your coat upstairs." He turned to go, but I grabbed his sleeve.

"Wait, that's it? You were barely civil to my parents the entire time you were here, and now you have to leave, and that's all you're going to say? 'It's cold out'?"

"What do you want me to say?" he asked, his eyes narrowing. "I get here and find Parker sitting at the same damn table, right next to you. What the hell? Then I find out you've been lying to me this whole time about who you are."

"That's not true! I told you my parents were wealthy and where I came from—"

"You didn't tell me you're a Muccino," he interrupted.

Ryker was angry, but so was I. "I've never lied to you about *who I am*," I said. "I'm Sage, and it shouldn't matter one damn bit what my last name is." I turned on my heel to walk away, but he grabbed my arm and yanked me back until we were nearly touching.

"You think it doesn't matter that your father runs seventy percent of the liquor business in Chicago?" His voice was incredulous. "Or that your whole extended family has a file ten inches thick down at the station?"

"My father has never done anything illegal," I hissed.

"That you know about," he retorted. "Don't be naïve, Sage."

"Naïve about what?" I spat, furious. "Don't you dare try to imply that my dad is a criminal." I tried to pull my arm out of his grip, but his hold was too tight.

"You think I want to disillusion you?" he gritted out. "I've just been blindsided by the fact that the woman I'm in love with is the daughter of a mob boss!"

I stared at him, my mouth agape, and I wasn't sure if I was stunned because of what he'd said about my father or what he'd said about being in love with me.

Ryker growled a curse, then he kissed me.

His lips pressed hard against mine, his palm cradling my jaw as his fingers slid into my hair. He lightly sucked my lower lip, sending a spark of heat through me, and I eagerly opened my mouth. His tongue slid alongside mine and before I realized it, he had me pressed against the wall. My fingers curled into the leather covering his shoulders and my knees felt too weak to hold me.

Ryker's leg nudged between mine, and the hunger and residual anger in his kiss made me breathless. The hard muscles of his thigh pressed against a very soft, very aroused part of me, and I moaned into his mouth.

When he lifted his head, I was completely turned on and utterly boneless. I was also vaguely considering the idea of finding the nearest empty room and having Ryker finish what he'd started. I didn't think he'd put up much of an objection, considering the fire in his eyes as he looked at me...or the hard length of his erection against my hip.

"Walk me to my bike?" he asked, his voice all rough and

evoking images of him tearing off my clothes. Or of me tearing off his. I was good with either.

"I thought it was too cold."

His lips twitched at my sass, then he slipped off the leather jacket and swung it over my shoulders. I was enveloped in Ryker's scent mixed with leather as I pushed my arms into the too-long sleeves. Sliding an arm around my waist, he kept me close to his side as we walked outside.

The wind was chilly and I shivered, huddling inside Ryker's coat. We stopped by his motorcycle and he pulled me into him, his hands inside the jacket and curled low on my hips. Ryker's body blocked the wind and I pressed against him, twining my arms around his neck. His hands slid to my rear.

"We'll finish this discussion later," he said.

"All right," I agreed. "Do you want to—"

"McCrady? Is that you?"

Ryker went rigid, his head jerking up to look behind me. "Fucking Christ," he muttered. "This day just keeps getting better and better."

I twisted to try and see who he was looking at, but his hands were vises around my waist.

"Go inside. Now," he ordered.

Ryker's tone was steel, precluding any argument. The look on his face scared me, and his eyes were cold and locked on to someone behind me. He turned me, pushing me behind him and toward the building. I hurried for the door.

"It *is* you! Well how about that?" The voice was coming closer and, despite the words, didn't sound friendly. If anything, the man sounded pissed. And what he said next made me stop in my tracks.

"What a surprise to see you alive," the man said to Ryker. "But that can be remedied."

CHAPTER FOUR

I was two steps from the door but spun back around. A man had approached Ryker while two other men flanked him like security guards. The one who'd done all the talking was shorter than Ryker, with salt-and-pepper hair and a hard face. His nose was crooked in a way that said he'd had it broken and not set back right.

"Whaddya say you take a ride with me, McCrady, and tell me where you been for the past four years?"

Alarmed, I tried to think what to do. These guys didn't look nice and they'd obviously mistaken Ryker for someone else. He was outnumbered, and was that a bulge I saw underneath their arms? Were they carrying guns?

Just then, I saw my mother and Parker come out of the building. My dad wasn't there—probably paying the bill still—and they were talking. Neither had spotted me yet, not in the dark. Hoping I was doing the right thing, I scurried back to Ryker, squeezing through the men and putting myself as a shield between them and Ryker.

"Hey, honey, can you do your business later?" I asked. "My parents want to talk with you."

Ryker looked furious and I knew I'd pay for interfering later, but I didn't care.

"Who's your girl here?" the man said. "You on a date, McCrady?"

I expected Ryker to correct the man, but he didn't. "It's none of your business, Leo."

"Sage! There you are! Come here, dear."

All of us turned to see my mother beckoning me.

"Am I interrupting a meeting with the parents?" the man asked, his sarcasm thick. His gaze turned to me.

"I don't believe we've met," I said stiffly.

"Pardon my manners," he said, offering me a slightly mocking tip of his head. "I'm Leo Shea."

"Sage Reese," I replied, polite but not friendly. I still stood in front of Ryker, blocking them from him. If they took him, it'd be over my dead body. "C'mon," I said to Ryker. "You can talk with your…friends…later."

I tugged his hand, pulling him out from between where the three men had hemmed him in.

"Catch you later, Leo," Ryker said.

"You can count on it."

Parker and my mother were talking, but I noticed Parker's sharp eyes were watching the exchange. Leo and his guards got into a waiting car and pulled away from the curb. I let out a breath of relief once they were gone.

"What the hell were you doing?" Ryker hissed in my ear.

Yeah. I'd been right. He was seriously pissed.

"What was I supposed to do?" I hissed right back. "Let them put you in a car and dump you in the river?"

"You were supposed to do what you were told and go inside."

"Wasn't that Leo Shea?" Parker asked, and I realized he'd come up behind us. I glanced at him.

"Mind your own business, Parker," Ryker snapped.

"Wasn't Shea indicted for drug trafficking a few years ago?" Parker asked, ignoring him. "But the case got tossed, right?"

Ryker's hand was nearly crushing mine as he stared at Parker. I winced as his hold got even tighter. Parker's gaze flicked to mine, then our joined hands.

"Ease up there, buddy," Parker said. "Sage needs both her hands to type."

"I'm not your buddy, so fuck off," Ryker shot back, but his grip immediately eased. "C'mon, Sage. I'll drop you off at home on my way in to the precinct."

Parker and Ryker were staring daggers at each other. I could practically feel the testosterone aggression pouring off both of them. With an internal sigh, I left them to it and hurried to my mother just as my dad exited the building. I gave them both a kiss and hug good-bye and thanked them for dinner.

"Shall we take you home, dear?" Mom asked, pressing her lips to my cheek.

"That's okay. Ryker will take me." I absently motioned with my hand toward his motorcycle as I turned to see if Parker and Ryker had come to blows. Not yet, but they didn't look far off, if body language was any indicator. They were actually talking, though, which I took as a good sign.

"Please tell me you're not pointing to that *motorcycle*," Mom said. The dismay in her tone had me whipping back around as an *oh shit* went through my head. Probably shouldn't have mentioned the bike…

"Uh, well, um, yeah," I stammered. "But it's fine. It's safe. Ryker's a good driver—"

"You've ridden on it before?" she asked, appalled. "In the *city*?"

"I can take Sage home," Parker interjected from where he stood. I hadn't realized our conversation had carried to them, but now I saw both Ryker and Parker looking at us. Ryker's expression was carefully blank. "It's on my way," Parker added.

On his way *where*, I had no clue, because Parker's apartment was the opposite direction from mine, but before I could say anything, my father spoke.

"Thanks, Anderson. Knew I could count on you." Dad led my mother to where their car stood waiting. In the next moment, they were in the backseat and the car was pulling away, leaving me with an angry Ryker and a Parker who was...

Yeah, I couldn't gauge his mood at all.

"Let's go," Ryker said to me, beckoning.

I avoided Parker's eyes as I hurried to Ryker, but Parker latched on to my arm as I passed him.

"Her parents think *I'm* taking her home," he said.

"And they're gone now, so it doesn't matter," Ryker said, taking my hand.

"So you're going to lie to her parents, ten minutes after you've met them?"

"*I* didn't lie to them. *You* did."

Both of them had a hold of me and neither one was letting go.

"I'm taking her home," Parker said. "I told them I would."

"That's too bad. Looks like your mouth got ahead of you. As usual."

"Stop it! Both of you!" I said, irritated. "Tonight has been a disaster from start to finish and the last thing I want to do is put up with you two in a pissing contest." I turned to Ryker. "Go on and go. It'll be thirty minutes out of your way to take me home and you said you had to get in to work."

"You're my responsibility," he stubbornly persisted. "I'll take you."

My already frayed temper lit up. "I'm not anyone's *responsibility*," I retorted, slipping off his jacket. "Least of all yours." I thrust his coat at him before spinning on my heel and stalking off. After a few steps, I stopped and glanced back. "Parker, you taking me home or what?" I could get a cab, but from here, the fare wouldn't be cheap and it was much preferable to ride in the clean confines of Parker's BMW.

Parker shot Ryker a look that may have been triumphant, but I didn't care. Ryker had pushed me too far tonight and I wasn't about to become the bone between two alpha dogs.

Nothing tonight had gone like I'd wanted it to and now it seemed like a huge mistake to be dating Ryker at all. He was a dangerous kind of guy, with honey-come-get-me looks and sharp edges all around. Were we one of those couples where the only place we really fit well together was in bed?

Parker and I didn't say much until we were on the road, then I took the opportunity to quiz him about Leo. Parker had acted like he'd known who he was and I didn't see a better chance to find out, especially since I had significant doubts that Ryker would be forthcoming with information.

"So you knew that guy?" I asked. "Leo Shea?"

Parker glanced at me, then back at the road. "Yeah. Supposedly, he runs a drug trafficking ring that helps get narcotics into Chicago and distributed. They arrested him a few

years ago, but the case got thrown out on a technicality. It
was a big deal at the time."

I vaguely remembered something about it, but watching
the news had never been one of my favorite pastimes.

"He called Ryker 'McCrady,'" I said. "I kept waiting for
Ryker to correct him, but he didn't. Instead, Leo said something about how he thought Ryker was supposed to be dead."

That earned a sharp look from Parker. "What happened?"

"I intervened because Leo said something about taking
Ryker for 'a ride.'"

Parker was silent for a few moments and I waited impatiently. "Well?" I said at last. "What do you think it means?"

His gaze was steady when he replied. "I think it means
that Ryker has a past he hasn't told you about. And I think
it's extremely unfortunate that Leo Shea knows you're involved with a man he knows as McCrady."

Yeah, that's what I'd been afraid he'd say. "You think
maybe Ryker worked undercover or something? And that's
why Shea knows him?" We'd both been thinking it. I just put
it into words.

"Yes, I do."

"I wonder if Ryker had anything to do with him getting
arrested then," I mused.

"Probably."

We pulled into the lot of my building and while I'd expected Parker to drop me off, he parked instead.

"You don't have to walk me up," I said. "I'll be fine."

"I'm sure you will," he said, beeping the car lock. "But
just in case, I'll make sure."

My nerves were jangling as we went inside and waited
for the elevator to take us up to my apartment on the third
floor. At work, there was always something to talk about.
Outside of work . . . all I could think about was how much we

hadn't discussed, like That Night (which was how I always thought of it inside my head).

"I didn't realize you knew who my dad was," I said.

"The firm does background checks on everyone," he said with a shrug. "Since you were using your mother's name, I assumed there was a reason and didn't see the need to pry."

The elevator dinged and we stepped inside. As usual, Parker looked impeccable even after a day of work. His tie wasn't even loosened and the smooth wave of his hair fell over his brow in an almost seductive kind of way.

I realized I was staring and jerked my gaze from him to the elevator doors as the floors slid by. When my floor opened, I tried again.

"Thanks for bringing me home," I said, stepping into the hallway ahead of him. But he just smiled in a benign sort of way and followed me.

"You're welcome."

I wanted to gnash my teeth in frustration and barely restrained myself from stomping to my apartment. I'd done a lot of work inside my head to get over my feelings for Parker, and being in close proximity to him outside of our usual environment and the rules that governed it wasn't helping.

"So are Ryker and you having a...disagreement?" he asked, smoothly taking my keys out of my hand and unlocking my door. He stepped inside and I had no choice but to follow him.

"We probably shouldn't discuss Ryker," I said, tossing my purse down on the kitchen table. "Our relationship is between us."

"Fair enough," Parker said.

I stood in the middle of the kitchen, arms crossed. I didn't want him there and wasn't about to play hostess.

However, it appeared I didn't have to, since he went to my cabinet where I kept my glasses and liquor and proceeded to help himself.

"Would you like one, too?" he asked, loosening his tie with one hand while he poured with the other.

My gaze was caught on his fingers as he tugged the silk and I had to shake myself back to awareness. Dragging my eyes up, I saw him looking at me, the tip of his mouth curving upward just slightly. As though he knew exactly what I'd been watching him do and the thoughts that had flitted through my head.

"If you're offering me my own liquor, then yeah, I guess so," I said, sounding more belligerent than I felt.

Parker didn't reply, just retrieved another glass off the shelf and splashed some of the amber liquid into it. Carrying it, he walked to where I still stubbornly stood and handed it to me. I had to uncross my arms to take it.

"Wouldn't Monique have a problem with you being here?" I asked, and yes, it was said in that bitchy tone that had most men looking for the nearest exit whenever they heard it.

"Why should I care?" he asked with a shrug, then clinked his glass against mine. "To a nice dinner with your parents," he toasted.

I eyed him as I took a sip. "It wasn't nice," I said. "It was awful and uncomfortable, and I have you to thank for most of that."

"It's not my fault Ryker still acts like a teenager instead of a grown man whenever he sees me," Parker replied coolly as he took another drink.

"Well, we're together now," I said. "So I'd appreciate it if you didn't antagonize him."

His expression went carefully blank at that, then he turned and walked to the windows. I didn't have the kind of view Parker did at his apartment, but the city and the lights were still pretty.

"Are you in love with him?"

I stared at his back, sure I'd misheard.

"What?"

"I asked, are you in love with him," Parker repeated.

"Again, none of your business." In dire need of the liquor in light of where this conversation was heading, I tossed back the bourbon in one swallow. I coughed a bit as the liquid burned a fire down my throat, but not as much as someone who wasn't used to it. Which probably said more about my alcohol consumption than I'd like.

"Are you in love with Monique?" I shot back. If he was going to get personal, then so would I.

"I'm not looking for love," he replied. "And neither is she."

I shouldn't have been as glad to hear that as I was.

"I knew it was you, Saturday," he said. "Right away. As soon as I saw you and Ryker on the boat."

Well, that put *that* question to rest, but I didn't know what to say in response. So he'd seen us. So what?

At last, I said, "I saw you and Monique. Does it matter?" I was tired and this conversation with Parker was going nowhere, not to mention I didn't even know why we were having it in the first place. I dropped onto the couch and kicked off my heels.

Parker didn't answer. He turned and watched me, his back to the window. His face was thrown into shadows, though his body was outlined against the backdrop of Chicago at night.

"I thought I could handle it, you and Ryker," he said. "These past few months, God knows I've been trying. But seeing it like that…his hands on you…his mouth on you." He paused and when he spoke again, it was a low rasp of sound. "I didn't like it." Swallowing the rest of his drink, he set the glass aside.

I stared at him in openmouthed shock. Hurt twisted in my gut, followed swiftly by anger, and I jumped to my feet.

"Tell me you did *not* just say that," I snapped. "What exactly do you expect me to do with this information?"

Parker's gaze was steady on mine. "I'm not expecting you to do anything. You're dating Ryker." He walked toward me, not stopping until only inches separated us and I had to tip my head back to look him in the eye. With my heels on, Parker topped me by a good three to four inches. Without them, he towered over me. "I just wanted you to know."

"You were the one who said there was never going to be an *us*," I said, poking him hard in the chest, which probably hurt me more than it hurt him, considering the layers of muscle beneath the expensive fabric of his shirt. "So the fact that you don't like seeing me with Ryker only tells me that *you* may not want me, but you also don't want anyone else—"

"I never said I didn't want you," he interrupted, his voice hard. "And trust me, I've been doing everything I can to get you out of my head, trying to convince myself things are better this way."

"So what are you saying? That you've changed your mind?" God help me if he said yes . . .

But he didn't answer. Instead, he moved past me toward the door, then stopped and turned back around.

"Ryker was in love with Natalie," he said. "Christ, he was about to propose to her. What he didn't know was that she was sleeping with me behind his back. I thought they'd broken it off. By that time, she'd already succeeded in pitting us at each other's throats. I found out she was lying to me, and I confronted her." He stopped, his lips pressing tightly together.

I waited, but he didn't continue. "And then what?" I prompted.

He scrubbed a hand over his face and took a deep breath. "I told her she had to choose, him or me. She said if I made her do that, I'd lose both her and Ryker. I didn't believe her, but I couldn't seem to resist her either. Ryker walked in on us, and went crazy. He knocked me out and the next thing I knew, she was gone and they were pulling her car out of the river the next morning."

My anger drained away.

"Ryker's never forgiven me," he said. "I've tried to tell him what was really going on, how she lied to us and was using us, but he's refused to listen to me. He's convinced I'm lying to him. Eventually, I gave up trying."

"Do you blame yourself for Natalie's death?" I asked.

His eyes were empty when he answered. "I should have listened to her, believed her. But she made me choose between being with her or lying to my best friend. I felt like I'd already betrayed Ryker. I wasn't about to keep doing it. It was a no-win situation."

It was heartbreaking to watch him as he told the story. The guilt emanating from him was like a living thing, despite the stoic way in which he spoke. Amy was right; it wasn't kind to speak ill of the dead, but Natalie sounded like she'd been one really messed-up person.

"Why are you telling me this?" I asked. "What does this have to do with me?"

"I just thought you should know the whole history before you got further involved with Ryker," he said.

"You mean, in case Ryker's really just using me to get back at you for what happened with Natalie." A suspicion I'd once had myself, though it had faded as the weeks with Ryker had passed.

Parker's expression didn't change. "The thought had occurred to me. He knows, or suspects, how much you mean
to me. Just like he knows where I dock my boat."

"So you're saying he planned on you seeing us together
Saturday?" I asked. "That's ludicrous. We've been dating
for months. Why now? And besides, that wasn't even his
boat."

"I just want you to be careful," Parker said. "I'd hate to
see you hurt."

"I think that's an awfully big reach—and a huge insult to
me—to imply he's just using me. You say you didn't like
seeing us together. Why? Because you think he's using me?
Or is there another reason?" I held my breath, waiting to see
what he'd say. What did I *want* him to say? Yeah, I didn't
want to think about that.

"You want to hear that I'm jealous," he stated.

"I didn't say that." But yeah, okay.

He moved toward me, his long legs covering the distance
between us in the span of one heartbeat to the next. Leaning
down, he put his lips by my ear. He was so close, I could
smell his cologne and feel the heat of his body. My eyes
drifted closed of their own accord.

When he spoke, his warm breath brushed my skin and I
shivered.

"I've wanted you since the day you walked in my office,"
he said. "And every day, every moment, since." I could have
sworn his lips touched my neck, and I forgot how to breathe.
Then he was out the door and gone.

* * *

I couldn't sleep that night. I was still upset about how dinner
had gone and I tossed and turned, doubts as to whether

I should continue seeing Ryker spinning in my head. Of course, he may not want to see me anymore either. It felt like one of those milestones in a relationship where we could either turn the next corner or it would go down in flames, and I didn't know which way it was going to go.

To my surprise, I heard the faint click of the lock on my front door opening. After a moment, I heard the familiar sounds of Ryker setting his weapon, holster, and handcuffs on the kitchen counter. A thrill went through me that he'd come, but also a whisper of caution. Was this a sign? Or just a booty call?

To avoid succumbing to the latter, I scrambled out of bed, hurriedly running my fingers through my hair to straighten it. Sliding my feet into my Ugg slippers—best things ever— I ventured into the living room.

It was chilly and I shivered. The pajama shorts and tank I wore provided little warmth without a blanket over me.

Ryker was standing in the kitchen, the outline of his body dimly lit by the one light I left on over the stove. He was looking at his phone, but glanced up when I got closer. He slid the phone into his pocket as his gaze raked me from head to foot and back. A shiver danced across my skin and it wasn't from the cold.

"I didn't know if you were coming," I said. "After dinner tonight, I didn't even know if we were still dating."

Ryker leaned back against the counter with a sigh. "I'd hoped we could discuss this later," he said. "It's late."

Nausea churned in my stomach. Oh God, was he breaking up with me?

"So you thought you'd pop by for a sleepover, and then break up with me?" I asked. "I don't think so. I'd rather we discuss it now." No sense prolonging the inevitable. "You accused my father of being a mob boss."

Ryker scrubbed a hand over his face, glancing away from me. I waited. That had been a pretty big accusation to level and I hadn't taken it lightly.

"Sage, the Muccino family is huge in Chicago. I don't have to tell you that."

I shrugged. "My father has five brothers. They all run their own businesses, started from the ground up. They help each other out from time to time." The list of cousins and relatives was endless on my dad's side.

"Our organized crime division has been keeping files on them for years," he continued. "You don't think your father's paid off government officials to get the kind of monopoly he has over the liquor distribution in Chicago?"

"My father is a good businessman," I said staunchly. "And just because they have a file doesn't mean he's done anything wrong. Obviously, if he had, they'd have arrested him. If anything, this only proves that he's an honest man because how could a criminal undergo such scrutiny without being arrested for something?"

I wasn't an idiot. My father had paid an army of lawyers over the years to keep the feds off his back. It seemed if you were Italian, lived in Chicago, and ran a very profitable liquor distribution company, you must be doing something illegal.

I wanted to talk about the *other* thing he'd said after dinner. The whole *in love* part. Was that really how he felt? Or had he just said that in the heat of the moment? I was dying to ask, but didn't want to be the one to bring it up.

"Let's say you're right," Ryker said. "Let's say your father is all aboveboard—"

"Because he is," I interjected.

"Fine, let's say he is. There's still the whole part about you...your family..."

I waited as he hesitated.

"Christ, Sage," he finally blurted. "You're worth millions."

"*I'm* not," I corrected him. "My father is."

"Really," he said dryly. "And who would be your parents' heir?"

My face heated and I was glad for the semi-darkness. "So what?" I asked, avoiding stating the obvious answer. "So what if my parents have money? What does that have to do with us? Most men like the idea of a wealthy wi— girlfriend." I stopped myself from saying *wife* just in time. Yeah, really didn't want to go there.

"Sage..." He broke off, shoving a hand through his hair and muttering, "God, how can I explain." When he met my eyes again, he seemed determined. "I was brought up dirt poor. Most of the time we barely had enough to eat, and what we did have was provided for by food stamps. I was the kid on the free lunch program at school."

"You've told me that," I said. "I still don't see why it makes a difference. You're an adult now, you have a steady job. It's not like being poor growing up was some kind of disease that tainted you."

"Of course you don't see why it makes a difference, because you've never been poor."

I pressed my lips together, staring at him. "So you're going to break up with me because I'm not poor?"

"I didn't say that, but I can't pretend that us being from opposite sides of the socio-economic scale doesn't change things, because it does," he insisted. "I'm a cop, and cops don't make shit for a living."

"I see," I said, though really I didn't. I didn't care if he was poor growing up or how much money he made now. "Listen, I'm not a gold digger. I don't care what kind of money you make. It's more important to me that you like your job, that you're good at your job, than what kind of salary it pays."

His lips twisted. "You say that now, and it sounds all nice and romantic and idealistic. But life's not like that. And you'd feel differently down the road."

I stiffened. "So...what? Is that it? Before, when you thought I was just a secretary with well-off parents it was fine, but now that you know my father's a millionaire, now it's over?"

"Listen, today's been shitty. Let's get some sleep, okay? We'll talk about it tomorrow." He pushed off the counter and wrapped an arm around my waist, but I dug in my heels.

"So were you lying?" I persisted, refusing to be moved from where I stood. "You said you were in love with me. Was that bullshit?" I wanted to know. That had been such an amazing thing to say, something no one had ever said to me before, and I had to know if he'd been telling me the truth.

Ryker's blue gaze held me captive as he reached to cup my cheek in his hand. "It wasn't bullshit," he said at last. His palm was calloused and warm against my cheek. Light from the fixture overhead glinted off the metal of his dog tags. The long-sleeved Henley he wore stretched across his chest and shoulders.

He kissed me, a sweet press of his lips against mine that seemed to say more about how he was feeling than anything else. I kissed him back, glad he hadn't asked me for a declaration in return. I wasn't ready to say it. Not yet.

The sweet kiss quickly turned into more, his tongue sliding against mine in a wet heat that went right through me. His hands moved to the hem of my tank and he dragged it up over my head, separating us. I tugged at his shirt, too, but he had to help me.

I felt like I couldn't get to him fast enough and when the

bare skin of his chest met mine, it was a sweet relief. He was kissing me again, his lips trailing down my jaw, then his hands circled my hips and he lifted me.

Surprised, I clutched at his shoulders as he sat me on the counter and stepped between my legs. I buried my fingers in his hair as his mouth fastened over my breast. The heat that had been building fanned into flame and I moaned.

His mouth caught the sound, his tongue teasing mine. My nipples rubbed against his chest, creating a delicious friction, so I did it again. I could tell he liked it as much as me, because his kisses grew deeper and more demanding. He was hard inside his jeans, pressing against the core of me.

Ryker pulled at the pajama shorts I was wearing, yanking the waistband down and lifting me so he could slide them off. I had a quick moment of *Oh God, on the kitchen counter? That's not sanitary.* Then he was unzipping his fly and I was all *Aw hell, that's what Lysol's for.*

The height was perfect and I was wet and ready for him, though his initial thrust made me gasp as he filled me.

"God, you feel good," he rasped.

Yeah, ditto.

He hadn't started moving yet, just buried balls deep inside me as my body stretched to accommodate him.

"Kiss me."

No problem. I was pressed against him from the chest down to where we were connected, and our kisses became as deep and wet as his cock moving in and out of me. I wrapped my legs around his hips and held on for the ride.

Ryker's hands were on my hips, holding me where he wanted me, and I didn't disagree with his choice. I had to breathe, though, so was forced to tear my lips from his so I could suck down more air. My skin was hot and so was his, a sheen of sweat covering us.

He moved me slightly and I gasped. "Oh yeah, oh God, yeah, right there," I half-moaned. Ryker was a good listener, and I could feel my orgasm hovering close. "Harder... faster...please..."

Ryker's head was buried in my neck, but I swore I heard him growl and felt the scrape of his teeth against my skin. But then he did as I'd said and I was beyond caring if he barked like a dog, just so long as he kept doing what he was doing.

Cries and gasps spilled from me as he pushed me over the edge, my body convulsing around his. He groaned, his cock growing even larger inside me, then he was coming, too, the pulsing of his cock prolonging my orgasm in the best way.

Both of us were gasping for air and I felt boneless, draped against him. Wow. That had been...just...well, words failed me, but I'd never look at the kitchen counter in the same way ever again.

"You're amazing, baby," he whispered in my ear, making my lips curve in a tired but sated smile.

"Ditto," I murmured, pressing a kiss to the skin underneath his jaw.

He fastened his jeans and picked me up off the counter, sliding an arm under my knees and the other behind my back.

"Wait, my pajamas—"

"You're not going to need them."

And he was right.

CHAPTER FIVE

My head was spinning the next morning, thinking through the conversation we'd had the night before. I was thrilled with Ryker's confession, but I wasn't sure how I felt about him. On one hand, I wanted to tell him I felt the same, because I did. I'd been happy these past few months and was coming to depend on him and need him more than I ever had someone else.

Yet he'd pulled the rug from underneath me with his hang-ups about my father and money. I didn't want to put myself and my feelings out there if he was going to end things just because I had wealthy parents. I'd been cautious about letting myself feel more for Ryker because it had seemed so surreal that a man like him would want to date someone like me—someone who was naïve, a bit sheltered, had a boring job, and was a total non-badass.

I'd gotten ready for work and was pouring a cup of coffee the next morning when Ryker appeared. Fresh from a shower, his hair was damp and all he wore was a pair of jeans. Literally. I knew he went commando when he stayed over and showered in the morning. That knowledge, combined with the view of his bare chest and arms, tempted me to set aside my coffee and christen my kitchen table the way we'd christened the counter.

"Good morning," he said, giving me a kiss that made my toes curl. Taking another mug from the cabinet, he filled it with coffee from the pot and took a sip.

I gazed longingly at the fly of his jeans, currently unbuttoned, and sighed a little. Time to get my mind off it. "So you didn't tell me... how does Leo Shea know you?" I asked. "And why did he call you McCrady last night?"

Ryker's mug paused on its journey to his mouth. "I can't really talk about it," he said, taking another sip.

"I figured maybe you used to do undercover work," I said.

"Something like that."

"So he thought you were dead, and now he knows you're not," I persisted. "Isn't that a problem?"

Ryker set down his mug and crossed his arms over his chest. I tried not to stare.

"Yeah."

I waited, but he didn't say anything more. "Are you going to tell me what's going on?"

"I can't," he said. "It's police business."

"Leo Shea knows who I am, and that I'm dating a man he knows as McCrady," I said. "I think that ship has sailed."

His lips thinned and I belatedly remembered that maybe I shouldn't have brought up that part.

"He wouldn't know anything about you if you'd done what I told you to," Ryker said.

"It seemed like the right thing to do at the time," I replied, taking another sip of my coffee.

"Putting yourself in harm's way?"

"No. Helping you," I corrected.

"I didn't need your help, Sage," Ryker said with a shake of his head.

"I wasn't willing to take that chance."

I crossed my arms over my chest and returned his glare. His lips twitched and he walked over to me.

Sliding his arms around my waist, he pulled my stiff body toward him. "Has anyone ever told you how sexy you are when you're mad?"

His gravelly, just-rolled-out-of-bed voice combined with the twin weapons of his signature half-grin and his heavy-lidded blue eyes made my irritation melt, though I pretended it hadn't. No sense letting him know how much power he had over me.

"What an incredibly sexist and patronizing thing to say," I retorted, looking down my nose at him the best I could while he towered over me. He pulled me closer.

"My apologies," he murmured, his lips by my ear. "Make it up to you tonight? Over dinner?"

A date! I loved when Ryker had time for us to actually go out. His hours were so odd sometimes that it seemed we only saw each other in bed. Which wasn't necessarily a *bad* thing...

"Like a *real* dinner? Or something we have to eat with our hands?"

"Real dinner," he promised, his lips brushing my neck down to my collarbone. "I promise there'll be silverware and everything."

"Okay then," I said, extricating myself from his hold though it was the last thing I wanted to do. He was half-naked and smelled like soap and warm, clean man. But if I didn't hurry, I'd be late for the bus, then late for work. "And just so you know," I couldn't resist adding, grabbing my purse and slipping on my heels before heading to the door. "You're not the only one going commando today."

The look on his face was priceless as I shut the door, making me grin for the next thirty minutes straight.

* * *

Parker and I didn't discuss what had occurred in my apartment or the things he'd told me. I'd thought about what he'd said... and *hadn't* said. He'd basically admitted he was jealous, without using that word, but hadn't answered when I'd asked him if he'd changed his mind about us. It was like one step forward and two steps back. And I was through doing that with him.

I had lunch with Megan, telling her my story of the dinner from hell and how upset Ryker had been, how angry I'd gotten, and how we'd made up last night, but I left out the part about Parker. I wasn't even sure how I felt about what he'd said, much less try to explain it to someone else. She listened sympathetically as we ate.

"So Ryker's okay with the whole parents-being-rich thing?" she asked when I'd finished.

"Maybe," I conceded. "At least he said it wasn't bullshit, that he was in love with me. That's good, right?"

"Are you in love with him?"

I grimaced. "I've tried to not think about it too much. It's been fun, yeah, but I keep waiting for him to wake up and be like *why am I with you when I could be with some hot model chick? Sayonara, babe.*"

"What if he has feelings for you, *and* is thinking long-term," she persisted. "Will you let yourself fall in love with him?"

I thought about it, thought about how I'd felt when he'd said he was in love with me.

"I think it's too late," I admitted.

Megan smiled. "Of course it is," she said. "I know you, and you can't sleep with a guy for four months and *not* fall in love with him. You wouldn't be you."

When I got back to the office, I had the unpleasant surprise of sharing an elevator with Monique. Wearing a red wrap dress that hugged her curves with a plunging neckline, I caught more than a few men looking at her twice.

"Monique, good to see you again," I said to her, faking polite conversation as Parker's comment about her wanting me fired echoed inside my head.

"Ah, yes, you are zee secretary, no?" she asked.

I gritted my teeth and smiled. "Executive Administrative Assistant."

She waved her hand in the international equivalent of *Whatever* as the elevator doors opened. She breezed out and I followed, nearly choking on the cloud of perfume left in her wake.

Monique pushed open the door to Parker's office, letting herself in before I could stop her.

"Pa*rrrrr*ker," she purred. "I'm so sorry I missed dinner last night. I want to make it up to you." She sat her skinny ass right on the edge of his desk, and I had a brief fantasy of shoving her onto the floor.

Parker had been working but glanced up now that she was sitting on his file.

"I'm sorry," I said. "She didn't stop to wait—"

"I am his girlfriend," Monique interrupted me. "I do not need to wait for zee secretary to say my name."

The look of disdain on her face made my hands clench into fists and I opened my mouth to tell her what she could do with her stupid name, but stopped when Parker spoke.

"It's fine, Sage," he said with a nod in my direction. "Close the door on the way out, will you?"

Our eyes met and I couldn't help remembering the things he'd said last night. Yet here he was, with his hand on Monique's bare knee.

"Of course. *Sir.*" If I could've slammed the door on my way out, I would have. Unfortunately, it was one of those cushion-close doors that drifted silently shut no matter how much force was used. Dammit.

I watched without looking like I was watching them, which meant I got nothing done for the next ten minutes as they sort of talked but mainly kissed. It was so unlike Parker to let something personal interfere with work that I had to wonder what was so great about Monique. Maybe he just felt more for her and was completely infatuated with her. Maybe French girls just did it better than American girls.

The green monster of jealousy set up shop right next to me, cracking its knuckles and digging its claws into my gut. I was stupid for believing Parker last night. He wanted what he couldn't have, and even that had been fleeting. He seemed perfectly happy playing suck-face with French Barbie.

"Wow. Is that—"

"Yeah," I answered Megan's unfinished question. She'd sidled up next to me, both of us staring through the glass. Parker and Monique were talking now, their faces close together. His hand was *still* on her leg... correction, now it was her thigh. I ground my teeth together.

"She's really pretty."

I shot Megan a glare at her unabashed praise and her cheeks flushed. "I'm just saying," she muttered.

"Well, she's a total bitch," I retorted. "She wanted Parker

to fire me because I was 'too pretty.'" I used quote-y fingers and a bad French accent.

"Oh my God, he *told* you that?" she asked, eyes wide. I nodded. "You know what that means, don't you?" she asked.

"What does it mean?" I asked, distracted by Monique putting her arms around Parker's neck. She was going to wrinkle his jacket and get her nasty-ass perfume all over him.

"Sage," Megan said.

"Hmm?" By God, if she even got a hint of lipstick on his collar, I was going to strangle her with her own nylons...

"Sage!"

"What?" I said, reluctantly turning away from the show.

"He's trying to make you jealous," Megan said.

"Pffft. Please," I said, waving her off and turning back toward the office.

"Listen to me," she said urgently. "He tells you that his girlfriend doesn't like you because you're too pretty? Then lets her come waltzing in here to put on a PDA just feet from your desk? That's not the Parker I know, but it sounds very much like he's trying to get your attention."

I turned back again to look at her. "Really?" I thought about it. "No, he wouldn't—"

"Oh yes he would," she said emphatically. "Have you *ever* seen Parker do anything remotely like this before?" She nodded toward his office.

"Well..."

"Of course you haven't," she said. "It's because he sees you're with Ryker and has finally wised up to what's between the two of you."

"But it's too late," I said. "I'm with Ryker. I love *him*, not Parker. Right?" Sudden self-doubt assailed me. I did love Ryker. I wouldn't have wanted him to meet my parents, wouldn't have let him sleep in my bed or make love to me on my (now spotless and disinfected) kitchen counter, if I didn't.

"You're the only one who can say if it's too late," Megan replied. "But I'm telling you, he's not into her. He's using her to get to you."

I glanced back into Parker's office. "I dunno, he looks pretty darn into her," I said. "Does she have her tongue in his ear?"

Megan shrugged and walked away. My computer dinged and when I looked at the screen, I smiled.

Toggling the intercom button, I said in a sweeter-than-saccharine voice, "Parker, five minutes until your four o'clock with Lowry in conference room two-twelve."

"Thank you, Sage."

I watched from the corner of my eye as Parker disentangled himself from Monique's claws. Though he'd supposedly been glad to see her, I could read the irritation on his face and in his body language as he gathered his things for the meeting. Monique was pouting and it looked as though she was arguing with him, but no way was I going to listen in. I had some pride.

Oh, who the hell was I kidding?

I toggled the button again, turning the volume low so I had to strain to hear.

"...can't cancel my meeting, Monique," Parker was saying.

"You have a secretary. Make her go for you."

"That's not what she does."

"Oh, really? Then what exactly eez it zat she does for you?" No escaping the petulant aggression in those words.

"Knock it off, Monique," Parker warned, straightening his tie. "I'm not in this to be nagged to death about Sage. We agreed to have a little fun together. That's it. This is twice you've shown up at my work. I've been patient, but that's about to end."

Monique was immediately contrite. "I am sorry, Pa*rrr*ker," she said. "I just miss you so. Maybe tonight we go out, drink and dance, no? To that place we like. What eez it called?"

His smile was thin and his answer perfunctory. "The Underground. Look, I'll give you a call." Politely giving her his arm, he helped her off the desk just as he glanced my way.

Quickly averting my gaze, I toggled off the intercom and pretended I was working on the computer as they came out of the office.

"I'll be back in about an hour," Parker said to me, his grip around Monique's elbow as he propelled her down the hall- way. I watched them disappear into the elevator.

So they'd been drinking and dancing together, eh? I wasn't sure I believed Megan's premise about Parker trying to make me jealous. Why should he? He'd already turned me down.

And had just told me last night that he wants me and al- ways has.

But that wasn't going to happen. I was with Ryker now. I worked for Parker, just as I always had, and I wasn't going anywhere. And I totally wasn't jealous.

Though the picture in my head of Monique in Parker's bed wouldn't go away.

Ryker called my cell a short while later. "I've been think- ing all day about what you're not wearing under that skirt," he said.

"Really?" I asked, all innocence. "I apologize for disrupt- ing your concentration. I'll try not to do it again."

"Don't change on my account," he teased.

I laughed. "Hmm. Riding a motorcycle commando doesn't seem like a good idea." I swiveled my chair around for a little more privacy.

He groaned. "Stop putting these images in my head. You're killing me."

A thrill of pleasure went through me. It felt good to be wanted, especially by a man like him.

"So you just called to check on the status of my panties? Or lack thereof?" I asked.

"No," he sighed. "Actually, I called because I need to postpone our dinner."

A sharp sting of disappointment at that, but I kept it out of my voice as I said, "That's fine. I understand. Some other time."

"I'm really sorry."

"It's fine."

There was silence for a moment.

"I can maybe come by later," he said. "When I get off."

I felt a flash of anger at that. No time for dinner, but he had time to screw. "I'm busy later," I said.

"Oh."

More silence.

"So what are you doing then?" he asked.

"I'm...going out," I said, thinking frantically. "With some girlfriends." Yeah. That sounded legit.

"It's awfully sudden," he said. "When you were planning on having dinner with me."

"Yeah, well, they asked but I said I had plans, but now I don't so..."

I was proud of my ability to make my bullshit sound so incredibly authentic, until he asked, "Where are you going?"

Okay, I had no clue what to say on that one, so I blurted

the first place that popped in my head. "The Underground."
I winced.

"Really? I wouldn't think that was your kind of place," he
said, still sounding suspicious.

"Drinks, music, and dancing, what's not to like?" I'd
never been there in my life and was just going off what
Monique had said. And if Parker had taken her there, it had
to be at least a little on the nicer side. For a club.

"Okay then, I guess I'll talk to you tomorrow," he said.

"Yeah, sure." *Don't sound anxious. Go for whatever-I'm-
not-going-to-wait-around-for-your-call.*

"Have fun," he said.

"I'm sure I will. Bye." I ended the call.

I was pissed off and hurt. I thought we were moving forward in our relationship, but I hated that he thought he could
just tell me he loved me then expect to drop by for sex like I
was some booty call girl. Not that he'd said the words *I love
you*, but he'd implied them.

And now I had to put together a Girls' Night Out at the
last minute.

Hurrying to Megan's desk, I caught her just as she was
hanging up the phone.

"What's up?" she asked. "Did Monique make nice and
offer to split an M&M with you?"

"Doubtful," I replied. "It goes straight to her hips, you
know."

We both grinned, amused at ourselves.

"No, seriously, I have to go out tonight," I said. "Well, actually, *we* have to go out tonight. Me and you."

"Go out? You mean like *out* out? On a Wednesday?"

"Yeah. And can you round up a couple other girls, too?
Maybe Maggie and Kelly? They're both fun." Both women
were single and worked in the Marketing department.

"I'll text them," she said, pulling out her cell. "And tell me again why we *have* to go out tonight?" she asked, her finger swiping over the tiny keyboard.

I sighed. "Because. I got pissed off at Ryker for cancelling our date. So I told him not to come by later because I was going out with friends."

Megan raised an eyebrow as she glanced up at me. "And is there a reason you don't want to have toe-curling sex with tall, dark, and dangerous?"

"It seems like I'm just the late-night booty call," I said. "He's too busy to take me out, but not too busy to come by, have sex, and fall asleep?" I shook my head. "I don't want that."

"I agree, that's total bullshit," Megan said. Her phone buzzed and she read the text. "Maggie and Kelly are in," she said. "They want to know where and when."

"Tell them The Underground at eleven."

Megan groaned. "I am going to regret this tomorrow, aren't I."

I grinned at her. "You bet. Meet me at my place, nine o'clock. We'll get ready together." I headed back to my desk as she groaned again. "And don't forget to hydrate," I called back to her.

"The things I do for you," she said.

I blew her a kiss and turned the corner.

A night out with the girls had been impromptu, but it sounded great. Maybe just what I needed to blow off some steam.

* * *

"No, don't use that. I've got some with glitter." I dug in my makeup bag, producing a stick of cream eye shadow and handing it to Megan. "It'll go perfect with that dress."

I loved Megan's cocktail dress. Turquoise and black beads in varying sizes were sewn on the fabric, creating a gorgeous combination. It had elbow-length sleeves, a wide neck, and was made out of a stretchy material that clung to her.

I'd chosen a champagne-colored tulle cocktail dress with a scoop neck and cap sleeves. The fitted bodice and mini-length skirt were wrapped in glittering beads sewn on in various patterns. With a cutout back, it was elegant and sexy.

"Need a refill?" I asked, talking over the music playing.

"Sure." She handed me her empty glass.

I headed into the kitchen, giving us both fresh margaritas before returning to my bathroom, where every inch of counter space was covered in makeup containers, makeup brushes, perfume bottles, curling irons, and cans of hair spray. Most of the time, my favorite part about going out was getting ready. It wasn't like glitter and smoky eye were really appropriate for the office, so it was fun to get all dressed up and go full out with the makeup and hair.

"Can you curl the back?" Megan asked. "It's hard for me to reach and make it even."

"Yeah, sure." I set down my margarita and took the curling iron from her.

We were quiet for a moment, listening to Taylor sing about having style, then Megan met my gaze in the mirror.

"I haven't told you something," she said.

Uh-oh. "That sounds serious," I said. "What is it?"

She winced. "I kinda...slept with Brian."

My jaw dropped. "Are you kidding? And you didn't tell me!" I was loud enough to even overpower Taylor. "When did—how—I thought you weren't speaking?" I moved on to the next curl.

"I told you Todd and I got in a fight about his ex," she said.

"Yeah..."

"Well, he came by my desk last night around six, trying to explain, and I thought things would be fine, but he still refused to stop talking to her. So I said we were through. And Brian was walking by at the time, so when Todd stormed off, Brian stopped to see if I was all right."

I moved to another curl, listening avidly. "And...?"

"And we got to talking and he asked me if I wanted to grab something to eat. So I said yes, and we went to eat and had a few drinks, then back to his place. One thing led to another..." She shrugged, her cheeks turning pink even as a little smile curved her lips.

I laughed aloud. "Holy shit!" I crowed. "I cannot believe it! So? How was it?"

Megan's face got even redder and she nodded. "Oh yeah."

"That's awesome! I'm so glad he lived up to your expectations." I was still grinning. "So...what now? Are you two seeing each other or what?"

Her smile faded a bit and she gave a little shrug. "I'm not sure. We didn't really talk about it, you know? We both had to be up early this morning, so I was up and leaving when it was still dark so I could get back to my place. I thought maybe he'd come by today, but he was too busy, I guess."

Internally, I frowned, but I kept my outward smile in place. "I'm sure that's what it was," I said. "I think there was some kind of server problem today. He was probably dealing with that." And that had better be the reason, because if he thought he could just toy with my best friend like that, then he had a serious wake-up call coming, courtesy of me.

Megan had been half in love with Brian for months now. If he wasn't planning on more to their relationship than a one-night stand, she'd be devastated. Then KLP Capital would be looking for a new IT guy because I was going to kill Brian.

"I say we go out tonight, forget about men, and have an awesome time." I finished the last curl and used my fingers to fluff her hair. "Hold still. Cover your eyes."

Megan carefully covered her face with her hands as I sprayed the hair spray until her head was immersed in a thick aerosol cloud.

"That's enough, don't you think?" she asked, coughing.

"You want these curls to stay or not?" I retorted, giving one last spray for good measure.

"I wish I had your hair," she sighed. "It's always got that perfect shampoo-commercial wave. Plus it's shiny and soft—"

"All of which can be replicated with a few select salon products and a curling iron," I said. "See?" Grabbing one more pump bottle, I sprayed a light mist of the contents over her hair. "Shine from a bottle. They think of everything."

"Okay then," she said. "Ready?"

I grabbed a bottle of perfume and did two sprays to my neck and one for my hair. "Ready."

It was cold outside the club and I shivered, wrapping my arms around my torso to try and keep warm. We hadn't wanted to deal with coats inside. Maggie and Kelly were already there, waiting in line. When Maggie saw us, she grabbed my arm.

"C'mon," she said, dragging the rest of us up to the front of the line.

"Hi," she said to the doorman, smiling widely at him. "My friends and I would really like to get in tonight. Do you think we'll be able to?"

The doorman took in her sleek bobbed blond hair, tight

black minidress, and sky-high heels, then he gave the rest of us the once-over as well before giving her a nod. Unhooking the velvet rope, he let all four of us pass.

Music accosted our ears the moment we walked in, immediately making it impossible to talk. The bouncer charging covers let us in for free and we made our way through the crowd to the bar.

"I'll get the first round," I said. "What do you guys want?" I took orders for two cosmos and a margarita (no salt).

"We'll look for a table or something," Megan shouted over the music. "They have some that aren't VIP only."

I nodded. Divide and conquer. It was the only way to get drinks *and* a place to sit. And considering the heels I had on, standing for the next three hours was out of the question.

Kelly stayed with me to help carry drinks, then we searched the crowd until we spotted Maggie waving at us from a table in the corner.

"Sweet!" I said when we got close. She'd scored a place to sit somehow, but that was Maggie. If you wanted to go clubbing, she was the girl you wanted to go with. Somehow, she just knew where to go, how not to have to stand in line, and all the ins and outs.

I downed my Grey Goose and tonic pretty quick and signaled a cocktail waitress for another. I was a decent dancer, but it was so much easier when I'd had a few drinks first.

We were talking a little, laughing as we people-watched, and bouncing to the beat. Another quick round later and Megan was pulling me onto the dance floor.

"This is my jam!" she said, bouncing and gyrating her way through the mass of people. Swirling neon lights lit up the dance floor in splashes of color amidst the shadows.

I was real relaxed now, and moving to the beat was a heck

of a lot easier without being self-conscious. The dance floor was crowded, but there was still room to move.

Megan and I were having a good time, then a couple of guys started dancing with us. They were both well-built and good-looking and Megan didn't seem to mind, so I let one of the guys put his hands on my waist.

"What's your name?" he said, speaking loud enough so I could hear him.

"Sage."

"Paige?"

"*Sage.*" Now I remembered why meeting guys at clubs was so irritating.

"What a great name!" he said with a grin.

"Gee, thanks." I fake-smiled back, wondering if he still hadn't caught my name.

"Can I buy you a drink?" he asked.

Free booze? "Sure."

I followed him to the bar, though, because I wasn't dumb enough to let some stranger bring me a drink, and watched as the bartender poured me another Grey Goose and tonic.

"So what's your name?" I asked, sipping my drink.

"Lucas."

"Nice to meet you, Lucas," I said. He seemed generically nice enough, and very easy on the eyes. His T-shirt was tight and his biceps tattooed. He wasn't quite a pretty boy, not with what I was pretty sure was a knife scar alongside his jaw and a glint in his eye that made me think I wouldn't want to meet him in a dark alley. "So what do you do?"

"I race cars," he said.

I may have choked a little on my drink. "You race cars?" I asked, sputtering only a little. That was one I hadn't heard before. Wow.

He nodded, his lips twisting in a slight grin. "Not like

NASCAR or some shit like that. Stock cars. I'm in town for a race."

"Isn't that illegal?" I asked.

Lucas just smiled. "It's only illegal if you get caught."

Another song came on and he took my drink from me and set it on the bar. "Let's dance, Sage," he said. "Because that dress is hot and you look too good not to show it off."

He took my hand and we squeezed our way back onto the dance floor. I saw Megan with the other guy and she was smiling, so I relaxed.

Lucas put my arms around his neck and his hands on my waist, which surprised me, but I couldn't back up. There was nowhere to go. I smiled stiffly as we danced, then started to get irritated at how close he wanted to be to me.

After I was sure I'd been violated at least a dozen times by his roving hands, I decided I'd had enough.

"Thanks for the drink, and the dance," I said, trying to extricate myself from his grip. "I'd better get back to my friends."

"Don't go yet," he said, gripping my arm and pulling me back. "We're just getting started."

"Actually, we've already started and now we're done," I said, yanking my arm free. I spun around to leave before he could grab me again and came face-to-face with Ryker.

Well, shit.

CHAPTER SIX

In his jeans and leather jacket—which I knew concealed his badge and weapon—with the gray T-shirt stretched tight across his chest, Ryker made Lucas look like a little boy playing grown-up badass. Ryker was the real thing. And he looked none too pleased to see me, though his expression became downright dangerous when Lucas decided to slide his arms around my waist.

"I love the playing-hard-to-get thing," Lucas said in my ear.

Oh, please. "Will you take the hint," I said, exasperated as I tried to shove him off me. I was through being polite. "I'm done dancing with you."

Ryker gave me a look of long suffering and sighed. "I just got off work," he said. "I really didn't want to get into a bar fight tonight."

"Then don't," I snapped. "I can handle this on my own."

"I can see that," he said, nodding to where Lucas was clasping my hand and tugging me backward.

"Dude, I saw her first," Lucas said, having spotted Ryker. "Go find another girl."

Ryker smiled, but it had an edge that made a shiver crawl up my spine. "But I like that one," he said.

"Tough shit."

Okay, yeah, I could see where this was going. A quick trip to Nowhere Good.

"Lucas, I'm done," I said to him. "Now let me go. Look over there," I pointed. "That little blonde is watching you. I'd bet she'd love a dance."

Like a kid shown another pretty toy, Lucas headed that way. I breathed a sigh of relief.

"See?" I said to Ryker. "Told you I could handle it."

"Why are you dancing with some tool like that anyway?" he asked, pulling me into his arms. It felt much better to have his arms around me than Lucas's and I melted against him like warm butter as he moved us to the music.

I shrugged. "Because he asked. He seemed nice enough. Just a bit... persistent."

"Guys like that come here looking for one thing."

I'd had enough booze to loosen my tongue. "Then I guess you found me at the right place," I snapped, "since that's obviously all you're looking for, too."

Ryker's eyes narrowed and he stopped dancing. "What?"

My brain had caught up with my mouth and now I wanted to take back what I'd said. Sort of.

"The only time we see each other anymore is at night. Specifically, when you come by my apartment to get laid." *Jeez, Drunk Sage, why don't you tell him what you really think?*

"You think that's why I come?" he asked.

In for a penny... "Isn't it? You barely talk to me about your job, you work all the time but I never know what you're doing, and any dates we talk about going on usually get cancelled. But somehow you find time to fit me in for—"

"A fuck," he interrupted, finishing my sentence.

My anger and bitterness had washed away now that I'd said what I'd been thinking, and I just looked at him. "Am I wrong?" I asked. "Because from my perspective, that's what it looks like."

"I just told you last night that I'm in love with you," he said. "Did you not believe me?"

"Yes... No... I don't know... Maybe." I heaved a sigh. "It's just so hard to believe, that's all."

"Hard to believe what?"

"You and me," I said, looking at him as though hello? Wasn't it obvious? "A guy like you and a girl like me. You're the bad boy all the girls swoon over and I'm just... well, I'm just me."

"So that's why you're so quick to think I'm using you for an easy lay?" he asked.

I shrugged. His reaction—or non-reaction—was making me feel stupid.

"You and I are... incredible together," he said, his hands moving to my ass and pulling me closer. "But frankly, sex is easy to find. It's the rest of it... the laughs, the fun we have... well that, not so much. And honestly, I wouldn't have stuck around this long if you *weren't* you."

His words made me smile and that hard little knot inside my chest melted away.

He put his lips by my ear. "Though that dress is worth fantasizing about taking off you."

A thrill of desire shot through me as another song came on with a grinding beat. "That depends on how good of a dancer you are," I teased.

"Oh, I can dance."

And boy, could he. Not the swing-me-around, spin-me-around kind of dancing. But the kind of up-close stylized dirty dancing I'd watched Patrick Swayze do with Jennifer Grey in one of my favorite movies of all time. I'd had dance lessons for years as a kid, but rarely had run across a man who could not only dance, but lead. Ryker was amazing and I wasn't surprised that we fit as well together on the dance floor as we fit in bed.

A sudden commotion off to my right made both of us turn. It looked like there was a fight going on. I squinted.

"It's that Lucas guy," I said.

It looked like the blonde had a boyfriend who had a big problem with Lucas hitting on his girl.

Oops.

Even though the fight started with just two guys, others were gleefully joining the melee. In seconds, we were engulfed in a crowd pressing against us. Some were trying to get out of the way, others trying to join. It took only a moment for me to be separated from Ryker.

The crowd swept me away and I lost sight of him. Things were getting crazy and I looked frantically for Megan, Maggie, or Kelly, but saw none of them.

It maybe wouldn't have been so bad if I'd been moved in the direction of the doors, but instead I was forced farther inside, closer to the fight. Someone pushed hard against my back and I in turn got shoved into someone else. I was unsteady on my feet and when someone pushed again, I tripped and went down.

Now I started to get scared. Legs and feet were all around me, someone instantly stepping on my hand. I couldn't get enough room to get back up and another person tripped over me, falling and landing half-sprawled on top.

People were screaming and yelling over the music which,

for some reason, was still playing. I could hear the sounds of men shouting and glass breaking somewhere close.

A knee connected with the back of my head, and I cried out in pain, frantically trying to get leverage to at least get to my knees or something, but I kept being knocked down as more people surged around me and another body fell.

Panic gripped me. Now I knew what it was like to be close to being trampled to death. If I didn't find a way to get up on my feet, people were going to start stepping on me rather than over or around me.

Sirens sounded in the distance, growing closer, but I was terrified it would be too late by the time they got to me. Someone's booted foot hit hard into my side, knocking the breath out of me with a sharp pain. For a few precious seconds, I couldn't move. Something caught in my hair, yanking it. I yelled, grasping for whatever it was and freeing my hair. But I didn't have enough hands or space or time to get up.

There was a sudden clearing of space around me and I tried to stand, my limbs shaking, but before I could, I was lifted off the floor and into a man's arms.

Ryker.

It was hard to see his face clearly in the bad lighting, but there was no mistaking it was him.

I clung to his neck as he fought his way through the crowd, yelling "CPD!" It was amazing how people paused just long enough at the sound of those letters for us to pass by. In mere moments we were out on the street.

I didn't know where he was carrying me; I only knew I felt safe now. After a few moments, he stopped and let me slide down to my feet.

"Are you all right?" he asked, his fingers beneath my chin lifting my face up.

I looked at him and gasped. In the light from the street-lamps, I could see a cut above his eye and one on his lip, and there was a bruise already darkening his cheek.

"You're hurt!" But he caught my hand as I reached for his face.

"I'm fine," he said. "Tell me where you're hurt."

I took quick inventory, but nothing was broken. "Just some bumps and bruises, I think."

"Sage!"

Turning, I saw Megan, Kelly, and Maggie rushing toward me. Relief surged. "Thank God you're okay," I said, hugging Megan.

"That was insane," Maggie said. "I didn't know if we were going to get out of there."

"So everyone's okay?" I asked. They all nodded. Sirens screamed as fire trucks and police cars pulled up. More people were streaming from the entrance to the building. We all turned to watch for a minute.

"I think it's time to go," Megan said. "Wanna share a cab?"

Maggie and Kelly were quick to agree, but Ryker stepped in. "I'm going to take Sage home, if that's all right with you ladies?"

Megan grinned and grabbed Maggie's arm. "You bet. Catch you later." They hurried to pile into a waiting cab.

"Don't you have to go with the cops or something?" I asked.

"There's plenty of them to handle it," he said. "You need me more."

A true statement, and I was relieved he didn't have to go. I was still shaky from the experience of nearly getting tram-pled to death. Ryker must have realized that, because he slid a supportive arm around my back and led me to where he'd parked his truck.

Forgoing the seatbelt, I scooted right up next to him as he drove and rested my head against his shoulder. He drove with one hand and put his arm around me, pulling me closer.

We didn't say much on the way back and it wasn't until we were back in my apartment that I finally relaxed. I grabbed us each a bottle of water from the fridge and then got some bandages and a clean cloth from the bathroom.

"Let me patch you up," I said, coming back into the kitchen. I'd barely set down my supplies when Ryker spun me around.

"Patch *me* up?" he asked, looking horrified. "Have you looked in a mirror? You're covered in bruises."

Glancing down at myself, I saw with some surprise that he was right. My legs were bruised and my dress was a sad, stained, and torn shadow of its former self. My face fell.

"Dammit. I really liked this dress."

"Screw the dress," Ryker said. "You were nearly killed tonight. If I hadn't been there—"

"Let's not think about if you hadn't been there," I interrupted. Though the image of Ryker swooping me up in his arms to rescue me like Superman in the movies would live in my memory for a long time.

"How about *I* take care of *you*." Drawing me toward the bathroom, he sat me down on the toilet lid, then crouched in front of me to slip off my heels.

He started the bathwater going, then disappeared back into the bedroom. When he came back, I saw he was barefoot and had discarded his shoes, jacket, holster, and weapon.

Standing me up, he slid the zipper down in the back of my dress, letting it puddle on the floor at my feet. Then he crossed his arms over his chest to drag the hem of his shirt up and over his head. The metal of his dog tags clinked as they dropped against his chest.

I reached around to unhook my bra, but he stopped me. "Let me."

He undid the clasp and slipped the straps from my shoulders and down my arms, then drew my panties down my legs.

I felt very exposed and slightly awkward, especially with his head inches from my—

"I've never had a cop draw my bath before," I joked, trying to ease my own discomfort. "Does the CPD do manis and pedis, too?"

"I'll do whatever you want me to, babe," he said, pressing his lips to my abdomen, just under my navel. Holy shit. Then he stood and I could breathe again.

"The hot water will help with the aches you're going to have tomorrow," he said, taking my hand as I tentatively put one foot in the water. Just this side of scalding...perfect.

I let out a long sigh as I sank down in the water. I winced a bit as the scrapes on my knees were submerged, but felt so much better already.

Ryker sat on the edge of the tub and reached for my soap and loofah. He lathered like a pro, then gently washed my hands and arms. Scooting down the side of the tub, he set my foot on his thigh as he soaped up my leg, mindful of the bruises.

It was super sweet of him and I enjoyed watching the play of muscles in his chest and arms as he worked. The water had steamed up the room so there was a light sheen on his skin.

Expecting him to join me in the tub when he was done, I was surprised when he stood, saying, "Soak as long as you want. I'll wait outside." Then he was out the door before I could say anything.

Okay, that was weird. Deciding to finish the bath, I

drained the tub and got out, hurriedly taking off my makeup and shrugging into the robe hung on the back of the door.

I found him sitting in my bed, ankles crossed as he watched the television. He glanced up.

"That was quick," he said. "Feeling better?"

"Yeah, but why'd you leave? I thought you'd join me." Discarding the robe, I saw his gaze drop and the Adam's apple in his throat moved as he swallowed.

"Thought you might want some time to relax," he said.

Climbing onto the bed, I lay beside him.

"I didn't get to thank you for coming to my rescue." Ryker had cleaned the blood off his face, but he'd be sporting bruises of his own tomorrow. "And here you said you didn't want to get into a bar fight tonight."

His lips twitched. "I hate bar fights," he said. "But for you, apparently it doesn't matter. When I saw you go down, getting to you was all I could think about."

"My hero," I said with a soft smile. His dog tags glinted in the light from the television and I wrapped the chain around my finger, giving it a small tug.

Ryker leaned over me, pressing his lips to mine. I was just getting into the kiss when I felt him draw the covers up over me. I reached for the fastening to his jeans, but he stopped me.

"What's wrong?" I asked.

He looked at me, his eyes serious and his hand cupping my jaw. "I want you to know, really know, that I'm in it for more than the sex. And if you can't believe me when I say it, then I'll show you."

My heart turned over inside my chest and something I'd been holding back felt as though it had been loosened.

"You already have," I said. "Showing up tonight like that, getting caught up in a bar fight, getting me out of there in one piece..." *I love you* hovered on the tip of my tongue but for some reason, I couldn't say it.

This bothered me, but now wasn't the time for a prolonged session of introspection, so I shoved the thought aside and kissed him again.

"But that doesn't mean I can't...relax...you," he murmured against my lips.

"What do you—"

Before I could finish he was sliding down my body, his lips fastening around a nipple and robbing the words from my tongue. His mouth was hot against my chilled skin and my eyes slid shut.

Ryker was a very physical guy, and he put his whole body into sex. So while his mouth was busy at my breasts, his hands were roaming, brushing down my sides to my hips, caressing my thigh and the tender skin behind my knee. He still wore jeans, the denim causing a soft friction that made me acutely aware of the more sensitive areas of my body.

His tongue flicked out, teasing my nipple, his thumb gently rubbing the other, and the dual sensation made me send up a prayer of appreciation for Ryker's ability to multitask.

He slid farther down, sending a shiver across my belly when his tongue dipped into my navel. Pressing openmouthed kisses to my hip, he nudged my legs farther apart, wide enough for his shoulders.

I made a noise and tried to squeeze my legs closed. I usually had to be a bit drunker for this. Ryker didn't understand. He was an all-in kind of guy, oral activities included, and was really, really good. But again, alcohol helped.

"C'mon, babe," he said, his voice a soft rasp. "Relax. I wanna taste you so bad." He braced his hands inside my knees, forcing them apart with too much strength for me to resist. Not that I was putting up a full-on fight, but still. Absurdly, his aggressiveness turned me on even more when the logical part of my brain said I should be mad about it. But the body doesn't lie and heat flooded my core.

Ryker groaned, his mouth fastened to my inner thigh as he sucked. Distantly, I realized I'd have a hickey there tomorrow, but it wasn't like anyone would see.

His hands moved to my thighs, spreading me farther, and before I could protest or try to resist, his mouth was on me.

"Oh God," I moaned, my head falling back on the pillow.

Thoughts of embarrassment or shyness went right out the window as Ryker proceeded to show me just how well he did this sort of thing. My hands clutched at his hair as his tongue did things to me that had to be illegal in at least nine counties.

I was saying things and moaning and God only knows what all when everything came to a head (figuratively speaking). Stars and comets and exploding nuclear bombs paled in comparison to the orgasm that overtook me and left me shaking and boneless in its aftermath.

Ryker crawled up my body, making pit stops on the way to press a kiss to my abdomen, then lick a trail up between my breasts to my collarbone, his tongue dipping in the hollow at the base of my neck. Finally, his lips met mine and I wrapped my legs around his waist, holding him close as we kissed so deeply I could taste myself on his tongue. Yowza.

He pulled back and I mewled in disappointment. Chuckling softly, he said, "Not tonight, babe."

Pulling me spoon-style against him, he tucked me close and pulled the covers up around us. Although I could feel the hard press of his erection against my backside, he didn't make any other move.

His hand lay against my stomach and I stared into the dark-

ness. Ryker was great, he really was. Tonight had been...
amazing. Eye-opening. I hadn't trusted his feelings for me before, but now I did.

The problem was...how did I feel about him? I loved
him, right? Yet, I'd been unable to say it, and I didn't know
why. That bothered me. But maybe I just needed more time.
I'd never told a man I loved him before, not like this.

Of course I told myself I didn't know why, though deep
down inside, I knew. But it was so pathetic, so pitiful, that I
didn't want to face it.

I still had feelings for Parker.

I stared at the darkened window, Ryker asleep at my
back, and felt tears sting my eyes. It was ridiculous. Why
should I feel anything for him? I'd put myself out there and
he'd turned me down without so much as blinking an eye.

Would I ever be free of the kernel of hope inside that
wanted more with Parker? I hoped so, but with a sinking sensation in my stomach, I thought that maybe I wouldn't. Not
unless I left him for good, and I wasn't ready to do that.

But when *would* I be ready?

I felt ashamed as I lay there. I had a man, a good man,
who said he loved me and wanted to be with me. Yet I
couldn't commit the same feelings to him. Part of my heart
was wrapped in a hopeless infatuation with someone who
saw me as much a part of his life as he saw his office furniture, and with about the same affection.

I had to change, had to *do* something, but I didn't know
what. Or if I did know the what, I lacked the strength to actually do it.

I fell into a troubled sleep, in Ryker's arms but thinking
about Parker.

* * *

Megan was bright-eyed and bushy-tailed the next morning. You wouldn't have known she'd been out partying until well after midnight.

"So how'd it go with Ryker?" she asked, leaning on my counter. "I thought he was too busy to go out last night?"

"I guess he decided to come there rather than go home after his shift," I said. "And it went well. Really well." I couldn't stop a little smile and Megan chuckled.

"So I take it you forgave him for making you feel like a booty call girl?"

I nodded. "Yeah. We talked about it. Everything's fine, I think. More than fine." But my words must not have been convincing because Megan frowned.

"Then why don't you sound like everything's fine?"

I hesitated, then decided to come clean. "It's just that, I care about him—I think I love him—but last night, when I wanted to tell him...I couldn't. The words just...wouldn't come out. It was like they were choking me or something. And I don't know why."

"You don't?" she asked, looking a bit sad. "Because I bet *I* could tell you why." She looked past me. "And he's headed this way."

I glanced up to see Parker striding toward me from the elevators, briefcase in hand.

Megan was already gone when I looked back and I spied her retreating back stepping around the corner. I sighed.

"Good morning, Sage," Parker said, stopping at my counter. I handed him a stack of messages.

"Good morning," I replied, wondering how he'd spent his evening last night and if he'd been with Monique. I wasn't about to ask, though. It was his business.

"We shouldn't have any more...unexpected visits from Monique," he said, flipping through the messages.

"Oh?"

"Yes, I believe we're through seeing each other," he said. "She shouldn't give you any trouble, but if you hear from her, please let me know."

"Absolutely," I said. He turned to head for his office. "Um...so she broke up with you?"

Parker stopped and raised an eyebrow at me. His lips twitched. "Really?" He said nothing further, just stepped into his office. The glass door swung shut behind him.

I felt a thrill of satisfaction at that. Monique was out of the picture. Good.

What Megan had said sat in the back of my mind all morning as I worked. It was confirmation of what I'd felt last night, but it was depressing to hear someone else say it aloud. And again, I didn't know what to do about it.

Idly, I opened my Magic 8 Ball app on my phone. "Should I quit?" I asked it, then shook it and waited as the answer floated to the top.

Signs Point to Yes.

Well, that answer wasn't a big surprise, but what would I do if I quit? It felt almost like I would be breaking up with someone—with Parker—which was just wrong and weird on so many levels.

I was turning this over in my head as I hurried back from lunch. I'd had to make a detour by the dry cleaner's to pick up a batch of Parker's suits and now waited impatiently for the pedestrian signal to change.

Standing on the curb in a group of people, I watched the traffic whiz by. The cookie I'd gotten at lunch was burning a hole in my purse. I dug for it. Why wait for mid-afternoon when I could have a cookie right now?

Especially when I was thinking about a man I shouldn't be thinking about.

Something slammed hard into my back and I stumbled. To my horror, I lost my balance and tripped off the curb, landing on my ass in the street—and directly in the path of an oncoming truck.

CHAPTER SEVEN

There was no time to get up and run, no time to scream for
help. I could only watch in terror as the truck barreled my way.

Horns blared and tires squealed. I squeezed my eyes shut,
instinctively curling into as small a ball as I could, waiting
for the bone-crushing impact.

Glass and metal shattered around me. A scream was
ripped from my throat, lost in the sounds of rending metal
on asphalt. There was a searing pain in my shoulder and a
burning sensation, then a quiet that seemed near silence after
the cacophony that had gone before.

I didn't move, too stunned and afraid to dare hope it was
over, that I had survived.

I heard voices, people shouting.

"Hey, lady! You okay? Can you hear me?"

Cautiously, I opened my eyes. What I saw directly above
me was the underside of a truck, a scant inch between my
head and the metal above. Somehow, I'd squeezed between

the road and the undercarriage. My shoulder hadn't been so lucky to stay utterly out of reach, though, and I could feel the wet, sticky flow of blood. Something had cut me.

"Help me," I croaked, my voice clogged with tears and shock. "Please, help."

Hands pulled on me and the asphalt scraped at my clothes and exposed legs, but I didn't care. I wanted out from underneath the truck.

"Holy shit, you're one lucky lady," a man said once I was clear. Another two men had helped get me out and they urged me to sit down as sirens screamed in the distance.

"Here's your purse," someone said, setting my bag beside me. Parker's suits were in a tangled mass underneath the front tire of the truck. "Is there someone I can call for you?"

I nodded and tried digging my phone out, but my hands shook too badly and the blood on my arm had run down to my fingers, making them slippery.

"Take it easy. I'll help you." There was a man crouched down next to me, a construction worker, judging by his orange vest and hardhat. He pulled out my phone. "Who should I call?"

"I-in my f-favorites," I stammered. My teeth were chattering from the cold. "Boss."

The guy looked at me strangely, but hit the button and dialed. After a moment, Parker must have answered. "Yeah, not sure who this is, but there's been an accident and the lady wanted me to call you." A pause as the sirens got louder so it had to be hard to hear. "Down here on Madison and Clark. You close by?" The man glanced at me. "I'd get down here as quick as you can." He ended the call and handed me back the phone just as an ambulance screeched to a stop.

I was flanked by two EMTs almost immediately. Then more ambulances arrived and people were helping the driver

of the truck and the drivers of two other smashed cars he'd
hit when he'd swerved to avoid me.

They moved me to sit in the back of the ambulance
and wrapped a blanket around my shoulders to ease my
shivering. They took my vitals as they peppered me with
questions, shined a light in my eyes, asked me who the current president was, what year I'd been born, blah blah.

"From what witnesses say, you're very lucky," one of
the EMTs said. "You need some stitches in your arm and
have some bumps and scrapes, but otherwise, you're going
to be just fine."

"Sage!"

I knew that voice and looked up to see Parker barreling
toward me, his face stricken. When he saw me, his expression eased somewhat, then he caught sight of the blood.

"What the hell happened? Are you all right?" he asked,
stopping at the edge of the ambulance's open door.

I'd held it together until then, but seeing him made the
floodgates open as relief poured through me. Tears blurred
my eyes and I reached for him. He had me wrapped in his
arms in an instant, and the warm strength of him eased the
residual terror of only an inch separating me from becoming
roadkill.

The EMTs told him the extent of my injuries and what
had happened. Parker's grip on me got progressively tighter
as he listened.

"... amazing story, that she's not hurt worse," the EMT
said. I knew we were all silently thinking "or dead."

Parker turned to me, his hold loosening. "So you just
tripped and fell?" he asked.

I shook my head. "No. I'm not that much of a klutz. It-it
was almost as though ... someone pushed me."

"Someone pushed you?" Parker echoed. "Are you sure?"

"I don't know," I said. "I mean, I guess it could've been an accident. It happened so fast..." I was getting blood on Parker's suit and winced at the stain. Doubtful that would come out, and I'd just gotten back on his dry cleaner's good side. Of course, Parker also didn't know that several thousand dollars' worth of his clothes was currently decorating Madison Street.

The EMT glanced behind him. "The cops are here," he said. "I'll send one over to talk to you."

Parker still had his arms around me, one hand stroking my hair—the bun I'd had it in was a distant memory—as I rested my cheek against his lapel. I was in no hurry to move. The guy had bandaged my arm to stop the bleeding until I could get to the ER for stitches and for the moment, I just reveled in the miracle that I was still alive.

"Call Ryker for me," I said to Parker. "Please." I needed to see him, feel *his* arms around me.

Parker didn't say anything, though his body stiffened. I twisted slightly so I could look up at him.

"I don't have his number," he said.

"My phone is in my purse."

His arms were slow to drop from around me, but he dug inside my purse and pulled out my phone. A moment later, it was at his ear. His eyes met mine.

"No, it's not Sage," he said curtly. "It's Parker. Sage has been involved in an accident. She'd like you to come."

There was a pause as he listened. "She's injured, but will be all right," he said. Parker gave him our location, then ended the call.

"He's on his way," he said to me.

"Thank you."

"Do you want me to stay as well?" His face was carefully blank.

"Can you?" I asked.

Parker's expression softened and he nodded. The shivering started again so I pulled the blanket tighter around me. Without a word, Parker stepped forward and drew me close to him. I sighed. The blanket was okay, but nothing helped more than the feel of his arms around me.

It must have been fifteen minutes or more before I saw Ryker coming toward us through the crowd. He caught sight of us and I straightened.

"God, Sage, you nearly gave me a heart attack," he said when he was close. Parker eased a few feet away as Ryker grabbed me in his arms to hug me. I gasped in pain as he inadvertently pressed on my shoulder. He immediately let go.

"Shit, I'm sorry," he said. "I just…I hadn't expected…" His words cut off as he kissed me, a quick, hard press of his lips against mine. He said nothing else, just rested his forehead against mine.

I felt better now, and it was strange, in a way. I'd needed Parker, but something inside hadn't eased until Ryker had arrived, too. Even as I knew it shouldn't be that way, near-death experiences had a tendency of making you not lie to yourself.

Ryker's thumbs brushed my cheeks, his breath mingling with mine. I reached out my hand behind him, searching, and felt Parker's slip into it. I gripped it tightly. Now I could breathe properly again.

After a few moments, Ryker cleared his throat and stepped back. His gaze caught on Parker. "Why are you here?" he asked.

"Ryker—" I began tiredly. I didn't want them to get into it. Not now. But Parker interrupted me.

"They called me," he said. "I'm a block away. Of course I came down to see if I could help."

"Was anyone else hurt?" I asked Ryker, figuring he'd know.

"The driver of the sedan has a broken leg and wrist," Ryker said. I saw his gaze drop to where Parker held my hand. "The rest are just banged up a bit. But I want to make sure *you're* okay."

"I'm fine," I said, then the pain in my shoulder reminded me that I wasn't. "Well, almost, I guess."

His eyes narrowed. "A couple of witnesses are saying that someone pushed you. That it wasn't an accident. These corners have street cams. We'll pull the footage and see what we find." He glanced over to where a group of cops were talking and I could tell he wanted to go talk to them, but was torn because he didn't want to leave me.

"You can go," I said. "I know you have to work. I just... I needed to see you."

"You need stitches. Are they going to take you to the hospital?"

"I'll take her," Parker said.

Ryker didn't like that at all, judging by his expression, but what could he say? He couldn't take me and I'd feel ridiculous riding in an ambulance to the hospital for mere stitches.

"Thanks," he said at last, the word sounding forced from him. He turned back to me, his palm gently cradling my jaw. "I'll be by when I get off, okay?"

I nodded and he kissed me again. A longer kiss this time, and while it was always a toe-curling experience to be kissed by Ryker, this time so blatantly in front of Parker, it felt more akin to a dog marking its territory. Not actually peeing on me, of course, just as a figure of speech. Because, eww.

When we came up for air, I saw that Parker had given us some space, walking a few yards away and turning his back to us. I looked up at Ryker, the blue of his eyes so startling beneath his dark lashes.

"I'll see you soon," I said. He took a step away, but I hooked his T-shirt with my fingers and tugged him back. "Thanks for not getting all weird about this," I quietly added.

He nodded, shot a quick glance at Parker, then he was gone.

I slid from the back of the ambulance until my feet touched the ground, then had to grab hold of something as my knees wanted to buckle. Parker was suddenly beside me.

"Hold on to me," he said, sliding an arm around my waist. I hooked my uninjured arm over his shoulder.

"My car's not far," he said. "I'd go get it and come to you, but this traffic won't let me anywhere close." It was true. The accident had snarled traffic in all directions.

"You have a four o'clock meeting today," I said.

"I'll reschedule."

"It's with Wuther Investments," I reminded him. "We set up this meeting weeks ago."

"Then we'll set it up again," he said. "I'm not worried about it."

He was so close, I was absurdly glad of the pain in my shoulder that didn't allow me to dwell on how much I liked the feel of his arm around me.

We made it to his car without incident, and the wait in the ER wasn't that bad. Finally, we were ensconced in a room, waiting for a doctor to do the stitches. I was apprehensive, drumming my nails on the table and fidgeting.

"What's the matter?" Parker asked. He was leaning against the wall, arms and ankles crossed. "Does it hurt? Because if you're in pain, I can go find someone—"

"I just hate stitches," I cut him off. "And they stick a needle right in there to numb it and..." I shuddered. I wasn't a huge fan of the ER anyway, or needles. I mean, who was?

The trace of a smile graced his lips. "I'll hold your hand," he promised. "And if you're good, maybe they'll give you a lollipop."

I rolled my eyes, but my lips twitched. A joke was nice after the harrowing accident. The memory made even my half-smile fade, and Parker seemed to sense my mood.

"Why did you call me?" he asked out of the blue.

I frowned, not following his train of thought. "What do you mean?"

"The guy who was helping you," he said. "You had him call me. Why? Why not call Ryker? Or your mom?"

I was momentarily speechless, staring at him. I hadn't really thought about it. I'd nearly died, literally faced death coming at me going forty miles an hour, and it hadn't occurred to me *not* to call Parker. When the guy had asked, I hadn't thought twice.

But now, with him looking at me and waiting for an answer, I felt foolish. Of all people, I'd called my boss? How... weird. No wonder that guy had looked at me all strange. He'd probably thought I'd hit my head, telling him to call my boss.

"I did call Ryker," I said, stalling. "Or, I mean, you did for me."

"But you called me first."

Shit. He wasn't letting this go.

"I-I..." My stammering made his eyebrow lift before I finally came up with something. "You were the closest," I blurted. Yeah, that sounded good. And was true, actually.

"I was the closest," he repeated, and the doubt in his voice made me double down on my fib.

"I knew you'd be able to come right away because you were in your weekly with Rafferty from Legal."

"So?"

"So that meeting never goes past an hour."

"That's because an hour is all I can stand with him."

"I know."

"So you're saying that's the only reason you called me?"

His persistence made me wonder what he *wanted* me to say. "Why else?" I asked. "It's not like you're my in-case-of-emergency person."

"Who is?"

"Who is what?"

"Your in-case-of-emergency person."

"My parents, of course," I said. Then curiosity made me add, "Who's yours?"

"You. Of course."

And that was the second time I'd been struck dumb by Parker in the span of mere minutes. Before I could think what to say, the doctor walked in.

"So I hear you've had quite a lucky day," he said to me, pulling up the little rolling stool to sit on and the tray with all the needles. He snapped on latex gloves and I gulped.

"Yeah, you could say that. So, um, how many shots do you think you'll need to do to numb it?" Those shots always felt as though they took an excruciatingly long time.

"Probably three or four," he said, looking at the slice in my arm.

I winced, my nails digging into the thin foam cushion of the chair I was sitting on. The doctor picked up the needle and I took a deep breath.

Parker was at my side, prying my hand from the chair and folding my palm inside his. I looked up at him rather than the needle, flinching as the medicine went into the wound. Gripping Parker's hand harder than I probably should have, I focused on his eyes, the clear purity of the blue that was a deeper shade than Ryker's.

He crouched down next to me. "So I found out Deirdre is dating someone," he said.

That got my attention. Deirdre was Parker's cleaning lady and cook who came by his apartment daily. Her cooking was phenomenal, and I knew this because I'd snuck a couple of bites a few times at Parker's place when he wasn't yet home from work and I'd been dropping off his dry cleaning or files he needed. I'd met her a few times, too.

An older lady in her mid-sixties, she had boundless energy that I'd kill for, and with her eight grandkids, she needed it. Her husband had passed away nearly a dozen years ago and she'd seemed perfectly content to fill her days with her kids, grandkids, and taking care of Parker's apartment. To hear she was dating someone was juicy gossip indeed.

"How do you know?" I asked him, wanting all the details.

"She wanted to know if she could make something ahead of time for Saturday night and if I'd put it in the oven. She said she had plans Saturday or she'd come by and do it. When I asked her what plans, she blushed and said she had a 'man friend' who was taking her out."

I laughed at the "man friend" descriptor—it sounded very Deirdre-ish—and shook my head.

"Well, how about that," I said. "Good for her. Did she say who he was?"

"No, but I have it on good authority that he's my butcher."

"Marco?"

Parker nodded.

"How do you know?"

"He told me."

"I bet they see each other all the time," I guessed. "She's always getting stuff there for you." Hmm. The Italian butcher and the cleaning grandma...it sounded like a Lifetime movie.

"Kinda what I thought," he said. "Think he'll give me a discount if things go well?"

"Doubtful."

Parker sighed in mock disappointment. "Yeah. I didn't think so either."

There was a tugging sensation on my skin and I realized the doctor had finished all the shots to numb the area and was now doing the stitches. I hadn't even felt it. I glanced over at him, but Parker caught my chin lightly with his fingers.

"Don't watch," he said. "Look at me instead."

Okay. Twist my arm.

He had on a deep navy pinstripe suit today with a crisp, white French-cuffed shirt. Silver cufflinks I'd gotten him for Christmas last year winked in the harsh fluorescent light. His tie was a gorgeous navy and silver diamond pattern with tiny paisleys in the center of each diamond. A busier tie than he usually wore, which meant he'd been in an exceptionally good mood this morning. Perhaps breaking up with Monique suited him just fine.

"All done," the doctor said, taking off his gloves with a snap. "The nurse will give you something for the discomfort and an antibiotic to prevent infection. The stitches will dissolve in seven to ten days. You'll have a thin scar, of course."

I thanked him as he left, then swallowed the pills the nurse gave me. The numbness was starting to wear off and it hurt something fierce.

"The pain medication will make you sleepy," she cautioned, "so no driving or operating heavy machinery, okay?"

"But Thursdays are backhoe night," I deadpanned.

Parker snorted a laugh, but the nurse didn't so much as crack a smile. Maybe she didn't know what a backhoe was.

Hands full of papers and pill bottles, we left the ER and

Parker drove me to my apartment. It was pushing six o'clock and my stomach grumbled all the way, complaining about my lack of afternoon snack. It would've embarrassed me, but the medicine had taken hold and I dozed in Parker's passenger seat.

"Wake up, sleepyhead. We're home."

I mumbled something, prying my eyes open. My hair was in my eyes, but even as I thought it, Parker was brushing it aside. His hand touched my cheek and my heavy eyelids fluttered closed again. I expected him to retreat, but to my surprise, he cupped my jaw. The warm slide of his thumb across my cheekbone felt like having a drink of water after running five miles on the treadmill (which I was just guessing at because I'd never been able to do more than three), and a small sigh escaped me.

When I managed to overcome the medication-induced lethargy enough to open my eyes again, it was to see Parker quite close, staring at me. Gone was the lightheartedness he'd distracted me with in the emergency room. Now his expression was grave, his lips pressed together and his brow furrowed.

"You're looking grim," I said, my voice soft in the quiet car. "Thinking of how much work you're going to have to do tonight to make up for this afternoon?"

"Thinking of how you were nearly taken from me. Again."

I was too tired and my brain was moving too slow to process how to respond to that, so I blinked at him. Once. Slowly.

Parker didn't seem to require a response, though. His fingers brushed my face, traced my brow, trailed down my cheek to my lips.

Unable to tear my gaze away from his, I waited... for

what, I didn't know. The things he'd said the other night, the insinuations and hints that he felt more for me—wanted more from me—were confusing. I thought I'd finally "gotten over" Parker, sort of, and now he was reeling me back in with almost effortless ease.

He was close enough to kiss, if I just leaned forward a few inches. It felt like a magnet was pulling me toward him, but something held me back and it took a moment for my sluggish brain to realize what that was.

Ryker.

Guilt hit and hit hard. I jerked back from Parker's touch, my hand flying for the door handle. In my haste to get out, I nearly fell on my face in the parking lot.

"Hey, slow down. I'll help you," Parker said.

"I'm fine. I just didn't expect the, uh, door to, uh, open that quick." *Gee? What did you think it'd do when you pulled the handle?* Good lord, I was spouting inane bullshit, but he was already rounding the car to my side.

"Here, let me take your purse," he said, lifting the strap from my shoulder. "Lean on me."

No, no, no. Bad idea.

"I'm okay," I insisted, heading for the door to the building. And it would have been a good exit, if my vision wasn't blurry and I missed the door handle by a mile when I reached for it. I heard a soft chuckle behind me.

"Yes, I can see you're perfectly capable when you're drugged up," he said, reaching around me to pull open the door.

I chose not to dignify that with an answer, and not because I had to concentrate too hard on where I put my feet as I walked down the hall to be able to form a coherent reply.

There were two sets of elevator buttons when I knew for a fact there should be only one. I hoped I was picking the real and not the ghost illusion when I pressed the button, and I let out a relieved huff of breath when I saw the correct circle light up.

"See?" I said, leaning against the wall. "I'm fi—" The wall moved and I lost my balance, toppling back into the elevator as the doors opened. Huh. I'd thought for sure that had been a wall...

Parker snagged me around the waist before I could fall, then helped me into the elevator the correct way...on one's feet.

"My, what fast reflexes you have, Mr. Anderson," I said, the words just popping out. I frowned. It seemed the medicine was not only making me groggy and see double, but had messed with the filter between my brain and mouth.

"Now that's one I haven't heard before," he said, helping me out of the elevator. His arm was still around my waist and I wanted to move away, but I also *didn't* want to end up on my ass.

"Comments about his speed usually aren't something a man wants to hear from a woman," he quipped.

I let out a very unladylike snort at the joke, then tried to swallow my laughter. Parker had just made a sex joke. This day was just full of firsts. The first time Parker made a sex joke, the first time I'd been high on painkillers around my boss, the first time I'd nearly gotten run over by a truck...

Okay, that last one wasn't funny at all.

By now, Parker was holding my purse up for me while I dug around in it for my keys. I'd yet to meet a man who wanted to brave the contents of a woman's purse, no matter how justified. It was taking too long, but he just stood there, patiently holding the knockoff Michael Kors.

At last, I triumphantly produced the keys. "Got 'em!"

Then proceeded to immediately drop them on the floor. "Oops."

Parker grabbed them before I could contemplate how to bend over without falling over, and unlocked the door. I followed him inside, really glad to be home. Heading for the couch, I plopped down on it and kicked off my shoes while Parker turned on a couple of lamps.

"You've got to be hungry," he said. "What do you want to eat? I'll go get it for you."

I tipped my head back on the sofa and looked up at where he stood behind the couch. He touched my hair again, moving it aside from my neck to my shoulder.

"Aren't I usually the one making the runs for take-out?"

His features softened with a small smile. "I'll make an exception. Just this once. Don't tell anyone."

"That you're really not a jerk?" I asked. Oops. Probably shouldn't have said that either, but his smile only widened.

"Is that what people say about me?" he asked.

"Not everyone," I hedged. "People know you're very... dedicated to your job." Which was true. Parker was respected at KLP, and most had a healthy fear of screwing up and getting on his radar. He dealt mainly with clients, so if Parker had to take time out of his busy schedule because of a personnel issue, it wasn't pretty.

"That's why I have you," he said. "You're my human credential."

"I'm your what?" I'd never heard that before. I twisted around so I could stop looking at him upside down.

"People know you're as sweet as can be, always nice and helpful. So if you can work for me and not quit your job—or kill me—then I can't be *that* bad, right? My human credential."

"Huh." I hadn't ever thought of it that way, but it was true.

I'd had the impression people had feared Parker a lot before I'd begun working there, but now things were better, though everyone still came through me if they wanted to see him.

"So what do you want to eat?"

I thought about it. "Pizza. Lots of cheese."

Twenty minutes later, I'd changed into yoga pants and a T-shirt and Parker was handing money to the delivery guy. The smell of fresh-baked pizza wafted through the apartment. I went to get off the couch and winced.

"Sore?" Parker asked, setting the box down on the coffee table.

I nodded as he sat down next to me. "Yeah. Everywhere. I guess my whole body just tensed up when I saw that truck coming." That plus getting kicked around in the nightclub last night, which I definitely *wasn't* going to tell him about.

He handed me a plate with three slices of pizza dripping cheese.

"I can't eat all that," I protested.

"Sure you can," he said, grabbing another plate for himself. He'd discarded his jacket and loosened his tie, but still looked incongruous taking a bite of his own slice. Setting down the plate, he went into the kitchen.

I watched him, wondering if I should daintily nibble on my pizza or scarf it down like I wanted to. Considering how much my stomach was growling, I decided I didn't really care if it was ladylike or not and took a huge bite. My eyes slid shut.

Heaven. Pure heaven.

I had a whole slice gone and was halfway through round two when Parker returned, carrying two wineglasses and an open bottle of red. He poured himself a whole glass and me half before handing it to me.

"Cheers," he said, clinking his glass against mine.

I'd slowed down by the time I got to the third slice, and my toes caught my eye. "Crap," I mumbled around pizza.

"What?"

"The asphalt scraped my polish," I explained, wiggling my toes so he could see what I was talking about. "Now I have to redo them."

"You're not going to be able to bend enough to paint your toes," Parker said, taking his fourth slice.

Well, shit. I hadn't thought of that, but he was right. I couldn't move off the couch without groaning. No way could I paint my toes. I'd just have to go around with them looking awful.

For some reason, this was the thing that broke me. Not the slice in the shoulder, not the scrapes and bruises from last night, not even the stitches. I was bawling because I couldn't paint my toes.

Parker took the glass out of my hand and the plate from my lap. I covered my face with my hands, embarrassed beyond belief that I was sobbing in front of him. He had to think I was insane.

But he didn't say anything, just put his arm around me and pulled me into him until my head rested against his chest in the crook of his neck and shoulder. He rubbed my back as I cried.

I didn't know if it was because the impending terror of seeing that truck had shaken me so much or what, but it seemed really hard to let this incident go. Months ago, Viktor Rowan had held a plastic bag over my head, nearly suffocating me, and that had been pretty damn scary. Or maybe it was that I'd had one too many near-death experiences in too short a span of time. Whatever the reason, it took several minutes for me to calm down.

Finally, when my tears had subsided and I was doing the

weird hiccup thing you did after crying too hard, Parker said, "If you wanted a mani/pedi, all you had to do was ask."

A bubble of laughter escaped, in spite of the crying jag. He handed me a tissue and I wiped my eyes.

"So where's your polish?"

I waved his question aside. "I'm fine. It's just one of those things."

"No. You always have your toes painted. It'll help you feel more normal, more in control. Just tell me where your stuff is. In the bathroom? Your bedroom?" He was already heading down the hallway.

"Parker," I called. "Really, it's fine…" But he'd disappeared into the bathroom. Oh geez, if he found my polish…

"Wow."

I cringed. Yep. He'd found it all right.

I liked nail polish. A lot. The last time I'd counted, I'd had over fifty bottles, and that had been at Christmas, nearly a year ago. I'd probably added twenty more in the time since.

Parker poked his head out the door. "You're going to have to help me out. What color?"

Like I was going to have him dig out a specific color. Please. They were organized by mood. Colors that made me happy, colors that made me feel sexy, colors to wear when I was feeling depressed, colors specific for certain holidays… no way could I explain that to him. "Um, whatever. You choose."

He returned bearing polish remover, cotton balls, and two bottles. "Okay," he said, sitting down again. "I have…" He looked at the bottom of one bottle. "*Tasmanian Devil Made Me Do It.*" He looked at the other bottle. "And…*A Good Man-darin Is Hard to Find.*" Glancing at me, he asked, "Which?"

I shrugged, unable to stop a smile. It was surreal, Parker eating pizza on my couch and picking out polish for my toes. Maybe I should have a near-death experience every day, if this was how Parker reacted.

He reached for my leg and propped it on his thigh so he could get to my toes, then began assiduously removing the scraped remains of *I Don't Give a Rotterdam*. His tie caught my eye and before I could think twice, I reached for it, loosening the knot and sliding the length of silk from underneath his collar. He paused while I did this, looking at me instead of my toes, and the air grew charged between us.

"I don't want you to get anything on your tie," I blurted, deliberately not following the path my mind was leading, where I was taking more off him than his tie. "Your dry cleaner hates me enough as it is."

Parker's lips twitched, then he returned to his work, removing the polish from one set of toes, then the other before choosing *A Good Man-darin Is Hard to Find*. I wondered if he knew that was the same polish I'd worn when I'd interviewed for the job as his assistant. Probably not. It wasn't like men noticed that sort of thing.

The touch of his hands on my skin was a decadent torture. His palm wrapped around my ankle as he steadied me before carefully applying the bright peach lacquer. Each nail was painted with a sure hand, then he set aside the bottle and blew warm air across my toes.

A shiver went through me and he must have felt it, because the hand circling my ankle loosened. His palm slid a few inches up my calf underneath the hem of my pants, just touching me in a gentle slide of his fingers against my skin. The warm air blew in a steady stream over my wet nails and my hands curled into fists.

This wasn't sexual. This was just Parker being nice. He'd

seen me fall apart over my stupid toenails. What was he supposed to do? Say, "Well, have fun with that. See you tomorrow!"

Yeah, because bosses painted their secretaries' toes all the time.

Okay, maybe that little voice in my head had a point, but even if *he* was thinking it, and *I* was thinking it, we weren't actually *doing* anything, so the guilt gnawing at my conscience was completely absurd, right?

The little voice was conspicuously silent.

The rattle of the lock in the door had me guiltily trying to pull my legs off Parker's lap, but his grip was suddenly strong around my ankles and I couldn't budge.

Which was why when Ryker walked in, he saw his girlfriend sitting on the couch with her legs in another man's lap.

Ryker stopped right inside the door, his gaze resting on us.

"Am I interrupting something?" he asked, and I winced at the thinly veiled accusation in his voice.

I tried to take back my feet, but Parker held firm.

"You're going to ruin the finest pedicure I've ever done," he said to me.

"It's the only pedicure you've ever done," I hissed back. My face was hot and I knew I was blushing under Ryker's scrutiny.

"What's going on?" Ryker asked. "Sage?"

"I brought her home and she was a little high on painkillers," Parker explained. "So I fed her some pizza and was polishing her toes."

Ryker's eyebrows flew upward. "You were *what*?"

"Relax," Parker said, carefully setting my legs aside and standing. "She was upset. You weren't here. I was just doing what I could to help."

Okay, so I guess the sexual tension I'd felt had been entirely one-sided. Good to know. Now to ignore the sinking feeling in my stomach. Stupid, stupid, to get sucked back in.

Ryker blew out a sigh, then to my relief, he let the matter drop. "Well, I have bad news," he said, shrugging out of his jacket and tossing it over a chair, though I had a hall tree *right there* to hang coats on. "The video footage showed exactly what you said. A man walked behind you, shoved you into the street, then disappeared into the crowd."

I'd been afraid that that's what had happened, but to hear it confirmed was just sad. I felt a little like my parents, wanting to ask, "What's the world coming to these days?" for a complete stranger to try and kill me for no reason.

"Any luck on finding out who it was?" Parker asked, but Ryker just shook his head.

"Not yet. We're trying some facial recognition programs, but that takes time. If we get a hit, they'll let me know."

Ryker dropped down on the couch beside me. "You can find your way to the door, I'm sure," he said.

Parker just smiled in a bland sort of way, then picked up his jacket.

I rolled my eyes and got painfully to my feet. "I'll walk you out," I said, following Parker to the door. He'd already opened it and stood in the doorway, waiting, by the time I got there.

"Thanks for taking me to the hospital," I said. "And for dinner. And the pedicure."

His answering smile wasn't so much on his lips as in his eyes. "You're welcome," he said, uberpolite but with a gentle undertone that inexplicably made me blush. "You don't have to come in tomorrow, if you're not feeling up to it. Take a day off."

"Thanks," I said, knowing I'd go in to work anyway. It was a nice gesture. "I'll see how I feel."

"Okay. Good night then. Don't forget to take your meds."

I nodded and he headed down the hallway. He was nearly at the stairwell before I remembered.

"Parker?" I called. He paused, glancing back at me.

"Yes?"

"Your suits from the dry cleaner's..." I hesitated.

"What about them?"

"The truck kinda...ran over them." I winced, thinking of how much it was going to cost to replace those. Parker didn't dress cheaply.

But his lips just twitched. "Better the suits than you," he said, then he was gone.

CHAPTER EIGHT

I think you need to up your life insurance," Megan said, spearing more lettuce with her fork. "Between the club and now the truck, I can't believe the awful luck you've had this week."

"I know, right?" I hadn't told her that someone had deliberately pushed me, just that it had been an accident. No sense worrying my best friend even more.

"So did Ryker go ape shit when he found out?"

I nodded. "Yeah, a little." I paused before adding, "Parker kinda did, too."

That made her stop chewing for a moment. I waited, wondering what she'd say to that.

"I'm not surprised," she said. "Who'd go pick up his dry cleaning and get his breakfast every day if something happened to you?"

"You think that's all it is?" I asked. "I was hoping, maybe…" I shrugged.

"You've been hoping that for a long time," she said. "I don't want you to mess up the really great relationship you have going on because you're looking for what isn't there with Parker."

"You're right, you're right," I said with a sigh. "I'm just...pathetic and stupid."

"No, you're not. Parker is pathetic and stupid, which is why you need to focus on your leather-wearing, gun-toting badass boyfriend."

I laughed at her description of Ryker and went back to eating my soup. I was mulling over what she'd said when a man caught my eye. Seated alone a few tables away, he kept watching Megan and me. I caught him at it, but he didn't look away like most people did when caught staring. He was nondescript, though not unattractive in a generic kind of way. His gaze was cold, though, and he didn't smile, which unnerved me.

Was it just another weirdo in a city full of them? Leo Shea and his threat to Ryker drifted through my mind. Maybe it hadn't been just a random act of violence yesterday when I'd been pushed in front of that truck.

I looked away, but kept tabs on him, breathing a sigh of relief when he remained at his table after Megan and I rose to leave. After yesterday, maybe I was seeing things that weren't really there.

We walked back to the office together and today I stayed well away from the curb. Megan did, too. She'd freaked when I'd told her what had happened yesterday, hugging me for a really long time, and she'd had tears in her eyes when she'd let me go.

The rest of the day passed without incident, thank goodness. Parker had been stopping by my desk more often than usual today, making me suspicious that he was using it as an excuse to check up on me, though he never said as much. He hadn't seemed a bit surprised to see me this morning, even after he'd offered me the day off.

"My tailor's coming by around six," he said one of these times. "Could you stick around and give me your opinion?"

This wasn't a new thing. Parker spent enough on his wardrobe that the tailor came to him rather than the other way around, and when he did, Parker always asked me to stay and provide a feminine voice as to his choices. I never minded. Secretly, I enjoyed it. What wasn't to enjoy? I got to see a gorgeous man modeling high-end suits and sport coats, then asking me what I thought. It never seemed like actual work to me.

But tonight was my rescheduled dinner date with Ryker. After the awful dinner with my parents, then the mini-fight we'd gotten in when he'd cancelled the first date, it seemed like a bad idea to have to tell him I needed to stay late for work.

"Um, let me check," I said to Parker, stalling. He raised an eyebrow in question. "Ryker and I had planned dinner for tonight."

"Ah," he said. "Then by all means, don't let me keep you." He gave me his signature bland half-smile that gave away nothing that he was thinking, then disappeared back into his office.

I swallowed my disappointment. I was doing the right thing. It probably wasn't that professional anyway to help your boss pick out his wardrobe. And lord knew I wouldn't be thinking professional thoughts. Best not to let temptation get in the way.

Ryker had texted and said he'd pick me up from work to head to dinner, so I met him outside. Even after four months, I still got a shiver of excitement when he pulled up on his motorcycle. With his black leather jacket, jeans, heavy boots, and aviators, he looked like every woman's wet dream and every father's nightmare.

"Hop on, babe."

Alrighty then.

I'd learned to pack a pair of jeans when I went to work for just such occasions as this. My skirt was neatly folded and packed in my oversize Tory Burch knockoff so I could straddle the bike behind Ryker. I wrapped my arms around his chest, adjusting my purse as I did so, and that's when I saw him.

The same guy from lunch.

He was standing on the sidewalk, maybe twenty feet away, and was lighting a cigarette. I watched as he cupped his hand around the end to shield the flame from the wind, then he pocketed his lighter and took a long drag. His gaze shifted to me and Ryker, then the corner of his mouth lifted in a satisfied smirk.

Before I had a chance to say anything to Ryker, he was pulling out into traffic and we were flying down the street. I twisted to look behind us and sure enough, the guy watched until we were out of sight.

* * *

"So that's weird, right?" I asked Ryker as I took a sip of my cocktail. The bartender had given me a blank look when I'd asked for Absolut Mandarin (my favorite flavor of vodka), so I'd smiled and said whatever he had that was Top Shelf would be fine.

"Why didn't you say anything to me?" Ryker asked, taking a swig from his beer bottle.

"I didn't have time. We were already leaving when I realized it was the same guy."

We were sitting at the bar in a bar & grill–type restaurant downtown. It was a little more *bar* than *grill*, but who was complaining? It was dinner out with my man so I shut my trap and kept my opinions about the overly juiced Cosmo with a sadly lacking Top Shelf vodka to myself.

"You think maybe it was just a weird coincidence?" I asked, hoping the answer was yes.

"I don't think you'd be that lucky," he said grimly.

Yeah. Me neither.

"So what do I do?" I asked. "What if I see him again?"

"Don't go anywhere alone," he said. "And if he approaches you, run in the other direction screaming bloody murder."

I frowned. "That doesn't sound good."

"Noise helps scare off an attacker," he explained. "They'd much rather a quiet and compliant victim than a noisy pain in the ass one."

I could totally do noisy pain in the ass.

"So how's work?" I asked. "Anything more about that Leo Shea guy? Did you have to tell somebody what happened?"

Ryker nodded. "I can't say much about it," he said. He had a drawn look to his face that worried me. "He's from an old case I worked on when I was with vice. Undercover. In a city the size of Chicago, never thought I'd run into him again. Probably wouldn't have either since he runs in pretty powerful circles. But the other night—"

"The other night I made you go to dinner at a fancy, expensive restaurant," I interrupted. "And he was there."

"Yeah."

"Okay, well, what parts of your job *can* you talk about?" I asked. I certainly didn't want to talk about *my* job.

"You don't want to hear about my job."

"Of course I do!"

"It's fucking depressing, Sage," he said. "You don't want to hear about the murders I see or the other shitty things that go along with being a homicide cop."

"If you don't tell me, then who do you tell?" I asked. "You can't just carry it around, all bottled up inside."

He eyed me, took another long pull of his beer, then said, "Fine. Today was rough because we got a call for a homicide scene where the dad shot his three kids, then his wife. He was on his way to his parents' house, probably to shoot them, too, when we got him. The kids were five, three, and six months."

I stared at him and swallowed hard. That was a nightmare that I had trouble wrapping my head around. And it was something Ryker dealt with on a daily basis. Words were inadequate for such horror, so I reached over and slipped my hand inside his, giving it a squeeze.

"I'm glad you got him," I said, "before he hurt someone else."

His lips lifted in a grim half-smile. "Me too." He squeezed my hand back.

"What about you?" he asked. "You feel okay today? Still sore? Did Parker the Prick take it easy on you today?"

I bit my tongue about the insult to Parker, knowing Ryker was wanting to take out some of his frustration.

"It was fine," I said mildly. "You know, he took me to the hospital yesterday and stayed until you got there, which I appreciated."

"And painted your toes," Ryker added, finishing his beer and signaling the bartender for another.

"It didn't mean anything," I said, which was true. By Parker's own admission, which still bothered me but I tried not to think about it. A recurring theme over the past few days, but whatever.

"I was wondering if you'd thought about getting another job?" he asked.

I nearly choked on the sip I was taking of the mediocre Cosmo. "Wh-what?" I stammered. "Why?"

"You don't want to be just a secretary your whole life, do you?" he asked. "You have a degree. You should use it, right? Isn't that what your parents want?"

"What do my parents have to do with my career choice? And since when is my being 'just a secretary' such a bad thing?" He'd hit on a sore spot and now I was struggling to keep a rein on my temper...and my hurt.

"I didn't think a Muccino would want his only daughter being at someone's beck and call when I'm sure he could pull some strings and get you a cushy job at a museum somewhere, that's all."

I knew my jaw was hanging open and I shut it with a snap. "First of all," I said through gritted teeth, "I'm an Executive Administrative Assistant, not some flunky who's at someone's 'beck and call.' Secondly, maybe I don't want my father pulling strings for me. If I want a different job, then I'll go get it myself. It's my life."

"Okay, okay, settle down," he said. "Don't get all pissed."

"Settle down?" I echoed, giving up on holding my temper. "Did you just tell me to *settle down*?"

Ryker sighed, taking a drink of the new beer the bartender had set in front of him. I didn't speak either and the silence was tense between us. Finally, I couldn't take it anymore.

"This is about Parker, isn't it," I said. "It's not the job. It's him. You wouldn't care one little bit if I worked for someone else, but because it's Parker, you want me to find another job."

He turned to look at me. "Do you blame me?" he asked, his voice bitter. "You're with him more than you're with me."

"I can't believe we're having this same argument," I replied, shaking my head. "I thought you were over this months ago. I chose you. Not him."

"I'm never going to be over Parker," he retorted. "And I certainly am tired of seeing him around you. Why is it such a big deal to get another job? If you want to stay a sec—administrative assistant," he corrected himself, "then you could, I'm sure."

"So just because you want me to get another job, I'm supposed to upend my life and do it?" I shot back, ignoring his question. "We've been dating for four and a half months, Ryker. I don't think you have the right yet to demand I switch careers, or jobs."

I suddenly did not want to be there anymore. Tipping up my drink, I swallowed the rest of the shitty Cosmo and hopped up from my barstool.

"I've got to go," I said.

As if to underscore my point, Ryker's cell phone buzzed. He glanced at the screen and cursed. "Looks like I'd have had to cut our dinner short anyway," he said.

Wonderful. I didn't even get the satisfaction of leaving him at the bar in return for him being an ass.

Shoving his phone back into his pocket, he stood, digging into his wallet and tossing money down to cover our drinks. We hadn't even had a chance to order anything to eat.

He took my elbow to steer me outside and I was just pissy enough to pull away from him. He didn't say anything.

When we neared his bike, I passed by it and waved to flag down a taxi.

"C'mon, Sage," he said. "I'll take you home."

"I can get my own ride," I said stiffly.

He grabbed my arm, halting me. "I don't want you alone. Not when someone may be following you."

"Then maybe you should've thought about that before you pissed me off." I jerked out of his hold and slid into the cab that had just pulled up, leaving Ryker staring after me.

"Where to?" the cabbie asked. I opened my mouth to give him my home address and heard the work one come out instead.

Huh.

Well, I supposed that was one way to salvage the evening, watching Parker model suits...if they were still there. It was a while past six o'clock.

I was irritated with Ryker and upset. I'd thought we'd moved past his overt animosity toward Parker. I was with *him* after all, not Parker. But it was as though he just couldn't let it go, and I was at a loss as to how to make him. What I *did* know was that I couldn't keep having the same argument over and over.

The cabbie pulled up to the building and I paid him before getting out. As I rode the elevator up, I figured even if Parker was gone, I had some work on my desk I could take home. That would help keep my mind off the argument with Ryker.

But I was in luck, as I saw the tailor and his assistant still in Parker's office. Parker was standing on a raised platform and the tailor was pinning the jacket he was wearing, measuring tape dangling from his mouth. As I got closer, I saw it was a tuxedo.

Wow.

I'd never seen Parker in a tux before, but the wait had been worth it. I drank in the black fabric stretched across his broad shoulders, the lines of the jacket perfectly cut to accentuate his frame.

Tentatively, I rapped on the glass door, then pushed it open. Parker turned around and caught sight of me.

"Am I interrupting?" I asked.

A wide smile broke across his face and I was momentarily transfixed.

"Absolutely not," he said. "Come in. Tell me, what do you think of this tux?"

I walked into the office, glad I'd been given an excuse to stare. From the back, he'd looked good. From the front, he was James Bond–level gorgeous.

"Um, yeah," I said, nodding. "That's…um…really nice." A massive understatement, but I didn't think it would be a good idea to gush about how amazing he looked because a) he was my boss and b) I had a boyfriend. Albeit a boyfriend I'd just had an argument with, but still.

"Just nice?" he asked.

I took in the perfectly knotted bow tie, crisp white shirt, cuffs complete with links all the way down to shoes so highly shined, they were military perfect.

"*Really* nice," I murmured with a sigh.

The tailor smothered a laugh and I whipped my head around to glare at him, but he was poker-faced as he hung some discarded garments on his rack.

"So what's the tux for?" I asked, wandering over to sit on the black leather couch in the corner.

"A fundraiser thing," Parker replied, turning to face me on the dais. The ever-patient tailor turned with him, adjusting his tape measure accordingly. "The Morris campaign for mayor."

"He's never gonna win," I said. "You know that. Not in this one-party town."

Parker sighed. "I know, but you still have to try. A lot of our customers are going, too, so it'll be good for business. Maybe pick up a few more while we're there."

"When is it?" Chances were my father was also donating to the campaign, but I doubted he'd attend any fundraisers.

The tailor had finished and was removing the tuxedo jacket from Parker's shoulders. I tried not to stare.

"Tomorrow night. Want to come?"

I didn't know what to say for a second. Parker hadn't ever invited me to something like that before.

"You can help me remember all the names of our clients that I should know," he said when I didn't immediately reply. "It's bad for customer relations when I have to ask them who they are."

True. Parker was amazing with numbers, but not always the greatest at putting a face with a name. Still, I hesitated. "You don't have a replacement for Monique yet?" I asked.

"I haven't been looking," Parker said, unknotting his bow tie and sliding it from beneath the collar. He handed it to the assistant. "Besides, no one except you can help me remember clients," Parker said.

Right. It was a work thing. Not like a . . . a date . . . or something.

"Yeah, I should be able to go," I said, wondering with a sense of unease how Ryker was going to take this. On the other hand, I wasn't going to quit my job anytime soon, so he needed to get over it already.

Parker moved behind the privacy screen the tailor had set up and I tried not to think about him getting undressed as he put his suit back on. Parker was discussing things with the tailor and I debated getting a drink from Parker's stash of scotch, wondering if he'd say anything about it if I did. I'd reluctantly decided against it when the tailor and his assistant finally packed up and left.

Glancing at Parker, I saw he hadn't bothered with his jacket or tie, and the top two buttons of his shirt were undone. I looked away from the patch of skin peeking out.

Just then my stomach decided to give a horrendous growl, reminding me that dinner with Ryker had been cut short before we'd actually gotten food.

Parker gave a low chuckle. "Sounds like you could use something to eat. Me too. I'm starving. Let's get out of here."

My cheeks were warm with embarrassment and I jumped to my feet. "Good idea." I'd just grab some work off my desk and then flag down a cab. Did I have anything at home to eat? A frozen pizza, maybe. I bet Deirdre had made Parker something awesome, as usual, which made me completely envious.

I'd finished stuffing the files into my purse when Parker came out of his office and locked the door behind him. Always the gentleman, he waited for me to precede him into the waiting elevator.

"Where are you going?" he asked when I punched the button for the lobby.

I frowned at him. "Um, home?" I'd thought that was pretty obvious.

"Deirdre told me she left a big pan of manicotti at home," he said. "You may as well come by and have some. I won't be able to eat it all. I never can. She cooks enough food for ten people even though I keep telling her it's just me."

Manicotti. Yum. Growing up with an Italian father meant pasta had been a staple in our house, lovingly hand-crafted and smothered in homemade marinara. Just thinking about it made my stomach growl again.

Parker laughed as the elevator doors slid open on the

parking garage level. "Then it's settled," he said. "Come on."

It was starting to feel dangerously comfortable and normal to ride in Parker's BMW, though following him into his apartment still fell under the title of *Surreal*. Yes, I'd been there many times before, but usually it was without him holding the door open for me to step inside.

I was immediately hit by the mouthwatering aroma of pasta baking, and I took a deep, appreciative sniff.

"Smells like we're just in time," Parker said. "Make yourself at home." He took his briefcase into his office as I looked around to try and figure out the best place to sit.

I didn't think making myself "at home" was the best idea, so I kind of stood awkwardly in the middle of the kitchen. He didn't say anything about it when he returned, though, just headed to the wine rack and chose a bottle of red.

"You're off the pain meds, right?" he asked, pausing before pouring the liquid into the second glass.

"Yeah. It makes me too sleepy and a little nauseous." Ibuprofen had been good enough to keep the pain in my shoulder under control, thank goodness.

After the fight with Ryker, a glass of wine sounded good. I was depressed about it now that my temper had worn off, and didn't know what to do. I swallowed a big gulp of what Parker poured for me while he took the pan out of the oven.

As I'd expected, the food was amazing. I moaned appreciatively as the first bite hit my tongue, my eyes drifting shut. I hadn't had homemade Italian in a while, and it felt like coming home.

Parker suddenly cleared his throat and my eyes shot open.

"Good?" he asked, his gaze dropping to my mouth.

"Mmhmm," I managed as enthusiastically as I could with my mouth full.

The wine was excellent and the food amazing, and before

I even realized, Parker was refilling my wineglass for a third time and I was finishing off my second helping of manicotti.

"I love Deirdre," I sighed when my plate was empty. Oh, wow, I was so full, and really regretted wearing tights today as the waistband felt like it was cutting into my now bloated stomach. Ugh. And after heavy Italian food and wine, I was lethargic and sleepy.

Hauling my ass out of the chair, I helped Parker clean up, then wondered what I was supposed to do—should I leave?—but he just grabbed the bottle of wine and our glasses. I followed him into the living room and he sat down on the sofa, setting the bottle of wine on the coffee table in front of it. So I sat there, too, and he handed me my glass.

I figured I should probably stop drinking as I could feel it had already gone to my head, but that's the thing with drinking—by the time you realize it's going to your head, you just don't care. And not caring about anything was an intoxicating feeling (no pun intended). Definitely a Catch-22, that, plus I'd never been great at knowing when to say when.

"I thought you and Ryker were having dinner tonight," Parker said. A non-question question.

"We did," I said. "Sorta. But we got in a fight before we could order and then he got called back to work, so there wasn't really food involved."

"A fight? What did you fight about?" Parker finished his wine and added more to his glass, then poured the rest of the bottle into mine.

"You." It kind of popped out and I winced.

"What about me?" He settled back against the couch, stretching an arm along the top behind me and turning his body slightly my way as he took another drink of his wine. I wondered if I should be talking about this with Parker, but it was kind of late to be worrying about it now. I gave a mental shrug.

"He wants me to quit. Says I should get a 'real job.'"

Parker froze for a moment, so briefly I wondered if I'd imagined it, then he swallowed the wine and set the glass aside.

"What did you tell him?"

"That we've only been dating a few months and I'm not going to turn my life upside down for someone when I don't know where it's going," I said, my irritation at Ryker plain to hear in my tone. I took a big swig of wine, tears stinging my eyes because even though I was mad at Ryker, I hated to be in a fight with him.

"Hey, it's okay, don't cry." Parker took my glass from me and pulled me closer with an arm around me, being careful of my shoulder that had the stitches. "Maybe he's just under pressure right now at work."

It was almost too easy to lean against him as I sniffed and tried to blink away the damn tears. "Yeah, maybe," I mumbled. "I don't understand why he can't just let it go. We're practically living together and he still acts like he's jealous of you."

Parker's hand was running a light path down my back, then up, but it paused.

"You're living together?"

I nodded, hoping I wasn't getting makeup on his pristine shirt. "Yeah. I think so. Mostly."

His hand resumed its path and I closed my eyes. I felt my body relax into his.

"If that's not something you want, then you should tell him," Parker said gently. "Don't let him rush you. There's no hurry."

I tipped my head back to look at him, which was a mistake,

because that's when I realized how close our faces were to each other. More importantly, how close his lips were.

Oh God.

He had his arm around me as I leaned against him and the scent of his cologne surrounded me. His face was tilted down, his blue gaze locked on mine, and I could feel the beat of his heart through his chest against my ribs. Or maybe that was my heart beating so rapidly.

Longing struck. That deep pang inside me that I thought I'd vanquished when it came to Parker. Turned out it wasn't vanquished, just buried real deep. All the thoughts I'd had about why I couldn't tell Ryker I loved him swirled with a sick feeling of guilt inside my head.

I pushed against him and he kept his hold on me just long enough to send a silent message before dropping his arms. Hurriedly I stood, albeit slightly unsteady on my feet. I didn't know if that was from the wine, what had almost just happened, or both.

Parker was up and gently held my arms until I was balanced, standing so close I could just lean forward an itty bit and lick that triangle of skin that his unbuttoned shirt revealed...

"I gotta go," I said, stumbling backward. I righted myself and made a beeline for the kitchen and where I'd dropped off my shoes and purse.

I was busy trying to shove my feet into my heels—when had it gotten to be so complicated a procedure?—when Parker spoke. I hadn't even heard him follow me. His voice was right at my ear and he rested a hand on my shoulder, startling me. I spun around to face him and his hand dropped.

"You seem kind of tipsy," he said. "Why don't you stay here for a while? I don't want to send you home like this."

But I shook my head. "I'm fine. Coming tonight was probably not the best idea."

"Why is that?"

He was still so close. I took a step back and hit the wall.

I swallowed hard before answering. "Because I can't do this," I said. I had to get through to him. This had to stop. "I'm with Ryker, and you're...toying with me...and I can't...I just...I can't—"

My throat closed up and I couldn't say anything else. My eyes begged him to understand. Parker meant so much to me, but it was too late. I wasn't going to dump Ryker—another man I deeply cared about—simply because Parker was putting moves on me. I didn't trust it and I didn't trust him.

Parker's hands cupped my face, his thumbs brushing my cheeks. "I swear, I'm not toying with you. You wanted more between us not long ago. Tell me you don't still feel that way."

I shook my head. "It doesn't matter. I'm with Ryker, and I don't trust you," I managed, barely above a whisper. Between the fight with Ryker and now...whatever this was with Parker...my emotions were raw. I felt buffeted between the two of them, like a leaf in the wind.

Parker flinched at my words, a barely perceptible reaction that someone who didn't know him as well as I did may have missed. His hands fell to his sides.

Grabbing my purse, I opened the door before I could re-think it.

"Thanks for dinner," I said, then I was hurrying down the hallway and out of the building as fast as I could go, not knowing if I was running away from Parker, running toward Ryker, or both.

CHAPTER NINE

I was utterly confused and miserable as I hopped out of the cab and headed for the front of my building. I didn't know what I was going to do about Parker, nor did I understand what had changed. Was it just the brush with disaster yesterday that had suddenly brought on this change of heart in him?

But it didn't matter, whatever it was. I wasn't going to let it derail my relationship with Ryker.

Which seemed to be well on its way to doing that all on its own.

"Miss Reese?"

I started at the sound of my name, right behind me, and whirled around. It was the man who'd been watching Ryker and me earlier. I stumbled backward a few steps.

"Who are you?" I asked.

But the guy just smiled in a way that sent a chill down my spine. "I work for Mr. Shea," he said, "and Mr. Shea is very interested in having a conversation with your boyfriend."

"He's not my boyfriend," I automatically lied.

He chuckled. "Nice try," he said, moving closer to me. I swallowed and held my ground. "Tell McCrady Mr. Shea wants to see him tomorrow, or he won't like the consequences."

"What consequences?"

Quick as a flash, the guy had a handful of my hair and a switchblade in his other hand, the flat of the cold blade pressing against my cheek.

I gasped in pain and fear, my pulse pounding. I didn't move and tears sprang to my eyes from the cruel grip he had on my hair.

"Consequences involving a dead girlfriend," he hissed. "Have I made myself clear?"

I didn't say anything—it was kind of a rhetorical question—and he waited another beat before letting me go. A car pulled up behind him, a dark sedan, and he slid into the front passenger seat, then it drove away.

I was shaking from fear, adrenaline, and anger. I was scared by what had happened, and pissed off, too. How dare Leo send someone to scare me, threaten me? The asshole.

I was still shaken up and fuming when I unlocked my apartment. I flipped on the light and nearly screamed. Ryker was sitting on my couch in the dark.

"What the hell?" I gasped, now even angrier that he'd scared me. "What're you doing here?"

"I came here as soon as I could get away from work," he said. "Imagine how worried I was when you weren't here." He stood and approached me until we were toe to toe. "Where have you been?"

Ah, shit.

"I went back to work," I said. "I had some stuff I could get done there." I moved past him and set my purse down, pulling out the files to show him. "See?" I tried to rationalize why I felt I had to prove my whereabouts to my boyfriend.

"Was Parker there?"

"Why does it matter?" I countered. "He's there every day."

"It's almost ten o'clock," he said. "You were at work all this time?"

"Why the interrogation?" I asked. "What did you think I was doing, Ryker?"

"Did you think I wouldn't notice what you *haven't* said to me?"

I swallowed, my mouth suddenly dry. "I don't know what you mean." I turned toward the cabinet, in dire need of a drink. Preferably of something alcoholic, but his hand closed around my elbow, pulling me back around to face him.

"I think I have a right to know how you're feeling about us," he said, "and if you were with Parker tonight."

"And if I was? What then? He's my *boss*. Being with him is kind of what I do all day. And this"—I jerked out of his grip—"is getting old."

Ryker growled a curse and shoved his hand through his hair. I ignored him, getting a bottle of bourbon I had and pouring myself a healthy shot.

"Besides," I said, after I'd had two swallows. The liquor burned a path down my throat to my belly. "Parker isn't who you should be worried about. Leo Shea sent some lackey to wait for me outside the building. He's the guy who was watching us earlier. He gave me a message for you."

Ryker's eyes sharpened and his body grew more tense, as though readying for a fight. "What happened?"

"He was waiting for me," I said. "Told me that Leo Shea wants to see you tomorrow. Or else."

"Or else what?"

I downed the rest of the bourbon before answering. "Yeah, that's when he pulled a knife."

Ryker was beside me in an instant, taking the glass from my hand and turning me toward him. "Are you all right?" he asked, anxious. His hands lifted to brush back my hair, inspecting my neck.

Tears clogged my throat, so I just nodded, swallowing them down. "He, ah." I cleared my throat. "He seemed really serious. Said if you didn't go, that you'd have a...dead girlfriend." Bitter anger filled my belly. I didn't want to be scared.

"I was afraid this would happen," Ryker said. "Any kind of weakness, Leo exploits it. He's not happy until everyone working for him is under his absolute control."

"But you don't work for him," I protested.

"I used to. And I was good at it."

"What did you do?"

Ryker hesitated, his hands dropping from me. "I was his enforcer. Kept his people in line. It was an ideal undercover position for gaining his trust and knowing everyone and everything that was going on."

And it sounded incredibly dangerous.

"How did you get out?"

"We made it look like I was killed," he said.

"So seeing you the other night must've really been a surprise," I said. "If he thought you were dead." No doubt an understatement, and helped explain why Leo had looked so pissed.

"You could say that," Ryker replied.

"So what are you going to do?"

"I'm not sure," he said. "I don't have a choice, if he's threatening you. I'll have to go see him tomorrow, see what he wants."

I nodded. I didn't see another way out either, especially if scary-knife guy knew where I lived and worked.

"Listen," he said, taking my hand in his and tugging me toward him until our bodies touched. "I'm sorry. About tonight. You... bring out my possessive side."

"I just can't keep having this same argument, Ryker," I said. His dark hair was tousled and I reached to push my fingers through the strands. "I'm with *you*. Don't you trust me?"

"Of course I trust you," he said. "I don't trust *him*."

My mind whispered that maybe he had a point, especially considering the things Parker had said and done the past few days, but I pushed the thought aside. "It takes two," I said. "And while I may not have said it outright, I wouldn't be with you—not like this—if it wasn't something more for me, too."

I still couldn't say the L-word, but maybe this would be enough. Yes, I needed to work through whatever it was I still felt for Parker, but my feelings for Ryker were real. He was a gorgeous man who oozed danger and Bad Boy from his pores, who had a decent job and was a good guy... and he wanted to be with me. Megan was right. I didn't want to screw that up.

He smiled, a full wattage complete with dimple, and it made me weak in the knees.

"Does this mean we get to have makeup sex now?" he asked, his eyes twinkling at me.

I raised an eyebrow, hiding my relief. "I'm not sure. Did we really fight? I mean, there wasn't any yelling or screaming involved."

Without warning, he swung me up in his arms and I squeaked in surprise.

"Oh, I'll make you scream," he said. "I promise."

Hoo boy.

* * *

"I don't want you to go to work today."

I looked up from where I was pouring coffee into two mugs. Ryker stood in the kitchen, shirtless and wearing just his jeans, which were zipped but not fastened. He was leaning against the wall, arms crossed, watching me. I pulled my brain out of the stupor seeing him like that always put me in.

"I have bills to pay, which only get paid if I work," I replied, determined to not get in another fight with him. I knew where this was coming from. He was worried. I couldn't blame him. If I was honest, I was worried, too. But I wasn't about to let that asshole Leo Shea keep me cowering in my apartment for the foreseeable future.

"Like your dad wouldn't help make ends meet if you need him to?" Ryker asked.

I shook my head. "That's not the point and you know it. I know why you want me to stay home, but that's not going to happen. We should be worrying about *you* and what your plan is."

"I've already been on the phone with my chief," Ryker said. "We have a plan."

When he didn't elaborate, I said, "Care to enlighten me?" My dry tone made his lips twitch.

"I'll tell you later," he said. "For now, let's get you to work safe."

"The bus *is* safe," I pointed out, but he was already shaking his head.

"No way. I'm taking you."

The look on his face and tone of his voice said he wasn't going to take no for an answer, so I didn't argue, even though I wasn't dressed for riding on the back of his motorcycle.

A few minutes later, he'd tossed on his shirt and jacket

and I was hiking up my skirt to climb on behind him. I had no time to change into jeans or I'd be late. Since it was getting colder, I had on nylons and I prayed I wouldn't get a run in them. Burying my face against the leather jacket covering Ryker's back to shield me from the wind, I closed my eyes and hung on.

Ryker had looked carefully around before we'd taken off, wanting to see if anyone was following us, I'd assumed. But we made it to my work without incident, pulling up right outside the door. People turned to look and I felt my face get hot. Being the center of attention wasn't really my thing.

The motorcycle had barely stopped, engine still running, before I was hurrying to get off so Ryker could be on his way. My skirt was so far up my thighs, I knew I was flashing people as I struggled to climb off the bike, then suddenly a hand was there to help me. Glancing up, I saw it was Parker just as Ryker turned off the engine.

"Classy way to bring a woman to work, Ryker," he said, his sarcasm thick. "Did you buy her the blue plate special for breakfast, too?"

"I was going to help her, asshole," Ryker retorted. "She didn't wait."

"It's fine," I interrupted, righting myself and jerking down the hem of my skirt, though not before both of them had gotten an eyeful.

"Take her inside and don't let her go anywhere today," Ryker said to Parker, whose eyes narrowed at the order.

"Why?"

I rolled my eyes. "He's overreacting," I said.

Ryker ignored me. "Because Shea knows she works here, and where she lives. He sent someone last night with a message for me. I don't want her going anywhere alone."

I couldn't really disagree with that—the thought of that

guy made me shudder—but neither did I want to be a burden or danger to anyone else.

"I'll be careful," I said, trying to placate him.

"I'm not into taking chances," Ryker said. "And if there's one thing I know you'll do, it's obey your boss."

The tension between the three of us grew tenfold with that little pronouncement and I glared at him.

"I'll make sure she's okay," Parker said.

I glanced up at him, but his face was unreadable and his eyes hidden behind sunglasses.

"I'm late for work," I said to whoever cared. I was going to walk away, but remembered Ryker and his appointment with Leo today and I paused. Leaning over to where he still sat on the back of the motorcycle, I hugged him.

"Be careful," I said in his ear. His hand curved around the back of my neck and I felt his lips brush my cheek, then I stepped back. Parker tugged me onto the sidewalk as Ryker fired up the bike. He sent one last glance our way, then shot down the street.

Parker took my elbow and guided me into the building. I put on the brakes in the lobby.

"Wait, I need to go get your breakfast," I said. "And your coffee."

"It's fine," he said. "I'll take an early lunch. And there's coffee upstairs."

Sensing that there was no point arguing, I followed him into the elevator. I knew what was coming and I was right, though he waited until we'd settled and had gotten coffee before calling me into his office.

"What happened last night? Who accosted you? What did they do?"

The questions were rapid-fire as Parker leaned back in his chair. His gaze was intent, his expression grim.

I didn't like being treated like a fragile flower to be locked inside a cabinet for safekeeping, but I didn't see that I could not tell Parker what he wanted to know.

"It was nothing," I lied, walking toward the windows so I didn't have to look at him as I told this whopper. "Just this guy being all scary and telling me that my boyfriend was wanted by the great Leo Shea. I was supposed to pass on the message."

"And if you didn't? Did he threaten to hurt you?"

I swallowed, staring out at the gray sky. "He said he'd kill me."

Silence.

"Did he have a weapon?"

"A knife."

More silence, even heavier than last time. Reluctantly, I turned around.

"Ryker's going to meet with Leo today," I said. "He said he and his...chief...had a plan, but he didn't tell me what it was."

"He's right. You need to have someone watching over you," he said.

I didn't reply, instead sinking onto a chair opposite his desk. "It made me angry," I confessed.

"Ryker?"

"No. Leo. How dare he send some flunky to do that? Try and scare me? And...I couldn't do anything about it. The helpless feeling...just made me angrier. I couldn't fight back, didn't know how."

"You shouldn't have to," he said.

"In a perfect world, I guess," I said with a shrug. "But it's not a perfect world, is it?"

"Far from it."

My gaze met his as he studied me for a moment. "Listen,"

he said, "why don't you come with me after work. I was
going to go work out before I go to that fundraiser tonight.
You're still going, aren't you?"

Shit. I'd completely forgotten about it. "Yeah, sure. I
didn't bring a dress to change into, though."

"It's okay. We'll swing by your place so you can change.
But back to my point. Come with me and I can show you
some pointers. Self-defense things."

"Really?" I asked, surprised. "You'd show me that stuff?"

He nodded. "It's not something mastered overnight," he
warned. "But it's a start, if you want to feel more capable of
defending yourself."

That sounded good. Really good. "Yeah. Yeah, I'd like
that."

Parker's lips lifted slightly. "Good. Then it's settled. We'll
leave at four-thirty."

I left his office feeling like I was actually doing something about Leo and taking control, which was way better
than how I'd felt when I'd walked in.

Unfortunately, I didn't have workout clothes with me,
so I hit up Megan. She always had some. Though she was
smaller than me, her clothes would do in a pinch, though
they might be a little tight.

"You're working out?" she asked.

"Don't look so shocked," I retorted, taking the black
shorts and tank top she handed me. "I work out."

"Only when I threaten you."

Okay, that might be true.

"So Parker's just going to let you go work out during
work hours?"

"Um, well…I'm kind of working out…with him," I
said.

Megan choked on her Red Bull. I slapped her on the back

a few times. "Are you serious?" she managed, once she'd stopped coughing.

"It's training," I hastened to explain. "He's going to show me some self-defense moves."

"Parker. Is going to show you...self-defense."

I nodded. "Yep."

She just shook her head. "You be sure to let me know how that goes."

"I'm sure it'll be fine," I said. "It's nice of him, actually. Lessons like that cost money, so if he already knows this stuff and doesn't mind teaching me, that's good, right?"

Megan just looked at me. "Right," she said at last, skepticism written on her face. "And how does Ryker feel about you learning self-defense from Parker?"

I glanced at my watch. "Gotta go."

"Yeah, that's what I thought," she called after me as I hurried away.

I heard from Ryker around mid-afternoon. I'd had my cell sitting on my desk and had kept an eagle eye on it all day, hoping it would ring. I snatched it up before the second buzz.

"Hey, babe," he said when I answered.

"I've been so worried," I said. "Is everything okay? What happened?"

"I can't talk about it over the phone," he said. "Just wanted to call and tell you that I'm okay, but can't see you tonight."

My disappointment was a lead weight in my stomach.

"Why not?"

"I'm looking into that video we got of your accident," he said. "Forensics finally finished enhancing and cleaning it up so I'm going by the station. But I need to make sure I'm not followed."

"Okay."

"Have someone take you home tonight," he said. "Don't go alone. I would if I could—"

"It's fine," I interrupted. "I have a work thing I have to go to anyway."

"All right. I'll come see you as soon as I can. Gotta go."

I nodded even though he couldn't see me. "Be careful."

"Ditto."

He ended the call.

I tried not to worry, but it stuck in the back of my mind for the rest of the day. Relief that he was okay, but worry over what he *hadn't* been able to tell me.

The workout place was literally just around the block, so Parker and I walked there. He kept me close with a hand around my arm while he walked on the outside of the side-walk. I noticed his eyes were moving constantly, watching everyone around us.

I changed into Megan's workout clothes, wincing a little as I looked myself over in the mirror. The shorts were crawl-up-my-ass short and the tank top was a size too small for my breasts. Some other women had on less, but I usually wore workout leggings, so felt a little uncomfortable. Shrugging it off, I pulled my hair up into a high ponytail and went to meet Parker.

CHAPTER TEN

He was waiting on one of the mats, talking to another guy who was just as big as he was. Parker had changed into a black T-shirt that had to have some spandex in it, the way it clung to him—not that I was complaining. He'd put on workout shorts, too, but they weren't tight like the shirt was. Dammit.

Parker caught sight of me and waved me over. His gaze ran from my head down to my bare toes still adorned in *A Good Man-darin is Hard to Find*, and I watched his Adam's apple move as he swallowed. The other guy was talking and I saw Parker's lips moved as he replied.

"Hey," I said once I was close enough. It felt strange to be with Parker in this setting, but he slid his hand around to the small of my back like it was no big deal.

"Sage, this is Mac," he said. "He's my sparring partner."

"Nice to meet you, Sage," Mac said with a smile as he

shook my hand. He had an accent I couldn't place, with brown hair and gray eyes.

"Same here," I said, feeling a little intimidated with these two huge guys flanking me.

"I'm going to show Sage a few self-defense moves," Parker explained.

"A little Krav Maga for the lady?" Mac asked.

"Hey, if you're going to teach self-defense, might as well do it right," Parker said with a shrug.

"What's Krav Maga?" I asked.

"It's a form of self-defense created by the Israeli Defense Force," Parker explained. "Its premise is not only defense, but counterattack to disarm and disable your opponent and come out the survivor of any physical confrontation."

"It looks like she could've used a lesson a few days ago," Mac said, eyeing the bruises and scrapes on my legs before his gaze landed on my stitched shoulder.

"Tell me about it," Parker replied grimly.

"You want to show her a demo?" Mac asked.

"Sure." Parker motioned for me to stand aside so I moved off the mat to lean against the wall.

Mac got behind Parker and wrapped an arm around his neck like he was putting him in a choke hold. Parker moved so fast I couldn't even track what he'd done, but he was out of the choke hold and Mac was down on the ground.

Parker held out a hand and helped Mac up. They faced off, then Mac attacked Parker. I sucked in a breath at the vicious jab, but Parker sidestepped it, then moved in close. They both moved fast, with their arms and fists and feet and every part of their bodies it seemed. I watched in wide-eyed amazement. I'd never realized Parker could do . . . all the stuff he was doing.

They finally hit a point where Mac tapped Parker's leg.

They were on the floor and Parker was doing something to his arm. When they stood up, they were both breathing hard.

"Nice," Mac said with a grin. "I let you win, you know. Didn't want to make you look bad in front of your lady."

Parker laughed. "That's mighty thoughtful of you."

Your lady. Hmm.

They did this man-grip handshake thing, then Mac nodded at me before heading off toward the men's locker rooms. Parker turned toward me.

"Ready?"

I gave a nervous huff of laughter. "I'm not sure I'm able to do anything like that." Talk about intimidating. Plus, I hated learning something new. I always felt like an idiot until I'd mastered it.

"That's what I'm here for," he said. "I'll teach you. Come on."

He took my hand and pulled me to stand on the mat. "Okay, the first thing you need to learn is that part of it is energy and will. You have to throw everything you have into your moves. Be decisive and intend to harm."

"Intend to harm?"

"Absolutely. If someone starts something with you, *you* want to be the one to end it. Not just defend yourself, but attack and disable them so they're out of commission."

That made sense. "Okay."

"So, last night, the guy pulled your hair, right?"

I nodded.

"Okay, well if someone grabs your hair, it's going to hurt no matter what. You might as well resign yourself to that. But here, let me show you how to get out of it."

Reaching out, he grabbed a handful of my ponytail. "The first thing you want to do is grab my wrist with both your hands." He showed me where to circle his wrist. "Then you want to create some distance between us, though it's going to hurt because I still have your hair. When there's distance, you use your feet. Vulnerable parts of the body. The knee, the groin."

"I'm not kicking my boss in the groin," I said.

His wide grin flashing perfectly white teeth made me lose my train of thought for a moment.

"I'd prefer you not either," he said. "This is practice. We'll go slow so you can get used to how it feels. When you get better, I'll put on gear and you can move faster and do real hits."

So we practiced. Using my hair, he'd pull me close, then I'd go through the moves he taught me, with him making corrections and suggestions. He was careful of my shoulder, which I appreciated. The stitches were healing, but I babied it since I was a complete wuss when it came to pain.

"Okay, now what if he does this?" Parker asked, using my hair to spin me around so my back was against his front. He put an arm across the front of my shoulders above my breasts and the other across my hips.

And I could feel every inch of his body against mine.

Sweet Jesus.

He was still warm from his sparring with Mac, his skin slightly damp with sweat, and I could smell his scent mixed with his cologne. A powerful aphrodisiac that made my bones want to melt.

"Now what?" he asked, his mouth at my ear.

Oh yeah. Self-defense. My mind was blank, unable to think of a single thing he'd taught me.

"Um, I-I'm not sure," I stammered.

"Move into the attack," he reiterated. "Remember? Put your hands here and you want to jerk your head back into mine."

I couldn't even concentrate on what he was saying, just let him put my hands where I was supposed to, then went through the motions as he talked me through it. If he noticed my sudden quiet, he didn't mention it, repeating the hold and moves until I wanted to yell at him to stop touching me. But it seemed I was the only one the close proximity was affecting, because he carried on as if nothing were amiss.

"And it's not," I muttered to myself. "Get a grip."

"What did you say?" he asked.

"Nothing," I said brightly. "Just…memorizing the moves."

I didn't think it could get worse. I was wrong.

"Okay, so let's go over how to escape the classic rape scenario," he said.

"Wh-what?" I squeaked.

He looked at me funny. "Most women want to know this move first," he said. "It's usually their biggest fear. Trust me, you want to learn it."

"Um, yeah, sure, okay."

Parker pulled me down onto the mat, urging me to lie on my back, feet on the floor and knees bent and spread as he crouched between my legs. Hooking his arms behind my knees, he pulled me closer so our lower bodies fit snugly together.

Holy Mary Mother of God.

Get a grip. Get a grip. Get a grip.

The mantra repeated inside my head. This was just Parker being helpful. This was *not* sexual. Just like painting the toes. Not sexual.

I only wished I could tell my body that because wow, was it ever throwing a party at being in this position. My heart was racing and heat curled low in my belly as Parker braced himself above me, leaning down until our chests were almost touching.

"If someone is going to rape you," he said, "this is how they'll be. Close and in your face. There won't be much space between you."

I nodded, not trusting myself to speak. It was all I could do not to wrap my legs around his waist, for crying out loud. Which would be bad bad bad.

"So here's what you'll do," he began. "Twist your hips to the side and leave the opposite foot on the floor. The other foot is going to go on my hip." He put his hands on my hips and legs, twisting me to show me what I should do. I forced my mind to concentrate. "Once you have some space, kick with your feet. Aim for the chin. It doesn't matter how big the guy is, you nail him under the chin, he's going down. Trust me."

He moved my hands. "If you can, lock your elbows and put your hands on my shoulders. Not my chest, but my shoulders."

Parker's shoulders were wide and hard underneath my palms. His body was wedged between my thighs and I could feel parts of him I shouldn't nestled against parts of me that were barely covered by my too-small shorts.

"Now lock your elbows," he said. "Or else I can just overpower you, like this." He pushed against me until my arms gave out and his chest rested against mine.

Our gazes caught and I couldn't look away, their blue so deep and clear and framed by thick lashes I'd kill for.

He froze, too. Against my will, my body relaxed, sending a message I had no business sending. My hips cradled his and my hands on his shoulders drifted to his arms, the biceps hard and flexed underneath my fingers. His response was immediate, pressing between my legs against my core. Arousal had danced in my veins since we'd started this whole thing, and now it flared to life.

"You're not fighting me," he said in a low voice.

I scrambled for what to say. "I, um, I guess I'm just tired." Which would've been a totally valid excuse... if my voice hadn't sounded take-me-to-bed-or-lose-me-forever.

Parker's eyes darkened and his gaze dropped to my mouth. He was hard between my legs and I was enjoying the feel of him way too much.

"We should go," I blurted. "Or we'll be late to that-that fundraiser... thing."

His eyes met mine again and for a moment he didn't respond. Then he was suddenly on his feet and pulling me up off the floor in one smooth move.

"I'm going to shower," he said. "My tux is in the car. I'll change at your place. Give me ten minutes, okay? Don't go anywhere without me."

My head was spinning from the abrupt change in topic and what had just happened. "Um, yeah, okay."

He waited a beat, his eyes searching mine for... I didn't know what. I smiled brightly.

"Thanks for the lesson, by the way," I said. "It was, uh, really helpful. I hope I never have to use any of that stuff." I gave a halfhearted laugh.

But Parker didn't smile back. "Me too."

I watched as he disappeared into the men's locker room before hightailing it to the women's to get dressed in my work clothes again. I didn't bother with the nylons and was waiting for Parker only a couple of minutes before he came back out. This time he had damp hair and smelled like soap and fresh cologne. He'd put his slacks and shirt back on, but hadn't bothered with the jacket or tie, and he carried a duffel bag.

"Let's go," he said, glancing at his watch.

He drove us to my apartment and by now it was full dark. I had a good hour before the fundraiser started, but knew it would take every minute of that time to get ready. So I hit the door running.

"Make yourself at home," I said, dropping my purse and coat on the kitchen table. "I'll hurry."

"Take your time," he said. "Fashionably late works for me." He'd brought in a garment bag that I assumed held his tux.

I showered in record time and blew my hair dry. I needed to figure out what I was wearing before I did my makeup, so I stepped out of the bathroom...only to stop short at the sight of Parker standing in my bedroom.

He was dressed in his tux and stood with his back to me in front of the full-length mirror in the corner of my bedroom. I was suddenly glad I'd taken the time to make my bed this morning.

He must've heard me because he turned around and I was abruptly aware that I was still wrapped in a peach towel.

Parker cleared his throat and took a few steps toward me. "I was messing with this tie," he said with a sheepish grimace. "Bow ties don't like me."

That's when I noticed the length of black silk around his neck. It was obvious he'd tried tying it several times as the fabric was slightly wrinkled.

"I can do it," I said automatically, reaching up to take the fabric between my fingers. That's when I realized what a bad idea that was.

Being so close to him wearing nothing but a towel was trouble waiting to happen, but it wasn't like I could back out now. I ignored the way he was watching me and prayed he wouldn't look down to see my breasts about to pop out above the towel. Concentrating, I began tying, the loops and method drilled into me by my mother, who thought that "all ladies should know how to properly knot a man's tie."

"You smell nice," he said. "New perfume?"

I avoided his gaze. "Yes, I wear something different at night than during the day."

"I like it."

I didn't know what to say to that, so I said nothing.

I jumped, startled, when his hands rested on my hips.

"What are you going to wear tonight?" he asked.

"Um, I'm not sure," I said, my voice much too high. Almost done with the tie...

"I'd say wear that, but I'd get in too many fights for the way men would look at you."

His words were low and roughened and went straight through me. I felt like there was a vise around my chest, squeezing the air from my lungs. I finished the tie, knotted perfectly, and glanced up at him with a tight smile.

"Yeah, I'd look pretty ridiculous showing up wearing just a towel."

But he didn't laugh. Instead, he leaned down and put his lips at my ear.

"Please tell me there's nothing but skin underneath this." His grip tightened on the fabric covering my hips.

"It doesn't matter because you won't see it," I retorted, irritated at him for touching me, and myself for my reaction. I should take a step back, but I didn't.

"I already have," he murmured, his mouth still near my ear. "Remember?"

Ah. He was talking about when I'd been falling-down drunk in New York and had decided to take a bath, a predilection of mine when I was three sheets to the wind.

"I try not to," I said.

"I can't forget it." His breath was warm against my skin, his nose nuzzling my hair.

My eyes fluttered closed at the touch, then flew open.

Covering his hands with mine, I pulled them off me and took a step back.

"Me coming out here in a towel wasn't a come-on," I said stiffly. "Don't treat it as such."

His expression shuttered. "I never said it was."

"I'm not going to sleep with you just so you can get back at Ryker for not believing you all those years ago," I continued, laying it on the line. "And you're not going to convince me your sudden interest isn't all about that and not about us."

I spun around and hightailed it back to the bathroom before I lost my nerve. Locking the door behind me, I caught sight of myself in the mirror.

"This is bad," I whispered to myself. Because I couldn't deny it. As much as I cared about Ryker and felt like our relationship was growing...my heart was still tied to Parker. And I didn't know how to cut the strings.

* * *

We weren't late...very. Just enough so that a few heads turned as we walked in. I held my head high and pretended I belonged at Parker's side.

Since he was wearing a tux, I'd chosen a black gown with long sleeves—handy for covering the stitches on my arm—which sounded boring. But it was made with sheer and Lycra netting with geometric embroidery. So the neckline plunged and the sides were cut out, sheer netting holding the dress onto my body. It was backless despite the long sleeves, cutting into a deep V down my lower back. It was classy and sexy all at once. I'd put my hair up to show off the back of the dress to full advantage.

When I'd stepped out of my bedroom, Parker had gone utterly still.

"Is this okay?" I'd asked, nervous when he hadn't said anything. I vividly remembered his disapproval of the cocktail dress I'd worn in New York.

"You look...I have no words," he'd said, which had made me smile. "No, wait. Yes, I do. Beautiful. Sophisticated. Elegant. Sexy as hell."

I was still riding high on the glow those compliments had produced as Parker walked us around the hotel ballroom. There had to be at least five hundred people there and I sipped sparingly on the champagne a passing waiter had given me, not wanting to have a fuzzy head when Parker was counting on me to help him remember our clients.

"So anyone famous here?" I asked in between greeting people.

Parker laughed lightly. "Doubtful," he said. "And you'd probably recognize them before I would." Which was true. He rarely paid attention to popular culture, whereas I could rattle off who was dating who in Hollywood quicker than I could recite the alphabet.

He spotted someone who raised their hand in greeting.

"Who's that?" he asked in an undertone as we headed that way.

I searched my brain. "Lucas Miller and his wife Shelly," I said. "He used to be the CFO for Bradley Investments. Then he quit for a comparable job at KCG. Rumor was he was having an affair with the boss's wife." I finished in a whisper just as we stopped in front of the couple.

"Lucas, so good to see you," Parker said, shaking the man's hand. "How are things at KCG?"

We chatted with them a little—"How's your oldest? Isn't he starting at Stanford?"—then moved on. Parker knew most of those who approached us, but occasionally needed a reminder.

"She's the marketing analyst for Dugen & Little," I said, nodding toward a woman standing in a group a few feet away. "Renee Jones. Her husband William is retired, paints in his spare time and fancies himself the next Van Gogh."

"Renee, what a pleasure to see you again," Parker greeted her. "And William, how's the painting going?"

I could tell by the smile on Renee's face and the way that William launched into an animated description of his latest work that it had been a nice touch, asking about the painting.

And so it went. It felt a little like a high school pop quiz, but I passed with flying colors. By the time Parker was seating me at dinner, I'd allowed myself a whole glass of champagne and was starting on my second.

In the back of my mind, I worried about Ryker. What he was doing and if he was safe. It gnawed at me and my helplessness was frustrating.

"Parker Anderson. It's been a while."

I turned to see a man standing behind me, shaking hands with Parker. Tall and broad, he had dirty blond hair, green eyes, and a strong jaw. His smile was easy and pleasant, and I nailed him for a politician instantly.

"Senator, yes, it's good to see you," Parker said. "I didn't realize you'd be here."

"I try to help out party candidates when I can," the man said, glancing down at me.

"This is my assistant, Sage," Parker said. "Sage, this is Senator Kirk."

"Pleased to meet you," I replied with a smile.

"Likewise."

Now that the smile was turned my way, I could see the appeal he had to have for voters. He looked as all-American as it was possible to be. Trustworthy, honorable, courageous...all adjectives I could easily see describing him. And I didn't detect the bullshit factor that politicians usually exuded despite themselves.

"Would you care to join us?" Parker asked, but the senator shook his head.

"I'm afraid I can't. I'm heading home for a quick visit—checking in on my new nephew and sister-in-law while my brother's out of town—then it's back to D.C."

"Excellent. How old is he?"

"Three months," he said. "It's their first."

"I hope she's doing well then. Best wishes to her, and you," Parker said.

"Thank you, I appreciate it. She seemed to be managing… last time I spoke with her." Something flickered in his eyes at that, so briefly I thought I must have imagined it. Then he turned to me.

"A pleasure meeting you, Sage." He smiled again, gave Parker a nod, then he was gone.

Parker took the seat next to me. "I didn't think I'd see him here."

"Haven't you donated to his campaign before?" I asked, remembering a listing on one of his accounts.

He nodded. "He's a good man, and God knows there are precious few of those in Washington."

"Is he married?"

Parker eyed me. "No, why? Did you like him?"

Was that a jealous note in his voice? Good gravy. I rolled my eyes and let it drop. *Men.*

Dinner was good and the dessert especially. I savored the flourless chocolate torte, popping a raspberry in my mouth and chasing it with more champagne. Parker was talking to the man seated next to him and I eyed the untouched raspberries on his plate, wondering if he'd notice if I snagged one.

He glanced at me, his lips curving slightly as he talked.

Picking up the pristine raspberry, he offered it to me. I reached for it, but he moved it beyond my grasp. Glancing quizzically at him, I saw him watching me, his conversation at an end as the man was now talking to his companion.

He offered the raspberry to me again and I could tell by the wicked gleam in his eye what he wanted. My eyes narrowed and I'd had just enough booze to lean forward and wrap my lips around the red fruit.

Parker's eyes darkened as my tongue touched his fingers. He brushed my lips ever so lightly, then I leaned back in my chair. The juice of the raspberry exploded on my tongue and my gaze was locked with Parker's.

The strains of a waltz filled the room and Parker stood and took my hand, drawing me to my feet.

"Dance with me."

I shouldn't.

But the words didn't come and I found myself on the dance floor in Parker's arms. We said nothing as he swirled me around, and I tried not to think. I wanted to enjoy the moment—a moment that had never been before and would likely never come again.

His arms were strong and solid, the scent of his cologne a lingering aroma that surrounded me. The touch of his hand was low on the exposed skin of my back, his fingers trailing up and down my spine. I couldn't look away from his eyes, the blue deep enough to drown in.

"We should go," he said after we'd danced to an endless stream of music.

I glanced around, realizing that the place was clearing out of people. "Yeah, sure," I said, my face flushing. I'd gotten a little too wrapped up in the dancing.

The valet brought around his car and Parker held the door for me as I slid inside.

"Thanks for coming with me tonight," Parker said as he drove.

"Mmmm," I replied, leaning my head back on the seat. I was pleasantly warm and in a good mood, my mind finally quiet. Worry for Ryker nagged at me, but I tried to ignore it. I watched Parker, the dim glow from the dash casting his face in light and shadows.

His lips twisted slightly and he reached across to take my hand in his. It was sweet and nice and I didn't pull away.

We ended up at my apartment and Parker took the keys from me to unlock the door. He checked out the inside while I stood in the kitchen.

"So what's your plan if someone had been in here?" I asked him when he returned. "You don't have a gun on you."

"Don't I?" he asked.

Hmm.

"But I guess with those moves you were pulling on Mac, you might not need a gun."

He stopped in front of me and I had to lean back to look him in the eye.

"You liked the moves?" he teased, bracing a shoulder against the same wall I was propping up.

"Pretty badass," I said with a shrug. No need to overdo it. Parker's ego didn't need stroking.

The sound of a key in the lock had me turning toward the door in time to see Ryker walk in.

Surprise and relief flooded me and I flew at him, wrapping my arms around his neck. His in turn circled my waist, holding me tight.

"You said you couldn't come tonight," I said, worry surging again with a vengeance. "Is everything okay?"

"No, everything's not okay," he said grimly.

I leaned back so I could look at him. "What's wrong?"

But he didn't answer that; instead he frowned, his hands moving from my waist up my back. "What the hell are you wearing?"

"I told you I had a work thing tonight," I said, moving back so his arms dropped to his sides. I wondered what my dress had to do with anything, and I hadn't liked the tone of his voice.

The buzz of Parker's cell phone interrupted us.

"Tell me what's going on," I said, lowering my voice as Parker answered.

"What the hell do you want?" The tight fury in Parker's voice caught my attention and I glanced over at him. "Go to hell."

My jaw dropped and I took an unconscious step toward him. Who in the world was he talking to?

Parker's head whipped around toward the windows.

"Incoming!"

Before I could figure out what *that* meant, Parker yanked me down to the floor in one smooth move, his body flattening on top of mine. Ryker reacted to Parker's shout instantly, dropping the same as Parker had. I opened my mouth to ask them what was going on, and that's when all hell broke loose.

CHAPTER ELEVEN

A hailstorm of gunfire shattered my windows and I screamed. Parker moved his body to lie even more fully atop mine, smashing me into the carpet, his arms and chest covering my head.

It seemed to go on forever, endless bullets whizzing by above us and shattering everything. A cacophony of glass and porcelain, stoneware and wood, all being destroyed. My entire apartment was disintegrating around me, and the only thing protecting me from being ripped apart, too, was Parker.

At last it ended, as suddenly as it began. I was so terrified, I was sure I was about to pee my pants. Was I okay? Was Parker? And Ryker? Oh God, what if one of them was hurt? What if *both* of them were hurt?

"Sage. Sage, are you okay?" Parker's voice in my ear. He was alive. He'd lifted off me slightly and I could breathe easier.

I nodded. "Yeah," I managed to rasp. I twisted, trying to

get out from underneath him. I had to check on Ryker, but felt Parker's palm on the back of my head. "Stay down," he ordered.

"But Ryker—"

"I'm fine," Ryker said. "You two all right?"

"Yeah," Parker answered.

"Let's get out of here. I'll cover you; get her in the hall."

Parker didn't reply but his arm moved to wrap around my waist, lifting me as he crawled toward the door, which was half hanging from its hinges. Ryker stayed behind, weapon in hand and his eyes trained on the view outside the broken windows, but we made it to the hallway without any more gunfire. Then Parker was on his feet and lifting me up to set me on mine.

Ryker was right behind us on his cell, barking orders in cop jargon of codes and numbers that I couldn't follow.

We were moving fast, my hand locked firmly inside Parker's, and we stopped at the stairwell door. Parker and Ryker glanced at each other and had some kind of unspoken communication. Parker nodded and Ryker moved in front of us, gun raised as he eased open the stairwell door.

Parker tucked me into him, turning us slightly away from the door, his body tense against mine. Knowing they were both expecting something bad made my stomach tighten with dread and I cringed closer to Parker.

But nothing happened. No one burst out of the stairwell and no gunfire erupted.

Then we were moving again, down the flights of stairs, where they repeated the process at the door to exit the building.

Sirens screamed in the distance, coming closer. Ryker and Parker finally spoke.

"Who gave you the warning?" Ryker asked.

"Viktor Rowan," Parker replied.

Ryker's gaze sharpened. "Tell me."

"He was taking credit for pushing Sage into traffic," Parker said grimly. "It wasn't just a random act."

Ryker cursed. "That's what I was coming to tell you," he said to me. "He was on the security footage."

"I thought Viktor was killed or arrested," I said in confusion. The last I'd seen him had been when the car he'd kidnapped me in had crashed.

Parker looked at me. "He escaped, Sage," he said. "That night when he had you prisoner in the car, they got the two men with him, but he disappeared. His security people were almost on us when we pulled you out and our guys would've been outnumbered. We had to leave and that's when he got away. Back to Russia, they think."

"And no one thought to tell me this?" I looked from Parker to Ryker. Neither looked the least bit repentant.

"I thought it was over," Parker said. "There's no earthly reason he should've come back to Chicago. Except, apparently, revenge."

"Revenge? For what?" I asked. "Because you helped the CIA bring him down? And aren't they the ones that screwed up by letting him escape?"

"Yeah, but I'm an easier target than the CIA, and he's not dumb," Parker said. "He's used you once before to get to me, and he's doing it again." He glanced meaningfully at Ryker, who muttered a curse.

"What?" I asked, swiveling my gaze between them. "What does that mean? That he's going to keep trying to kill me?"

I saw my answer written on their faces as police cars, fire trucks, and an ambulance piled into the parking lot.

"Here," Parker said, swinging his tuxedo jacket over my shoulders. "It's cold out here." I tugged the fabric closer around me to ward off the tremors wracking me, which I didn't think were entirely from the chill in the air.

Ryker's palm curved around the back of my neck and he kissed me, a firm press of his lips and a gentle touch of his tongue against mine, then he was stepping back. He seemed reluctant to leave me, but went to meet one of the officers as they exited their vehicles.

The adrenaline was gone, leaving exhaustion in its wake, which made it nearly impossible to remain standing. I kept shifting my weight from foot to foot to stay awake as the police took our statements. I watched Ryker talking with them and pointing across the street. I figured that was maybe where they'd deduced the shooter had been.

Parker came back to where I was waiting once he'd finished his round of questioning.

"You look like you're about to drop," he said.

I was so tired and wanted to lie down so bad, it made me want to cry. And my pretty dress was ruined. And a truck had nearly run me over only two days ago. And everything I owned had just been obliterated by a man whose new mission in life was to kill me.

As far as weeks went, I'd had better.

Parker read the misery on my face because he wrapped an arm around my shoulders and pulled me into a hug. His brand-new tuxedo shirt was torn and dirty from crawling through the debris on the floor. His body was warm against mine and I sniffed back tears, catching the faint scent of his cologne that remained.

"Sage."

I heard Ryker's voice and took a step back out of Parker's embrace.

"Come on," Ryker said, taking my hand. "You can stay with me."

"Can I get any clothes or anything?" I asked, trying to get my tired brain to think through the logistics. "I need pajamas, and work clothes, and my makeup, and shoes—"

"Go on and take her home," Parker interrupted me. "She's exhausted. I'll bring by a suitcase of her things."

I was about to protest—the thought of Parker picking out my clothes felt weird—but Ryker was already talking.

"Sounds good. Thanks." Then he was moving me away toward his truck, which thankfully wasn't far away.

I didn't say much on the ride to his place. I think I was in too much shock to really absorb what had happened. I'd nearly been killed today—again—and was heading deep into denial mode, which was the only way I thought I could cope.

Ryker reached across the expanse of seat between us and took my hand. I unlatched my seatbelt and slid across the seat, needing to be close to him. He didn't say anything, just laid his arm across my shoulders and let me rest my head on his chest.

McClane, the policy dog academy dropout, was super excited to see me, jumping up to rest his paws on my chest as his tail *thump thumped* against the wooden floor.

"Hi, McClane," I said, with a noticeable lack of enthusiasm, trying to avoid the tongue bent on licking my face. Eww.

"Off," Ryker commanded, having to say it twice more before the dog obeyed. He had a mind of his own, hence the "dropout" rather than "graduate."

I followed Ryker into the kitchen, not really thinking about anything at all, if I could help it. I sat in one of the four wooden chairs at his table and watched as he poured a shot of Jack into a glass, then handed it to me.

McClane planted himself at my feet, his dark eyes gazing

up at me. His tail wasn't thumping anymore, and if I didn't think it would sound crazy, I'd say he looked worried. He was definitely subdued, maybe sensing my mood. He whined a little and rested his head in my lap. Tentatively, I laid my hand on top of his head.

"Aren't you going to have any?" I asked Ryker, taking a sip of the liquor as he sat in the chair next to me, but he shook his head.

"I need to get back over there, see if they found anything," he said. "They were canvassing the area for where the shooter may have been."

I tensed up at the thought of being alone, and Ryker seemed to read my mind.

"I won't leave until Parker gets here," he said. "And you have McClane, too. He won't let anything happen to you."

"I don't need Parker to stay with me," I said. After some of the things he'd said and done the past few days, I didn't think being alone together was a good idea, not that I really wanted to mention that to Ryker.

"It'll be fine," Ryker said gently, reaching for my hand. "Look on the bright side. You've survived, twice. You must have nine lives."

"That means I've used up two of them," I said glumly. Actually, probably more than that, considering. And my arm hurt. Somehow my stitches had pulled and now I was regretting not having any ibuprofen on me.

"Next time, we'll get him."

"There's going to be a next time?"

Maybe he would've answered, I don't know, but there was a sharp rap at the door and McClane about knocked over my chair getting to it. Ryker and I followed at a more normal pace.

It was Parker and he was carrying my suitcase.

Ryker let him in and McClane hurried to say hello. I watched, one eyebrow raised, to see how well Parker would take to the behemoth jumping on him and resting his dirty paws on Parker's shirt.

Parker shot the dog a look and McClane stopped in his tracks, his paws skidding on the wood floor, then he settled back on his haunches, his ears perked forward and his tail thumping the floor. I frowned in disappointment. Apparently, Parker was also the dog whisperer.

It seemed an uneasy truce had been declared between the two men, as Ryker didn't have anything smartass to say as Parker set my suitcase down and scratched McClane behind the ears.

"I need to get back to the crime scene," Ryker said to him. "I may be a while. I don't really want to leave Sage by herself."

"I'll stay," Parker said.

"I don't need a babysitter," I protested, embarrassed that my boss was being asked to watch over me. "I'll be fine with McClane." I gestured to the supposed guard dog, who'd now given up all pretense at dignity and had flopped onto his back, legs in the air, waiting to see if Parker would scratch his belly.

Hmm.

"You have your weapon on you?" Ryker asked, ignoring me.

Parker reached behind his back and produced the same gun he'd had at the office. I guessed he hadn't been bluffing when he'd searched my apartment earlier. Ryker nodded and Parker replaced it.

"What are you doing?" I asked Ryker in an undertone. "I thought you couldn't stand Parker, remember?" Maybe if I reminded him of this, he'd tell Parker to leave.

Ryker glanced at Parker, then back to me. "Personal issues aside, I know he'll keep you safe. That's more important right now."

Oh, *now* he decided to play the adult. I wanted to gnash my teeth in frustration.

Ryker took a step forward until he was in Parker's space and they stood eye to eye. "But no more painting toenails." The threat in his voice was greeted with a slight twitch of Parker's lips, but other than that, he said nothing.

"I'll be back as soon as I can," he said to me.

"No, wait, I don't want—" I was cut off by him kissing me again, and this time it wasn't a sweet kiss. It was the second time in as many days that he'd kissed me in front of Parker and I was starting to feel like an exhibitionist.

"Stay here. Stay safe," he rasped, his lips grazing my cheek. Then he was out the door and gone.

I avoided looking at Parker, instead glancing at the clock. It was late, and I was exhausted.

"You don't have to stay," I said. "Ryker's overreacting. The dog will be fine for a few hours until he gets back."

"I'd feel better if I stayed," he said. "Inside is preferable, but I can sit in my car if you'd rather."

I looked at him. "Of course not." Like I'd make him do that.

I felt awkward, not least because here was Parker in Ryker's house. Deciding I wanted to go to bed, I went to grab my suitcase, but Parker got there first.

"Here, I'll help you," he said, picking up the suitcase. "Where am I taking it?"

I hesitated. It felt really strange for me to say I'd be sleeping in Ryker's bed, though it shouldn't. Surely Parker had to know Ryker and I had sex, right?

"Um, his bedroom is back here," I said, leading the way.

I was uncomfortably aware of his eyes on my back and I couldn't wait to get out of the ruined dress.

"I take it things are going well," Parker said as I flipped on the light. "I thought he might've had a problem once he found out who your father was."

"He did, a bit," I admitted. "Apparently, he doesn't like the fact that my father has money. Says we're from 'opposite ends of the socio-economic status.' Or something like that."

Parker snorted in disgust, picking up the suitcase and laying it flat on a chair before unzipping it. "Ryker's always been hyperaware of money. That he reacted so badly when he saw who your father was doesn't surprise me a bit." He started unloading my clothes, hanging a bunch of them in the closet next to Ryker's.

"I can do that," I said, reaching for my makeup bag and hairbrush.

"I wasn't sure what to get, so I brought some of everything," he said.

That was obvious. I'd be looking slightly...eclectic for the next few days, I decided, taking out a pair of red heels. By the time I'd set them in the closet and turned around, Parker's arms were full of satin and lace.

My jaw dropped in dismay. "I'll take those," I squeaked, blushing to the roots of my hair. Yes, he'd indeed thought of everything, and I didn't want to imagine him going through my drawers.

The corner of Parker's mouth lifted slightly as I snatched the assorted bras, panties, and pajamas from him. The hook of a bra caught on his shirt and yanked me back.

"Hold on," he said, pulling me closer as he fiddled with the hook. It seemed to take a long time to fix and I was much too close to him.

"We could've died tonight," he said after a moment, finally freeing the bra.

I looked up from the lace to find him gazing down at me. I swallowed.

"Yeah." Wow, what a thoughtful response. I wanted to kick myself for sounding idiotic. "But we didn't," I hastened to add. "You saved us."

"That flash of time when you think you're going to die," he said. "That's when everything you've ever regretted doing or not doing flashes through your mind."

Obviously, Parker's brain worked differently than mine because all that had been going through my head had been *Oh shit oh shit oh shit!*

"And?" I prompted when he didn't continue. "If you regret not giving me a raise, we can fix that first thing tomorrow."

He didn't crack a smile at my feeble attempt at a joke.

"All I could think about was you," he said. "And how much I regretted turning you down."

I stared at Parker, wondering if the pain in my shoulder and the events of tonight had coalesced to make me hallucinate. But he still stared intently at me, as though waiting for my response.

My response was . . . I got royally pissed.

"I've had it," I retorted. "You've got to stop saying these things, doing these things." I poked him hard in the chest. "You had your chance and you. Said. No. You don't get to just change your mind now. It doesn't work like that."

"Then you tell me how it works," he said.

"I don't know, but not like that." I spun away, opening a drawer in the lone nightstand and shoving all the stuff in my arms inside. My cotton pajama pants were peeking out of the suitcase and I yanked them out along with the matching shirt.

"Besides," I continued, "how do I know you're not doing exactly what you're accusing Ryker of? How do I know that I'm not some pawn between the two of you, a prize going to the 'winner'?" I used quote-y fingers for *winner*.

"You know I'd never use you like that," he said.

"Do I? Because it seems to me that you never looked at me twice until I started dating Ryker, and now you've decided we should be something more. Well, forget it, Parker. I don't need that. Ryker and I may not work out, but for now I'm with him. I care about him. A lot." I ended my tirade.

God, it hurt to say no to him. I'd wanted him so badly for so long, but I couldn't get the suspicion out of my mind that he was like a child with a toy—a toy that was only desirable if someone else wanted it. And in case the analogy wasn't obvious, *I* was the toy.

Parker walked to where I stood, getting so close I could feel the heat from his body. Looking up at him, my mouth was suddenly dry.

"You care about me, too," he said, his voice a low thrum of sound that went straight through me. "And you forgot these. My favorite."

He dangled a scrap of lace in front of me and I wanted to drop through the floor in sheer embarrassment. A black lace thong that was meant to be worn for a very short period of time.

Snatching it from him, I scooted past him into the bathroom, where I took a shower. I took my time and finally emerged with wet hair and clad in my pajama pants and T-shirt. I'd hoped Parker would have gone and Ryker returned, but when I tiptoed into the living room, it was to see Parker sitting on the sofa. His arm was dangling and he was absently scratching McClane's belly, who looked like he'd died and gone to doggy heaven.

Though I thought I'd been silent, Parker turned around, spotting me before I could tiptoe away again.

"How are you feeling?" he asked, getting to his feet.

I was self-conscious. My wet hair and scrubbed-clean face left me feeling as though I'd forgotten to put on my armor.

"Fine," I said. "Just, uh, going to bed. It's been a long day." A massive understatement. "And I'm really tired."

"Do you need anything?"

I shook my head. "No. You don't have to stay, you know," I reiterated. "I'll be fine with McClane."

Parker ignored me. Putting his arm around my waist, he turned me around and guided me into the bedroom. I was taken aback to see he'd straightened the sheets and turned down the bed.

"I didn't know you provided turndown service," I joked as I crawled underneath the covers.

"I'm full of hidden talents," he quipped, tucking the blankets around me.

Leaning down, he pressed a kiss to my forehead that was achingly sweet. I took a deep breath, inhaling the faint aroma of his cologne that still lingered on his skin. Then he was stepping away and shutting off the light.

"Parker," I called just as he was about to close the door.

"Yes?"

"Thanks for the self-defense lessons... and the dance." It had been the best part of what had ended up being a truly memorable day, though not for reasons I wanted to dwell on. Both because I didn't want to think about what a close call we'd all had... or at how my susceptibility to Parker had guilt eating at me.

"It was my pleasure," he said. Then he was gone.

CHAPTER TWELVE

My phone's alarm woke me in the morning and it took me a minute to remember where I was. I glanced to the side and saw Ryker, asleep.

I'd been quick enough with my alarm that he still slept. Lying on his stomach, the covers barely covered his ass, which I knew was bare because Ryker slept naked. His back drew my eye and I saw old scars from two bullet wounds. With his face turned toward me, I could see dark shadows under his eyes.

Easing out of bed, I tiptoed to the bathroom, doing my business and brushing my teeth and hair. I swallowed a couple of Tylenol capsules to take care of the lingering aches and pains. After washing my face, I went back into the bedroom and saw Parker had texted me.

I'll pick you up on my way to work.

Guess I wouldn't have to worry about having to borrow Ryker's truck.

I texted back okay, hitting Send just as Ryker's hand wrapped around my wrist and tugged me back onto the bed.

"I didn't mean to wake you," I said.

"It's fine," he said, his voice husky with sleep. "C'mere."

Time was short, but I couldn't resist a naked Ryker. Turning onto his back, he pulled me on top of him, the sheet getting tangled around our legs.

"How's your stitches?" he asked, his fingers brushing lightly against my arm.

"They're okay," I said. "Better than last night. You look tired." I smoothed a hand across his whiskered jaw.

"It's been a long couple of days," he said.

"Everything okay at work? With Leo? Are you done with him now?"

Ryker didn't answer right away. His eyes looked into mine and his arms circled my waist, holding me close.

"No, I'm not," he said at last.

That alarmed me. "What's wrong? What happened yesterday?"

"The FBI has gotten involved," Ryker said, pushing my hair behind my ear. "I was in meetings about it yesterday. They're chomping at the bit to get another crack at this guy and vice wants to redeem themselves since the case got tossed."

I had a bad feeling in the pit of my stomach. "What does that mean?"

"It means...they want me to go undercover again."

The knot in my stomach turned to lead. I didn't know much more about cops than what I'd seen on television, but even I knew that being undercover was one of the most dangerous things they did.

"What did you tell them?" I asked.

"I said I needed to think about it," he replied. "It's dangerous and..."

"And what?" I was afraid to hope that I'd figured in to his decision at all.

"And I'd have to not see you," he finished.

"Not see me?"

"I can't be coming back here if I'm undercover," he explained. "They'll have me under constant surveillance once I go back in. I can't chance leading them here to my house or anywhere near you."

"But they already know we're dating," I protested. "Hello, they showed up practically at my *door*."

"So I'll tell them we broke up. I'm not leading a man as dangerous as Leo Shea right to you."

I didn't want to think about not seeing Ryker or knowing how he was doing for God knew how long.

The light blue of his eyes held my gaze and his hands slid up my back underneath my T-shirt. I lowered my head and kissed him, a sweet kiss that rapidly turned into more. Apparently, it didn't matter if Ryker was tired, judging by the hardness pressed against my thigh.

"I need to get ready for work," I murmured as his mouth moved down my neck.

"I'd say this'll be quick, but that might not be much incentive," he replied. "Instead, I'll just say I'll make it worth your while to be late."

Thoughts of protesting flew out the window as he pushed my pajama pants down my legs and flipped us so I was on my back. In another moment, my T-shirt was dragged over my head and I was as naked as him. Before I could enjoy the full frontal view he was displaying, he was scooting down the bed and spreading my legs.

"Ryker—" I didn't know what I was going to say, but it turned out not to matter. His head was between my thighs, his mouth on me, and thinking coherently was beyond my abilities.

Ryker was an oral kind of guy and I was a very lucky girl. And loud. My fingers were buried in his hair, holding on for dear life when I came, and the aftershocks were still rippling through me when he slid inside me in one deep thrust.

His dog tags pressed against my breast as he pulled me up to sit astride him. My body felt boneless, but he didn't need me to do much. His hands gripped my hips as his cock moved inside me. The slide of his flesh against mine had the familiar tension inside my body coiling again.

"Oh God, Ryker..." I sounded like a porno film on steroids, moaning his name, but he didn't seem to mind.

He moved faster, his mouth fastening to my breast, and stars exploded behind my eyes. My nails dug into his shoulders as I cried out, then he was pulsing inside me, his hands digging into my hips.

The sweet feel of sated lethargy crept over me as Ryker kissed me, a slow, deep kiss made even more intimate with him still inside me. His dog tags were warm from our bodies, the metal pressed between us.

"I've got to get ready for work," I murmured against his mouth.

He made a disappointed sound, but released me. Glancing at the clock, I mumbled an *oh shit* and hurried into the bathroom for the fastest shower I was capable of. I couldn't put my hair up without using both hands and lifting my arm up hurt this morning, so I brushed my hair and left it long.

Wrapping a towel around myself, I came out of the bathroom to get some clothes from the other closet and saw

Ryker had again fallen fast asleep. Not that I blamed him. Sex on top of being exhausted? Yeah, I'd be out, too.

McClane was lying on the floor in the open doorway, looking at me. I shouldn't have made eye contact because he began to whine. Crap. He probably had to go outside.

"Fine, let's go," I whispered, moving past him into the hallway.

I tucked my towel closer around me when I let him out the back door. The wind was cold and I shivered. Time to get dressed. But before I could make it into the back bedroom, there was a knock at the door.

Not wanting to wake Ryker, I hurried to the door and glanced through the small window. Parker stood on the porch.

I paused in indecision, not wanting to answer the door in just my towel, but then he raised his hand to knock again and I jerked open the door.

"Shh," I hissed. "Ryker's asleep."

Parker slid his sunglasses down an inch, looking at me over the tops. His gaze traveled from my bare shoulders to my painted toes and back up.

"His loss," he said. "I'm really starting to like the terry cloth look on you."

My face heated and I stepped back, but instead of retreating to his car like I'd expected, Parker followed me inside. Sliding his sunglasses into the inside pocket of his suit, he gave me a half-smile.

"The stitches look better," he said.

I glanced down at my arm. The angry red from last night had faded.

"Yeah. It's better today," I replied. "Listen, I'm almost ready. I just need to get dressed."

"Need any help?"

The question was all innocence, but I knew better and flashed him a narrow-eyed look, but he didn't look evenly remotely abashed.

"I can manage," I said, pivoting on my heel and trying not to feel Parker's gaze on me as I left the room.

Although chilly this morning, I knew it would warm up later today, so I found a long-sleeved dress in peacock blue and put it on. Nude heels went just fine with it, and if I was at home I'd have accessorized with a scarf or a statement neck-lace. But Parker hadn't packed any of those things, so I felt not quite put together when I emerged from the bedroom. I'd grabbed my makeup bag, figuring I could put my makeup on while riding in the car.

"Okay, I'm ready," I said, grabbing my purse. "Oh, wait." I'd almost forgotten McClane. I let him back inside and re-filled his food and water bowls, then met Parker at the front door. A few moments later, we were pulling away in his BMW.

I'd ridden more in Parker's car the past few days than I had the previous years I'd worked for him. The car was im-maculate and expensive, and after I unzipped my makeup bag, I hesitated.

"Mind if I put this on in your car?" I asked.

Parker glanced at me, his eyes once again hidden behind a pair of designer sunglasses. "You're not going to dump it all over the seats, are you?" he asked.

I hid a grin. "That's not generally how it's done, no."

"Then it's fine with me."

Flipping down the visor for the mirror, I made quick work of it, forgoing eyeliner since I was in a moving vehicle. The mascara went on, then the lipstick, and I was zipping every-thing back into the bag.

"I'd forgotten this last night," Parker said, reaching over

to open the glove box, which put his arm in too close a proximity to my bare knee. The fabric of his suit brushed against my skin, which felt way more intimate than it actually was.

I was on edge after yesterday. Something had shifted between us, becoming more comfortable, and it scared me. I didn't want a closer relationship with Parker, not now. And yet I couldn't deny that I was glad to see him, that being with him made me happy inside. It wasn't something I wanted to examine too closely. There was no reason to alter my life just because Parker'd had a supposed change of heart. Who was to say he wouldn't have another change of heart once he had what he wanted, and where would that leave me?

Exactly.

To my utter embarrassment, he handed me my packet of birth control pills. How thoughtful of him. Really. Dear God...

"Um, thanks," I mumbled, my face on fire. I stuffed the pack into my purse.

"So I take it you and Ryker resolved your differences?" Parker asked.

I glanced at him, but he was watching the road.

"Yeah. Things are okay." I frowned. "How'd you know?" Surely it wasn't *that* obvious that I'd had sex this morning? Did I have beard burn from Ryker? My hands itched to flip down the visor and look in the mirror, but I didn't.

"Just a guess," he said.

There was a silence that wasn't at all comfortable, then he asked, "Did he say anything about Leo?"

I nodded. "He said he had been working undercover and that's how Leo knew him... and that they want him to do it again—go undercover."

"Is he going to?"

I frowned, thinking. "He didn't say, actually. But yeah, I think so. We were talking about it, then kinda got... distracted—"

"I really don't want to hear the details," Parker interrupted, his tone dry.

I cleared my throat in embarrassment. "So, um, yeah, anyway... I guess if he does go back undercover, we won't see each other for a while."

"How long is 'a while'?"

I shrugged. "He didn't really say."

"Did he say anything about the shooting last night?"

I shook my head again. "No."

Parker muttered a curse under his breath. "So he's just going to go undercover and leave you alone in his house?"

I could feel a headache coming on, and didn't bother answering him. His jaw was clenched and his lips pressed tightly together, but he didn't say anything else.

He pulled into a Starbucks drive-thru, ordering breakfast for us and his usual double tall latte. I opened my mouth to tell the faceless speaker my order, but Parker was already speaking.

"...and a grande nonfat pumpkin spice latte, no foam, add extra whip," he said.

I looked at him in surprise.

"That is what you want, isn't it?" he asked.

"Uh, yeah," I said, shocked that he knew what I'd order. "How'd you know?"

The voice gave Parker the total and the car inched forward in line. "You have the pumpkin spice lattes in the fall," he said. "And you always add whip. I figured after yesterday, you might need more than the usual amount."

I guess I shouldn't have been so taken aback that Parker had known this. He was the smartest man I knew, was incredibly observant, and he never forgot a thing. I just hadn't realized I'd ranked on his lists of Things to Observe and Things Not to Forget.

Parker paid, handing me my cup before pulling back into traffic.

"I was afraid Ryker would let us down," he said. "So I called my contact at the CIA and told him what happened. They're sending a cleanup crew to your apartment to repair the damage, by the way, free of charge."

Gee. How generous of them. Considering it was their fault Viktor was loose at all, it was the least they could do. "What did he say?" I asked.

"You're not going to like it."

That didn't sound good. "What?"

"They want to put you in protective custody until they can track Viktor down."

"What?" My screech made him flinch. "You're kidding, right? Protective custody? For how long? And why just me? Why not you, too?"

"Someone needs to be the bait to lure Viktor out so they can catch him."

It took me a second to realize what he meant. "No way," I said. "That's just...that's wrong! They can't make you risk your life—"

"I volunteered."

My jaw hung open as I stared at him. "Why would you do something so crazy?" I blurted.

"You think I'm just going to wait around until he kills you?" Parker snapped back. "I don't think so."

He pulled into the parking garage, navigating through the levels to his reserved space. I took his coffee and mine so he could grab his briefcase from the back. Transferring the bag containing our breakfast into his briefcase hand, he settled his other hand on the small of my back as we headed for the elevator.

This was new.

"What are you doing?" I asked.

"What do you mean?"

I punched the button for the elevator and turned, realizing he was standing really close to me, sandwiching me between the wall and his body. He was tall and his shoulders were wide, completely obscuring my view of the garage behind him. But he wasn't looking at me. He'd propped his sunglasses on top of his head and was scanning the parking garage level we were on.

"The, um, you know... touching thing." Talk about awkward. And the bigger problem wasn't that he was touching me, but that I liked it when I knew I shouldn't. God, this was turning into a psychiatrist's wet dream.

"It's a helluva lot easier to shove you to the ground if I already have a hand on you," he replied, still observing the quiet garage filled with silent cars. He moved and his jacket shifted. That's when I saw the glint of metal at his side and figured it out.

Parker was protecting me.

The elevator doors slid open and he hustled me inside, keeping his body between me and anyone who might be aiming for us. Reaching behind, he hit the button and the doors closed.

"You can't keep doing that," I said.

"Doing what?" Parker asked, his body relaxing slightly.

"I don't want you getting hurt because you're trying to protect me."

He looked at me now. "But it's okay for Ryker to protect you?"

"He's a cop," I said. "That's kind of his job, I guess..."

"You know I'm a Marine, right? Just like him. Just because I don't wear my dog tags doesn't mean I've forgotten what they mean."

Okay, now it looked like I was heading into totally-offended-Parker's-manhood territory. I was temporarily at a loss. This was ground I'd never been on before.

"I didn't mean to imply—"

"Sure you did," he cut me off.

And it hit me. He was feeling...inadequate. Because of Ryker. It was surreal. Parker was nearly revered at KLP Capital. I felt more than a twinge of pride that I was his assistant. And now his ex-bff-turned-cop, my boyfriend, was making him competitive? Over me?

The elevator doors opened and we exited as normal, Parker heading straight into his office while I went to my desk. I was starving and the cheese Danish he'd bought me was devoured almost immediately.

It didn't take long at all for Megan to show up at my desk.

"Oh my God, I heard what happened!" She rushed around my desk to throw her arms around me. "I'm so glad you're okay!"

I squeezed her back, despite the twinge in my stitches. "I'm fine, thank goodness. But I definitely wouldn't want to live through that again."

She pulled back, looking at me seriously. "The news said someone shot up your apartment? Some kind of gang drive-by thing. Is that true?"

I nodded, deciding I'd just go with the gang story the CIA had apparently leaked to the media, and she gasped in horror.

"That is so...I just can't...thank God you're okay." And she threw her arms around me again. "Why are you even here?" she asked when she released me. "Please tell me Parker isn't making you work today."

"I'm sure he would've given me the day off if I'd asked," I said. She pressed her lips together, but didn't say anything. I hurriedly spoke again. "I'm fine. Really. I wouldn't know what to do with myself if I weren't here."

This seemed to satisfy her. "If you're sure," she said. "Hey, it's the end of the month so we're ordering in lunch today. Chinese. No one has time to go out. Want me to order something for you, too?"

"Yeah, that'd be great." I gave her my order for sweet and sour chicken along with some money.

"Anything for Parker?"

I hesitated. Usually, he ate out somewhere unless it was a Monday. But he didn't have a client meeting scheduled today and if Viktor was targeting him like he was targeting me...

"Yeah. Get him Szechuan chicken, please." The thought of someone shoving Parker into traffic made me shudder. I'd just come up with some excuse that would make him have to stay in today. I didn't know what I'd do tomorrow, but resolved to take it one day at a time.

Work was the usual and my arm wasn't too bad. For all that had happened the past few days, I was for the most part physically relatively unscathed. As for mentally or emotionally... well, let's just say that it was a relief to be buried in work so I didn't have time to think about anything else.

At about a quarter to noon, Parker came out of his office. "I'm heading to lunch," he said as he walked by.

"Wait," I called out, jumping up from my chair. He paused as I scurried around the counter. "I, um, need your help... on this report."

Parker looked at me strangely. "What report?"

I thought fast. "The report for Contracts. They, um,

need to know which customers have holdings in the Asian markets."

"Why?"

Good question.

I gave a fake little laugh. "Like they're going to tell me. I don't know; I just got the request in and they need it by this afternoon."

Parker glanced at his watch, frowning. "And you can't do it on your own?" he asked.

I shrugged. "You know I get confused with some of the Asian stuff." Parker wasn't fluent, but he knew enough Chinese to get by, whereas it was all Sanskrit to me.

"Okay, fine," he said, heading back toward his office. "Send me what you have so far."

That wouldn't take long, since I had nothing.

"Sure!" I said brightly to his retreating back. "Thanks a lot. Really appreciate it."

He glanced back and arched a brow before going back into his office.

Hurrying to my computer, I created a quick-and-dirty spreadsheet and threw a few companies onto it, then sent it to Parker. I felt kind of bad for making him do made-up work, but then I thought of what could happen to him outside and the feeling went away. This whole idea that he was going to work with the CIA to lure Viktor out was appalling.

A half hour later, I took the Szechuan chicken into his office. "Hungry?" I asked, setting the plate down on his desk.

Parker glanced up at me, then sat back in his chair.

"And Contracts called," I added. "Greta said they didn't need the report anymore. They found an easier way to pull the data." No more guilt over making him do unnecessary work.

"Really," he said. "That's funny, because I called Contracts to get some clarification, and they didn't know anything about a report they'd requested."

Shit. I kept a bland smile on my face as I folded his napkin and carefully set the silverware down.

"You probably just didn't talk to the right people," I said. "Anyway, thanks for your help. Sorry it ended up being a time-waster."

"Yes, let's talk about that," Parker said. "You just happened to order take-out that quickly?"

My smile faltered a bit but I forced another laugh. "I know, right? That new place across from Starbucks is *crazy* fast."

"Sage..." Parker sighed and I gave up the game, standing in front of his desk like a kid caught sneaking candy. "What're you doing?"

I stared at my toes, the peachy orange so cheery against the deep gray of the carpet, and didn't answer.

"I have a meeting tonight with my CIA contact," he said after a moment, "to decide the best course of action."

"You mean to see how they can best use you as bait?" My voice was bitter.

"Better me than you," he shot back.

My hands were clenched into fists at my sides and I wondered if the CIA would even care if Parker got killed doing this.

Getting up from his chair, Parker rounded the desk and stood in front of me. Taking my hands in his, he said, "Sage, I know you're not happy about this, but it's my decision. They'll keep you safe, and the sooner we can get Viktor, the safer all of us will be."

I was still staring at the floor, afraid to look up at him and what he might see in my eyes. The thought of Parker putting himself deliberately in harm's way, for *my* sake, left me with conflicting emotions. On one level, it stunned me that he would do that, but then again, he'd said he was a Marine. Maybe it was an honor type of thing and not as personal as it felt.

It also took a lot of courage. Viktor was former KGB and had the kind of mercenaries and assassins at his disposal that I could only imagine. Parker's "mission" seemed doomed before it had even begun.

"Hey, look at me," he said softly. His fingers tipped my chin up until our eyes met. His gaze took in the tears clinging to my lashes. "I'll be fine."

"You don't know that," I said. "Ryker's going undercover, and now you're doing this, and I-I..." I pressed my lips tightly together, unable to put into words how terrified it made me that both the men in my life were putting themselves in grave danger.

Parker didn't reply and something seemed to catch his eye behind me because he released my hands and took a step back. A moment later, the door to the office opened. I turned around as Ryker stepped inside.

Rounding his desk, Parker said, "She'll be back in a few hours, Ryker. No need to check up on her."

"I didn't come here for Sage, asshole," Ryker retorted, glancing at me. "I need a few minutes with your boss, babe. Alone."

I opened my mouth to ask questions, but something about the look on his face made me nod and turn away. I closed the door behind me and settled in at my desk.

They were both still standing and the differences between the two men were striking.

Though they were the same height, Parker was dressed in a tailored Tom Ford suit, the deep charcoal a stark contrast to the white shirt he wore. His tie was one of my favorites, a deep eggplant shot through with silver. A matching pocket square peeked from his lapel.

In contrast, Ryker looked even rougher than usual. He hadn't shaved, and his aviators were hooked on the front of the gray tank he wore. The black leather jacket and jeans were a given. When he moved a certain way, you could see the glint of metal at his side.

And yet, differences aside, they carried themselves with exactly the same confidence-bordering-on-arrogance.

I felt not the slightest twinge of conscience when I reached for my phone, toggling the switch that would turn on the intercom in Parker's office. I pretended to work on my computer while I listened.

"...I do for you?" Parker was asking Ryker.

"This isn't about me," he replied. "This is about Sage."

My ears perked up.

"What about her?"

"I need you...to watch her. Look out for her."

"I'm doing that anyway. Viktor's not going to give up."

"Viktor's not the only problem," Ryker said. "I have to do a job. There's a slight chance it could put her at risk."

"What kind of job?"

A pause.

"Leo Shea."

I was a little surprised Ryker told Parker the truth.

"You're going after him again?"

"Yeah."

"And he knows about Sage."

"Yeah. In case she didn't tell you, Leo sent a flunky to her apartment building the other night."

There was another pause and I snuck a glance into the office. Ryker was walking toward the windows, looking out at the view of the city. His arms were crossed over his chest. Parker stared after him.

"He'd come after her, you think?"

"If my cover should get blown, maybe. Let's hope that doesn't happen."

"Are you going to have any backup or are you going in alone?"

"Unfortunately, it isn't like the Corps. I don't have buddies to watch my back. I'm on my own. When you're in deep enough, there's not a lot they can do to protect you."

"How dangerous is this?"

"They're fucking drug and arms dealers, protecting a billion-dollar business. How dangerous do you think it is?" Ryker's sarcasm was bitter.

"You think this is a good idea? You and Sage..."

Ryker turned to face Parker. "Me and Sage what?"

"I thought things were getting serious between the two of you."

"How is our relationship any of your business?" Ryker's tone had been matter-of-fact before, though not particularly friendly. Now it was hostile.

"I care about Sage. If you get your ass killed, it affects her." His voice was as hard and cold as Ryker's.

"Glad to know you give a shit."

I could almost feel the tension in the room as I watched them through the glass, unable to look away.

"Actually, I do," Parker said, coming out from behind his desk. He pushed his hands into his pockets. "You were the one who decided we couldn't move past Natalie."

Ryker said nothing, his gaze returning to the window.

"Isn't it time we bury the past?" Parker asked.

"Interesting choice of words."

I could see the tension return to Parker's frame. "You may

have decided you don't give a damn about me, but I still care what happens to you." He was next to Ryker now, who finally turned to look at him. "So if you get in a bind, you need backup, you'd better fucking call me, or so help me, I'll kill you myself."

A beat passed. "You want to move on?" Ryker asked at last. "Then prove to me you've changed. I'm trusting you to take care of Sage, keep her safe. That's all. Don't make me regret it."

Silence.

"Understood."

I was mesmerized, watching them. Yeah, they were talking about me, but there was a lot going on there between them and I couldn't help hoping this was a first step toward reconciliation.

Ryker headed for the office door and I quickly flipped off the intercom. I got up and rounded the counter as he let the door swing shut behind him. I saw Parker moving behind his desk, his gaze on us.

"So what was that all about?" I asked, pretending of course that I hadn't listened to the entire thing.

"I'm heading in tonight," he said. "I don't know when I'll see you. It may be sporadic, and at weird times, but I'll do what I can."

I shook my head. "It's fine. I'd rather you not put yourself at risk." My throat was thickening with tears that I was desperately trying to swallow down. "Um, so this guy thought you were dead. Is he going to just… accept… that you're not and let you back into his organization?"

Ryker hesitated. "I'll be fine."

He was deliberately lying to me from what he'd said to Parker about how dangerous it was, which told me even more. My stomach turned over and I didn't trust myself to speak.

"Take this," he said, handing me a slip of paper. "It's the number for Malone, my partner. If you absolutely have to reach me, call him. He'll know where I am."

He moved closer, sliding an arm around my waist and his lips by my ear.

"I'll find a way to communicate with you," he said. "Trust me."

"Okay," I whispered. "Kiss me."

It didn't matter that we were in an office, standing by my desk, his lips met mine and the real world melted away. I put everything I had into that kiss, trying to convey what I was afraid to put into words—my fear, longing, worry, and yes, love. I'd fallen in love with Ryker without even realizing it, not until I was faced with losing him.

I wondered if he felt the same.

My fingers were sliding through his hair, a hand curled around the back of his neck, and our bodies pressed tightly together when he finally raised his head.

His eyes were dark and serious as he looked at me. "Don't worry," he said, the corner of his lips tipping up in a half-smile. "I'm a tough sonofabitch. I'll be okay."

My answering smile was a little watery and weak, but I tried.

Digging in his pocket, he handed me a set of keys. "This is to my truck and house," he said. "No one will find you there, and McClane will watch over you."

I nodded again. "Okay."

"And it'll help," he said, his hands tightening on my waist, "to know you're sleeping in my bed."

That made my chest tight and I couldn't speak. He smiled again and brushed his lips to my forehead, then he was striding toward the elevators. I watched until he'd disappeared inside.

I glanced into Parker's office as I turned back to my
desk. He was watching me, the expression on his face one
of grave resignation, and it pushed me over the edge. Tears
fell and I hurried to the restroom to lose my composure in
semi-privacy.

CHAPTER THIRTEEN

Parker drove me to Ryker's apartment after work and walked me inside. McClane greeted me as enthusiastically as he always did and I had to dodge his leaps.

"No!" I commanded, trying to be as authoritative as Ryker.

The curt reprimand had the dog obediently plopping his ass on the floor, tail thumping as he stared up adoringly at me. I sighed.

"So where's this meeting of yours?" I asked him, setting my purse on the couch. McClane immediately began sniffing the leather and I watched him, hoping he didn't think it was an oversize chew toy.

"Actually . . . here."

I frowned. "Really? Why? I mean, I'm glad, because I really want to know what's going on, but isn't it a bit strange to have them come here?"

"It's where you are," he said, shrugging off his jacket

and tossing it on a chair. I automatically grabbed it up and brushed a few stray dog hairs from the fabric, then hung it in the nearly empty coat closet by the front door. "Plus, like Ryker said, this place has no connection to either of us. It won't be on Viktor's radar."

I processed this as I let McClane out the back door and refilled his doggy dish with his dinner. Opening the fridge, I surveyed the contents, wondering if Ryker had anything I could scrounge for dinner.

But the shelves were pretty bare. An old pizza box, a few beers, some bottled water, lots of condiments, a couple of eggs, and that was about it.

"Looks like he could use a Deirdre," Parker said from behind me. He reached over my shoulder and grabbed a beer off the shelf.

"We all could use a Deirdre," I replied, taking a beer for myself. "Looks like I need to go to the store."

"I can take you."

I shut the fridge and turned around, raising an eyebrow. "*You're* going to take me to the grocery store? *You* are."

"Sure. Why not?" He used the edge of the counter to pop the lid off the bottle, traded me bottles and did the same with the second before taking a swig.

I narrowed my eyes, taking a sip of the brew before I spoke. "Have you ever even *been* to a grocery store?"

His lips curved in a half-smile. "There's a first time for everything."

I couldn't help a smile back. "Do we have time? I don't want you to miss your meeting."

"Trust me, he won't be here until late. Let's go. I'm starving." He took another long drink and set the bottle aside.

Okay then.

I directed him to a supermarket a couple of miles away,

feeling a sense of the surreal as I grabbed a cart and started pushing it down an aisle, Parker by my side.

"So this is where food comes from..." Parker said in mock wonderment. I glanced up at him and grinned, his answering smile genuine enough to take my next couple of breaths.

I wasn't a gourmet cook, but I got by, courtesy of some lessons from the cook we'd had at home since shortly after I'd turned four. Her name was Rita and she'd insisted I needed to learn a few dishes to make when I lived on my own.

I grabbed the ingredients for one of those meals, plus a few other things that I considered staples—real half-n-half for my coffee, peanut M&M's, and a bottle of wine. Okay, two.

Parker pulled out his wallet for the cashier.

"What are you doing?" I asked. I was digging in my purse for my money as he handed over his credit card.

He gave me a look like I was an idiot. "Paying. I may not come here often, but I'm relatively sure they prefer you to pay before you walk out the door."

"I mean why are you paying for my food?" I asked in exasperation. The cashier had already swiped the card and was handing it back by the time I'd found my wallet, unzipped it, and dug out my card.

"Because I wanted to," he said simply, taking the groceries from the bagger and walking away before I could argue further.

I followed him out the door and back to the car, trying not to think of how...domestic this whole scene was. After months of the return to ultra-professional at the office, it was too welcome a feeling, and I realized I'd missed the short time of intimacy Parker and I'd had.

We were almost back to Ryker's when he asked, "So what did you think about what Ryker said, this job he's doing?"

I glanced at him, decided to play dumb. "He said he'd be okay, that I shouldn't worry."

Parker gave me a look. "You really think I don't know you were listening?"

My face got hot. "I only use that in emergencies."

"Like when you were listening to me order your birthday present?"

"I wanted a scarlet pashmina. You were ordering coral. I look awful in pink." I loved that scarf and had worn it all winter. A fabulous blend of silk and cashmere, it was a great splash of color in the drab winter months. And the orangey-pink that he'd been about to order would have been hideous.

Parker snorted, his gaze back on the road. "I told you to just order your own present and put it on my card."

"Which is exactly what I did for Christmas. You were quite generous."

His lips twitched. "Back to the original subject," he said. "You heard him say that Leo might give you trouble."

"I'm much more concerned about Ryker than myself," I said. I'd been trying not to think about what he was doing tonight, knowing if I did, I'd be nearly incapacitated with worry. "And I think you are, too."

Parker didn't answer, pulling in to Ryker's driveway and turning off the car. We took the groceries inside and Parker put them away while I started dinner.

"I didn't know you cooked," Parker said, snagging a snow pea and popping it in his mouth.

I shrugged. "Not everyone has a Deirdre."

"So why do you try to pretend you're not related to your dad?" he asked as I layered chicken and vegetables in a pan.

"Yeah, how long have you known about that?" Parker had

even spoken to my parents before, but I hadn't realized he'd known the truth.

"Since you were hired."

That got my attention. I slid the pan into the oven and set the timer. "You've never said anything."

"I am now. So what was it? Too many people wanting handouts? Friends who weren't really your friends? Favors you never wanted, but then they expected something in return?"

"Yes, yes, and yes," I replied. "All of the above. I just wanted to be... normal, for a change. Make it on my own."

"I'm surprised your dad didn't have more to say about it."

"My dad is self-made. I think he understands. But he still insists on helping out here and there. I don't mind. They're my parents and I love them. It makes them feel better to know I live in a decent place, that I'm safe."

"And how would they feel if they knew you were putting yourself in danger by refusing protective custody?" he asked.

I reached for a bottle of wine. Way better than beer. "It's my life, Parker. My decision." I twisted the opener into the cork and tried pulling it out. It wouldn't budge.

"What happens to you affects everyone who cares about you," he said, taking the bottle from me. "So not just your life. Not really." He pulled, easily leveraging out the cork, then handed the bottle back to me.

"Ditto," I shot back, shooing McClane away from sniffing the counter. As if I was going to hide away like a coward while Ryker and Parker were putting their lives on the line.

My cell rang and I dug it out of my purse and answered.

"Dear Sage, how are you? I heard you've had a couple of close calls recently."

The sound of Viktor's thick Russian accent in my ear

made me stiffen and my gaze flew to Parker's. He knew instantly something was wrong.

"Why are you doing this?" I hissed. "I've done nothing to you."

"Your boss did, and where I come from, payback is always personal."

The cell was suddenly snatched from my hand.

"You have something to say to Sage, you say it to me," Parker growled into the phone.

I watched his face as he listened, his expression a mask of cold fury.

"You want her, you're going to have to come through me." He ended the call, then turned off the phone.

"Why are you doing that?" I asked.

"I don't trust those Russian hackers," he said. "You'd be amazed at what they could do with a cell signal, including finding you. We'll get you a burner phone tomorrow." At my questioning look, he clarified. "Untraceable."

"What did he say to you?" I asked, almost afraid to know the answer.

"You don't want to know." Grabbing the wine bottle, he poured us each a glass. Taking his, he went into the living room. I picked up mine and followed him.

A familiar tension marked the lines of his body as he perused the shelves along one wall, and I wasn't sure if he was really seeing the books that lined the shelves or was still thinking about Viktor.

Dinner was done before long—a blend of roasted chicken and veggies with olive oil, fresh rosemary and thyme—and I dished it up, serving us both on the small dining room table. Both of us seemed lost in our own thoughts as we ate. I was worried about Ryker, and the call from Viktor had scared me more than I wanted to admit. McClane lay at my feet, hoping for a scrap to fall, his big brown eyes following my every movement.

"It's ironic," Parker said after he'd had a few bites. "The first meal you've ever cooked for me...is in Ryker's house."

It was an odd thing to say, lending more meaning and intimacy to the impromptu dinner than I'd considered.

"Well, how is it?" I asked. He'd eaten nearly half his plate already, so I was assuming I knew the answer to that one.

"You could give Deirdre a run for her money."

I was absurdly pleased at the compliment, prompted though it may have been. He'd mentioned Ryker, though, and I wondered if he had him on the brain as much as I did.

"I hope you and Ryker can patch things up," I said. "And I'm sorry he brought me into it. I've tried to tell him you're just my boss, but..." I shrugged, at a loss as to what to say.

"Am I?"

"Are you what?"

"Just your boss."

The blue of his eyes seemed deeper in the soft lighting as he gazed at me, waiting for my answer. We were sitting across from each other, but given how small Ryker's table was, he was still too close.

"What do you want from me, Parker?" I asked tiredly, setting down my fork. My appetite was suddenly gone.

McClane began to growl, easing up onto his haunches as he stared into the darkened hallway. My panicked gaze went from him to Parker, who was already up, gun in hand.

"Call off the dog, Parker. It's me." A man stepped around the corner and I recognized him as the CIA agent who'd been undercover as an assassin for Viktor. His real name was Sasha.

Parker relaxed, sliding the weapon under the waistband of his slacks at the small of his back. He'd discarded his tie and turned back the cuffs of his shirt and I couldn't help the thrill of feminine appreciation for how sexy he looked doing that. Which was wrong wrong wrong, on so many levels.

"Relax, McClane," Parker said, setting his hand on top of the dog's head. To my surprise, the canine obeyed, his ears coming up and his tongue hanging out as he looked curiously at the new arrival.

"Sorry for coming in the back door unannounced," Sasha said, still eyeing the dog warily as he approached us. "Keeping as low a profile as possible."

"Is anyone watching this place?" Parker asked, leading him to the living room. I followed, taking a seat on the couch. Sasha sat in a chair and Parker settled next to me. McClane plopped his butt on my feet.

"Not that we've been able to ascertain, but it's only a matter of time before they follow you—or her—here," Sasha said.

"Any progress on finding out where Viktor is?" Parker asked. His thigh was pressed against mine and he leaned forward, bracing his elbows on his spread knees.

"Not yet," Sasha said. "He's been expelled from all his contacts in Russia after how badly he messed up the ZNT deal. After how much money was seized and accounts frozen by us, it's amazing they let him live."

"So he's a man with a vendetta and nothing to lose," Parker said. "That's not good."

"Plus, he's decided you're to blame," Sasha continued, nodding toward Parker. "The Russian Mafia stay in power for a reason. He'll want to kill anyone who's close to you, starting with Sage. And he's more than capable of doing it."

The words lodged in my brain like a flashing neon banner. I had no idea what to say. I felt like I was living inside a movie. But was I the heroine who couldn't die? Or the tragic victim who'd be avenged?

I didn't want to find out the answer to that question.

"So what are you planning to do to protect Sage?" Parker asked.

"We want to put her in protective custody, if she'll agree." Sasha looked expectantly at me, but I was already shaking my head.

"Not unless Parker agrees to go, too," I said.

Sasha looked at Parker. "That can be arranged."

"I'm not hiding out while that lunatic is tracking Sage," he said.

Sasha sighed tiredly, leaning back in his chair. "Then what do you expect us to do, Parker," he said. "I can't *make* her do jack shit."

Parker turned to me. "Sage, please—"

"Please what?" I interrupted. "I'm not doing it unless you do, too."

"You know I can't do that," he said.

I shrugged. It was a no-brainer to me. I wasn't about to go into hiding and let Parker take the fall.

"So what's Plan B?" Parker asked.

"We have people working on tracking Viktor down," Sasha said. "While he's unable to get assistance from his former compatriots, he does have ties to organized crime in the U.S., too. Even here in Chicago, I'm sure."

"He'll have to have gotten the weapons and people he used last night from somewhere," Parker said.

Sasha nodded. "We're working on it. We have some intelligence, sources on the inside here in Chicago. If he contacts them for supplies or crew, we'll know about it."

A former KGB guy with nothing to lose and an ax to grind. That didn't sound bad or anything. McClane must have sensed my disquiet because he whined a little, turning to rest his head in my lap. I petted him absently as I thought.

Maybe protective custody wasn't such a bad idea…

But then I pictured Parker, injured or dead because of me, and I knew I couldn't. I'd go crazy with worry over him, piled onto the worry I was already dealing with for Ryker.

Sasha stood. "I'll be in touch," he said. "Stay aware. Stay alive. Call me if you change your mind."

"We'll do our best," Parker replied, standing as well. We watched as Sasha slipped out the back the same way he'd come.

"Well," he said once Sasha had gone. "It looks like I'm going to be living here for a while."

I looked up at him in surprise. "What?"

"It's not like I can just leave you here alone," he said. "You're a sitting duck."

McClane took umbrage to that, making a noise and glaring up at Parker as though he'd understood what had been said.

"McClane can protect me," I said, scratching him behind the ears. His eyes rolled back in his head in doggy bliss.

"One bullet can take down a dog, though he might give you a few seconds' lead time to get away," Parker said grimly.

"Rather than waiting for him to make a move, why don't we draw him out?" I asked. It was much preferable to think of taking action rather than waiting for something to happen.

"It's dangerous," Parker said.

"It's going to be dangerous no matter what," I countered with a shrug.

The corners of his lips lifted slightly as he stared at me, and he said nothing.

"What?" I asked after a moment, self-conscious. Had I sounded ridiculous or something? I thought it was a solid plan. But he just shook his head.

"I haven't ever seen this side of you," he said. "I like it."

"You mean my foolhardy, crazy, self-destructive side?" I asked dryly.

That got a laugh. "I wasn't going to call it that," he said. "More like courageous, daring, and taking the initiative in a badass kind of way."

Pleasure curled in my belly at the compliment and our gazes caught. A beat passed and my smile faded.

Then McClane sneezed all over me.

"Aw, yuck! McClane!" I shoved his head and snotty nose off me and jumped up to go wash my hands. Dogs were gross and he didn't look the least bit sorry.

"Let's get some sleep," Parker said, glancing at his watch. "We'll think of something in the morning."

I was exhausted, so that sounded like a good plan to me.

Parker stretched out on the sofa while I took Ryker's bed. McClane hopped up and made himself at home, stretching out diagonally and crowding me until I had to shove his butt over. As tired as I was, I couldn't sleep, but it wasn't just worry for myself that kept me awake. I wondered where Ryker was, and if he was safe. I finally fell asleep in the small hours of the morning.

* * *

"No, you're not coming with me."

I narrowed my eyes at Parker and crossed my arms over my chest. We'd been arguing for several minutes now because he was going to his apartment to change and pick up some things and I didn't want him to go alone.

"Viktor knows where I live," he said, grabbing his keys, wallet, and cell phone. "I'm not leading you straight to him."

"So *you're* just gonna walk right in then?" I asked in exasperation.

"I'll be fine," he said. "And if Viktor is there, then this thing will be over before it even gets started." As if to emphasize his point, he racked the slide on his gun and pushed it into the band of his slacks at the small of his back.

"Stay here," he ordered me. "Don't go anywhere. Don't answer the door. Don't even look out the windows." He looked down at McClane, standing at my side and tail wagging like mad. "McClane, watch."

I had doubts as to McClane's ability to understand, much less obey, such a command. But the dog sat immediately next to me, his ears perked and his eyes on Parker's.

"I'll be back," Parker said, heading for the door.

"What about work?" I called after him.

"I told them we're taking a few vacation days," he said.

"Wait...together?" I asked, appalled. "People are going to think—"

"Gotta go. Lock this behind me." And he was out the door.

Shit.

I shut the door and locked it, feeling more unnerved than I wanted to admit at being left by myself. I glanced down at McClane, which was a mistake because his tongue lolled in a doggy smile and his tail started thumping.

"I'm not scratching your belly," I said. "You need to be alert. Not in a doggy coma."

He tried the puppy dog eyes on me, but I was immune.

I decided I needed something to do, so I went rummaging in my makeup bag for nail polish. I always kept a few bottles in there and I grabbed *You Pink Too Much*. After the week I'd had, I definitely needed some sparkle in my life. And since I was on "vacation," I was going to paint my toes *and* my fingers.

"You're such a rebel," I muttered to myself, hunkering

down in the living room with my supplies. I flipped on the television and found a random station with an old sitcom playing. That was good. Something light.

Turning on my cell, I saw I had several voice mails from my parents. Crap. They'd either heard it on the news or the building manager had already called my dad. His name was on the lease as well, and I could only imagine what he'd be thinking when they called to tell him that not only was my apartment riddled with bullets, I was nowhere to be found. I dialed my mom's cell.

"Sage! Oh my God, we've been worried sick!" My mother was as beside herself as I'd ever heard her and I winced.

"I'm sorry," I said. "There was kind of... an accident. But I'm okay." I didn't dare tell her about nearly getting run over by a truck.

"An accident!" she screeched. "Sage, the police said it was gang violence and the building manager said that apartment is a total loss! Now are you going to tell me what happened? Or do I have to put your father on the phone?"

"No, don't get Dad, please," I said hurriedly. My father would go even more ape shit than my mother. "It's just... well, there's this guy, this criminal..." and I proceeded to give her the *Reader's Digest* condensed version of who Viktor was and what he was doing now.

"But Parker is watching over me," I said, hoping to allay her fears. "And the CIA is on the lookout for him, so it'll be fine. It just may take a few days." I hoped that was all it took.

"Sage, I don't like this," she said. "You should go home for a few days while your father and I are out of town."

"You're out of town?" I asked. "Where'd you go?"

"Oh, your father got a wild hair—you know how he is

sometimes—and decided he wanted to go visit his uncle Louie."

"So you're in New Jersey?"

"For the time being. Probably only for a few more days," she said. "So why don't you go home? Rita will cook for you and you'll have the whole place to yourselves."

"'Yourselves'?" I repeated.

"Well, for goodness' sake, make sure you take Parker," she said in an are-you-an-idiot tone. "Now, are you going to go? Or do I have to use my mom voice?"

I kinda thought she was already using her mom voice, but agreed anyway. "Okay, we'll go," I said. "Just...don't tell Dad until you get back, okay?"

She gave a heavy sigh. "All right. Call me tomorrow."

"Will do. Love you."

"Love you, too, dear. And I'm thankful, *very* thankful, that you're all right."

I hung up feeling a little warmer and fuzzier. Moms tended to have that effect, I supposed.

I packed while I waited for Parker, my spirits a little better to think of going home rather than staying at Ryker's house, sans Ryker.

Ryker.

Crap. What would he do when he found out I wasn't here? Would he be worried? Think the worst? Probably.

I hesitated, staring at my cell. "Screw it," I muttered, picking it up and hitting the button I'd programmed for Malone, Ryker's partner.

"Hey, it's Sage," I said. "Ryker's girlfriend."

"Oh yeah, hey. How're you doing?" he asked.

"I'm okay, but...I really need to see Ryker." I hesitated. "He said I should call you if it was an emergency, that you'd know where he was."

"I do," he said. "But it's dangerous. Are you sure?"

"I wouldn't be calling if I weren't."

"Okay," he said with a sigh, then rattled off an address, which I quickly jotted down.

"Thank you," I said. "I swear, it'll be quick."

Suddenly, McClane began to growl. I whipped around to look at the dog, who was staring down the hall. His ears flattened on his head and his teeth bared. The growling grew louder.

"Oh God," I whispered. "Someone's in the house."

CHAPTER FOURTEEN

Send the police," I hissed at Malone. "I've gotta go." I hung up. There was nothing he could do anyway, and a phone in my hand would only hamper me.

Shoving the phone in my pocket, I wrapped a fist around McClane's collar. His growl was deep in his throat, but he quieted. The hair was standing up on his back and his obvious alarm made a cold flood of adrenaline rush through my veins.

I took a few careful steps forward. McClane stayed at my side, pressed against my legs. The floor creaked underneath my feet and I froze.

A man walked around the corner.

"There you are," he said with a smile. "Easiest job ever."

He raised a gun, pointing it at me, and I stopped breathing.

McClane leapt at him, teeth snapping and growling. His jaws fastened around the man's wrist as the gun went off. The bullet went wide and I watched in horror as McClane attacked the man with vicious intent. Panic and fear flooded me and I remembered what Parker had said.

It only takes one bullet to stop a dog.

The dog was going insane and the guy was fighting him tooth and nail. He cried out in pain and I saw the red stain of blood.

The only way out was past them and I tried to squeeze past the melee of dog and man fighting in the hallway, but a hand wrapped around my ankle and jerked. I fell hard to the floor, my knees and elbows slamming onto the hardwood. The breath rushed out of me in a huff. We hit the wall and something fell, glass splintering into a thousand pieces.

In desperation, I kicked back and must have hit him because I heard a grunt. McClane was still going berserk and I crawled forward on my hands and knees to scramble to my feet.

Rushing to the front door, I yanked it open, grabbing the truck keys from the table. "McClane! Come!" I had no idea if he'd obey me, but sure enough, he did and we bolted outside.

I ran for the truck. McClane needed no command to jump inside, and I followed. Seconds later, the engine roared to life and I slammed it into reverse. Thank God there was no one behind me because I didn't even look before backing up. I glanced in the rearview mirror as we sped down the street and saw the man standing in the doorway, watching us.

"Oh God, oh God, oh God," I said aloud. My hands were shaking and I just wanted to pull over and have a nervous breakdown, but I was too scared to stop.

I reached out, needing some kind of reassurance, and buried my fingers in McClane's fur. He whined a little and I glanced over.

"Oh no!" There was blood on him.

I skidded the truck to a halt on the side of the road and shoved it in park. "McClane, c'mere." I ran my hands over him and that's when I saw it. He'd been cut somehow, from the glass maybe, and it was deep, his fur matted with blood. I had to get him to the vet. But where?

Pulling out my phone, I Googled for vets nearby, then shoved the truck back into gear. Following the map on my phone with one hand, I drove to the nearest veterinary clinic. McClane put his head down on the seat.

"It's okay, McClane," I said. "You're going to be okay." I didn't know if I was reassuring him or myself, probably more of the latter since he obviously couldn't understand me.

When we pulled into the clinic, McClane didn't get off the seat, his dark eyes just staring soulfully at me.

Leaving the door open, I ran inside. "Please help me!"

Two workers came out right away, and between the three of us we got McClane inside. They took him into the back and I stood staring at the swinging doors, feeling like they'd just taken a family member away from me. I started bawling.

A worker put her arm around me. "He'll be okay," she said, rubbing my shoulder. "Our doctors are the best."

"But I don't even like dogs!" I sobbed. They were slobbery and smelled and McClane jumped on me with his dirty paws...and today he'd saved my life. I cried harder.

She guided me to a chair in the waiting room and I sat down heavily. A moment later, she thrust a box of tissues into my hands.

"I'll let you know how he is," she said sympathetically. "As soon as I hear anything."

I nodded, wiping my face and snotty nose. I'd stopped crying and a hiccup escaped. If something happened to McClane, Ryker would never forgive me, I was sure.

Unable to just sit there, I began to pace. The lady came back with some forms for me to fill out and I jotted my name, address, and all other relevant information. I figured I'd better use my name instead of Ryker's, not the least of which was because I didn't know his actual address.

A half hour went by before someone came out to talk to me.

"Is he going to be okay?" I asked.

The doctor smiled reassuringly. "He's going to be fine. He needed surgery, though, and stitches. We should keep him a day or so for observation."

Relief flooded me. Thank God. McClane would be okay. I sat down again and the doctor gave me a little pat before disappearing back behind the swinging doors.

I had blood and dog hair on my hands so I searched for the bathroom, washing up and taking a dampened paper towel to my tear-streaked face.

As I was coming back out, I heard someone talking to the lady behind the front desk, and I paused around the corner to listen.

"...had an injured dog," he was saying. "A German Shepherd. Have you seen her? She's my sister and she called me, very upset. I came as quickly as I could."

Me. He had to be talking about me. Except I'd called no one and I didn't have a brother.

I peeked around the corner and had to stifle a gasp. It was the same guy. He'd cleaned up from his tussle with McClane and looked exactly like what he was purporting to be: a concerned brother come to collect his distraught sister.

"Yes, she's here," the woman said. "The dog had to have surgery—"

I didn't wait to hear what else she was going to tell him. Backing up, I went down the hallway, searching for an exit.

A door blocked my path, but it was unlocked and I hurried through it, spotting an EXIT sign at the rear of the building.

I was almost there when I heard a "Hey!" from behind me. Instinct made me turn and look in time to see the guy pointing his gun at me. I dove through the door just as the shot sounded. It ricocheted off the slamming door and I hit the ground running.

Running for your life isn't the same thing as running for anything ever before. No matter what race I'd run as a child or teen, or how fast I'd wanted to clock a mile on the track, none of it compared to knowing that if I *didn't* go faster, I'd be dead.

The door to the truck was still hanging open and I could only be grateful for the few precious seconds that saved me as I jumped in and started the engine. As before, the old truck roared to life immediately and I gunned it, seeing the guy once again in my rearview mirror. This time, he fired at the truck. I screamed, ducking down, but then was quickly out of range.

I drove aimlessly for a few minutes, just trying to get myself under control. The tears had dried up, thank God. It was becoming dangerously clear that if I didn't keep my wits about me, I'd end up dead.

Parker. I needed to call him.

Pulling out my cell, I hit his speed dial. To my dismay, the call wasn't picked up but went to voice mail.

"Parker, it's me," I said. My voice was shaky and I took a breath to try and steady it. "Someone came to the house. I don't know how, but he found me. McClane got hurt and I took him to the vet. I think the guy is following me somehow..." And it hit me. Shit. My phone. Parker had even warned me about it. Maybe that's why Parker hadn't answered. His phone was off, too.

"I'm going to get rid of my phone," I said. "I'll call you again from another."

Ending the call, I tossed the phone out the window, then kept on driving.

The only thing I could think of to do was head to my parents' house, but before I went there, I had to tell Ryker what was going on.

Though it was early afternoon, I headed for the bar where Malone had told me I could find him. It was in an older section of downtown where the buildings were closer together and the sunlight didn't quite reach all the dark nooks and crannies of the street.

I was lucky enough that someone pulled out of a parking spot on the street just as I pulled up, so while it took me three tries, I was able to parallel park the truck. Hopping out, I glanced around before hesitantly going inside.

It was an old Irish bar, with Guinness signs prominently displayed on the walls and windows. The bar, floors, and furniture were made from heavy, dark wood that would have cost a fortune nowadays to use but had obviously been there since the place was built.

A couple of pool tables were in the back, and two men were playing a game on one. They didn't glance up from their game, but the man sitting at the bar did. Old and wizened, he looked as though he might've been grown on the barstool upon which he sat, planted when the place had opened and not moving from that spot ever since. He was nursing a beer. Considering the hour, I wasn't surprised that not many people were in the place.

"Jameson, straight up," I ordered from the bartender. He raised an eyebrow, but gave me what I wanted. I dug a crumpled ten from my jeans' pocket and handed it over, then tossed back the shot in one swallow.

I asked for a water, which I took to a far table in the corner, cloaked in shadows. I could keep my back to the wall and have a good view of the room as well as the door. A hallway led to the back and I saw a dimly lit EXIT sign, so if I had to leave quickly, I could.

I was exhausted. The adrenaline was gone, as was the terror that had propelled me to stay one step ahead of whoever this guy was following me, and I wished I could lie down and sleep for a week.

A woman walked in from the back—I wasn't sure where she'd come from as the back door hadn't opened—and went to the bar. She was really pretty, with deep red hair and eyes so green I could see their color even from where I sat. She was also tiny, not only in stature, but she had little bones and was that kind of petite I'd always envied. My legs were too long and my bones too big to ever be that little, even if I lost twenty pounds. Not that *that* was happening anytime soon. I was just saying.

I watched her out of interest and boredom as she joked with the bartender. He set a shot of whiskey on the rocks in front of her, but she didn't toss it back like I had. I wasn't paying much attention to their conversation until I heard something that made my ears perk up.

"...McCrady's back," the bartender was saying.

The woman went absolutely still. "Don't fuck with me, Barney." But the bartender just shook his head.

"I know better'n that, Branna," he said. "You think I wanna end up on your shit list? I swear to God. He's back."

"He's supposed to be dead," she said.

The bartender shrugged. "I know. Turns out he was running from the feds. He's back in town now, wanted a job back with Leo."

"What'd Leo say?"

He shrugged. "Seems to have welcomed him back with open arms. Thought I'd better give you a heads-up, though."

My attention was completely captivated now and I watched avidly to see what Branna would say. Turned out, she didn't have to say anything because just then, Ryker walked in.

The breath caught in my chest. He looked different, but I couldn't really pinpoint why. He still wore the same type of clothes—jeans, leather jacket, boots, and aviators, though I noticed the dog tags were missing. But his face was cold and absolutely devoid of emotion.

He came in the front door, it swinging shut behind him, and he paused, taking in the scene. Ryker didn't seem to see me in the corner at all. His gaze landed unerringly on the woman called Branna.

After a pregnant pause, he walked toward her, stopping when he was right in front of her.

"Branna," he said by way of greeting.

She said nothing…just slammed him with a right hook that made me flinch as bone met bone.

Ryker didn't seem surprised. He took the hit well, rubbing his jaw slightly, but he didn't back down. Turning, he faced her again.

"You've got some set of balls, McCrady," she gritted out, "showing up here again after all this time."

"Wouldn't want to be predictable," he said.

There was a moment of breathless tension, then she threw herself in his arms and they were kissing like two lovers who'd been parted and were suddenly reunited.

My stomach felt like someone had shot a fist into it. I couldn't breathe, watching as Branna and Ryker kissed like there was no tomorrow.

Oh God. I didn't know what to think as I watched from

my dark corner. What did this mean? Who was this woman? I knew he was undercover, but this seemed... more than that. You couldn't make up the kind of passion that sizzled between them. At least, I couldn't have.

They finally came up for air, but were still wrapped in each other's arms. The bartender had moved on, to give them some privacy I guessed. I strained to hear their conversation, but couldn't. But did it really matter? Their faces were close together and his hands were on her ass. I felt as though I'd swallowed a lead ball.

Shrinking farther back into the shadows, I waited as Branna walked in the back and Ryker asked the bartender for something. As he waited, he turned and leaned with his back to the bar. As though I'd called his name, his eyes fell on me.

There was a beat and something passed across his face, perhaps a hint of surprise, then it was gone and he was striding toward me.

"What's going on?" he asked when he reached my table. "How the hell did you find me?"

"Sorry to upset your plans," I replied, my voice tight with hurt I was channeling into anger. "Malone told me where you'd be."

"Do you have any idea how dangerous it is for you to be here?" he growled, showing not a flicker of embarrassment that I'd caught him kissing another woman.

"So I figured. Thought I'd tell you that... my dog got hurt," I said, opting to not name McClane. "He was helping me out in a pretty big way"—*hint hint*—"and he's going to be okay, but he'll be at the vet for a few days, so I'm leaving town."

"Where are you going?" he asked.

"I'm going home," I said, and now he should be hard-pressed not to know I was pissed. "It looks like you have someone to keep you occupied anyway." I tossed him the truck keys. "You might need these."

In a flash, he had me by the arm and was propelling me into the corner until my back hit the wall. He towered over me, in my space until we were almost touching. I felt his hand at my hip, pushing the keys back into my jeans' pocket.

"Don't do this," he hissed. "I told you why I'm here."

"Yeah, you did," I said. "So who the hell is Branna and why were you kissing her?"

Ryker hesitated. "She's ... someone I used to know," he said. "A friend."

I raised an eyebrow. "That's one hell of a friend."

His grip on my arm tightened. "I can't do this now," he said. "I'm asking you to trust me. Can you do that?"

I ignored his question and asked one of my own. "Are you going to sleep with her?"

He didn't answer, his lips pressing into a thin line. I gave a short, humorless laugh.

"Wow. Okay, whatever. I have my own problems right now, so you ... do whatever you've gotta do."

"Branna does some contract work for Leo," he said. "She's smart and dangerous. If anyone were to see through my cover, she would. It's vital that she trusts me."

"That's an excuse I haven't heard before."

Ryker ignored my snarky comment. "She and I were close," he said. "She was an excellent source and loyal to only herself, not Leo. When I went away, that was the end of it."

"Yeah, but you're back now," I replied. "And it looks like she wants to take up where you left off."

"McCrady."

We both turned to see the woman we'd been discussing

standing a few feet away. Her eyes narrowed when she saw me.

"Leo's here," she said to McCrady, her eyes still on me. "He's asking for you."

"Leo's here?" Ryker asked. "It's the middle of the day. Why is he here?"

Branna just shrugged and nodded at me. "Who the hell is this?"

"Just an ex," Ryker said. "I was just showing her out." He tugged on my arm, but a voice stopped him.

"What do we have here?"

Dread filled my gut at the familiar voice, and sure enough, Leo appeared behind Ryker.

"Looks like we have quite the party going on, thanks to you, McCrady," he said. "Bring the girl back, too."

I could tell Ryker was pissed, and I didn't know if it was directed toward me, or Leo, or the whole situation. Either way, he didn't have a choice and I followed Leo, some guy who was standing with him, and Ryker down the hallway. Branna brought up the rear.

A stairway was nearly invisible at the far end and we went down and into another short hallway. A door was standing partially open and we went inside the brightly lit room.

It was an office, a nice one, done in plush carpeting and with comfortable furniture, including a sofa that sat against one wall and a heavy wooden desk with two armchairs in front of it.

Leo sat in the chair behind the desk while the guy who was with him stood to the side, facing us.

"So I thought you and this one broke up," Leo said. "That's what you told me last night."

Ryker shrugged. "I can't help it if she's having trouble

accepting that it's over. She followed me here. I was just trying to get through to her when you walked in."

Okay, I didn't really like the picture he was painting of me being some lovestruck, needy female who couldn't let him go, but I didn't have a choice. So I kept silent.

"Perhaps I can help with that," Leo said. "We can even kill two birds, so to speak."

"How's that?" Ryker asked.

"There's the matter of your sudden reappearance," Leo said, "and your loyalty. Some members of my... organization... have expressed doubt that you are who you say you are."

I thought one of those "members" was probably the man standing next to him, judging by the look he was giving Ryker. My stomach twisted into knots. They didn't believe him, and he had no backup. If Leo decided to kill him right then, there was nothing anyone could do about it.

"So I'm proposing a test," Leo said, sitting back in his chair. "Something that will prove to me, and my people, that you're on the up and up."

"What kind of test?"

Leo reached inside his middle desk drawer and pulled out a handgun. He held it out to Ryker, butt first.

"It's an easy test, especially for someone like you," Leo said. "All you have to do"—he looked at me—"is kill her."

For one wildly hopeful moment, I thought he meant Branna. Then I realized... nope, he meant me.

I instinctively took a step back, but Branna was behind me and there was nowhere to go.

"You want me to kill my ex-girlfriend?" Ryker asked, skepticism in his tone.

"It would solve my problem, and incidentally, yours as well," Leo replied.

"She's just some secretary I picked up at a bar and fucked a couple times," Ryker said. "She's got nothing to do with this."

Okay, now I was obsessive *and* easy. I shot him a glare that he didn't see.

"Then you should have no trouble doing your job." Leo nodded at the weapon he still held and Ryker finally took it. Now I started to panic.

"Hey, listen, I just met this guy and we seemed to hit it off, but you don't want to see me anymore, that's fine," I babbled. "I'll just be on my way and let bygones be bygones." I took another step back toward the door, but was stopped in my tracks by Leo's sidekick pointing a gun at me.

"You kill her," Leo said. "Or Johnny here will do the honors. Either way, she's not leaving here alive." He glanced at me. "Sorry, honey. Don't be offended. It's nothing personal."

"Well, that's a relief," I snapped.

"McCrady, make up your mind," Leo said. "Kill her . . . or I'll have serious doubts as to your level of commitment."

I eyed the gun in Ryker's hand as a cold sweat broke out all over my body. "If you think I'm just going to stand here and let you shoot me—"

"That's exactly what you're going to do," Leo cut me off. "McCrady, decide."

Ryker raised the gun, its muzzle pointed directly at my head.

My mouth went utterly dry. I stared at the gun, then at him. His jaw was set in tight bands and his hand was steady.

"Please, don't," I said, my voice unsteady. The gun looked very deadly, and I was hyperaware of everyone watching. I knew Ryker's life was on the line, too, and had no idea how else he could get out of this without exposing his real identity. Surely he wouldn't hurt me. Surely...

And yet, my plea seemed to fall on deaf ears. There wasn't a flicker of emotion in his eyes as he looked at me. Not even when he pulled the trigger.

CHAPTER FIFTEEN

My heart stopped for a shattering moment, but nothing happened. No sound of a bullet, no ripping pain through my head or my chest, nothing at all. Just the dead click of a hammer against an empty chamber.

"Some weapon," Ryker mused, looking at the gun. With one flick of his thumb, the magazine ejected into his hand. "It would be much more effective if it were actually loaded." He tossed the gun at Leo, who caught it. "Did I pass your test?"

Leo laughed in delight while I struggled to remember how to breathe.

"I knew you were still the same cold sonofabitch," he said, still smiling. "That's good enough for me."

Ryker had almost killed me. In cold blood.

I couldn't wrap my head around that, shock settling in bone deep.

"You really want to mess up your carpet?" Ryker asked Leo, cool and calm. As though he hadn't just pointed a gun at me and pulled the trigger. "I'll take her somewhere else and get rid of her."

Leo waved his hand. "Of course. No, I don't want to replace the rug. It cost a hundred and fifty dollars a foot."

Ryker took my elbow and sense finally kicked in again.

"Let me go, you bastard!" I fought him, swinging my fist and connecting with any part of his body I could reach. I fought dirty, nails scratching and biting, but he hauled me around, back to his front. His arm was tight across my chest and I couldn't breathe.

"Sorry, Leo," Ryker said. "She's a bit of a wildcat."

Leo laughed. "Then I see why you liked her in bed."

Ryker hustled me out the door and into the hallway. I was panic-stricken and terrified, with no real plan or thought to how I was trying to get away. I just kept fighting him. But he subdued me easily.

"Knock it off, Sage," he snapped. "You'll only hurt yourself." I stopped when I felt cold steel at my throat. Ryker was holding a knife against my skin. Tears burned my eyes. I couldn't believe he was doing this. Was I really so easily expendable in the face of his job?

"How can you do this to me?" I hissed through my teeth. "Are you out of your mind?"

"Collateral damage," Ryker said. "I told you not to come here."

"Need some help?" Branna asked, and I realized she'd followed us out a few steps.

"Nah. I got it," Ryker said.

That's when I realized he was holding me in exactly the same position Parker had taught dirty how to get out of when he'd done the self-defense training. We'd practiced it over and over until I had it right, though I hadn't hit with full force. At the time, I'd been afraid perhaps I wouldn't be able to hit with full force when needed, but I shouldn't have worried. My fear and anger were such that I *wanted* to hurt Ryker.

I went still, waiting until I heard Branna go back into the office and the door shut. Ryker's hold on me loosened fractionally as he took me up the stairs and I obediently went up the steps, his hand in my hair and knife at my throat.

"Play along," he hissed in my ear, taking me by surprise. "We're being watched."

Play along? Part of me felt utterly relieved. Ryker wasn't going to kill me. The other part of me was still terrified, and now, furious. First, he'd all but said he was going to sleep with Branna so she'd trust him again, then he'd agreed to kill me to cement his position with Leo. Had he known the gun was empty? How could he possibly have been sure? And now he wanted me to play along in this deadly game? No problem.

When we got to the top, I took a deep breath, praying I did this right.

Whipping my head back into his chin, I shoved his knife hand down while I spun away and out of immediate danger. Remembering what Parker had said about disabling your attacker, I struck, just like he'd taught me to. A sharp jab to the solar plexus, then a knee in the nuts.

A grunt of pain told me I'd made good contact and both his hands dropped from me.

"Give Branna and Leo my regards," I hissed, then didn't waste any more time, but turned and ran for the front of the building and burst through the door.

The dim sunlight outside was like a spotlight compared to the murky confines of the bar. Wanting to get away as quickly as possible, I climbed into the truck, feeling more lost and more alone than I'd ever felt in my life. It had been a huge mistake to come here. Ryker was in deep with men who'd kill me without thinking twice. If that gun hadn't been empty of bullets, we might both be dead.

I couldn't handle this. Couldn't handle a cop boyfriend who had to go to lengths like cheating on me and pretending he'd kill me for his job—if he'd been pretending and it hadn't been just luck that the gun wasn't loaded. It had seemed so real, the coldly calculating way he'd looked at me before pulling the trigger. I'd never imagined he could so utterly become someone else like that.

He could go to hell, for all I cared. I was going to do what I could to say alive. Which meant getting the hell out of Chicago.

* * *

I pulled into my parents' house an hour later. It was a relief to be home. A place I finally felt safe after the last few days. I'd completely forgotten to buy one of those "burner" phones Parker had said he was going to buy, but couldn't bring myself to care.

Schultz met me at the door. Our driver for as long as I could remember, he seemed surprised to see me, but he recovered quickly.

"Miss Sage," he said. "How good to have you home."

"Thanks," I said, mustering up a smile.

"I'll let Rita know you're here," he said. "Do you have any bags?"

"No, but thanks." I handed him the keys to the truck and he looked dubious at the ancient relic, but I was too tired and disheartened to explain as I brushed past him into the foyer.

My bedroom was upstairs and that's where I went. The queen-size bed still overlaid with a sky-blue coverlet gave me a measure of comfort to be somewhere familiar.

I took a shower in my bathroom and dressed in sweat pants and a long-sleeved T-shirt. My feet were bare as I padded downstairs to the kitchen. Whatever Rita was cooking smelled mouthwatering and I followed the aroma.

"About time you came home for a visit," Rita admonished the moment she saw me. I gave her a hug.

"Good to see you, too," I said with affection. She squeezed me tight despite her gruff greeting.

"I have fresh linguine for dinner," she said, "and clam sauce."

"Sounds amazing," I replied, letting her go. I headed for the wine cellar, choosing a bottle at random and bringing it back upstairs to uncork. Rather than let the red breathe, I poured a glass immediately and took a long swallow as Rita looked on with disapproval.

"Your father drinks like that when he's having business problems," she observed, stirring a pot of creamy sauce.

"Yeah, well, it must run in the family," I said.

"Want to talk about it?"

"Not really." What was there to say? Too much to tell and too sad of an ending to bother.

She nodded, staying quiet. I loved that about Rita. Whereas my mother would keep at me like a dog with a bone, Rita would hold her peace until I was ready to talk.

"You and Schultz sticking around even though my parents are gone?" I asked.

"Well, I'd thought about driving down to Bloomington to see Jeffrey and the girls." Jeffrey was her son. He was divorced with two children. "But now that you're here—"

"No, don't even finish that sentence," I interrupted. "I'll

be fine. I can manage here by myself. You go on and visit Jeffrey. Are you driving yourself?"

"Well, Schultz was going to go, since you know it makes me nervous to drive by myself, but I hate to leave you here alone."

"Stop it," I admonished her. "I'm a grown woman. I live alone, for goodness' sake. You'll make me feel guilty if you don't go."

It took a few more reassurances that no, I wouldn't starve if she left and yes, I didn't mind being alone, before she agreed to not change her plans.

I made her sit and eat with me when dinner was ready, but Schultz refused. He was old-school, maintaining that there should be a respectful distance between employer and employee, but Rita'd had a soft spot for me since the day I was born, so she was easy to persuade.

"C'mon," I cajoled. "No sense in me eating alone if you're here." That plus puppy dog eyes and I had her. So easy.

We chatted about inconsequential things while we ate. She said I was too skinny, I said she nagged too much. Same old, same old, and it felt wonderful. I could pretend all the bad things that had been happening to me weren't real, just for a little while.

She and Schultz left after we'd cleaned up dinner. I reassured her again that I'd be fine as she gave me a list of dishes she'd premade and kept frozen for unexpected times like this. I finally pushed them out the door and waved as the car disappeared into the darkness.

I showered and pulled on a pair of pajamas that had seen better days: shorts and a tank that were so soft, though almost threadbare. Curling up in my old bed in my old room, I stared into the darkness.

Worry for Parker gnawed at my belly. I hadn't heard from him all day and couldn't reach him on his cell. What had happened? Had Viktor been waiting in his apartment? Had he been ambushed the way I had? What if he hadn't made it?

And Ryker. Now that I was alone, I could let the hurt and betrayal wash over me, and tears leaked from my eyes to stain the pillow. Why had he done it? To save himself? Should I condemn him for that? It was hard to demand someone give their life for yours, but I could still see him pointing that gun at me and feel the stark terror when his finger had moved on the trigger.

I fell into an uneasy sleep sometime after midnight, tossing and turning and watching the moonlit terrace outside my window for intruders. Even so, I missed it when someone did come in, and I suddenly woke with a start to see the outline of a man standing at the foot of my bed.

I drew in a breath to scream, but he moved fast, pressing a hand over my mouth.

"Shh, it's okay. It's me."

Parker.

Oh God. Relief washed over me, not only because it wasn't the same guy who'd tried to kill me today, but because it was Parker... and he was alive and safe.

Pulling his hand away from my mouth, I yanked him down toward me until I could fling my arms around his neck.

"Where the hell have you been?" I managed to ask. "I've been worried sick."

"*You've* been worried," he said, sitting down next to me and wrapping his arms around my waist to pull me closer. "I've been out of my mind, thinking you were dead."

"A man came," I said, "he had a gun. But McClane stopped him."

His hold tightened. "God, Sage, when I saw the blood on the floor and realized you were gone..."

Parker's voice was rough in my ear, and I could have let him go, but I didn't. I'd tried not to contemplate the worst-case scenario all day but it had still been there, lurking in the back of my mind. The sweet relief I felt that he was here with me was overwhelming.

He pressed a kiss to my hair, then my forehead. I moved back slightly and his lips brushed my cheek. The touch sent a shiver through me and we both went still. The air between us grew thick and so heavy; it was hard to breathe.

I'd had a death grip around his neck, but my hold loosened. His shoulders were wide and muscled under my palms. My hand moved to the back of his neck. The thick softness of his hair tempted me and I slid my fingers into it.

His hands tightened on my hips. He'd stopped kissing me, but his lips were so near mine I could feel the warmth of his breath.

We didn't move and I hardly breathed. My heart was racing so fast I thought for sure he could feel it. I wanted him to kiss me so badly, I thought I'd die if he didn't. Yet I didn't move. I wanted Parker to make the decision, not me. I didn't want to be rejected again.

He breathed out, and I breathed in, his chest pushing against mine. Moving his head just slightly, his mouth brushed the corner of my lips—not in a kiss, just skin against skin. I held back a moan, my nails pressing into his nape.

I was breathing much too fast, but couldn't slow it down. His cheek was slightly roughened with whiskers and I closed my eyes, savoring the moment of closeness.

"I should let you go," he said, his lips moving against my skin. "I promised Ryker."

A flash of Ryker pointing the gun at me went through my

head. I wondered what he was doing now...and if he was in Branna's bed.

"Ryker's out of the picture," I said, which was an understatement. But I didn't think Parker would take very well to hearing that Ryker had nearly killed me today.

"Thank God," he murmured, then his lips finally met mine.

It was pure pain and pleasure, the sweet culmination of such a strong desire, and I savored every moment, committing the taste and feel of him to memory.

Parker. The man I'd committed nearly every waking moment to for over a year. Kissing me the way I'd watched Ryker kiss Branna today, as though we'd been waiting our whole lives for this moment. And it felt like I had.

Lips and tongues and hands, breathing the same air, bodies touching and desperate passion fueling every kiss, every caress. This was the only moment that mattered.

Parker had touched me before—in New York, in my apartment—but he hadn't *kissed* me before. The intimacy of it suddenly struck me, perhaps more intimate even than having sex. The feel of his lips coaxing mine, the gentle brush of his tongue, sending an electric current through me.

His hands moved to the hem of my tank, tugging it up over my head. My breasts ached for his touch and he didn't make me wait, his palms cupping their weight as his thumbs brushed the hardened tips. I whimpered, wanting more, and impatiently yanked at his shirt until he relented, pulling back to tug it over his head.

I'd heard it said that sex was better when it was with someone you loved, and maybe that's what was different, because every brush of his skin against mine, every touch of his hand, seemed amplified with meaning. I wanted to *show* him how I felt, how much he meant to me, and what our relationship had become without having to hide behind the persona of work.

Parker pressed me back, lowering me until my head touched the pillow. He followed me down, his chest against mine, still kissing me as he settled between my legs. His jeans were rough against my thighs, but I could feel him against my core and it sent a rush of heat through me.

Pulling back slightly, Parker looked me in the eye, his hand brushing the hair back from my face.

"I thought I'd lost you," he murmured, "in every way. And I've been so stupid, all this time. It's you. It's always been you."

I couldn't help a small smile. Words I hadn't even realized I'd been waiting to hear.

"You're making up for it now," I said. His eyes were hard to see in the dim light, but I could make out the gleam in them as he looked at me.

"This changes everything," he said. "You know that. It's not just sex. Not with you and me."

"I know." But it was a relief to hear him say it.

He kissed me again, his hands skating down my sides to the waistband of the shorts I wore. Pushing them down, he had to break our kiss and sit up to pull them off. When I was naked, I reached for him, but he took my hands in his, slotting our fingers together.

I was self-conscious with him looking at me. Why had he stopped? Had he changed his mind?

"What's wrong?" I asked, nerves knotting inside my belly.

Parker shook his head. "Nothing's wrong. I just wanted to take a second and memorize this moment. I don't ever want to forget it."

If there was anything he could have said that would've

made me melt more, I didn't know what it could possibly have been.

Releasing one of my hands, he rested his palm on my stomach, slowly moving it up my abdomen and between my breasts. His gaze followed the path of his hand. Warmth spread at his touch as if by magic.

Stretching across me, he turned on the small lamp by my bed. I blinked in the light, though it was dim.

"Lights on?" I asked. Not that it was necessarily a bad thing, but I looked best in dim light, especially naked. Full dark was even better.

"I want to see you," he said simply.

Considering the view I was treated to, Parker shirtless and kneeling between my legs, I couldn't disagree.

I reached for the fly of his jeans and unfastened the button. It only took a few moments for him to shed the last of his clothes, then he was climbing back into bed with me and I had one of those pinch-me-I'm-dreaming moments.

"Is this real?" I whispered. "Or am I dreaming it?"

"Do I feel real?" He was braced on his arms, his body resting atop mine, chest to chest, my hips cradling his, the hard length of his erection pressing insistently between my thighs against the most sensitive part of me. His eyes stared intently into mine as his knuckles brushed my cheek.

I was too full of emotions to speak, but I didn't need to. He read it in my eyes.

He kissed me and it was like a drug. Now that we *could* finally kiss, I didn't want to stop. But I wanted more. My hands were busy mapping the planes of his back and his lips trailed to my jaw and down my neck. Eyes drifting closed, I let my senses overwhelm me with him—his scent, the texture of his skin, the weight of his body, the touch of his tongue.

My heart was beating so fast it felt like the flutter of a

hummingbird's wings inside my chest. I sucked in a sharp breath at the gentle rasp of his tongue on my nipple.

"You're so beautiful," he murmured, pressing soft kisses between my breasts. "I've imagined this so many times. My imagination didn't do you justice."

I memorized the words and the way he said them, wanting to have them later to replay inside my head. That Parker had felt this way about me all this time was still a shock to me, a revelation that left me reeling.

I didn't want to wait, couldn't wait, any longer. It seemed Parker wanted to take it slow, whereas I was burning from the inside out.

"Please," I managed, lifting my hips slightly, hoping he'd get the hint. I wasn't exactly capable of more speech at the moment.

Parker's hand moved between my legs. My nails dug into his shoulders and I tugged him back up to kiss him. Our tongues tangled and I moaned into his mouth when his fingers parted my folds to stroke me.

I was wet and ready for him and he groaned, his kisses growing fierce as he slid a finger inside me. The thought was running through my mind in an endless stream that it was unbelievable that we were here together like this. Parker was kissing me, touching me, after all the time of wanting and wondering and obsessing.

My orgasm hit with the force of a tidal wave, unexpected and overwhelming. A keening sound was coming from my throat, but I was helpless to stop it. Tearing my mouth away from Parker's, I sucked down air. His lips brushed my cheek, his finger still moving inside me.

Impatient for him, I pushed his hand away from my body and reached for his cock. It was hot and hard in my hand, and I wrapped my fingers around his length.

"I want you," I said.

Finally, he was as impatient as me, moving so he was positioned at the entrance to my body. My hands skated up his arms, the muscles there flexed and hard as they supported his weight above me.

"Look at me," he said.

Our eyes met and it felt as though we were sharing the same soul. He pushed inside me, filling me, and now we shared the same body. The idea of two people becoming one had always seemed to me a rather romanticized view of sex. Not anymore. Now I understood what people meant when they said that.

I couldn't look away. I didn't even blink. His eyes were a deeper blue than I'd ever recalled them being. His face was so dear to me, I had to touch him. My hand cupped his cheek and he turned, pressing his lips into the center of my palm.

He began to move and I wrapped my legs around his waist, lifting my hips to meet his thrusts. Slow and deliberate, I could feel every inch of him sliding out of and into my body. It was an exquisite torture.

I wanted him to kiss me again, so I threaded my fingers through his hair and drew him toward me. His kiss was deep and I lost myself in him. Pleasure and emotion tangled into a haze as he made love to me. He whispered in my ear and fit his palm at my hip, his hand sliding down my thigh to hook behind my knee and lift my leg higher up his side. Time lost meaning and I clutched at his ass, urging him faster and harder.

Our bodies were damp with sweat and I was moaning and gasping, hovering on the blissful edge. Parker thrust harder, my name on his lips as he came, sending me flying again. Our bodies were in complete sync, the pleasure so acute it brought tears to my eyes as I held on to him.

We were both breathing hard as the waves of ecstasy ebbed. I felt utterly boneless, completely overcome with not only the physical connection we'd just shared, but also at the emotions coursing through me. *Post-orgasmic glow* was too mild a phrase to describe how I was feeling. Parker's head was buried against my neck, his breath hot against my skin. My legs still circled his waist and I could feel the pulse of his heartbeat against my chest. It was...utterly lovely.

Right up until I got a toe cramp.

"Ow ow ow ow ow." I cringed, frantically squirming to try and get to my toe.

"What's wrong? Am I hurting you?" Parker asked anxiously, lifting himself off me.

"Toe cramp," I hurried to explain, pushing myself up and grabbing my foot with the offending toe. "Ouch. Dammit." Okay, not exactly how I'd pictured the aftermath, but what could I do. I sighed in relief as the cramp eased, then glanced at Parker, who was staring at me. I shrugged, embarrassed. "Sorry. Couldn't help it."

He burst out laughing, his eyes dancing as he looked at me. "Well, I'm glad your toe waited. A few minutes earlier would have been extremely inconvenient," he teased. "Are you okay now?"

"Yes, I'm fine," I said primly, though I was having a hard time hiding my grin. "Classy, right?" I rolled my eyes.

Parker surprised me with a swift kiss. "Yes, you are. And also unexpected. I love how you constantly surprise me. I never know what's coming."

Taking me in his arms, he twisted to lie on his back, tucking me into his side with his arm underneath my head. Still smiling, I nestled closer to him. I had the passing thought I should get up and go clean up a little and wipe the stickiness from the inside of my thighs, but I loathed the thought of moving too much. So I stayed where I was.

Parker's fingers idly drew unseen patterns on my shoulder, his touch trailing lightly up and down my arm. I listened to his heartbeat and watched the slow rise and fall of his chest as he breathed.

"How did you know I was here?" I asked.

"I looked everywhere for you," he said. "I called Megan, knocked on your neighbors' doors, even tried to reach Ryker. This was the last place I thought to look. It should've been the first, I guess. It makes sense that you'd go home. Where are your parents? Out of town, I take it?"

"Yeah. I told my mom a little of what was going on. She said I should come here. So I did. After that guy found me at Ryker's, I didn't know where to go and I couldn't reach you..."

His arm tightened around me. "I'm sorry. I shouldn't have left you like that."

"It's okay. Was everything okay at your place?"

He hesitated. "Not...really, no."

I lifted my head to look at him, alarmed. "What does that mean?"

"It means there's now a dead guy in my apartment."

"What!" I sat straight up.

"It's okay," Parker said, tugging me back down.

"It's not okay! What happened?"

"It was an ambush," he said. "But I knew it was coming, and Viktor underestimated my ability to fight back."

"Did you call the police?"

"No. I called Sasha. He sent a cleanup crew to take care of the body and the damage to the apartment."

"But tell me what happened," I persisted, not fooled by his vague reply. "Are you hurt?"

He looked down at me, an eyebrow cocked. "Do I seem hurt to you?"

I felt a blush creep up my neck and he laughed slightly. Reaching for the lamp, he switched it off. "Go to sleep, sweetness."

My eyebrows went up at the endearment, even as something warm curled inside my chest.

I snuggled against him again, wondering if I'd be able to sleep. I was incredibly happy... but Ryker lingered in the back of my mind.

Why had he done what he did? Was he safe? Despite what had happened, I was worried about him. But I no longer felt I could trust him, or what he said he felt about me. He'd talked about being with Branna as though I should just understand. Did he have feelings for her, feelings that ran deeper than what I'd thought we'd had? Had anything he'd said over the past few months been real? He'd slid into the skin of McCrady so easily... as easily as he'd kissed Branna while I watched.

CHAPTER SIXTEEN

Someone banging on the door downstairs woke me up. I sat up, confused for a moment as to where I was. Parker was no longer beside me and I heard the shower running in the bathroom.

The banging came again and I jumped up and grabbed the robe hanging on the inside of my closet door. Throwing it on, I belted it as I hurried down the stairs.

It was really early; the sun wasn't even up yet. The outside lights on the house illuminated things enough for me to see as I glanced out the window before opening the door.

Ryker.

I hesitated, but then he started on the door again so I yanked it open.

"Thank God," he said when he saw me, looking relieved.

But the anger from yesterday came surging back. "How the hell did you find me?" I asked.

"You have my truck," he said, as though it was obvious.

"So?"

"I've put a lot into that truck. It's LoJacked."

Ah. That explained it. Modern technology and GPS.

"Why are you here?" I asked. "Did Branna not satisfy you? Or have you come to shoot me again? Maybe you'll get lucky and the gun won't be empty this time." I went to slam the door, but he shoved his foot in it and forced his way inside.

"Babe, listen to me—"

"Don't call me that," I cut him off, furious. "You should leave."

I turned away, but Ryker grabbed my upper arms and spun me back around, holding me too firmly for me to get free.

"I knew the gun wasn't loaded," he said. "My life depends on knowing my weapons. I could tell by its weight the second he handed it to me that it wasn't loaded. It was just a stupid test of Leo's. Do you honestly think I'd fucking *shoot* you?"

"You pointed a gun at me and pulled the trigger! What the hell was I supposed to think?"

"What's going on?"

We both turned to see Parker standing at the foot of the stairs. His hair was wet and he wore only his jeans, but his gaze was shrewd as he took in Ryker's hold on me. He must have heard the yelling.

"What the fuck are you doing here?" Ryker asked. I saw him take in Parker's bare chest and feet and his jaw tightened.

Parker's stride was eating up the floor. "What the hell is she talking about, Ryker?" he asked, ignoring the question. "You shot at her? Are you fucking kidding me?"

"The gun wasn't loaded," Ryker said. "I could feel the magazine was empty."

"What if there'd been a bullet in the chamber? Did you think about that?" Parker looked livid.

A bullet in the chamber? Nausea curdled in my stomach.

"It was empty," Ryker insisted.

"You took a chance and got lucky. Now get your hands off her." Parker shoved Ryker and he let me go, stumbling back a couple of steps.

A dangerous glint came into Ryker's eyes and it scared me. The tension between the two men was white hot and only needed a spark to set it off.

"No," I said, putting myself between them and putting up a hand in front of each. "We're not doing this. There's enough going on without you two being at each other's throats."

They looked at me and for once seemed to see sense. Ryker turned away and heaved a sigh, shoving a hand through his hair. I saw Parker's body relax slightly as he, too, eased off.

"Why are you here?" he asked Ryker. "Aren't you supposed to be working undercover? What if Leo had someone follow you here?"

"He didn't. I'm here because I was worried about Sage and had no way to reach her. And to tell you that Leo's organization is the one supplying Viktor."

"What?" I asked just as Parker said, "How do you know?"

"Because I'm the one he hired to find you," Ryker said grimly.

"That's convenient," Parker said.

"Exactly." Ryker replied. "If we can get your CIA contacts to work with us, we can set him up with fake intel and they can nab him."

"Yeah, that should work," Parker said after a moment's thought. "But won't that blow your cover with Leo?"

Ryker's face was expressionless. "You may think I didn't care if I killed her," he said, "but you're wrong, man. I love her, and I'm not about to let Viktor keep stalking her if I can do something about it."

Oh God. I stared at him, caution whispering in my mind. He said he loved me, but what about Branna? What about how icy cold he'd been to me? Had I been utterly wrong about what had happened yesterday? What if Ryker *hadn't* been lying to me about his feelings? He was putting his life on the line to help us stop Viktor . . . because he said he loved me.

And last night I'd slept with Parker.

Ryker took my hand and tugged me toward him. Still in a stupor of shock and confusion, I let him pull me in and wrap his arms around me.

"I'm so sorry," he murmured in my ear. "I knew you were afraid and there wasn't a damn thing I could do about it. I just prayed you'd trust me. If I'd hesitated, he'd have killed us both."

"And Branna?" I asked, unreasonably hoping he *had* slept with her. It would make things easier.

"She and I are through," he said. "She knows me as someone completely different. Not the person I really am. Not like you."

The nausea in my stomach increased threefold. It wasn't that I regretted what had happened between Parker and me—I was utterly in love with him—but if I hadn't thought Ryker and I were over, it wouldn't have happened.

But now Ryker thought we were still together and if he knew, he'd think I'd cheated on him. Which I guess technically, I had, but that hadn't been my intention. I'd believed we were over. I'd told Parker so.

At the thought of Parker, my gaze lifted, searching over

Ryker's shoulder, and I found him. He was staring at us, his lips pressed in a thin line and his hands clenched in fists at his sides.

"Say you forgive me," Ryker said in my ear. "All I've been able to think about is the look on your face when you ran out."

"Um, I-I don't know," I stalled. "I need time." What was I supposed to do? Break up with Ryker right now? When they were about to go into a dangerous situation with Viktor? When he was already toeing the edge in this deadly game with Leo?

Ryker had said he loved me and I loved him, too—but I'd been in love with Parker for so long, I couldn't give him up now that things had changed between us. It was bad timing, that's all, but when this was over with Viktor and Leo, I'd explain to Ryker that it wasn't going to work out between us.

Standing there, wrapped in Ryker's embrace as I stared at Parker, I felt like the worst kind of fraud. Not only did I feel like I was deceiving Ryker, but what must Parker be thinking right now? What if he thought I'd lied to him in order to sleep with him? He'd unwittingly betrayed Ryker before at the hands of a lying female. What if he thought I was cut from the same cloth as Natalie?

"So what's the plan?" Parker asked, finally looking away from me to Ryker. "When are you supposed to get back to Viktor?"

I eased out of Ryker's arms, a flush creeping up my neck, and I couldn't look Parker in the eye. If I did, I was afraid Ryker would know, would see my feelings written on my face.

"As soon as possible. Leo's the go-between. Where do you want to do this?"

"Let me call my contact. See what they say," Parker replied. He gave me a long look and took the stairs two at a time.

"Um, yeah, I'd better get dressed," I said, backing away. Ryker caught at my hand.

"You know I'd never hurt you," he said, squeezing my hand. "I just had to make it look good."

"Yeah, I get it."

His lips lifted in a crooked smile. "That move you did to get away, that was totally badass. Where'd you learn that?"

"Parker taught me a little self-defense," I said. Even saying his name made guilt rise like a bile in my throat.

Ryker's grin faded. "Lucky that you remembered what to do then," he said.

I nodded, slipping my hand from his. "Yeah, lucky. Um, I'd better dress."

I felt his eyes on my back the entire way up the stairs.

Looking through my closet, I was suddenly hauled around.

"What's going on, Sage?" Parker asked, anger etched on his features. "You said Ryker was out of the picture."

"I thought he was," I said. "He pulled a gun on me yesterday. I didn't know it was a setup. And there was this girl there that he'd had some kind of relationship with the last time he was undercover and it was like they were taking up where they left off... and yeah. I thought it was pretty over between us."

"Do you love him?"

That wasn't the question I was expecting. I thought he'd ask if I loved *him*, not Ryker.

"I do," I said, deciding honesty was the best way to go. "But—"

"I'm not doing this to him again," Parker interrupted,

backing away from me. "Last night was a mistake. It should never have happened. I was out of my mind, crazy with worry for you. You were terrified, nearly killed, and running for your life. Neither of us was thinking straight."

I stared at him, my stomach dropping to my toes. "What are you saying?"

"I'm saying we're going to pretend it never happened."

"But last night you said—"

"It doesn't matter what I said. He loves you, and you love him. I won't let history repeat itself. I can't."

Before I could utter another word, he was gone.

I stared in shock at the empty space where he'd been, unable to believe what had just happened. My chest ached and pain stabbed me with every breath I took. After last night, how could he just throw away what we had together? We had a connection, something that went deeper than anything I'd ever felt before. He had to have felt it, too.

Or maybe he hadn't.

It was hard to breathe and my knees were too weak to hold me. I sank to my knees on the floor of my closet and crossed my arms over my middle, holding on tight. I choked on a sob and realized I was crying. How long had I been crying?

I had to pull myself together, when all I really wanted to do was curl up in a ball in my closet and sink into a pool of miserable self-pity. Had Parker not felt like I did? I was in love with him and I'd assumed he loved me back, or else why would he have done what he had last night, said the things he'd said?

But he didn't love me. All this time I'd kept my love for him alive, even when I shouldn't have, unable to kill that last tiny shred of hope that wished so desperately for more between us. Last night I'd thought it had finally paid off. The realization that I'd been very, very wrong stripped my dignity to the bone, leaving me feeling vulnerable, naked, and exposed.

I pressed the heels of my hands to my eyes, halting the flow of tears. I had to be angry about how Parker had misled me, used me, and discarded me. Otherwise the heartbreak and hurt would cripple me.

After splashing water on my blotchy, tear-stained face, I brushed my teeth and hair, then dressed in jeans and a black, long-sleeved shirt.

Tennis shoes seemed the wisest choice, and I braided my hair in a French braid, the familiar workings of my fingers comforting me. Though it took me two unsuccessful attempts before I finally got it on the third try. My hands were trembling and whenever I let my mind wander to last night, it felt like I couldn't breathe.

I took a deep breath before leaving my room, giving myself a pep talk. "You can do this," I muttered. Facing both Parker and Ryker felt like a daunting task. Parker had made me ashamed and embarrassed about last night and how I felt about him. And what to do about Ryker? If I told him the truth, he'd probably kill Parker...and me. Maybe it was best to just do what Parker had said and pretend it had never happened.

Even if it was impossible for me to forget.

They were both downstairs sitting in opposite chairs in the front parlor talking when I stepped into the room. I tried not to think about anything, my emotions numb. They glanced at me as I took a seat away from them both.

I looked at Ryker, keeping my gaze averted from Parker. "So what's the plan?" I asked, wincing a little at the leftover roughness in my voice from crying. I cleared my throat. "Where are we going?"

"You're not going anywhere," he said. "You're staying here. Parker and I will take care of Viktor."

I bristled at this. "Why should I stay behind while you two get to go? I want to see Viktor go down, too. He tried to kill me, for crying out loud!"

"I know, but let's be real, Sage. You're not trained for this. Let us do what we know how to do, and keep you out of it."

What he said made sense, but I hated not being able to be there when they got Viktor. That man had terrorized me on several occasions and I wanted to see justice done, up close and personal.

"It makes the most sense, Sage," Parker said in his let's-be-reasonable voice.

I stiffened, then completely ignored him, directing my response to Ryker. "Fine. I'll stay. But only if you swear you'll call me as soon as it's done."

Digging in his pocket, he handed me his cell. "Here. Keep this. I've got a burner phone I'm using while I'm on the job."

"Okay." I clutched it in my hand, wondering how I was going to sit and wait for hours to find out what had happened. And if they were safe.

They both stood and that was when I saw they were armed. Parker had his weapon in the small of his back and he took it out. He popped the magazine and checked the bullets before slamming it home again. I hurriedly looked away just as he lifted his gaze.

Both men flanked me and I could nearly feel the testosterone in the air as the prospect of what was to come had them on high alert. They looked like men you didn't want to fuck with, both sporting a day or more's worth of stubble on their jaws, tight T-shirts that stretched across layers of muscle, wide shoulders, and biceps that said pumping iron was a leisurely hobby they did as easily as breathing.

"It'll be okay," Ryker said, sensing my growing worry

and unease. Sliding a hand to the back of my neck, he pulled me close for a kiss. At the last second, I turned my head so his lips landed on my cheek.

"Yeah, be safe," I said, giving him a tight squeeze before nervously stepping away.

He looked at me strangely, but didn't make a comment. "Okay, let's go," he said to Parker, then headed out the parlor door into the foyer.

The last thing I wanted was to be in the same room with Parker, so I started to follow Ryker, only to be caught up short by Parker hooking his finger in a belt loop at the back of my jeans. It was the wrong move. I was tired of being pushed around, by both of them, and I spun around, knocking his arm away from me.

"Sage, I just want to say—"

"I don't want to hear what you have to say," I hissed, cutting him off as I fought back tears. "I listened too much last night. And if we make it out of this alive, I quit. I am so through with you and being your secretary."

I stormed away before he could respond. Anger was so much easier to deal with than the heartbreak that pulsed inside me.

Ryker was waiting at the open front door, his gaze narrowing when he saw me. I pasted on a smile and tried to calm down.

"Be safe," I said, hugging him again.

"No worries," he said, brushing a kiss to the top of my head. I let him go, then clenched my fists at my sides so I wouldn't reach for Parker despite myself as he walked by. What if something happened to him? Maybe I'd regret what I'd said, but what else could I do? I'd bared my soul to him last night and it hadn't made a bit of difference. I had nothing left to give him.

Our eyes met and he paused just for a moment. I said nothing and neither did he, the unsaid things piling between us like a brick wall. Then he was gone, following Ryker out to a black SUV. I watched them both get in, my heart lodged in my throat. My vision blurred as they drove away, the SUV disappearing down the long driveway.

I didn't know what to do, how to while away the time. My nerves were already shot and the sun had risen barely an hour ago.

I needed to talk to someone and before I'd even thought twice about it, I'd picked up the phone and called Megan. When she answered, it was obvious I'd woken her.

"Oh geez, I'm sorry," I said. "I didn't mean to wake you. Just…call me later—"

"No, it's fine," she interrupted with a yawn. "What's going on? You okay?"

I hesitated, then blurted it out. "I slept with Parker."

"Really? Oh my God, that's great! That's what you've been wanting, right? How was it?"

Her enthusiasm made me grimace. "It was good, I mean, in and of itself. Really, *really* good. But then today, Ryker showed up and I thought we were broken up, but I guess we weren't—"

"Please tell me you did not tell him what happened," she interrupted.

"No, I didn't. I was going to break up with him, but then Parker like…took it all back."

"What do you mean? How could he take it back? It's sex. There are no takebacks in sex."

"I know, but he did. He said it was a mistake and we should never have done it." Saying the words made my eyes water and I had to blink several times.

"What a complete asshat!" Megan fumed.

"I know, and I got so angry and just...tired, you know?" I sighed. "I've been feeling this way about him for so long and then I thought we were finally getting somewhere, and it was so...great, then boom! It's gone. So...I quit."

"You quit?"

"Yeah. I told him I was through with him and I quit." I still couldn't believe I'd actually done it.

"Okay, so how are you feeling about that?" she asked carefully.

"I-I'm fine," I stammered. "I mean, it's good, right? Ryker's been wanting me to quit and everyone says I do too much and should, you know, find a different career and..." But by now I was having a hard time getting the words out past the tears, so I stopped talking altogether.

"Aww, honey," Megan said with a soft sigh. "That's what I was afraid of. Are you sure about this?"

Sniffling, I rummaged in the kitchen for a tissue to wipe my eyes and nose. "It's too late," I said, my voice thick. "I don't know what to do. It-it hurts...so much—" I couldn't continue. My self-pitying misery overtook me.

"I know it does—"

I heard a voice—a male voice—in the background murmuring something I didn't catch.

"Who's that?" I asked.

"Um, well, it's um...Brian."

"Oh God, I'm so sorry!" Shit, I couldn't believe I'd interrupted her and Brian, who'd apparently slept over. I smiled despite my inner misery. "Okay, ignore me, get back to what you were doing—I mean *who* you were doing—and I'll talk to you later."

"No, it's fine! I can talk—"

"Forget it. I would be the shittiest friend alive if I kept you on the phone. Now, go. I'll talk to you later," I insisted.

"Are you sure?"

"Yes, I'm sure. I love you. Bye."

"Okay, love you, too."

I hung up the phone, smiling a little. At least one of our love lives wasn't completely screwed up.

Looking at the clock, I saw only twenty minutes had crawled by. Damn. Today was going to be a really long day.

And it was. I played two movies in the theater downstairs, neither of which I could concentrate on for more than five minutes. Giving up after the second one, I wandered the house, which took some time. We had a really large home, over eight thousand square feet, and I drifted from room to room, outside to walk the grounds and around the pool, down to the edge of Lake Michigan, then back.

The sun was setting and I was trying to eat something— I'd been too upset to eat all day—when Ryker's cell phone buzzed. I grabbed it up immediately.

"Hello?"

"Dear Sage, how lovely to hear your voice."

My hands went ice cold. Viktor.

"H-how did you get this number?" I asked.

"The detective's number, you mean? Easy to learn once you know his real name."

Bile rose in my throat. Ryker. His cover had been blown.

"I must say, Sage," he continued. "I am disappointed in you. You are supposed to be with Parker, and yet I hear you have been fucking the cop."

I swallowed hard. "What do you want?"

"I am glad you asked," he said. "I love games, Sage, and when I found out about this love triangle you are at the center of, I had the most wonderful idea for a game."

"What are you talking about?"

His voice changed, from light and playful to cold and deadly. "I have them both. Parker and the detective."

Oh God...My eyes slid shut in dismay and I pressed my lips together so I wouldn't make the sound clawing its way up my throat.

"So here is what we shall do," he continued. "You are going to do some work for me, and in return, I'll make their deaths slightly less painful. Do a good job, and I might even let you save one. Understand?"

"How do I know you're telling the truth?" I asked. "You could be lying to me." I wasn't stupid. I needed proof before I did anything he said.

"Oh, you would like proof?" he asked. "I can provide that."

The phone abruptly switched from voice mode only over to camera. I saw him, someplace I couldn't discern. It was dark behind him. Maybe a warehouse?

He turned the phone and I sucked in a breath. I could see them, Parker and Ryker. Their shirts had been removed and they hung from ropes tied around their wrists. Their feet just brushed the floor, but not enough to take any real pressure off their wrists. A naked lightbulb swung listlessly above them, dangling from a wire.

"Don't listen to him, Sage," Parker called out.

A man standing to the side moved suddenly, swinging a short stick, like a policeman's baton, and it smacked into Parker's ribs. His body flinched and he flung his head back at the vicious blow, but didn't cry out.

"Hang up the phone. Go to the cops." That was from Ryker, who got the same treatment. He grunted, jerking when the baton hit him, and my hand flew up to cover my mouth. Tears stung my eyes.

"Oh God..." I murmured.

"Let me show you what happens to them should you decide to go to the authorities," Viktor said.

I watched, barely breathing. Something happened that I couldn't see, then both men were shaking, their entire bodies taut. Even from the fuzzy image, I could see they were in a massive amount of pain.

"Stop it! Stop!" I cried. "I'll do whatever you want. Just stop hurting them!"

Their bodies went suddenly slack and I realized what it had been. Electricity. Viktor was sending voltage through them somehow.

"An excellent choice, my dear," Viktor said, swinging the camera back around to himself.

"What do you want me to do?"

* * *

I sat outside the bar inside Ryker's truck, waiting. My nerves were shot and I didn't know what I could do other than follow the directions I'd been given.

At precisely nine o'clock, a car pulled into the lot. Taking a deep breath, I got out.

The car I'd been waiting for parked and a man got out. He took a moment to light a cigarette as I approached him.

"Detective Malone?" I asked, calling out to Ryker's partner. "Is that you?"

The man turned with a start, but relaxed when he saw me. I saw his gaze move over my body.

"I am for you," he said with a smile. He focused on my face as I got closer and his grin faded. "Sage? Is that you? What're you doing here? Did you see Ryker yesterday?"

"I have a message from Viktor," I told him. "He said you're no longer required."

He frowned. "What the fuck does that mean? And how do you know Viktor?" A panicked look came into his eyes and he looked around, searching the shadows and empty parked cars in the lot. "Where is he?"

"I don't know," I said. "I'm just supposed to give you that message."

"Why? What's going on?"

I tried to take a step back, but he grabbed my arm. "You're not leaving until you tell me how you know Viktor. What did he say?"

"Let me go!" I jerked away just as I heard a popping sound. Then Malone was no longer there. Confused, I looked down to see his crumpled, headless body lying on the ground.

My cheek was wet. In a daze, I swiped at my face, my hand coming away with blood and gore. It was all over my clothes, too.

I stumbled backward into another car, hitting it hard and nearly falling in my haste to get away. Malone was dead. Shot right in front of me.

Turning, I ran back toward the truck, slipping and falling once. The gravel bit into my hands, but then I was up and climbing into the driver's seat. I threw the truck into reverse and backed up, hitting something in the process, but I didn't stop to check. Shoving it into gear, I floored it, gravel spraying from the wheels as I sped out of the lot.

I was too numb to cry, too much in shock to process what had just happened. I pulled the phone from my pocket.

"Excellent job!" Viktor crowed. The call had been live the entire time I'd been speaking to Malone. "It's rather apropos, my final words being delivered by a beauty such as yourself. Death comes in all kinds of packages, though honestly I think I did him a favor, sending you. Much better than one of these thugs—unexpected and poetic, if I do say so myself."

"I did what you said, now let them go," I demanded, my voice shaking only a little.

"I said you might be able to save one of them, not that I'd let them go, but let's make it more interesting, shall we? Come to this address, and we'll continue our game." He rattled off an address in the southeast part of Chicago. "Let's make it ten minutes," he said, "or they'll start losing their fingers, one by one. Tick tock, little Sage." The call ended.

"Goddammit!" I exploded, tears of rage and fear spilling down my cheeks. I'd known he wouldn't live up to what he'd said, but what else was I supposed to do? And now I was on a time limit before he hurt them again.

My dad had grown up in that part of Chicago and I had cousins all over the place. I was vaguely familiar with the address, but even in light traffic, I was twenty minutes away. I floored it.

Stoplights were nonexistent for me as I blew through too many red lights to count. I prayed I wouldn't get stopped by a cop as I took every shortcut I knew, making turns at speeds that were outright dangerous, not to mention foolish. But I had no choice. I believed absolutely that Viktor would do as he said. He'd cut off their fingers and laugh while he did so.

The truck tires squealed as I made a hairpin turn, glancing frantically at the clock. Two minutes.

I was going sixty-five in a twenty-five zone, swerving around cars and into oncoming traffic. Horns blared in my wake, but I took no notice of them. My entire focus was on the road and the ticking of the clock inside my head.

The docks were close and I swerved into the address he'd given me, slamming the truck into park and jumping out. I hit the pavement at a dead run, aiming for the door I could see set into the bleak warehouse. And I was only steps from it when something slammed into me from behind, knocking me to the ground. My head cracked against the pavement and everything went black.

CHAPTER SEVENTEEN

A blinding pain woke me, then another, before I realized someone was slapping me. First one cheek, then the other. I tried to lift a hand to stop them, but couldn't. My hands were tied behind me.

My eyes blinked open and I flinched as another blow came toward me, but it stopped at the last second.

"Oh good, you are awake. I was afraid Lee had hit you too hard."

Viktor was the one hitting me and I glanced to where he indicated. A body lay on the floor, a pool of blood spreading beneath him. Not far from him was a metal barrel with a fire burning inside. It cast weird shadows around the room.

"You're certainly leaving a lot of dead bodies in your wake," I said.

"Yes, well, good help can be so hard to find."

I was sitting on a chair, my wrists tied behind my back, inside what I assumed was the warehouse. Glancing around, heart in my throat, I spotted Parker and Ryker. They were maybe twenty feet away and now I could see they were tied to a set of bedsprings suspended above them. No blood marred their wrists or forearms and I breathed a sigh of relief.

"Yes, you made it just in the nick of time," Viktor said. "And I had hoped to at least get a pinky as my trophy. Ah well. Perhaps later."

"Not if I have anything to say about it, you bastard," I ground out.

Viktor laughed. "You are entertaining, Sage, I will give them that. But your loyalty is quite lacking."

I pressed my lips together and didn't reply.

He began to pace slowly, back and forth as he talked. "So please tell me, how did this come to be? Last I saw you and Parker, you were quite the hot item. I believe my driver reported a steamy scene in the backseat of the car. And you two did share a room together."

I half-listened to him as I took stock of the huge room. The ceiling was high, at least twenty feet, and there was a glimmering light from the hallway to my right. I thought maybe that was an exit. Unfortunately, three guys stood between me and the exit, not to mention getting Parker and Ryker free and out of here was probably beyond my capability.

"And yet," he continued, "you're dating the detective." He shook his head sadly. "I can't help but think you're not being true to yourself, Sage. I think the detective is merely little fling on the side, that you know you belong with Parker. Or am I wrong? Does the lawman bring out a side of you your boss cannot? Do tell me."

"This isn't a fucking soap opera," I spat. "You're insane."

He backhanded me with enough force to knock me from

the chair. I lay on the floor, gasping and blinking the blackness from my vision. Blood ran freely from my mouth, the inside of my lip cut from my teeth.

"Viktor, what the fuck are you doing?" I heard Parker call out. "You should be getting out of town while you still can. You don't think the CIA is going to track me down? You stick around here, you're going to miss your chance to get out of the country."

"The CIA doesn't even know I'm alive," Viktor said. "I'm not worried about them. What I do want, what I *crave*, is a bit of revenge."

"They'll kill you if you go back, is that it?" Parker asked. "Given your history, I'm sure the CIA would offer you clemency and protection if you'd tell them what you knew."

Viktor's laugh was bitter. "As if anyone can protect me from them. I'm living on borrowed time as it is. I might as well make the most of it. And torturing those who caused my downfall is the best revenge I could possibly have."

He grabbed my braid and hauled me upright. The pain was excruciating and I scrambled to ease the pressure, getting to my feet with my hands still tied.

"Let's play that game. The one Americans are so fond of," Viktor said. "What is it called? Oh yes. Truth or Dare." His cold eyes focused on Ryker. "You first, Detective. Truth? Or Dare?"

Ryker's head was bowed, his chest covered in sweat and bruises, but he looked up. He looked at me, at the blood dripping from my mouth, then focused on Viktor. "This oughtta be good, asshole. Dare. I choose dare."

"I thought you would!" Viktor said with a wide smile. "A cop is known for their bravery, their courage. A dare is a natural choice, after all."

Viktor walked to the fire burning inside the barrel and

picked up something from the floor. A tire iron. My heart stuttered in my chest. He held it into the flames.

"This is a test of not only your courage, but your ability to endure pain," he said. Taking the tire iron from the fire, I saw the end of it glowed with heat. He walked over to Ryker.

"I'm going to press this into your side for ten seconds," he said. "If you ask, I will remove it. But then she"—he pointed at me—"will endure the rest of the time you could not. If you refuse, she'll endure all ten seconds. Understood?"

I was horrified. "No! Please, Viktor! Don't—" But Ryker was already nodding.

"Fine."

"No!" I screamed as Viktor pressed the tire iron to Ryker's flesh. Every muscle in his body went rigid, his face contorting in pain. He gritted his teeth, grunting, but didn't flinch away. I could smell the stench of burnt flesh and tears streamed down my face.

"You sonofabitch!" I yelled, jumping to my feet, but two of the guys had their hands on my shoulders instantly, shoving me back down.

Ten seconds was an eternity when someone you loved was hurting.

After what felt like way more than ten seconds, Viktor stepped back. There was a livid brand in Ryker's skin and his head hung again. I couldn't tell if he was conscious or not.

"Tell me, Parker, do you care that Sage is fucking someone else?"

Parker glanced at Viktor, then stared straight ahead. "Sage and I aren't together."

Viktor looked at me. "Is he telling the truth?"

I gave a jerky nod.

"I suppose there's an easy way to find out," Viktor said, returning to the fire. My gut twisted as I watched him again heat the tire iron.

"Please, don't hurt them again," I begged through lips gone numb. I had no real hope that he'd listen, but I had to try.

"Oh, this one isn't for them," he replied, inspecting the glowing metal. "This one is for you."

"Don't even think about it, Viktor," Parker furiously cried out. "I'll kill you!"

Viktor ignored him, approaching me until he stood at my side. "He's not in much of a position to argue, is he, my dear?" he said to me.

I didn't answer, my eyes glued to the metal. My whole body was quaking in terror.

"Tell me the truth, Parker," Viktor said loudly. "You still want Sage, don't you? Tell me the truth or I put out her eye."

He held the tire iron next to my face and I leaned away, but then was forced back upright by the guard. He forced my head to stay still and I could feel the heat emanating from the tire iron as it moved closer.

"Stop it! Yes! I still want Sage, now stop!"

At Parker's yell, Viktor froze. I couldn't breathe. The metal was only an inch from my eye and I didn't even blink. After a moment, Viktor stepped back and I thought I'd lose control of my bladder, I was so relieved.

Too scared to even cry, I sat in the chair, gasping for breath and shaking from head to toe.

"Let us hear it then," Viktor said, waving a hand at Parker. "Why let the detective take her?"

Parker's lips pressed together and I knew he didn't want to answer.

"Answer or I will not hesitate this time," Viktor said, raising the tire iron and pointing it at me.

"She loves him." The words sounded pulled from Parker's chest. "I let her go because she loves him."

"A faithless woman." Viktor looked at me. "Fickle and inconstant in her affections. I would wager she feels nothing for you and enjoys playing the femme fatale, isn't that right, Sage?"

I shook my head, "No—"

"Don't lie, Sage," Viktor interrupted. He looked at the guard. "Cut her bindings." The man hastened to comply and the ropes fell from my wrists. I rubbed the torn skin, staring warily up at Viktor.

"Give me your hand," he said.

I hesitated.

"Now!" he yelled.

I jumped and thrust out my left hand. Taking it in his, he turned it palm up.

"For you, I choose Truth," he said. "Tell me, Sage. Do you love the detective?"

"Y-yes," I stammered. My hand trembled and he tightened his hold. I glanced at the still-glowing tire iron.

"And Parker? Do you love him, too?"

I glanced over where Parker and Ryker were tied. Both men were watching.

"O-of course I do," I said, trying to pull my hand away.

"And have you had sex with them both?"

Oh God. This wasn't how I'd planned on telling Ryker.

"Say the truth..." he prompted, moving the heated iron closer to my palm.

"Yes," I blurted, keeping my voice down.

"I'm afraid I didn't hear you. What was that?" The iron was only inches away.

"Yes! I said yes. Now let go of me."

"Not so fast, my dear," Viktor said. "Two men have endured great pain because of you. They deserve to know which one you want. So tell me, who shall it be? The detective? Or Parker?"

I stared up at him, aghast. Was he asking so only one wouldn't be killed? What would happen to the other if I said one of their names?

"I-I don't know," I stammered.

"*Tsk tsk*," Viktor scolded. "Let me assist you in making up your mind." Without warning, he pressed the metal into the center of my palm.

I screamed at the pain, excruciating and white hot. Then it stopped.

"That's just a taste," Viktor said with a cold smile.

"Stop playing with the girl, Viktor," Parker called out. "I'm the one who screwed you over. Come play with me instead! Or are you not man enough that you have to pick on little girls?"

Viktor didn't respond to the taunt.

"Cops will be here any minute, Viktor," Ryker added. His voice was strained and I knew he had to be in a lot of pain. I was shocked he hadn't passed out.

"Tell me," Viktor insisted. "Or I will put a hole in the center of your palm with this." He brandished the iron. "Choose. Who do you love the most, dear Sage? They deserve to know."

I frantically shook my head, terrified of what he'd do no matter whose name I said.

"This will be painful, I'm afraid." He gave a mock sigh of regret and lifted my hand higher.

Parker and Ryker both started yelling at him, taunting and threatening, the bedsprings rattling above them, but all I could see was the glowing metal touching my hand...

I screamed again and tears streamed from my eyes. The

pain was worse than before and I could smell my own flesh burning. I struggled to get away, but the guard held me and it was hurting so bad and I couldn't take it...

"Parker!" I screamed.

The iron left my skin immediately and the guard let go of me. I collapsed onto the concrete floor and curled on my side. Cradling my hand to my chest, I tried to slow my breathing. I was hyperventilating and my vision was edged in black. If I blacked out, God only knew what Viktor would do to get me to awaken.

"Gentlemen, we have an answer," Viktor said. "Congratulations, Parker. It seems the lady prefers you to the detective."

I pried open my eyes, matted with sweat and tears, and watched Viktor approach Ryker.

"My apologies, Detective," he said. "But it is preferable to know, wouldn't you agree?"

Ryker didn't reply.

Despair overwhelmed me. What was going to happen to us? Surely there was something I could do? My hands were free now, but the two guards still flanked me.

My gaze drifted to the hallway and where I thought perhaps an exit was located. Maybe if I could get away, make a break for it, I could get help.

"...women are worthless," Viktor was saying. "She deserves to be punished, treated like the whore she is, for what she's done to the two of you." He turned and spoke to the guards. "She's a whore. Treat her as such."

Understanding dawned just as the two men looked down at me, and suddenly I was out of time for planning.

Panic made adrenaline surge through my veins and I scrambled backward and onto my feet. Then I was running.

One of them growled something in Russian, but I could

hear both of them coming after me. Behind that, I heard Viktor's laughter.

I ran as if the hounds of hell were after me, down an endless hallway, all while praying I was heading for an exit.

A door blocked my path and my heart leapt. I slammed into the crossbar and shoved it open... right into an identical warehouse from the one I'd just escaped from.

"Gotcha!"

Hands locked around my arms and I screamed bloody murder as they pulled me back into the dark hallway. The door slammed shut in front of me.

I began fighting in earnest, but one session of self-defense wasn't enough to free myself from two well-trained men who each had a hundred pounds or more on me. In moments, they had me on my back on the floor. One had my arms pinned over my head, the other forced my legs apart and knelt between them.

"Hold her," the one kneeling said.

The guy on top of me started unfastening his pants. I couldn't free my arms; he was too strong. But my legs were free.

I kicked out and my foot caught him in the chest, but did nothing. I remembered what Parker had said about getting them on the chin, that even the biggest guy would go down, and changed my aim. But he pushed closer, using his chest to pin mine down, and I couldn't get my legs in between us.

I was screaming at them, yelling obscenities and telling them to get off me. The guy on top swung his fist at my face, connecting near my temple. Pain exploded in my eye and head. Dizziness was a cloudy fog and my screaming was cut off as I struggled to stay awake.

Maybe you don't want to be awake for this, I thought. It would probably be better to be unconscious. It would be easy. My brain felt weird, my limbs heavy. Oblivion beckoned.

I felt him tugging at the fastening to my jeans and I moaned, trying to move away. Then he was pulling them down over my hips—

Suddenly I was free, the pressure on my chest, hips, and wrist gone. I opened my eyes with effort. Everything was blurry, but I saw a man standing over me. He bent down toward me and I cringed away with a sharp cry of fear.

"Shh, it's okay. It's me. You're okay."

"Parker?" I stared at him in disbelief, blinking to clear my vision. "How— Where's Ryker?"

"I'm here."

I swung my gaze to my left and sure enough, Ryker was crouching next to me.

"Hold on to me, babe," he said, putting his arms underneath mine and lifting me. I clung to him, resting my head against his chest.

I felt Parker pull my clothes back up, his hands sliding around my waist to fasten my jeans.

"Here, let me take her," Parker said. "You can barely stand yourself."

That made me sit up. "You're not okay," I said to Ryker. "He hurt you."

"I'll be fine," he said, but made no further comment as he handed me over to Parker, who stood, lifting me in his arms.

My head was spinning and aching and my hand hurt so badly, but I was able to see the men who'd been about to rape me. They were on the ground and neither was moving. I didn't know how Parker and Ryker had gotten free or what they'd done to those men; I was just glad they had.

When we reached the warehouse, Parker sat me down in the chair I'd occupied earlier, and I saw cops had begun pouring into the building. Parker stood right behind me, his hands on my shoulders. Then my gaze fell on something else and I froze.

It was Viktor, lying flat on his back on the floor, the tire iron protruding from his chest.

"I see you found her."

Tearing my eyes from the sight of Viktor, I saw Branna standing next to Ryker. She was looking at me, but her attention refocused on him.

"You need to get to the hospital," she said. "They need to look at that burn."

"I will. Just gimme a minute," he said to her, his eyes on me.

My head had cleared but I felt numb, like I was in shock or something. I'd always heard about it, but hadn't experienced it. Now I understood what people meant. I didn't know what to say or how to react to anything. The entire horrifying experience was too awful to contemplate, so I didn't.

Ryker crouched in front of me.

"Babe, you okay?" he asked.

I looked at him and gave a tiny nod. "I think so. My hand..."

"Let me see."

He took my hand gently in his, turning it palm up. The mark was as livid as the one against his side. It hurt too much to flatten my hand and I felt self-conscious with both Parker and Branna watching, so I pulled away, cradling it back against my chest.

"I'm sorry," I choked out. "I didn't know what he would do to either of you, no matter what name I said." Tears dripped, but I ignored them.

"Let's not talk about it right now," he said.

I nodded. "Okay."

EMTs came flooding in, surrounding the three of us, and I was separated from them. I looked around, trying to spot either of them in the crowd, but couldn't.

"Where are they?" I asked the woman working on me. "I need them. I can't—I can't—" Breathing became impossible, catching in my chest, and my lungs wouldn't inflate properly.

"Calm down, you're all right," she tried to assure me.

"C-can't," I gasped. "P-Parker and Ry-Ryker. Need them, please…"

"We have a situation here," she told a partner. "Who are the other victims? Either of them Parker or Ryker?"

I had to find them. Were they safe? Did Viktor have them again? Was he hurting them?

I struggled to my feet, pushing away the woman when she tried to stop me.

"I have to find them!"

"Ma'am, please, sit down." A man wrapped his arms around me, imprisoning my arms at my sides.

Panic flooded me. "No! Get off!"

"Sage! It's okay, listen to me."

Parker was suddenly in front of me, his face filling my vision.

"Let her go; you're scaring her," he demanded. The arms holding me dropped away and I fell into Parker's embrace, sobbing.

"Don't leave me," I begged. "Please don't."

"I won't. I swear. I'm right here."

"Ryker?"

"He's right behind you, not ten feet. You've gotta let him go, though," he said gently. "He needs to go to the hospital, okay? He'll be okay. I promise."

I believed him. Parker wouldn't lie to me.

I settled, tuning out everyone and everything but Parker. He held me while they messed with my hand and I barely paid attention to what they were doing.

"Did they give her anything?" the EMT asked Parker.

"I don't know." He pulled back slightly to look at me. "Sage, did they give you something? A drug?"

I shrugged, not caring, and leaned forward to rest against him again. He was warm and solid and alive.

Hands pulled back my hair while others lifted my arm to inspect the skin.

"Here," Parker said, his voice rumbling in his chest. "There's a mark on her neck. Some blood."

"We need to get her to the hospital," the woman said. She placed her hands on my shoulders and pulled at me.

"No!" I clutched at Parker, panicked.

"I'll come with her," he said. His arm tightened around my waist.

That made perfect sense to me. It was strange. In some corner of my mind, I could tell I was being unreasonable. But I couldn't stop it. I *needed* Parker and nothing was going to keep me from him.

Parker stood, making me stand with him, and we took a step. My knees gave out and I would have fallen if he hadn't had a hold of me.

"Easy now," he murmured.

My legs were like spaghetti, completely useless. Parker mostly carried me outside to the ambulance and helped me climb in the back.

They had me lie down and they wanted my blood for a test. So long as I could see Parker's eyes, I didn't care what they did. He held my good hand and I lost myself in his eyes, until nothing remained but their pure blue, shining in the darkness...

CHAPTER EIGHTEEN

Everything was dark when I awoke. My mind was lethargic and slow. I licked my dry lips, blinking slowly as I turned to look around the room.

Was I alone? Where was Parker? Ryker?

Anxiety edged my listlessness, and I tried to sit up in the bed I was lying in.

"It's okay, Sage. You're safe."

Parker. He was sitting in a chair next to the bed, holding my hand.

I fell back onto the bed.

"Where am I?" I croaked.

"The hospital."

"Why do I feel so weird?"

"You were given a drug. They weren't sure what it is, so they aren't counteracting it, just watching you until it wears off."

"Ryker. Where's Ryker?"

I started to cry, images of him being burned by that tire iron so vivid in my mind, it was like I was watching it on television.

"Shh, it's okay." Parker tried to soothe me. "Don't cry. He's fine, I promise."

But I was inconsolable, curling onto my side and crying as though my heart were breaking.

"You gotta come, man," I heard Parker saying. "It's the drug. It's making her unstable. She needs you."

I opened my eyes, distraught now that Parker might think I didn't need him.

"Don't leave," I whispered, tugging him closer. "Come here." I pulled at him until he climbed into bed with me.

"It's all right," he said, drawing his fingers through my hair. "The drug will wear off soon."

"Viktor won't come?" I asked.

"No. He won't come."

I breathed a sigh, closing my eyes.

"Sage, you remember tonight, when Viktor asked you if you'd choose?"

"Mmmm."

"Do you remember what you said?"

I frowned. "He hurt me. My hand..." It felt numb now and was wrapped in something. I couldn't bend my fingers.

"Yes, he did," Parker said. "Do you remember who you chose?"

"I love you."

"Yes, you said that."

"I love Ryker."

"Yes, you said that, too."

I squirmed, tears leaking from my eyes. "He was hurting you. Hurting both of you. I was afraid he'd kill you."

"He didn't. We're fine. I swear to you. Just tell me...do you remember choosing? Do you remember?"

I heard the door open and gasped, jerking around in fear. But it was Ryker. He was at my side in an instant.

"I'm here," he said, taking my hand.

I pulled him down so I could hug him, talking through my tears. "He hurt you," I managed. "I saw him..."

"Don't think about that anymore," Ryker said.

"Can you stay with me?" I asked. "Do you have to work again?"

He winced, but nodded. "Yeah. I can stay."

I relaxed again, lying back on the bed. Parker rose, but I clutched at the T-shirt he wore.

"No, don't!" He paused. "Stay," I said. I was afraid. Afraid to let either of them out of my sight. They'd left me before and had nearly died. They could so easily be dead right now.

Parker hesitated, then lay back down next to me. I still had hold of Ryker, who sat awkwardly on the other side of me. My fingers were wrapped in gauze and he held my hand as though it was made of glass.

I let out a deep sigh, feeling the knot of anxiety inside my chest ease. *Now* things were okay. So long as I could see them and feel them, I'd know they were both safe.

My eyes were heavy and I couldn't keep them open anymore. The room spun slowly on its axis. I could feel the comforting presence of the men I loved and before I realized, I was out.

* * *

When I woke up again, it was still dark, but this time I didn't panic. I could feel the steady rise and fall of Parker's chest as he breathed. Ryker was lying on my other side toward the end of the bed, his head resting on my stomach and his arms thrown over my thighs. Both of them appeared to be sound asleep.

It was a slightly odd situation and the memory of what had come before was hazy. I remembered being upset and unreasonably afraid something would happen to them. Somehow I'd gotten them not only in the same room, but into the same bed with me.

Huh.

I trailed my fingers absently through Ryker's hair. The gauze had left enough of my skin uncovered so I could feel the silky strands. I marveled that they were here, they were alive. All of us were. But how? They'd been tied, strung up, and the men had taken me away—

I shuddered, my mind shying away from remembering.

Everything that had happened was hazy. I stared at the darkened ceiling and tried to remember. Viktor had been torturing Ryker and Parker, electrocuting them, then using the tire iron. Parker had told him about Ryker, then Viktor had begun quizzing me.

The tire iron had branded me—so much pain—and I'd told Viktor I'd slept with both of them, that I loved both of them, and he'd wanted me to choose.

And I'd said Parker.

I'd actually picked one of them, not knowing what was going to happen, if Viktor would kill the man whose name I spoke, or if he'd kill the one that I didn't. How could I have done that? What kind of person did that make me? Not only had I technically cheated on Ryker, I'd chosen Parker in a life-or-death situation.

Self-loathing and regret filled me. Yet again, I'd sacrificed my dignity because of my complete infatuation with

Parker—a man who'd tossed me aside after only one night with me. I loved him—couldn't seem to stop loving him—but that love was unrequited. He'd said he wanted me, yes, that things would change between us. But they hadn't, and his silence on love was deafening.

Ryker deserved better, and would no doubt be quick to end things once daylight came. And as for Parker, it was about time I gave up the obsession. It had been nothing more than a one-night stand, though I'd thought I was giving him my heart along with my body. It looked like Ryker meant more to him than I did, which I shouldn't resent, but I did.

Maybe they'd be friends again. Maybe they'd both blame me for putting them in this untenable situation and find a common ground because of it. It would suck for me, but I'd be glad for them.

The sun slowly rose and I memorized this moment, being with the two men I loved, each in a different way. I loved Ryker as much as I could with a heart that had been taken by another man. If I ever wanted it free to give to someone else, I needed to cut ties with Parker.

But for now, while he was asleep, I could savor being with him one last time.

The room brightened bit by bit, and despite my best intentions to stay awake, I drifted off.

* * *

They were gone when I woke again, and the crushing disappointment overwhelmed me for a moment. I squeezed my eyes shut against the sting and took a deep breath.

"Are you feeling better?"

A nurse had entered—that's what had woken me—and I snapped my eyes back open.

"Um, yeah," I said. "Can I go now?" I was already climbing out of the bed, holding the hospital gown closed with my good hand and searching for my clothes. I'd abruptly decided I wanted to be home alone to lick my wounds in peace.

"Your bloodwork came back clean and we've given you a prescription for the ointment you'll need for your hand," she said, handing me a sheaf of papers. "You'll have a scar, that's for certain, but otherwise you're fine and free to go."

I hesitated. "The, uh, the men who were here with me. Are they...all right?" I'd almost asked if she knew where they were but decided at the last second that I didn't want to know. I didn't want to be tempted to go find them.

She nodded. "We treated the burn on the one man. The other had cracked ribs and a dislocated shoulder. Both had various minor cuts and contusions, but overall they were in good shape. They were discharged as well."

I swallowed hard and forced a smile, even as I realized Parker and Ryker had left me. Maybe they'd grown tired of my neediness last night. "Thanks. I'll be out of your hair shortly."

"Is there someone I can call to come pick you up?" she asked.

I shook my head. "I'll be fine."

"Would you like me to get a wheelchair and wheel you to the entrance?"

So no. "Um, thanks, but no," I said politely.

The nurse nodded and left. There was soap, toothbrush, and toothpaste in the bathroom and I cleaned up the best I could, finger-combing my hair. I found my clothes and was in the process of trying to fasten my jeans one-handed when the door opened and Ryker walked in.

We stared at each other for a moment, then he realized my predicament and walked toward me.

"Need some help?" he asked. He didn't wait for a response, reaching forward and fastening the button.

"Thanks," I said. "I-I thought you'd left. The nurse said you'd been discharged."

He shook his head. "I got cleaned up, took a shower. That's all." He paused. "I wasn't going to leave you alone."

"Can you tell me what happened?" I asked. "How did you and Parker get caught? How'd you escape?"

"What do you remember?" he asked.

I shrugged. "It's hazy and confused. Some of it feels like a dream, or a nightmare. I remember him hurting you, hurting Parker, then they had me pinned down in that hallway and were going to..." I cleared the sudden lump from my throat.

"Leading Viktor to us was the plan," he said. "We didn't realize until too late that he'd set a trap."

"What kind of trap?"

"You," he said simply. Reaching in his pocket, he took out a cell phone and pressed a few buttons. I heard my voice, tinny through the speaker.

"It's too late. I don't know what to do. It-it hurts...so much."

I felt the blood leave my face. Those were words I'd said to Megan on the phone yesterday morning.

"Viktor said he had you," Ryker continued, pocketing the phone. "And that was his proof. We had no choice but to go in."

"Oh God...it's my fault—"

"No, Sage, don't think that way. It wasn't your fault. Plans turn to shit all the time. Malone—my partner—had been paid off by Viktor. I still can't believe it. He's the one who tipped him off and got him access to tap your line. Which also explains why he'd do something as colossally stupid as sending you to Leo's bar in search of me. He was hoping that would blow my cover."

"But then how did you escape?" I asked. "Viktor had you tied up..."

"Parker damn near broke his arm," he said. "I know he dislocated his shoulder getting free. He went after Viktor and they fought, but it was a pretty short fight."

I remembered the iron shaft sticking out of Viktor's chest, and swallowed.

"By that time, Branna had arrived with the cavalry. He and I came after you."

"Branna?"

"I told you she's loyal only to herself, she doesn't actually work for Leo. She knew Leo had found out so she went to the cops. Turns out, she was working with someone else, some politician on the Senate Homeland Security Committee. So the feds have been investigating Leo, too, through her."

"So she's on your side?" I asked.

"Yeah. I guess so. For now."

We stood in silence for a minute as I processed all this.

"Want a ride home?" he asked.

"Yeah. Yeah, I do."

We walked outside and I didn't object when he put his arm around my shoulders. Leaning into him seemed to be a good idea.

He helped me into his truck and a half hour later, we pulled up into my apartment building.

"Parker said your place should be fixed up," he said.

The name was like an acknowledgment of the thick tension between us. The engine was idling, but I made no move to get out of the truck and Ryker didn't turn it off. We just sat there.

"So you slept with him," he said at last.

I nodded. "Yeah," I managed to say. "I thought you and I were done. That you were with Branna and had almost killed me."

"A rebound thing then?" he asked, a note of cautious hope in his voice. "Trying to get back at me?"

Had it been? Maybe. It was possible. So much had happened and my emotions had been left reeling. It was hard to say what I felt, and impossible to know what I wanted.

"I quit my job," I said, glancing over at him. His aviators masked his eyes, but I saw his body relax slightly. "I...I won't be seeing Parker anymore."

"You said his name, you know." He rested an arm across the top of the steering wheel. "When Viktor told you to choose, you said Parker."

I didn't reply, just stared out the windshield the same as he did.

"Did you mean it?" he asked. "Were you choosing him? Or were you screaming for help?"

And there it was. My out. If I chose to take it.

"I think," I began, choosing my words with care, "that I would understand if you want to call it quits between us."

"Is that what you want?" he turned to look at me. "Because I sure as hell don't."

He reached for me and dragged me onto his lap. "I'm not giving up," he said. "I gave up once before and I shouldn't have. This time it's going to be different."

He kissed me, his fingers sliding into my hair and his tongue tangling with mine. Sweet relief and an echo of heartbreak expanded inside my chest. I couldn't make sense of my jumbled feelings, so I shut off my brain and kissed him back.

I didn't know how long we kissed—time didn't have

much meaning—but when we finally came up for air, it felt as though something had shifted between us.

"I have to go to the station," he said, pressing his lips to my cheek, then next to my eye. "But I'll be back, okay?"

I nodded. "Okay."

I watched him drive out of the lot before going inside and up to my apartment. As Parker had promised, the place was once again pristine. I guessed those CIA guys knew how to do that sort of thing. It was amazing. I was just glad I hadn't had to pay for it.

The first thing I did was take a shower, then dug out fresh gauze from my medicine cabinet for my hand. I needed to get that prescription filled, but was too tired to mess with it.

My refrigerator was sadly lacking in anything edible, so I stretched and got my cookie jar from the top cupboard. The sweet scent of peanut M&M's hit me when I lifted the lid. Aw yeah, just what I needed.

I took the whole jar into the living room and sat on the sofa. My gaze wandered the room. I could barely see some spots where holes in the walls had been patched and the paint didn't quite match, but overall it was an incredible transformation.

Two episodes of *The Big Bang Theory* and almost the entire cookie jar of candy later, there was a knock on my door. I checked the peephole before opening the door, too surprised to even think of not opening it.

"What are you doing here?" I asked Parker.

"Can I come in?"

"Um, yeah. I guess." I moved aside and he stepped past me. Closing the door, I followed him into my apartment.

"I should thank you," I said to him. "Ryker told me you dislocated your shoulder to get free and come help me."

"Did he tell you why we went in there in the first place?" he asked.

I nodded. "Ryker's partner was a dirty cop. Viktor paid him for access to tap my phone line. And he recorded me talking, made it sound like he had me."

"Ryker and I came to an understanding in that moment," he said. "The past between us didn't matter. What *did* matter was saving you. It was the first time we'd agreed on anything in over a decade."

"I'm glad," I said. And I was. It would be good for them both if they could be friends. At least the pain I'd gone through hadn't been in vain.

"But I also realized I'd been an ass," he said, moving closer to me. His hands cradled my face. "You finally trusted me, and I threw it away because of Ryker. Because of the past. A past I can't change. But the future...the future is still up for grabs."

I couldn't speak, just staring up at him in stunned silence. His blue eyes gazed deeply into mine and the calluses on his thumbs brushed my cheeks.

"I love you," he said. "That became crystal clear to me last night. I didn't *have* to kill Viktor. I *wanted* to. He'd hurt you, and I'd had to watch him do it."

"You...you love me?"

"I have for a long time, I think," he said. "It just took me this long to realize it. You and I have something special and rare, a connection that's deeper than anything I've ever known. You feel it, too, don't you. You've probably known a lot longer than I have."

I was so confused I stepped back, away from his touch. "First you told me no, then you told me you were wrong, then you said sex between us would change everything. And I believed you, and I wanted to be with you. Then Ryker showed up and you said it had been a mistake and should never have happened. Now you decide you love me and that we have a 'special connection?'"

Anger replaced confusion and I turned, grabbing the first thing I could lay my hands on: my cookie jar. I threw it with all my strength at the wall. The ceramic hit with a crash, splintering into a thousand pieces with M&M's flying everywhere.

"Why do you keep doing this to me? I can't take it anymore!" I flew at him, wanting to hurt him the same way he was tearing me up inside. "Why are you doing this?" I was yelling at him and hitting his chest. "Why?"

He grabbed my wrists, forcing me to stop. "Sage—"

I struggled in his grip. "You can't keep doing this! You can't—"

"Sage!"

He pushed my arms down, locking my wrists behind my back and holding me tight against him. I couldn't fight him anymore and I was crying and why oh why was he doing this to me?

Suddenly, he was kissing me, hard, his lips pushing mine apart. Our mouths collided with a fierce passion, my anger melting into a fierce desire. My wrists were free, but I didn't push him away. Instead, my arms circled his neck, holding him tighter and closer.

His arms were a vise around my waist and I began clawing at his clothes, yanking on his shirt. He broke off kissing me long enough to pull it over his head, then he jerked mine off, too. He didn't bother unfastening my bra, the fragile lace tearing until the fabric fell to the floor. His mouth covered my nipple and I gasped, my head falling back. The scrape of his teeth made me moan.

My fingers tangled in his hair and I pulled until he lifted

his head to kiss me again. Skin against skin was a potent drug and my knees went weak.

Parker pushed me backward and my back hit the wall. I grappled with his belt, tugging it loose. I needed him.

He brushed my hands aside, pushing the yoga pants I wore down my legs and dragging my panties down with them. I kicked them aside, but slipped on the fabric. Parker caught me, saving me from hitting the floor, and lifted me. I eagerly wrapped my legs around his waist, swinging my hair to the side so it was out of our way, then I kissed him again.

I barely paid attention as he carried me to my bedroom. He set me on my knees on the bed and I attacked his jeans again, making quick work of the fastening and zipper.

Parker wore nothing under his jeans, which was all kinds of hot. I pushed the denim down, my hands clutching at his ass. His erection pressed against my abdomen and I couldn't help rubbing against him like a cat. His hands were buried in my hair as he kissed me.

He pressed me back onto the bed and I clutched at his shoulders. I was wet for him, burning for him.

"This isn't going to be gentle," he said, his words rasping in my ear.

"I don't want gentle."

He thrust inside me without another word, filling me. I heard him moan at the sensation even as I gasped.

"Oh God oh God," I moaned. "Yes, please—"

His mouth cut me off, his kiss deep. Then he was pulling me up until I straddled his hips. It pushed him deeper inside me and I couldn't get enough. His hands gripped my hips as he pistoned into me. With every thrust, his cock slid over my clit, pushing me into a frenzy of desire.

"Tell me again," he whispered. "Tell me you love me."

"I love you," I gasped. "Love you love you."

He kissed the words from my lips.

"I love you, too. Come for me, sweetness."

My heart was pounding so hard it felt like it would leap out of my chest. My body tightened, straining for release. His mouth fastened to my breast, his tongue flicking over my nipple, and it was enough to send me over the edge.

I cried out, my nails digging into his skin. He thrust harder and faster into me and a keening sound came from my throat. A rush of heat washed over my skin, and then he was coming inside me, his cock pulsing and his body shaking with the force of his orgasm.

Our bodies were covered in a layer of slick sweat, both of us gasping for air. His tongue stroked mine, playing and teasing, and I could taste the salt from his skin.

Parker lay back on the bed, keeping me on top of him. I rested my head on his chest, listening to the pounding of his heart.

I was completely wiped out—mentally, emotionally, physically. It seemed Parker was, too, because he didn't try to talk, merely reached over to turn down the covers, then moved us over and drew the blankets up over our naked bodies. I was asleep within moments.

* * *

I was awakened abruptly by Parker flipping me onto my back, his body covering mine.

"What—"

"Move and your head will have another hole in it."

The voice came from above us and I could see a man standing in the room. He held a gun to the back of Parker's head.

"Get the girl and let's go."

Two men in my bedroom, both armed.

I looked at Parker and I could see in his eyes that he was readying himself to fight. He looked at me and it seemed as though time stood still. His muscles coiled with tension.

A sudden blow caught him in the back of the head and I screamed, then he was being pulled off me. I followed him as they rolled him over on his back.

"Parker! Oh my God—"

"Let's go."

I was yanked from the bed and they threw my clothes at me.

"Get dressed or your boyfriend dies."

The one who'd knocked out Parker stood over his unconscious body, gun pointed at his head.

I scrambled to put my clothes on and shoved my feet into tennis shoes. When I was done, the second guy motioned with his gun and I preceded him out of the bedroom.

Leo Shea stood waiting in my living room.

"The cop wasn't with her?" he asked.

"Nah, some other guy."

"What are you doing here?" I asked. "What do you want?"

"I want the sonofabitch who's been spying on me, pretending to be someone he's not," Leo replied. He turned to one of the men.

"Tape her up."

I struggled, but all too quickly my arms were bound with duct tape and another strip placed over my mouth.

"What should we do with the guy?"

Leo glanced at the bedroom door, then shrugged. "Kill him."

I screamed at him, muffled behind the tape, and flung myself away from the guy holding my arm. Rearing back, I headbutted Leo right on the bridge of the nose.

He roared in pain as I was quickly subdued by one of the men.

"You fucking bitch!" His fist came flying and there was nowhere for me to escape.

CHAPTER NINETEEN

It was pitch black inside the trunk, and cramped. They'd duct-taped my arms behind my back and used more around my ankles, but it was the strip over my mouth that terrified me. It felt as though I'd suffocate. Breathing slowly through my nose, I forcibly calmed myself. Panicking would be bad. Panicking could kill me.

I couldn't tell where we were going or how fast. My senses were all turned around. I didn't know what they were going to do to me and I didn't want to try and imagine it. Instead, I tried to think of what to do next.

Parker.

A sob built inside my chest but I swallowed it down, knowing that a nose clogged with tears might kill me.

The car doors slammed and I braced myself. The trunk popped open and sure enough, those same guys appeared above me.

"You get her legs," the tall one said.

One took my shoulders, the other my legs, and they hauled me out of the trunk. I couldn't tell where we were, but knew we were no longer downtown. There was water nearby; I could smell it and hear it. And it was dark, the only streetlamps few and far between.

I was terrified they were going to throw me into the water and let me drown, but they carried me inside a building. A small one, from what I could see—the wooden floor creaked and groaned beneath their feet.

We went down a flight of stairs but I was headfirst, which was awful. I was afraid they'd lose their grip on me and there'd be no way for me to cushion my fall. But we made it to the bottom with me still in one piece.

The guy with my feet set them down so he could open a door, then they carried me through the doorway and set me on the dusty wooden floor none too gently. Then without a word they left, closing the door behind them.

I let my body relax. I was on my side and I rested my head on the floor. My right eye was swollen nearly shut and my head hurt so bad I wanted to vomit. The trip inside hadn't helped that, and I took a moment to just breathe. If I threw up, I'd choke on my own vomit.

"Sage?"

Jerking my head up at the sound of my name, I frantically peered into the dark shadows of the room, fear licking at my veins. After a moment, I could see well enough to make out a figure huddled in the corner.

Branna.

She was inching toward me the best she could, though I could tell she'd been bound in the same fashion, only her mouth wasn't covered.

When she got to me, I saw she'd been beat up, her face

more bloody and bruised than mine. There was blood on the white tank top she wore, too.

"Looks like they didn't exactly take it easy on you," she said dryly. "Hold on," she said.

Turning around, she was able to move her hands near my face. Realizing what she wanted to do, I scooted closer, letting her fingers brush against me until she got hold of the tape. I braced myself, but even so, it didn't prepare me for the blinding pain of the tape being ripped off.

I gasped, biting back a cry. Some of my hair had been stuck in the tape and had gone with it. My eyes watered and I gulped down air, relieved to have the tape off. I laid my head on the floor and just breathed for a moment.

"Are you all right?" she asked.

"Do I look all right?" I croaked, then coughed. The smell of dank mildew in the room was nearly overpowering.

"What's going on?" I asked, my voice thick. "What does Leo want?"

"He wants Ryker," she said, turning back around. "He must be wanting to use you as leverage. It'll be okay. Just stay calm, all right?"

"How can it possibly be okay?" I asked in disbelief.

"Turn around," Branna said. "We'll put our backs together and maybe we can get the tape off."

They'd wrapped it around my entire lower arms several times and I had doubts that we'd make much headway, but I did as she said.

"How long have you been in here?" I asked.

"A few hours," she said. I could feel her working at the tape, trying to tear the edge.

"What will they do to us?" I asked, my imagination conjuring scenarios I didn't want to think about. Not that I cared anymore. Parker was dead. They'd killed him.

But before she could answer—if she'd have answered—the door opened. The short counterpoint guy of the duo entered and I saw the glint of a knife in his hand. He reached for me and I pulled away with a sharp jerk.

"Hold still," he snarled, grabbing my legs. With one swift slice, he cut the tape, then yanked it off me. I was very thankful I was wearing jeans and not a skirt. Grabbing my elbow, he hauled me to my feet.

"Leave her alone," Branna said. "It's me Leo wants. The girl's got nothing to do with this."

"Oh, you're comin,' too," the guy said. "Leo wants both of youse."

The guy sounded like he'd watched too many Bugsy movies. Or maybe that's just how an Italian gangster thug sounded.

Tall and skinny came back with a guy I hadn't seen before. One held a gun on Branna while the other cut the tape off her legs so she could walk.

"This way."

I tested the bindings on my arms, but they were as tight as ever. Branna hadn't been able to make more than a small dent in them and I hadn't torn hers at all.

They sat both of us in two folding chairs about a foot apart. The lighting was better but the smell wasn't. I could hear the lapping of water against the wall outside. We were right on the lake then.

I heard steps on the stairs and watched as Leo descended. More footsteps sounded from upstairs. I could hear them walking around.

"So, Branna," Leo said, stopping to stand in front of us. "You see I brought you some company. And now I have the two women *Detective Ryker* cares about the most."

Branna didn't say a word.

He held a cell phone in front of her face. "Call him."

"My hands are tied, dipshit," she said, her lips twisting with scorn.

Leo backhanded her and I jumped at the sharp crack of sound. But Branna just looked bored, despite the blood trickling from her mouth.

"Untie her," he ordered.

Shorty hastened to do his bidding. Branna rubbed her arms once the tape was removed.

"Now do it," he said.

"You sure have a hard-on for Ryker," she said, taking the phone from him. "Does he do it for you?"

He went to hit her again, which was his mistake. She grabbed his arm and wrenched it. There was a sharp crack of bone breaking and Leo grunted in pain.

She twisted and stabbed her elbow into his solar plexus, then tossed him over her shoulder and into the wooden chair. It splintered under his weight with an ear-splitting crash and he hit the floor.

The guys flanking me had been stunned, but now they sprang into action and attacked her. I watched in dismay, then leapt up and threw myself into the mix, hoping to take one of them out just by getting in their way.

It worked for a moment, as they couldn't get a clear shot at her, then the tall guy slugged me hard, right in the gut.

I grunted in pain and bent over, the force of the blow knocking the wind out of me. For a moment, I couldn't breathe at all as my stomach felt like it was on fire from the inside out.

The sound of a gun's slide being racked made me force my body back up. Leo was up, one arm cradled to his chest and blood flowing from a cut on his head, but he was pointing a gun... at me.

"Stop!" he yelled.

The two men paused, as did Branna, who was facing off with them, gun in hand.

"Stand down, or I'll shoot her," he said.

I wasn't sure Branna really cared, and the way she eyed me for a moment, I was sure she was considering just shooting me herself, then the rest of them.

"Shit," she muttered, then tossed her gun onto the floor.

My good eye was glued to the gun in Leo's hand, my other eye swollen shut. I was breathing too fast and felt like I was going to pass out. His hand moved over the trigger—

Gunshots sounded from upstairs and my gaze flew up at the ceiling.

"You," Leo said to the tall guy guarding me. "Go see what's going on."

Picking up the gun Branna had thrown down, the guy nodded and went running up the stairs. I heard another shot and saw the spatter of blood. His body came tumbling back down, lifeless.

"Mr. Shea," a voice called from upstairs. "I advise you to disarm yourself, if you want to live. We're coming down there."

Leo had only one guy left and himself. I could tell when he'd made the decision because he lowered his weapon.

"It seems I'm left with little choice," Leo called back.

More creaking on the stairs and I watched warily as men came down. Lots of them. I'd expected the cops, but what I saw instead made my jaw drop.

"Dad?"

My dad was among the men; he seemed to be in charge of them, actually, as he was the only one not brandishing a semiautomatic rifle. Only one of the men looked familiar, but I couldn't place him. He was holding a handgun rather than a rifle.

My dad's gaze landed on me and relief broke over his features. "Sage, honey," he said, hurrying toward me.

I glanced at Leo, who'd gone very pale. "This...this is your...your *daughter*?" he asked.

By now my dad was inspecting my damaged face and his expression was so unlike my father's usual cheery façade that it sent a chill down my spine.

"She is," Dad said. "And it seems you've been mistreating her." He glanced at Leo. "That's quite unfortunate. For you."

If possible, Leo turned even paler. "M-M-Mister Muccino, please believe me. I had no idea this was your daughter. She never said—"

"Leo, you've always been an asshole, but I've tolerated you in this city," my dad interrupted. "But I'm afraid you've overstepped this time." Dad motioned to a couple of the men with him. "Take him outside for now." They immediately moved to do his bidding, dragging a babbling and pleading Leo up the stairs.

The man who didn't appear to be like the others made directly for Branna, and it suddenly struck me who he was. That senator Parker had introduced me to. He must be the guy Ryker had said Branna was working for.

Though they looked far from an employer/employee relationship. He had an arm around her and was kissing her. Huh.

My dad dug in his pocket to produce his pocketknife. A few quick slices and my arms were free. Dad took my hand and helped me to my feet, wrapping an arm around me.

"How did you find me, Daddy?" I asked.

"I had someone keeping an eye on your apartment ever since you told your mother what happened."

"She wasn't supposed to tell you," I said.

"Your mother doesn't keep secrets from me," he said. "Especially secrets that concern the safety of my daughter."

"Who are all these men?" I asked. "Why is Leo so scared of you?"

But my dad just smiled. "We'll talk about it later, honey. For now, let's get out of here. The smell is disgusting. I should've known Leo would pick a shithole like this."

I didn't argue, letting him lead me up the stairs. We passed crumpled bodies on the way, but I kept my gaze straight ahead.

When we got outside, I saw Leo standing with some of my dad's men. He looked over at us.

"What shall I do with him?" Dad asked me.

Leo was the man who'd ordered Parker's murder. I knew exactly what I wanted.

"I don't want him breathing," I said, my voice flat. "Ever."

A ghost of a smile flitted across my dad's face. "That's my girl," he said softly.

My dad opened the door to a waiting limo and I slid inside.

I felt numb. Parker was dead in my apartment, in my bed. My dad seemed to be exactly what Ryker had said he was, and I'd grown up blissfully oblivious. My body was broken and bruised, and my soul...my soul had died back in that apartment with Parker.

"Take me to Ryker's," I said to my dad. Ryker needed to know what had happened...and that Parker was dead.

I didn't ask if Dad knew where Ryker lived. I had a feeling he did. And sure enough, forty minutes later, we were pulling up to Ryker's house.

The truck was in the driveway and the lights were on.

My dad walked me to the door. It flew open almost immediately.

"Sage," Ryker said, looking surprised. Seeing my dad, his brow creased in confusion, then he got a good look at my face. His jaw tightened. "What happened?"

"Your job happened," my dad said. "Leo Shea thought he'd use Sage to get to you. Fortunately, I was keeping a closer eye on my daughter than you were."

Ryker said nothing, though a wince crossed his features.

"Leo's left town," my dad said. "I trust the police won't devote a tremendous amount of resources looking for him?"

"No," Ryker rasped, and I knew he understood what my dad wasn't saying.

"Excellent. Then we have an understanding. I'll continue to allow you to see my daughter, against my better judgment, but she asked to come here. However, if you continue to take such poor care of her, you and I..."—he paused meaningfully—"will have a problem."

Ryker didn't flinch at the threat, but I elbowed my dad.

"Stop," I chastised him. "Go on and go. I'm exhausted."

"All right, honey." He brushed a kiss to my forehead. "Get something on that eye."

He walked away and I fell against Ryker, tired to the bone and too heartbroken to cry. He pulled me gently inside and closed the door behind me.

I took a deep, steadying breath. "There's something I have to tell you," I began...

Sage Reece almost lost the two men she loves:
tough cop Ryker and sexy businessman Parker.
But when a beautiful, cunning woman from their
past returns, Sage must make the most
dangerous play of her life . . .

Please see the next page for a preview of

Play To Win

**Available
from Piatkus in Spring 2016**

PROLOGUE

P arker and I have been sleeping together."

The words fell with the force of a bomb against Ryker's ears as he stared at the woman he loved. Shock had turned his muscles to stone and he couldn't move, could barely breathe.

This couldn't be happening. He couldn't possibly have understood her correctly. She was lying, or this was a really bad joke—

"I've been in love with him for a while," she continued as though completely unaware of the stake each word was driving into his chest. "And he loves me, too. We were going to tell you before, but…" Her words trailed away and she shrugged.

"But what?" he asked, his voice like a rake on gravel.

"But I love you, too," she said, tears filling her eyes but not yet spilling over. They clung to her lashes like diamonds sparkling in the sun. "And I don't want to lose you."

She moved closer until she stood within a hairbreadth of her abdomen touching his. Lifting her hands, she placed her palms on the bare skin of his chest. Ryker squeezed his eyes shut, his senses assaulted by her—the heat of her touch, the smell of her skin, the brush of her hair against him as it stirred in the breeze.

"We can be happy, the three of us," Natalie said, her voice a soft murmur of sound. She pressed her lips to his skin, and against his will Ryker's cock twitched, hardening from her mere touch.

"Parker put you up to this, didn't he," Ryker said. That was the only explanation. The woman he knew was sweet and trusting. She'd believe anything Parker told her. God only knew what he'd said to seduce her and make her think they were in love.

"Parker's your best friend," she said, her lips moving against his skin. "The three of us together...just think about it."

But Ryker had stopped listening. Grasping her upper arms so tightly she gasped, he pushed her back so he could see her eyes.

"Tell me the truth," he growled, trying to keep his temper in check. "Parker filled your head with all this crap about the three of us, didn't he? He said whatever he had to in order to get you into bed. You love *me*. You want to be with *me*. Right?" He shook her slightly before he stopped himself. "Tell me!"

"Y-yes," Natalie stammered, her eyes wide. "It was Parker. I-I didn't know what to do. And he said we could be happy, the three of us, wanted to show me what it would be—"

"He wants you for himself," Ryker interrupted, abruptly releasing her. Turning away, he shoved a hand through his hair. "I can't believe it. My best friend, stabbing me in the back."

It was unreal. Incomprehensible. Parker and he went back—way back—and had looked out for each other through street gangs, schoolyard bullies, drill sergeants, and enemy fire. Parker knew how much Ryker loved Natalie. He'd even talked with Parker about how he was thinking of proposing, once Natalie had gotten over the loss of her husband, missing in action and presumed dead.

And he'd thought she was there or, at least, almost. She'd told him she loved him. They'd made love...

Then Parker had seduced her. To do something like that to someone as trusting and vulnerable as Natalie made his blood boil. Parker had finally shown his true colors. It had just taken a woman to bring out what Ryker had always suspected was there—a narcissistic asshole blinded by his own wealth and privilege. It must've amused him, all these years, playing the savior for the charity case kid from the shitty part of town.

He felt Natalie's hands on his back, lightly stroking his skin, gentling him.

"I love you," she said, "and only you. I don't know why I let him get inside my head like that. Forgive me? Please? You're the one I want."

The words were a balm to his fractured soul, though nothing could heal the searing pain of Parker's betrayal. The thought of Parker with Natalie—

No. He couldn't think about it, *wouldn't* think about it. It didn't matter what she'd done or been coerced into doing, Ryker couldn't live without her. His every breath was for her. If she left him...he'd have nothing and no one. He needed her more than he cared about his broken pride or wounded psyche.

"Of course I forgive you," he rasped. "It's you and me. Together. Nothing will come between us. Especially not Parker."

Taking a deep breath, he turned around and took her in his arms, his lips finding hers in a searing kiss that melted his anger and turned his guts into a molten river of want.

She let him make love to her, their joining more desperate on his side than it had been before. As though his soul knew he was losing her, inch by inch.

* * *

It was only a week later that his worst fears were realized.

Ryker didn't announce his presence when he walked into Parker's place. He hadn't been able to reach Natalie for the past hour, though they were supposed to meet for dinner after he got off work. On a suspicion he didn't want to dwell on, Ryker had come here.

He hadn't spoken to Parker since Natalie had confessed. Unable to know for certain what he'd do if he saw Parker, Ryker had avoided him all week.

Now he stood, frozen in Parker's bedroom doorway, aghast at the tableau in front of him.

Natalie, naked, her limbs entwined around Parker's hips. The sounds of her gasps and moans filled the air, pouring into his ears like acid. The sheets tangled around their legs and the sight of Parker pumping between her thighs sent fury raging through him.

With a roar, he attacked, grabbing Parker and hauling him off Natalie. He tossed him, and Parker hit the wall with a thud and grunt before falling to the floor.

Parker's gaze met Ryker's, shock and confusion followed quickly by horror.

"What the fuck are you doing here?" Parker asked.

"Besides watching you fuck my girlfriend," Ryker spat. "I'm here to kill you, asshole."

He went for him, but Parker fought back, blocking Ryker's right hook and retreating.

"It's over between you two," Parker said. "You've got to accept that."

"Fuck you," Ryker growled, going after him again. This time he landed a good hit to Parker's jaw and gut before Parker was able to retaliate, the blows to Ryker's solar plexus making him lose his breath, forcing him to pause.

"You've gotta stop," Parker said, breathing hard. "She's not worth this."

Nothing Parker said could have enraged Ryker more and he yelled as he attacked again, this time his fury such that Parker's blows didn't stop him. Blood flowed and his knuckles ached, but all he saw through the haze of red in his vision was Natalie's body being desecrated by Parker.

"Stop! You're going to kill him! Stop!"

Natalie's words broke through the rage at last and Ryker went still, his chest heaving from exertion. Parker lay on the floor, blood staining the skin around his mouth and nose. His eyes were closed and he didn't move.

"Oh God oh God oh God…" Natalie was murmuring over and over. She'd dropped to her knees, her hand tenderly brushing back the hair from his face. "I think he's just unconscious," she said at last.

Lifting her gaze to Ryker's, he was stunned to see the tears streaking her face.

"I can't do this. I can't watch you two tear each other apart," she said.

"You have to choose," Ryker said, his voice flat. "Him or me. You can't have both." Because now he knew. He knew by the look in her eyes that she hadn't told him the truth.

"I told you I wanted you," she said. "But I want him, too." Her gaze was unflinching.

"I can't live like that."

Slowly, she got to her feet. "You can," she said. "For me, you can." Her eyes were mesmerizing. Her hold over him utter and complete. "Or else you'll lose me. And him. Forever."

"I don't understand."

"Don't push me, Ryker," she said. "You won't like what happens."

The look in her eye sent a chill through him, and Ryker was suddenly struck at how she stood over Parker's unconscious and bleeding body, naked but without any apparent self-consciousness.

"This ends now," he said. "You choose. Him or me."

She didn't answer, just silently gathered her clothes and dressed. When she was done, she stood in front of him.

"Kiss me," she ordered.

Hesitant relief flowed through him, but he was too cautious to believe she'd chosen him. Still, he couldn't resist her. Hope was too strong a pull and he leaned down, sealing her lips with his.

At last he lifted his head, his eyes too lazy to open. When they did, he stumbled back in shock.

For it wasn't Natalie in his arms, staring at him with a look of utter satisfaction on her face. It was Sage.

* * *

Ryker woke up with a start, sitting straight up in bed. A sheen of cold sweat covered him, but he didn't notice. All he could see inside his head was Natalie and Sage, the thin, sharp blade of betrayal cutting him deep.

Getting up, he went into the kitchen, forgoing any lights. He knew his way in the dark. McClane padded beside him, his nails clicking on the floor as he trailed his owner.

Ryker absently filled a glass with water and took a deep swallow, letting the night air cool his sweat-slicked skin. Even now, years later, he remembered the horror of that night and the morning that had followed. The police had called with news that her car had been found in the river and they had sent in a recovery team to find the body.

He hadn't spoken to Parker since that night until four months ago, when he'd walked into Parker's office...and laid eyes on Sage.

Now he was on the brink of losing the woman he loved, again, to the same man who'd betrayed him all those years ago.

Ryker wasn't going let that happen. He wouldn't lose Sage to Parker, and he'd do anything to keep history from repeating itself.

Do you love historical fiction?

Want the chance to hear news about your favourite authors (and the chance to win free books)?

Mary Balogh

Charlotte Betts

Jessica Blair

Frances Brody

Gaelen Foley

Elizabeth Hoyt

Eloisa James

Lisa Kleypas

Stephanie Laurens

Claire Lorrimer

Sarah MacLean

Amanda Quick

Julia Quinn

Then visit the Piatkus website and blog

www.piatkus.co.uk | www.piatkusbooks.net

And follow us on Facebook and Twitter

www.facebook.com/piatkusfiction | www.twitter.com/piatkusbooks

piatkus

Do you love fiction with a supernatural twist?

Want the chance to hear news about your favourite authors (and the chance to win free books)?

Keri Arthur
Kristen Callihan
P.C. Cast
Christine Feehan
Jacquelyn Frank
Larissa Ione
Darynda Jones
Sherrilyn Kenyon
Jayne Ann Krentz and Jayne Castle
Lucy March
Martin Millar
Tim O'Rourke
Lindsey Piper
Christopher Rice
J.R. Ward
Laura Wright

Then visit the Piatkus website and blog
www.piatkus.co.uk | www.piatkusbooks.net

And follow us on Facebook and Twitter
www.facebook.com/piatkusfiction | www.twitter.com/piatkusbooks

piatkus